GHOSTS OF EARTH

THE FORSAKEN COMEDY
BOOK TWO

KEVIN KAUFFMANN

GHOSTS OF EARTH

Kevin Kauffmann

Ebook ISBN: 978-1-964658-02-5

Print ISBN: 978-1-964658-03-2

Any references to historical events, real people, or real places are used fictitiously. Names, characters, and places are products of the author's imagination.

Front cover image by Andy Belanger.

Book design by Peter J. Wacks.

First printing edition 2014.

Second printing edition 2024.

www.kevinkauffmann.com

10 9 8 7 6 5 4 3 2

CONTENTS

1. Paved with Good Intentions   1
2. Lines in the Sand   23
3. The Conscientious Objector   43
4. A Snake in the Garden   75
5. War and Pieces   115
6. Any Port in a Storm   157
7. When in Doubt   189
8. Rhyme and Repetition   213
9. Alea Iacta Est   249
10. Hellfire Upon Us   289
11. Vengeance for the Devil   319
12. No Rest for the Wicked   353
    Epilogue   389

    Dramatis Personae   393
    Watch For...   397

CONTENTS

CHAPTER 1
PAVED WITH GOOD INTENTIONS

I n the time before...

"LUCIFER."

The firstborn had been squatting down in the dirt and teaching his students when he heard the voice behind him. With a smile, Lucifer turned from the simple apes and saw the glorious sight of another angel. He greeted his brother with warmth and affection, rising from the soil that had dirtied the white cloth hanging around his hips.

"Tamiel! Just who I wanted to see! Come, look at what they can do now," Lucifer said, beckoning his brother to come closer. The other angel stepped forward, his own white cloth dragging along the ground and his shoulder-length black hair flowing in the wind. Tamiel was young, made centuries after Lucifer, but he did not **act** like a baby brother.

"Why do you keep wasting your time on these animals? Don't you have better things to do?" Tamiel crossed his arms as the firstborn sighed heavily and shook his head.

"Truthfully, no. Father can only give me so many errands, since he has **you** *to do his bidding,"* Lucifer teased, nudging his brother with an elbow.

"I don't do his bidding any more than you do, Lucy. Now what are you doing here?" Tamiel crouched down so he could have a better look at his brother's pets.

"Teaching, **oh perfect one**. *I'm tired of seeing these apes falling all over themselves and getting eaten by mindless creatures,"* Lucifer gestured toward his students with a wave of a hand. *The primates, which looked like oversized chimpanzees with less hair, were huddled in two groups of four. They looked at the new arrival with suspicion, glancing back at Lucifer for some sign, and held bones and branches the size of their arms in their wrinkled hands. Lucifer nodded toward Tamiel and crossed his heart with his hand.*

"He is a friend, gentle ones," Lucifer said, smiling at his students as warmth radiated from golden eyes. *"He will not hurt you."*

"Can they understand you, Lucy? They seem pretty mindless to me," Tamiel said, scratching at his cheek with his index finger. At first it was an absent-minded gesture, but then Tamiel noticed that one of the apes was mimicking his behavior. When he stopped his finger, so did the ape. Its black eyes were staring straight into his.

"Hah, **now** *do you see?"* Lucifer asked, leaning over to nudge Tamiel's shoulder. *"They are* **eager**. *If you had been watching like I have, you would have seen how much progress they have been making. It's, well, exciting."*

"Lucy, he was just... scratching his cheek. It's not **that** *promising,"* Tamiel argued, trying to dismiss the creature's behavior, but Lucifer took hold of his arm.

"Then you're not paying attention. A thousand years ago, they were crawling around on all fours. A thousand years ago, their thumbs were practically useless. In a very, **very** *short time, these creatures have made huge strides,"* Lucifer explained, causing Tamiel to look back at the huddled creatures.

"Wait, are you trying to say they're becoming like us?" he asked, turning back to his brother with skepticism.

"Well, not exactly. I don't think they're ever going to sprout wings or

anything. They're still corporeal beings and they have a **long** way to go. But, I mean, something is happening here. Something **real**. I'm not sure Adonai really appreciates it." Lucifer stood and Tamiel followed him to his feet, and they both realized the apes had stood up with them.

"What do you mean he doesn't appreciate it? Father set up this whole evolution experiment from the beginning, you know. And since when did you call him by his true name?"

"I'm trying it out. I figure our dear father might need someone on a more... equal playing field. We keep treating him with absolute respect and I think his ego is going to get out of control. And, well," Lucifer started, seeming to draw within himself. "Things aren't going... too well with these ones."

"What do you mean?" Tamiel asked, looking at Lucifer's students. They seemed to be waiting for instructions, but then Tamiel noticed something strange about their behavior. Unlike the other animals, which had developed their bodies into having natural weapons, these apes seemed to be rather weak. Then, Tamiel finally realized why they were holding the heavy branches and bones from fallen beasts.

"What... exactly have you been doing, Lucifer?" Tamiel asked, his tone serious now that he had an inkling of his brother's plan. This was no good; Tamiel could even see small shards of rocks embedded in the branches.

"I told you. I'm teaching them," Lucifer said before looking at Tamiel out of the corner of his eye, and the favored son squared up to him.

"We're not supposed to interfere. Whether they live or die is no concern of ours."

"Why not? These creatures have so much potential, but it's getting **wasted**! Just because they don't have sharp claws or teeth, or thick hides to ward off predators!" Lucifer shouted, turning to his brother and pointing back at the creatures in the dirt. "They're worth more than just... a life of being **food**! If we nurture them, if we teach them, they could be **astounding**! You know how long I've been teaching them to use tools like this? Two weeks! You know how many of them have died? **None**."

"Lucy, you have to stop this before it's too late. Father is not going to take kindly to your meddling. If they're going to die, that's it. That's the game. That's how Adonai wants it," Tamiel explained, but Lucifer rushed forward and grabbed him by the shoulder.

"Well maybe he's **wrong**. I can tell, brother. I can tell that they can think and feel and, if they don't die, that they are capable of so much. I only had three students the first day, Tamiel. They brought **others** for the next lesson. They **understand**; they **learn**. If their every day wasn't a fight for survival, they could—I don't know, maybe they could stand by us," Lucifer pleaded, but Tamiel removed his brother's hand.

"They're monkeys, Lucy. You want to know what I know? **This** won't end well." Tamiel stepped back and sighed heavily. "I know you're excited about all of this, but this is father's territory. You have a lot on your plate, and I know it's stressful..."

"You know what's stressful, Tamiel?" Lucifer interrupted, putting his hands on his hips. "It's seeing these creatures struggle for no damn reason. There's so much pain here and we can prevent it. I can't **watch** that! I can't watch these beautiful creations suffer and die just because Adonai is playing a little game."

"It's not a game, Lucifer," another voice responded, drawing the attention of the quarreling brothers. When they turned away from Lucifer's students, they saw a shorter angel wearing a yellow tunic, his hair golden and curly. Held in his left hand was a golden staff with twin snakes wrapped around the handle, their mouths joined together at the top.

He did not look happy.

"Please tell me you're here to remind us of some errand, Gabe," Tamiel said, but the smaller angel took a harsh sniff and worried his thumb against the staff.

"Afraid not, brother. Your conversation drew some unwanted attention. He sent me here to get you, Lucy," Gabriel admitted, twisting the end of his staff in the dirt beneath him and avoiding eye contact.

"Gabriel, I can explain," Lucifer started, but the golden angel shook his head before making eye contact.

"My opinion doesn't matter, brother, and you know that. You'll have to explain to **Him**."

Now...

THE MAN in the red hood and brown cloak stirred at his place in the tavern, but no one took notice. Only the cloaked man beside him seemed to care, shifting in his seat, but the rest of the customers continued with their habits. A scrawny man—with a receded hairline despite barely making it past his twentieth year—trembled as a chill tore through him. He at first thought it was another symptom, but when he turned to investigate, he found a trio of men had thrown open the door. He felt the itch nibbling at his mind once more, but he did everything he could to stop from scratching the raw skin.

If they knew he was sick, there would be trouble.

"Where's the owner of this establishment?" the short man at the entrance bellowed. His head was bare, but plenty of black, wiry scruff hung from his upper lip and chin. If he did not keep the door open, the hair would have hidden his mouth, his gums half-filled with yellowed teeth. He would have looked comical if not for the heavy armor and wolf-pelts covering most of his body

"I'm here, I'm here," a pudgy, middle-aged man said between bouts of coughing, rushing out of the kitchen to greet his new guests. After wiping his brow, the innkeeper finally saw who it was and stopped midway along the bar.

"Good, then we won't have to chase you too far," the short man said as he stomped toward the innkeeper, his subordinates following behind. Although they were each bigger by a foot and covered in similar armor, it was plain to see they were not bright enough to lead. When the smallest man made his way to the bar, he plopped himself down on a stool and knocked on the wood.

"You were here last week..." the innkeeper trailer off, his voice weak, but that only made the short man twist his ugly face in annoyance, making him even uglier.

"Are you saying you don't enjoy my company, Baro? That would be such a *shame*." His rank breath came out forcefully, but with an effort to ignore the stench, the innkeeper shook his head and erratically waved his hands in front of him.

"No, not at all, Cesare! I... uh, I thought you were here to collect taxes," Baro explained, but the other man gave him a crooked smile.

"I *am*. You owe us. We protect you, you know," Cesare explained, and Baro stumbled into the wall behind him.

"I—I already paid you for this month! I can't... I have no money to give you," he explained, drawing a laugh out of the tax collector. Cesare waved his hand at the people sitting in the tavern, which was only a third of the usual crowd.

"That *can't* be true." He argued, nodding at his men to come forward. "You have all of these fine gentlemen here. They must be paying you *somehow*."

"They—there hasn't been much business," the pudgy innkeeper tried to argue, but Cesare slammed his gauntlet onto the bar.

"I don't *care*! My friends and I, we make sure you're *safe*. We expect payment for our services," he said, pointing at the thin man sitting a few spots down the bar. Cesare's companions crept toward the man, who was doing everything he could to hide his illness, and he shook with anxiety as the brutes towered over him.

"I'm sure this one could help with your... problem," the biggest enforcer implied, knocking against the man's temple with his finger. At the touch, the peasant forced his eyes closed and started to rock back and forth on the stool. The itching was becoming unbearable.

"I... I—I have nothing. I only have enough to eat," he explained, the burning in his limbs becoming painful. Something needed to happen soon or he would lose his mind.

"He has enough to *eat*, Baro," the tax collector explained, waving at the peasant. "Has he already eaten?"

"N—no, I haven't been able to give him..."

"Then he can go without food for the night. Or you can give him a bowl of that slop you call a stew. On the house, as it were. You wouldn't want to see him go hungry, would you?" Cesare asked, a wild smile showing the gaps between his remaining teeth. The innkeeper shook his head and gripped the counter behind him with both hands.

"N—no, of course not, Cesare. But, you can't keep doing this. If the citizens of Napoli knew they couldn't come here without being robbed—" he started, but Cesare threw away his stool.

"This is no *robbery,* Baro, and I demand you recant your petty accusation!" he shouted, slamming his fist against the bar once more, but he settled down after a long moment.

"We give you a service, and we expect to be paid. Nothing more. Now, we will collect your taxes from your customers. You will give them slop and that piss water you serve in order to make it less of a loss for them. You may even want to take care of them *after* this, just to make it up to your fine clientele," Cesare explained, turning to the other denizens of the tavern. "After all, *they* have to make up for your mistakes."

"Please," Baro started, but he was interrupted by another bout of coughing. At the sight, Cesare scoffed and then turned, looking at the peasants of Napoli. Under his gaze, most of the men cowered and seemed to shrink.

Then Cesare saw something he had not expected; there were two cloaked men sitting calmly in a dark corner of the tavern. Seeing a glint of something underneath their cloaks, Cesare licked his lips and started toward them.

"So give us what you have, serf," the big enforcer said in the meantime, jabbing at the scrawny peasant's right arm. It was enough to make him start shaking.

"I—I... please don't touch me. I—" he tried to explain, but then the enforcer clapped a hand against his shoulder, causing an inferno of pain underneath his skin. At the sensory explosion, the peasant crashed to the ground and writhed about, taking his dirty nails and scratching at his skin over the rough material of his tunic.

"Hah, look at this one, boss," the other brute said, momentarily turning to Cesare, but the tax collector waved off the comment. From just the rich red material of the first mystery man's hood, Cesare knew he could claim extra taxes. Once he came to a stop, Cesare held out his hand and smiled.

"I'm sure you heard us over there, gentlemen. Hand over your coin purses and we won't have to get rough," he said, licking the front of his teeth and tasting the rot of his gums. He was still smiling when the man in the grey cloak yawned and lifted his head slightly, most of his face still hidden behind his hood. There was scruff on his chin, as if he had not shaved in a few days.

"I would just walk away," the man suggested, his voice low and almost apathetic, an unfamiliar accent on his tongue. "He's usually grumpy when he wakes up."

"Wha—" the tax collector muttered, but then he scoffed at the statement and shook his head. "Oh, maybe you didn't hear us over there. We protect you citizens of Napoli. We need to be paid. If we are not *paid*, you can't expect us to *protect* you."

"No disrespect intended," the man in the grey cloak said with a sniff, "but we don't particularly need protection."

All the hairs on Cesare's lip twitched at the gall of this stranger, but, before he could react, he heard a shout behind him.

"Boss!" the deep voice of the larger enforcer rang out, forcing Cesare to turn and investigate. Once he did, he found that the scrawny peasant had torn off his clothes and was raking dirty nails across his arms and thighs, blood seeping from torn skin and black tissue spread out along the rashes.

"*Another* one? Bah, this plague is getting worse and worse. Kill him and then drag him out back. We'll burn his corpse outside of Baro's tavern," Cesare explained before turning back to the strangers. "See? We're protecting you."

"We *don't* need it," the man in the red hood finally spoke, his words rough to Cesare's ears. "*They* don't need it, either. Go terrorize another tavern."

As he spoke, the man lifted his head and drew back his hood, revealing matted black hair that fell to his shoulders. An angry green eye stared at Cesare, but he was more interested in the yellow armor peeking from beneath the man's brown cloak.

It had to have some value.

"You don't *understand*," Cesare said, his hand drifting to the handle of his short sword. "I mean to collect the taxes you owe. By talking back to me, that is only increasing my price."

"I'm letting *you* know that we're not paying it," the stranger said, rising to his feet. "And you're not going to kill that man over there. He's under my protection."

"What... *impudence!* What makes you think you can talk to me like that?" Cesare asked, drawing out his weapon and forcing its point against the skin of the stranger's throat. Instead of showing fear, the stranger leaned into the blade—somehow forcing Cesare's hand back—and glared at him with that green eye.

"I just *did*, didn't I? And you," the stranger said before leaning back and turning to the enforcers watching the scene play out. "Back away from that man and get out of here. You're not collecting taxes today."

"You have no right to speak to my men like that! You will die!" Cesare shouted, throwing his sword at the stranger's throat, but his strike was stopped almost immediately. When he looked down the blade, Cesare found a massive, bandaged hand gripping the metal. Stammering, he looked back up into the face of the stranger, who wore a slight grin.

"Will I?" he asked before twisting his hand and snapping Cesare's blade off at the hilt, causing the tax collector to fall onto his back. Still smiling, the stranger stepped over Cesare to face the two brutes rushing at him. Cesare turned over and watched as the stranger seemed to glide between the men, blood flowing in an arc that splashed onto Cesare's face.

Throwing himself back, Cesare wiped away the crimson stinging his eyes as crashes of steel against steel echoed throughout the room. After he was finally able to see, Cesare's gaze fell on one of his enforcers staring at the roof with dead eyes, blood sporadically pumping out of a gash in his neck.

The other enforcer was still fighting the stranger, but then Cesare realized the living monster was merely playing with the brute, knocking away each of the heavy strikes aimed at him. Hoping to see vengeance for his subordinate, Cesare watched as the stranger, tired of his game, slammed an abomination of a hand into the enforcer's jaw. The force of the blow snapped his neck and sent the man tumbling toward Cesare, something the tax collector was unable to avoid.

After crying out in pain, Cesare realized he could not move; his subordinate's heavy corpse was pinning his legs to the floor.

"Seems you were wrong, tax man," the stranger said, lazily approaching Cesare. The small man tried to roll the heavy body off his legs, but before he could make any progress, the stranger held a cracked blade to Cesare's throat. The effort was enough to make his black hair fall to the side, showing the plagued tissue which covered the left side of his face.

"Wha—what kind of demon are you?" the terrified man asked, but that only drew out a weary laugh. Bringing his hand to his forehead, the stranger massaged the skin.

"You know, sometimes I ask myself the same question. Tell you what," the stranger said before sinking the Cesare's own short sword into his throat and letting the blood flow.

"Ask them for me. Name's Niccolo."

"WAS THAT NECESSARY?" Cadmus asked, disdain barely perceptible over the fatigue. After Niccolo flicked away a fleck of flesh that had already seeped into his bandages, he surrendered with a shrug.

"Nah, not necessary, but I'm hoping that if he does say something to them, they could at least... know where we are." Turning away from the reaper, Niccolo made his way to the owner of the tavern, stepping over bodies as he went.

"What do you want?" Baro asked, numbed by the fear of another violent display. He had never thought he would meet a demon, but obviously he was wrong. As he leaned over the bar, Niccolo chuckled and shook his head.

"Blood, but not yours," he said, opening his jaw and hearing it click back into place. "You seen anything weird lately? I'm looking for a grey-skinned man. Covers eyes in a black blindfold. Another guy is huge, blonde hair, covered in black armor."

"I—I..." Baro stammered, wracking his brain for anything the killer had mentioned, but he had nothing. "No, I've never heard of these men."

"Figures," Niccolo said, sighing as he looked down at the bar. When he looked back up at innkeeper, he bit his lip. "That cough of yours, how long have you had it?"

"Th—my cough? I... I've always been a little ill. I've had it for years," Baro explained, confused as to why a demon would care, but it seemed to bring relief.

"You can't understand how that makes me feel. I thought... well, it doesn't matter what I thought. When they come to investigate all of this, just claim it was some bandits, alright?" Niccolo suggested, waiting for Baro to nod, and then turned to the plague victim still writhing on the ground. Pain was etched into every line of his face.

"I can take it," Cadmus said as he drew closer, his cloak sweeping along the ground. However, Niccolo shook his head and retrieved a small dagger from his belt. He avoided eye contact on purpose.

"No, Cadmus, I started it. I'll end it," he stated before leaning down and holding the man's shoulder. At his touch, the peasant stopped writhing and was able to open his eyes.

"What... who are you?" he asked, tears streaming away from his red-rimmed eyes. Niccolo sighed, reaching with his blighted hand and touching the man's face.

"I'm the one responsible. What's your name?" he asked, his touch soothing the man's pain, even while rot actively spread from where his fingers touched the skin.

"My name? I... Tommaso. What's going on?"

"This is my fault, Tommaso. I'm sorry," Niccolo said, defeated, and he plunged the blade into the man's ribcage. He gasped out at the pain, grabbing his mutated wrist in some sort of protest. Although he breathed shakily, Niccolo forced himself to look the man in the eye.

"If you go to Hell, let them know that Niccolo sent you. Barbas should help. That's the most I can offer you," he said before pulling out the blade, along with the man's life. Still the corpse stared at him with glassy eyes, which Niccolo closed with his bandaged hand. After collecting himself, Niccolo rose to his feet and then walked to the doorway.

Cadmus would have tried to argue, tried to convince Niccolo that it was his job as the Pale Rider to reap these souls, but he knew his friend too well.

Niccolo would not let him take this guilt.

That wasn't necessary. You don't have to kill every one you find, Plague said telepathically, breaking through Niccolo's thoughts. Stroking his bandaged hand through the creature's mane, Niccolo tried to argue his point.

Look, he was already too far gone. And if it wasn't for me, they wouldn't be coming down with this sickness. He could tell that Plague didn't approve even before he huffed with a reply.

You have no idea if that's true. Yeah, you're the Horseman of Pestilence, but not every sick person is your responsibility.

C'mon, Plague. You just said it yourself. I'm the Horseman of

Pestilence. We can hide all we want, but I am **destined** *to bring disease and rot to this world. When Cadmus and I went through that portal, well, I started something. I wasn't thinking—* Niccolo was mid-thought when Plague turned his head and huffed from his nostrils.

Even after a few months, Niccolo still wasn't used to the plainness of the eyes that stared at him. In a fortunate turn, Plague could hide the blight in his skin. It irritated him to no end, but green fog pouring out of his eyes would be conspicuous.

Shut the fuck up. We both know what you were thinking and you need to stop blaming yourself. I'm getting annoyed with this martyr act of yours. I know you still want vengeance. Focus on that instead. Then Plague turned his attention back to the road.

Breathing in slow, Niccolo looked at the sunset to his right and memories of Lucifer came to the surface. After a moment, the sight of Azazel's grinning, blindfolded face replaced it. Immediately, Niccolo turned back to his horse with a scowl.

Don't put thoughts into my head. I don't want to think about it.

Don't give up, then. He took Lucifer from you and he needs to pay. Don't worry about the little humans you can't save. Focus on killing that goddamn satyr. I'm sure it'll make us feel better.

Well, genius, we can't find the fucker, so drop it! Niccolo grabbed the reins tight and jerked back to force the point home.

"Don't take it out on him, Nico," Cadmus said from Mercy's back, who was keeping step with Plague.

"He... he was—" Niccolo tried to explain, but Cadmus finished the statement for him.

"*Probably* making a good point. You don't need to take out your anger on your friends." The truth of it earned a neigh from Plague.

"Thank you, Cadmus." Plague's voice was too deep and reverberated in the still air, and he turned his attention back on Niccolo without missing another beat. "But we're here for you, little man, and you don't need to go down this path."

"Goddamnit, why can't you guys just leave it alone? I help kill innocent people just by *existing*, and we're nowhere close to avenging Lucifer. We're failing and... I'm allowed to be frustrated," Niccolo looked into the distance.

"No one is saying you are not allowed to feel, Niccolo," Mercy rasped, the pale horse finally breaking into the conversation. "However, there is plenty of blame to spare, and it is not just your burden. There is no point in feeling that guilt when there is nothing you can do about it."

"Look," Niccolo started, but then the horse turned his blank stare on him.

Mercy didn't hide his vacant, white eyes.

"You think I do not *see*?" his voice rattled. "We will kill the traitors, Niccolo. It has only been a few months, and immortality is on our side. We will drop the subject."

They rode in silence for a few minutes, each of them lost in their thoughts, but Niccolo was not at peace. No matter what they said, Niccolo had the Devil's blood on his hands.

"So what did you see this time?" Cadmus asked, breaking the silence. Niccolo looked up, but a glance at Cadmus was enough to show there was no use in trying to hide it.

"How did you know?"

"I've known you for *how* long, Nico?"

Giving up on keeping it secret, Niccolo thought back to the dream and tried to find the best way to describe it.

"It was back, back at the beginning this time. Scratch was... he was teaching these animals how to use... I don't know, it looked like clubs," he explained before letting out a heavy breath. "Then this other angel showed up."

"Other angel?"

"Yeah, his name was Tamiel. From what I... from what I *felt*, it seemed like the two of them were close," Niccolo said, sensations from his dream distracting him from reality.

"Tamiel... I've never heard of him," Cadmus muttered. "What did he look like?"

"Hah, well, he kinda... kinda had hair like me. Except, well, *pretty*," Niccolo said, earning a scoff through all of Cadmus' stoicism.

"Well, they're angels, you know."

"Yeah, yeah. It seemed like he was important to Adonai. Maybe more than Lucifer himself." Niccolo tried to recall the feelings once more. During the dreams, Niccolo really felt like he *was* Lucifer.

"Then, the dream ended with Gabriel showing up and telling them that... I think that Adonai wanted to talk to Scratch for some reason," Niccolo said, clenching Plague's reins a little tighter. "I think he was creating humans, Cadmus. I think that's what I saw. What started the rebellion."

"It's not outside reason," Cadmus added, and Niccolo turned to his friend with a groan.

"*Isn't* it? Why the hell am I seeing these visions? They come out of nowhere and now when I dream I'm suddenly seeing Scratch's memories?"

"You were close to him."

"*So*? If *anybody* was going to get his memories, it was the one who reaped him. That's *you*, Cadmus," Niccolo argued, shocking the reaper out of his argument.

"I..." Cadmus hesitated, trying to think through the situation. "Look, Nico, I don't know. We've been circling around the question for months now and we don't know a damn thing. We're *both* new at it. I have no idea why you got his memories instead of me, and I have no idea where that flash of light came from in the Overlook. This is uncharted territory."

"If... if I had answers, Nico, I would give them to you," Cadmus said, looking toward the woods on his left.

After seeing Cadmus shrink into himself, Niccolo's anger fell away. Releasing his grip on the reins, Niccolo put out his human hand and stroked Plague's mane again.

"I'm sorry. I know that you aren't hiding the answers. I just wish I knew what was going on. We're blind up here and the best idea we can come up with is to change cities. It was... unfair of me to do that to you."

"What do you expect you'll find once we get there?" Cadmus asked, changing the subject with a low voice and forcing Niccolo to look at him. Now that Cadmus brought it up, Niccolo realized he had no idea what to expect.

"I... I don't know. It just—it just feels right. I need to see what it's like now. It's been two hundred years," he explained, his thoughts falling back to his father's smiling face. At first, he brightened at the memory, but then he remembered their last confrontation in the courtyard. Shoving the thought from his mind, he tried to remember the good parts of his life. He tried to remember Marco; he tried to remember his lost youth.

He remembered Camilla's smiling face and decided to hold onto that memory.

"Everything you knew..." Cadmus began, but Niccolo shook his head, gathered the reins to his horse and then sighed with determination.

"Oh, I know, but after three months of living in Napoli and seeing all those peasants and vassals and nobles, I just need to see something familiar. I need to see merchants in the squares, the Arno, all of the old streets," Niccolo rambled on, his nostalgia making him feel better for the first time since finding his way to Earth. He turned to Cadmus and gave him a crooked smile.

"Hell, if we're lucky, I can still show you around," he said before looking ahead, feeling the last rays of the sun on his face. Now that he was going home and his friends had cheered him up, being back on Earth was not so bad. For the moment, Niccolo decided to forget about his revenge.

Seeing his smiling face, Cadmus returned one of his own and looked ahead, trying not to worry about the leper's visions. There was nothing he could say that would help his friend, and Niccolo seemed to be in a better mood now that Firenze was in the near future. Echoing in his mind, the rattle of Mercy's voice tried to console him.

You did the right thing. The truth would only hurt him.

"It's... this was a mistake, Cadmus."

"I'm sorry, Nico," the reaper said softly, standing while his friend knelt. It was a spring morning—light from a cloudless sky flooded their surroundings—the grass beneath them a brilliant green. Bells rang from the chapel nearby and the bustle of Firenze could be heard even from here, but neither of them could focus on the life around them. Niccolo just stared at the ground beneath, the shade of the grave marker swallowing his huddled shadow. Even if he had the courage to read the names on the stone, wind and rain had eroded the letters. It made no difference; Niccolo knew exactly who was buried beneath them.

Camilla.

"I don't... I'm not sure why I thought this was a good idea," Niccolo admitted, sniffing back the snot in his nose. He wiped his right hand across his face and leaned back, looking over the small gravestone. It wasn't customary for the times to have a headstone, but after Camilla's service, the church had deemed it appropriate to leave some marker.

"Maybe this was your way of gaining closure. There's no shame in that, no shame to admit that you're in pain," Cadmus said, placing his hand on the leper's shoulder.

"The best... the best I could have hoped for... was that she had a good life." Niccolo wiped away the tear that was about to fall from his right eye. "That's all I wanted for her."

"We can't know, but maybe she found some satisfaction in her work," Cadmus argued while squatting down next to him, but Niccolo scoffed at the thought.

"*Really?* She became a *nun*. You didn't know her, but Camilla was *never* devoted to faith or piety. It must have been Hell for her."

"Maybe she *found* her faith, Niccolo. You can't know."

"I *can*. She didn't find *faith*. Joining a convent was the only option I ever gave her. This is *my* fault. I poisoned her husband, died, and left her completely alone," he explained and, before Cadmus could argue, pointed at the grave marker. "Because I was arrogant enough to believe that she'd fall back in love with me, I ruined her life."

"Nico—"

"I *ruined* her life. I turned her into a *nun*. In the course of my life, I destroyed *two* houses. Three *families*, if you really want to get into it."

"No, I'm not going to let you blame yourself for your father's mistakes," Cadmus declared, but Niccolo wasn't going to drop the subject.

"Why the fuck *not?*" Niccolo shrugged off the hand on his shoulder and rose to his feet, his anger out of place on such a sunny day. "I probably got this rot on my arm by being irresponsible, or, Hell, maybe this was the beginning of my career as the Horseman of Pestilence! Because of *me*, my father's line ended."

"*He* banished *you*," Cadmus stressed as he pushed off the ground with the handle of his scythe. "Stop trying to make yourself the goddamn center of the universe. If you want, you can feel guilty about Camilla or, if you *really* want, Simonetti, but your father made *his* mistakes. *He* ruined your family. Not you."

"He," Niccolo hesitated, looking at Firenze in frustration. "I don't know. It's just... we were so influential back then."

"Glory fades, Nico," Cadmus said, his voice softer now that Niccolo was done with his tantrum. "Time is no empire's friend."

"I just... I just wish I could have been there. I wish I could have had that other life," Niccolo muttered. It seemed like only a few weeks ago he had a different future, happiness within his grasp.

"Well, now you have another one. We don't have to forget the past, forget our loved ones, but we can choose to acknowledge that it is behind us," Cadmus stated, his hand landing gently on Niccolo's back. "We have to look to the future."

"Some of us have an easier time with that," Niccolo said with a bitter laugh. When Cadmus seemed confused, Niccolo raised an eyebrow. "How is that future sight working out for you?"

"Oh... *that*," Cadmus mumbled, bringing back his hand so he could grab the handle of his weapon. At Niccolo's comment, blue flashes of foreign memories flitted around the inside of Cadmus' mind. Shaking his head, he tried to focus on the present. "The honest answer is that it's *not*."

"You've had it for months, now," Niccolo said, crossing his arms as he turned to face Cadmus. "The seers' powers can't be that unruly."

"Well... they are," Cadmus said, the massive amount of information giving him a headache. "There's just so much there, and it's not exactly like they agreed with each other. I have two worlds of futures bouncing around my head and... talking about it isn't making it better."

"Oh, look who doesn't want to talk now," Niccolo teased, nudging Cadmus with his elbow. At the touch, Cadmus was shaken out of his preoccupation.

"There's a difference between that and opening up, Nico," Cadmus said, standing up straight and then looking around the cemetery. It would have been a pleasant little church courtyard if not for the memories attached to it.

"Well, I don't know for sure, but I'm thinking they're both a little painful," Niccolo said as he looked down at the grave marker again. Everything Niccolo had loved was buried beneath him.

"Look, there was no way you could have known she would end up here," Cadmus tried to placate him, but Niccolo shook his head softly before replying.

"Yes, there was. I was just being stubborn. She paid the price," Niccolo admitted, his voice lower now that his anger had evaporated. He stared for a moment longer, but then lifted his head and looked at the church. Cadmus had been right; there was no point dwelling on this. Under his breath, for the first time in centuries, Niccolo prayed that Camilla had made it to Heaven for her services.

"You know—" Niccolo started, but then he was interrupted by a voice coming from the woods nearby.

"It's about fucking time. Could you two have gone any slower?"

Niccolo turned quickly and grabbed the bow from his back, the string drawing itself as he grabbed a barbed arrow with his other hand. Keeping his weapon ready in front of him, Niccolo observed the two men walking out of the woods, noticing that each of them had brown skin, dark black hair and stood a little shorter than average. In the moment, Niccolo thought they may have been a threat, but one of them seemed awfully familiar.

"Ph—Phenex? Is that you?" Cadmus asked from the side, which brought an end to Niccolo's hostility. The kind demon was giving them a warm smile that set Niccolo at ease, even if flames danced in his eyes. However, when Niccolo looked at his companion, he saw a stranger.

"Cadmus, it's good to see you," Phenex said, extending his hands out in welcome. "We've been waiting for two months for you to show."

"Could have been a couple *days* if you let me hunt for them," the stranger complained. Noticing Niccolo's scrutiny, the stranger scoffed and crossed his arms. "And what the hell are you looking at, Nico?"

"Who... are you?" Niccolo asked, causing the man to bristle with anger.

"Are you *kidding*?" The man stepped forward, his eyes turning yellow, black hair sprouting from his face, and long fangs descending from his gums. Before Niccolo could react, the werewolf had a rough hand wrapped around Niccolo's throat and lifted him off the ground.

"Marchosias. Stop it," Phenex commanded in a disappointed tone, but the werewolf held Niccolo by the neck for a second longer.

Then, with a low growl, he lowered Niccolo, stepped away and transformed back into an angry little man.

"You could have," Niccolo started, a dry cough interrupting the statement, "you could have just said so. I've never seen you without the wolf getup."

"Well, excuse me for your ignorance." Marchosias turned back to Phenex with a sneer. "Why are we babysitting again?"

"We're not babysitting. We're playing our part," Phenex said before turning back to the Horsemen with a yawn, covering his mouth with his hand. "Oh, excuse me. I was napping before you arrived."

"What are you two doing here on Earth? Did you come through the portal after us?" Cadmus asked, but Marchosias just laughed and shook his head.

"No, we're not as monumentally stupid as you bastards. After Azazel skipped town, we had to pick up all the pieces. Eventually, when there was time for it and all the blood had been spilled, Moloch gave us an option," Marchosias explained lazily. Now that he had recovered, Niccolo placed his bow onto his back and set his hands on his hips, shifting his weight to his right side.

"Wait, an option?"

"Yes, Niccolo," Phenex said with a nod. "Originally, Lucifer had tasked it with closing the portal if it was ever opened, but Moloch told us that it could stabilize it instead. After some deliberation between Astaroth and the remaining kings, we decided we couldn't just close the portal. Too much was going on behind the scenes and we couldn't leave the two of you up here all alone."

"All alone?" Cadmus asked, his hands wrapped tight around his scythe. Seeing his reaction, Phenex shook his head lightly.

"No, we couldn't have two of the Horsemen up here with no one to support them. There would be no hope for the Apocalypse if you were stranded up here," he replied, but that only served to make Niccolo more confused.

"What are you saying?" he asked, crossing his arms to seem

intimidating. Instead, Marchosias groaned and rolled his eyes before looking at his companion.

"Enough with the cryptic bullshit, Phenex," he urged before turning back to Niccolo.

"We're taking you back to Hell."

CHAPTER 2
LINES IN THE SAND

"This is bullshit!"

"What happened?" Tamiel asked as he approached Lucifer, who was stomping away from the massive golden doors of Adonai's chambers. Before Tamiel could come any closer, his brother let out a roar of anger, three voices issuing from his throat and alabaster wings materializing from his back. His harmonious voices resonated with the marble beneath their feet and vibrated the air around them. Tamiel was worried for the first time in his long life as he watched the firstborn's fury shake the decorative pillars of the massive antechamber, the other angels present recoiling from their sibling.

After a terrible moment, the eruption of sound was over and Lucifer breathed heavily, his wings looking magnificent in the light of heaven. Warily, Tamiel stepped forward with a hand outstretched, braver than he should have been.

"This is unacceptable," Lucifer said between breaths, staring at the ground. "He doesn't understand."

"Maybe," Tamiel offered, drawing within striking distance of the firstborn, but he hoped that Lucifer would see reason. "Maybe we don't understand **his** wishes; it's not our place."

"And why not, Tamiel?" Lucifer almost spat out, standing up and letting his wings dissolve in a flash of light. "Are we supposed to accept that Adonai has infallible wisdom? You and I **both** know that's not true. We've seen him make mistakes before."

"Look, it's not up to us what he chooses to believe, what he chooses to do. Our place is to follow his orders, whatever they might be." Tamiel hoped to calm Lucifer, but the firstborn was incensed by the argument.

"Maybe that needs to change! Do you know what he wants me to do, Tamiel? Do you know why I rushed out of that ostentatious throne room?" Lucifer asked, pointing back to the golden doors with an arm trembling with rage. "He wants me to kill them!"

"Well," Tamiel began, trying to spin the statement, but Lucifer interrupted him.

"Not just stop **teaching** them. He wants me to take their **lives**. Because I was such a **terrible** little servant, he wants me to personally go down there and kill the very creatures who inspired me to want more from this world," Lucifer shouted, pacing in the middle of the antechamber. As he did, three dozen angels watched, taking sanctuary by the massive columns that supported no roof.

"It's **his** world, Lucy," Tamiel said, crossing his arms, but that did nothing for Lucifer's temper. When the firstborn quickly turned back to stare his brother in the eye, Tamiel realized Lucifer was more fragile than he had thought.

"And what good has **that** done for the world? He wants to see them suffer, he wants the beasts to chase them around and eat them because it brings joy to his malicious, ugly face!" Lucifer shouted, resulting in a glare from Tamiel.

"Hey, let's keep the face out of it," he warned, causing Lucifer to look at him in annoyance.

"Don't focus on the unimportant shit. You're better than that. This is cruelty, Tamiel. This is torture. He's keeping these animals down just because he wants to giggle at their suffering. They don't deserve it. You **saw** them down there," Lucifer stressed, closing the distance between them. "You can't deny the potential is there."

"Whether or not they have potential isn't something we need to worry about. I agree that... I agree that they might deserve more than their lot, but father's decision has been made. They need to die."

"By **my hand**? That's an insult."

"Well, to be fair, you did mess up his experiment," Tamiel argued with a shrug, but then a powerful hand closed around his throat.

"Stop being the perfect one and **listen** to me," Lucifer demanded, light shining from his eyes as he pinned Tamiel by the neck.

"Then say something before I rip your arm off," Tamiel threatened, his own eyes glowing bright. Instead of backing down, Lucifer maintained his hold.

"I'm not going to do it," he declared, which shocked Tamiel so much that he lost his anger. Upon seeing the reaction, Lucifer released his brother and backed away.

"What in his name are you talking about, Lucy?"

"I will not give into his childish demands. The creatures deserve to have a fighting chance and, since **he** won't back down, I will be their champion," Lucifer declared, his voice rising in volume as it split once more. His wings spread out from his back as light swirled around him, his holy strength becoming evident.

"You're mad," Tamiel muttered, fear gnawing at him as he realized the implications. "You can't just deny father's wishes! We exist to serve him! If you don't obey, he will tear apart the world to find you."

"He will not have to look far, brother. I'm not going to hide away from him. If he calls for my head, so be it. He'll have to earn it. Those of you who have been **eavesdropping**," Lucifer lingered on the word as he looked at their audience and found awestruck faces, "do not be afraid. You are not my enemy. I count you all as my family. I have no doubt that you feel the same for me."

"Very soon, events will unfold that we cannot predict. We are going off of **Adonai's** plan," Lucifer said as he turned back to Tamiel, who was flustered by his antics. "I have deemed it unacceptable what Adonai is doing here, and if you agree, you have a brother in arms. I understand if *you do not join me, but if our father sends you against me, I will not hesitate. I will do what is right and what is just."*

*"Make your own decisions, brothers and sisters. I cannot choose for you." With a pause, Lucifer stared straight at Tamiel. "At least **I** offer a choice."*

"Lucy," Tamiel started, but words abandoned him once Lucifer placed radiant hands on his shoulders.

"I'm not going to be a slave another second, brother. I would hate to see you in chains while I am free."

Before Tamiel could react, Lucifer patted his shoulders and then walked past him, away from the golden doors. Tamiel could only watch as his brother marched to his doom, his footfalls growing weaker as he walked along the marble tiles.

Then the Morningstar exited the giant antechamber and left Tamiel alone with his thoughts.

His spirit burning with righteous anger, Lucifer was halfway through the divine courtyard when he realized the full implications of his declaration. Panicking slightly, Lucifer staggered to his left and reached out with his hand, finding purchase on the rounded edge of a nearby statue. Supporting himself and distracted by his thoughts, Lucifer didn't even realize what was keeping him standing.

"That is your first act of rebellion? You fondle a statue of our sister?" a soft voice came from behind him, causing Lucifer to realize he was holding onto the statue's breast. Sighing, Lucifer looked over his shoulder and realized who had come to mock him.

"Lilith..." he murmured, seeing a woman approaching him with a pleasant smile.

Waves of scarlet red hair fell to the middle of her torso, a great deal of which she had loosely braided to rest over her right shoulder. Although she wore a modest wrap of white material, Lucifer had no problem seeing the curve of her hips beneath the folds of her clothing. However, he was in no mood to ogle anyone.

"No doubt Paimon will be flattered, but Father will be less than impressed," Lilith continued, walking forward with her hands held behind

her, which only served to improve her posture. Lucifer shook himself out of his daze and tried to gather his wits.

"Trust me, sister, my weapons against Adonai will not be statues of my sister's likeness. I'm a little more resourceful than that," he argued, trying to muster confidence he did not have. Lilith merely gave a lilt of a laugh.

"Resourceful? You? The angel who just declared all-out war against his creator right outside his door? I'm actually quite surprised Adonai did not strike you down right then and there." Lilith drew within a few feet of the statue and admired the handiwork. It was a triumphant statue of a woman in form-fitting armor, the fingers of her raised hand extended into long claws.

"Perhaps he is afraid," Lucifer suggested, but Lilith looked at him in dismay.

"Of his first creation? Doubtful." She turned back to look over the gleeful smile etched into the stone face of her sister. "I am more inclined to believe he did not notice."

"He will, Lilith. I'll see to that," Lucifer said, his voice more resolute now that someone was arguing against him.

"You are so **defiant**, Lucifer. You must tell me how you can muster the nerve to take on a deity who created you from nothing," Lilith mused as she reached out to touch the statue's face with her hand.

"You have not seen what I have seen, sister. Adonai has gone too far and he needs to be stopped," he stated, but that only earned a scoff.

"You mean that **he** has insulted you for the last time? I know how the two of you bicker. It's no secret that you have begun to test the limits of his patience. Why do you choose to hide behind these causes of yours?" she asked, drawing her hand away from the statue and facing Lucifer directly.

"I'm not hiding anything, Lilith. These creatures do not deserve to suffer, and I cannot stand it anymore. If Adonai doesn't stop it, we could see something amazing, I just know it. I don't care what happens to me. I just... I just want to give them a future."

As he finished the statement, Lucifer's indignation evaporated and he lowered his gaze to the tiles beneath him. After a moment, he felt a gentle *touch underneath his chin and lifted his head to find Lilith looking at him with a smile.*

"That was all I needed to hear, Lucifer. Your cause is now mine," she said, just slightly cocking her head to the side, strands of crimson swaying with the movement. Lucifer stammered, but then he took her hands in his.

"Lilith, that's... I wasn't trying to recruit you. I don't want to put you or any of our sisters into harm's way." He had tried to backtrack, but Lilith grunted and narrowed her gaze.

*"You think we cannot defend ourselves, brother? This statue of Paimon wasn't placed here because she waited in a tower for one of our **brothers** to save her. She won that honor by leading the charge against the Nephilim. That same spirit flows through me, Lucifer, and I will not have you speaking down to me again." Lilith crossed her arms and looked into his eyes with determination.*

Seeing her strength, Lucifer had to chuckle at his oversight.

*"I meant no offense. I just don't think that I... this is not a battle I hope to win. Now that the anger is gone, I can see that it was foolish of me," Lucifer said before setting his hands on her shoulders. "This... rebellion, as you put it, might just go down in history as a warning to others. I will stand for these creatures, I **have** to, but there is every chance that I will fall."*

"And that, Lucifer," Lilith said before standing on her tiptoes, her gaze soft now that he had admitted his fears, "is why I will not let you stand alone."

CADMUS LOOKED to his right and found that Niccolo had shifted in his saddle. These dreams of his were becoming more common, and they certainly weren't helping Niccolo's mood. However, as curious as he was, Cadmus decided to ignore his friend's awakening and focused on the road in front of them. Niccolo would share when he wanted to, but they had more pressing concerns. Their new companions, walking along as the Horsemen rode, were not particularly shy.

"How do you like being on Earth after all this time, Cadmus?" Phenex's voice said from the left. Shaken out of his preoccupation, Cadmus considered the question for only a moment.

"Well, it's not awful, but you may want to ask me in a few days. Before the two of you arrived, Nico and I were more concerned with being alone up here rather than enjoying our... holiday."

"Well, sometimes you have to take a moment to appreciate your surroundings. I hope it wasn't *all* bad," Phenex said with a gentle smile. Cadmus' spirits were lighter while in the man's presence, but when he looked down at Mercy's neck, he sniffed in the fresh countryside air that he couldn't quite bring himself to enjoy.

"There were a few moments... a few moments where I forgot what we were doing up here. I died over twelve centuries ago and I," he said, pausing as he realized who he was talking to, but then continued anyway, "I didn't realize how much I missed the light. Just feeling the sun on my face..."

"Oh, *that* I definitely understand," Phenex said, closing his eyes and basking in the heat of the late morning sun.

"I don't," Marchosias muttered from the other side of Niccolo's horse, but Phenex exaggerated a roll of his eyes at him before turning back to Cadmus.

"He's always liked the night a little more. Back when we were alive, he'd stay inside as long as he could," he said, stretching his arms above him. "It's his loss, I think."

"We lost more than just sunlight," Marchosias said, his voice low and, to Cadmus' surprise, emotional. After noticing Cadmus looking at him, the man grunted and walked a little faster, putting Niccolo's horse in between them so he could evade attention. Taking the hint, Cadmus turned back to Phenex, whose smile had disappeared.

"Maybe we shouldn't talk about that. No point in bringing up the bitter memories," Phenex said, shrugging as he walked along the road. It took little time for him to recover and soon he was smiling back at Cadmus. "You said twelve centuries?"

"I—yes," Cadmus admitted, but then he looked at Phenex with a raised eyebrow. "I thought we weren't bringing up the bitter memories."

"We're not. I want to focus on life, not death, my dear friend," Phenex stated with a light chuckle. "You know, that's about the same time that Marchosias and I were living."

"I... know," Cadmus stated, breaking eye contact and staring at Mercy's neck. Phenex made a few uncomfortable noises, but then sighed heavily.

"Ah, you figured out who we are, then," he said under his breath, but soon he took a deep breath. "Well, like I said, no point in the bitter ones. I am a little curious, though. How did you find out?"

"Well," Cadmus hesitated. He didn't want to offend or hurt the man more than necessary.

Just tell him. The man respects truth, Mercy commented. After wordlessly thanking his friend, Cadmus turned to the small man walking beside him.

"I died several decades after you. Your fame had grown in those years and I... my family respected your teachings until the... the end. When I fell, when I heard about the men Astaroth kept in his company..." Cadmus intended to finish the statement, but Phenex let out a soft breath and patted him on the knee.

"I understand. I'm sorry that you had to suffer for my mistakes. I wish you could have avoided that," he said, compassion in his eyes.

"You don't need to be sorry. I never truly *believed*. I just... respected you. When I heard that you were down in Hell, too, it made the transition a bit easier," he explained, earning a scoff from Marchosias on the other side of the road.

"At least *you* had it easy, reaper," he grumbled, which caused Niccolo to break out of his thoughts and turn to him with a glare. They kept their staring contest for a long moment, but Marchosias broke first and looked straight at Phenex.

"Screw this, I'm going to go scout ahead."

Marchosias' bones grew and stretched his frame, his clothes disappearing only to have black hair sprout along every inch of skin.

His jaws projected forward, long teeth grew to fill them and after just a moment, the small man had been replaced by an eight-foot-tall werewolf.

"Stick to the woods, Marchosias, we don't need extra attention," Phenex cautioned, earning a huff of annoyance.

"Yeah, and don't go too far. We'll whistle if we need you," Niccolo teased. Almost immediately, Marchosias issued a violent growl and bared his teeth.

"You speak to me like that again, leper, and I'll make sure you never whistle again," he said, heaving his entire diaphragm with each breath.

"I'll keep that in mind. Thanks for taking care of us, Scruffy." Niccolo's condescension earned a long glare from the werewolf.

Deciding that it was all pointless, Marchosias lowered to all fours and bounded into the woods, quickly absorbed into the shade.

"What is his *problem*?" Niccolo was still watching the disappearing werewolf when he heard the sigh from Phenex.

"He would resent it if I explained, Niccolo. Don't worry, he'll open up eventually." Phenex shrugged before continuing. "Trust just doesn't come easily with him."

"And what does it take to earn that?" Plague asked, entering the conversation abruptly. Phenex looked surprised for an instant, but then smiled at the black horse.

"Like I said, don't worry. I've known him a long time and can tell he already likes you. He just doesn't want to admit it, yet."

"Already likes us?" Cadmus asked, drawing a nod from Phenex.

"We've never liked authority and he's particularly reckless. That you stood up to Azazel and rode through the portal without a second thought really impressed him. He acts like he's annoyed about *babysitting*, but trust me, he'd ignore you if he didn't like you."

"That's... comforting." Cadmus set about reevaluating their past interactions, but Niccolo wasn't satisfied.

"That's bullshit. I still don't like all of that babysitting talk he goes on about. It's not like it's *our* fault that you want us back in Hell."

"Oh, he's more annoyed at *me* for making him wait in Firenze for you. Thought it was a waste of time that I wouldn't let him hunt for you with that nose of his."

"Why *didn't* you let him go after us? That werewolf form seems to be pretty useful," Cadmus said, but Phenex shrugged at the missed opportunity.

"At all costs, we didn't want to draw attention. J—" he said, catching himself before he revealed too much. "*Marchosias* is good at what he does, but we couldn't risk anyone reporting sightings of him, or, worse, any mysterious murders if he got out of hand. I usually have to convince him not to go too far, though he returns the favor often enough."

"*That* I can sympathize with," Cadmus said, earning a sympathetic nod from Phenex.

"I can see that. And, I actually wanted to let you come to us because I thought that, well, I thought you may have some unfinished business up here. I wanted to give you the time for that before we dragged you back into this conflict." Phenex offered a smile of consolation to his companions.

"That's nice of you," Niccolo said, light on the sarcasm.

"I thought so," Phenex replied with a slight tug at his lips. "I figured that if we stayed by Camilla's grave that you would show up eventually. At that point, we could continue on without any distractions."

"How *did* you know about her?" Niccolo asked with skepticism, drawing out a belly laugh from Phenex.

"Nico, the *first* thing we did was talk to Barbas. The old man is worried sick, by the way. He'll be excited to see you." Then Phenex looked further down the road and came to a stop. "Hmm, if we make it, that is."

"What?" Cadmus asked before turning to see two cloaked figures at the crest of the hill in front of them, the stranger on the right holding something like a spear at their side. Preparing for hostility, the reaper lifted his scythe and let it thrum with power. Meanwhile, Niccolo grabbed the bow from his back and stared hard at the strangers.

"Is there some reason you're standing in the middle of the road?" Phenex called out, stepping ahead of the Horsemen, as intimidating as his small stature would allow. It seemed like the unarmed figure was about to draw back its hood when a black shape burst out of the woods and slammed into the stranger holding the odd weapon.

Marchosias, covered in his mystical shadows, had decided to go for a preemptive strike.

Miraculously, the cloaked figure was able to deflect Marchosias' claws with the handle of the strange weapon and sent the demon tumbling into the dirt on the other side of the road. Though she was unharmed, the stranger's cloak had opened and revealed light armor over a tall and narrow woman's frame.

Shaking his head mightily and sending dust into a cloud around him, Marchosias jumped up to stand on his hind legs and let out a deafening roar before looking down at his enemies.

The living shadow was about to jump toward the unarmed stranger, but, before he could, three long blades burst out of the figure's sleeve and pierced the werewolf's shoulder, forcing him to his knees. If not for the woman's hood falling back from the effort and revealing a familiar face framed by golden hair, it would have been a vastly different situation. Instead, they just stood there in shock.

"Pai... Paimon?" Niccolo asked in surprise, unable to process the information. At his voice, the second woman turned away from Marchosias, whose shoulder was still impaled on her fingers, and gave a weary smile.

"Hey, sweetie. Mind calling off the mutt?"

"I COULD HAVE RIPPED out your throat, Paimon!" Marchosias snarled as he sat down on his log.

After discovering the strangers were Paimon and Cimeries in disguise, the group had decided to walk a few minutes into the woods and discuss everything in private. They were set about in a circle; Marchosias on his log, Phenex on the dirt beside him, Niccolo and Cadmus standing to their left, Paimon sitting on a stump opposite the demons, and Cimeries leaning against an old pine tree with her arms crossed in front of her.

"I would have liked to see you try, pup. You're lucky that Cim had the presence of mind to not stab you through the heart," Paimon said, squinting slightly to hint at Marchosias' mistake.

As she spoke, Niccolo observed the demon king and found that something had changed about her. No longer was she a seductress with a light sense of humor. Most of her hair was tied into a loose braid and her body was covered in light, linen clothing. Her usually-smiling face was currently stern and devoid of mischief.

"I thought I was attacking humans, you bitch. If I had known, there would have been blood." Marchosias gnashed his teeth, but Paimon was ready for him.

"There *was*. *Yours*. Now can we get off this topic?" she asked, fatigue in her voice. Shifting his weight slightly, Niccolo cleared his throat and waited for her to look at him.

"What happened to you during the battle, Paimon? We heard that you went off with Azazel."

"Yes, Nico, I did. He told me that he had a plan in place, something that could help save Lucifer. Well," she said, anger rising to surface, "he had a *plan* all right. He stabbed me through the heart and left me on the steps of the palace."

"So he tried to kill you?" Cadmus asked, earning a bark of laughter.

"No, Cadmus, I'm a little stronger than that. It just took me out of the fight, and that's all Azazel wanted. Well, that and my blood."

"Your blood?"

Before Paimon could answer, Cimeries entered the conversation, still looking at the ground past her crossed arms.

"When they arrived in Hell and decided on leadership, a spell was crafted to guard Lucifer from lesser demons. Unless someone with royal blood attacked him, he was safe from death."

"Royal blood... Since Azazel wasn't a king, he had to find some way around it," Cadmus explained, Paimon nodding along in approval.

"That's right. I'm not sure if he meant for it from the start or if it was just a backup plan, but the satyr knew what he was doing. He did make a mistake, though," she said before offering a murderous look. "He *should* have killed me."

"Is that why you're here? Vengeance?" Phenex asked, earning another nod from the demon king. However, she didn't stop staring at Niccolo.

"Absolutely. I'm not going to let his betrayal slide. Neither will Cimeries. Beleth and Azazel need to pay and I'm sure the rest of you can agree."

Even if they didn't say a word to each other, Niccolo knew they didn't need them. Paimon could see the same hunger in Lucifer's second son.

"We're supposed to take them back. Astaroth and Beelzebub want to regroup—" Marchosias started, but Paimon whipped her head around and interrupted.

"That's the *last* thing we need to do. We need to kill those bastards, then we can worry about the rest of it!"

"What are you, insane?" Marchosias barked, leaning forward on his log. "Hell is in shambles right now and we need to consolidate before anything else happens. Azazel turned dozens of demons feral, obliterated any chance we had at winning the Apocalypse and if we're going to have a chance—"

"You still think we *have* a chance, Marchosias?" Paimon interrupted, jumping to her feet. "Azazel took everything from us and we don't have any hope *left*. It's chaos down there and everyone is scheming for control. Astaroth and the others are doing what they can, but Hell is too massive and there aren't enough Fallen to spread around. Asmodeus hasn't stopped burning demons alive looking for anyone *vaguely* attached to Azazel over the last ten thousand years! The Leviathan is currently enjoying a *feeding frenzy* in Beleth's province!"

"Which is why you should be down there right now!" Marchosias shouted, rising to his own feet and transforming partially so they were the same height, his fangs dripping saliva as he talked. "You're one of the goddamned *kings*, Paimon, and you're running away with your tail between your legs!"

"You're talking to *me* about running away, you fucking coward? Maybe I *should* cut out that heart so you can't preach your hypocrisy," Paimon threatened, her fingers extending to claws and her teeth growing out of her gums.

Before they could continue, flames burst all around them and forced them out of their confrontation.

"That's *enough!*" Phenex shouted, his body floating three feet off the ground and wreathed in flames, the forest turning into an inferno in front of them. "*We have enough problems without being at each other's throats! You both revert to normal right now.*"

"Phenex—" Paimon started, but flames erupted from the kind demon's eyes and sent intense waves of heat toward them.

"*Now,*" Phenex declared, which was enough for them to retreat and take their human forms. Although Paimon wasn't afraid of him, Phenex would not have used his powers unless they were out of control. As the flames died down and Phenex drifted to the forest floor, silence fell over them.

"Is it really that bad down there?" Cadmus asked, his soft voice easily heard over the crackle of dying fires. Paimon turned to him and sighed heavily.

"We've lost it, gentlemen. There's no saving Hell. Without Scratch, without some big leader to unite them all, there's no way we can even make a dent in Adonai's forces. Don't get me wrong,

Astaroth is trying, but it's herding cats down there. I figured... I figured it might just be better to focus on goals we can actually accomplish. Before I die in the war," Paimon said, sniffing back tears, "I just want to make sure those traitors pay."

"Paimon," Niccolo said softly before walking forward and kneeling in front of the demon king. As tears fell down her cheeks, Paimon could only look in wonder as he grabbed one of her hands with his, the mutated left hand underneath.

"What's with the bandage?" she asked with a short laugh. Shrugging, he looked down at the ground.

"Didn't know what to do with it once we were up here. If the angels caught wind that we were up here... Thought it might be better to hide it," he explained, Paimon shaking her head.

"Don't hide your strengths, honey," she said, smiling down at him. He returned it for a second before letting it fade.

"Neither should you. But Paimon," he said, releasing his grip on her hand and scratching his diseased cheek. "You should know that we have no idea where they are. You would think a nine-foot tall armored warrior with a horrific, mutilated horse and a blind demon with goat legs and a tail would stand out, but *nobody* knows where they are. Not one hint. It might be better to just go home and lick our wounds."

"A human trying to give me wisdom... You might as well be saying *goo-goo gah-gah*. You don't need to tell me this," Paimon argued through the tears, earning an eye-roll from Niccolo.

"I'm going to let you have that one, but just this once. And you're right, I don't need to tell you this, but *trust me*, there's nothing out there. I would give anything to know where they are and rip Azazel's spine out and choke him with it, believe me, but it's just—"

"We can find him, Nico. We just need to talk to the right person," Paimon said, mischief returning to her eyes for the instant.

"Right person? Who would know?" he asked, drawing back from her as Paimon wiped away the tears on her face.

"Tamiel," Cimeries said from her post by the tree, but she left Paimon to explain.

"He's an old one," she started, but Niccolo interrupted.

"He's an angel," he muttered, surprising everyone but Cadmus, who merely worried the scythe in his hands.

"He... was. How did you know?" Paimon asked shakily and, seeing her vulnerability, Niccolo lost his ability to speak. He turned to Cadmus to save him, the reaper noticing after a few seconds.

"Ever since the Overlook and that white light," Cadmus began, drawing their attention, "Niccolo has been seeing visions of Lucifer's past. Recently, some of those visions have shown an angel named Tamiel."

"What else do you know about him?" Paimon asked, falling off the stump and crawling to Niccolo, grabbing his face with both hands. Stumbling back, Niccolo tried to tell her everything.

"N—not much. He tried to talk down Lucifer from starting the rebellion. That's... that's all I know so far," he said, nervous with Paimon's blank eyes so close to his face. After a moment of staring at him, Paimon backed away and bit her lip as she looked into the middle distance.

"He did that; that's true. Why are *you* getting Lucifer's memories..."

"We have no idea," Cadmus said, gripping his scythe tighter. "But it's good to know that he's not imagining it." The group quietly considered the implications of what those visions could be, but eventually Cimeries pushed off the tree she was leaning on.

"That doesn't matter. Tamiel can lead us to Azazel and Beleth. That's why we're here, and that's where we're going," she stated, setting down the blunt end of her pike on the moss near her feet.

"Are you saying he's on their side? Is this an interrogation?" Phenex asked, which made Paimon burst into laughter.

"Tamiel *never* chose sides. That's why he's on Earth. And, if you knew him, you'd know he would be caught *dead* before helping out Azazel."

"Wait, he's on Earth because he didn't choose a side?" Niccolo asked, which made Paimon turn to him.

"After the war, Adonai wasn't in a kind mood. If you didn't fight on his side, you were going to get punished. Those of us who rebelled ended up in Hell. Those of us who didn't want to fight each other, they ended up on Earth, banished from Heaven and Hell to live among the creatures and beasts of the world," she explained, sighing heavily at the end of it, which Cimeries took as her cue to shoulder the burden.

"They are called *watchers*. Left with nothing else, stripped of their wings, their only choice was to observe the changes in the world." Cimeries' voice was empty of emotion. "I have known two in my time. One came to me in need, the other in shame."

"You met a watcher?" Cadmus asked in shock.

"More than that, reaper. They are not so impressive in person. In any case, this does not matter. We must find Tamiel," she declared, tapping her pike against the forest floor to drive the point home.

"How do we find him?" Niccolo asked, abandoning all thoughts of returning to Hell. If this angel from his dreams could give him revenge, nothing would stop him.

"Cim can lead us to them," Paimon said. "He's north of here, only two days' travel if we hurry. With the power we have at our disposal, it's nothing. Phenex and Marchosias are fine and the two of us can ride with you."

"It's going to be awfully suspicious if we go full speed, not to mention that *they* are pretty obvious," Cadmus added, and Paimon turned to him in dismay.

"Are you still trying to hide? It doesn't matter if people know you exist!" she shouted, but Niccolo joined his fellow Horseman in the argument.

"As soon as they know that the Horsemen are riding, Heaven will think the Apocalypse has started, Paimon. It's already hard enough to hold back our presence as it is," he replied, looking down at his hand as he did so. "Just being here has caused a plague that is tearing apart Italia."

"Heaven is not going to do a *damn thing*, Nico," she claimed, turning to face him directly.

"The deal is that the Apocalypse starts when *all* of the Horsemen ride. That's what the angels are looking out for. If you don't remember, you killed Ajax and they're not even close to choosing his successor. Even if that wasn't the case, it's hard enough to get Diogenes to do *anything*, so telling him that he shouldn't go up to Earth isn't exactly a fight. We can't ride through the middle of cities with our powers on full display and expect Heaven to ignore us, but as long as we keep our heads down, we should be fine."

"Is that true?" Cadmus asked, turning to face Phenex and Marchosias. Instead, Mercy's voice crackled into the air.

"That is my understanding, master. Without my siblings, true Hell on Earth cannot be unleashed," his voice shook through the air, disturbing their audience. However, Niccolo's thoughts were only on one thing.

"So that means... that means that I don't have to worry about my duty. I can... I can go after Azazel?" he asked Paimon, who leaned forward with a smile.

"*We* can go after the satyr. We just need to get directions from Tamiel."

"You talk about finding an ancient, hidden angel like it's nothing, Paimon," Marchosias said, returning to the conversation. "We're supposed to believe that Cimeries can find him in the middle of wild country?"

"You should. She was quite a hunter when she was alive, and she knows just where to look. *And*, if you *really* want to feel useful, Marchosias, you can always use that cute nose of yours to sniff him out."

"Keep with the dog jokes. See what happens," he growled sarcastically before rubbing his face with both of his hands and turning to face everyone in their hellish group. "So is that what we're doing now? We're just going to abandon Hell and claim revenge on the guy who manipulated eleven kingdoms into letting him escape? The guy who can turn souls into feral animals? We're going to go after the demon who killed *the Devil* without a fight?"

"If he had actually *fought* Scratch," Niccolo said with a grudge, "he would have died. I think we'll be fine."

"It would be nice to know what he's up to," Phenex conceded, running fingers through his beard. At his betrayal, Marchosias let out a loud sigh and looked at the ground.

"So I'm the only one who thinks this is a stupid idea?" he asked. He watched the reaction on each person's face before setting his eyes on Cadmus, who was staring at the ground as he held onto his scythe. "Even you, reaper? You're going to be as foolish as the rest of them?"

At the question, Cadmus broke out of his stupor and looked hard at the werewolf. However, his mind was not on the discussion, but the visions swarming about in his head. It was even worse than usual, but he could divide the sea of futures distinctly into two camps. Even if it was the riskier option, Cadmus knew this decision was already made for him.

"Call me a fool. They need to die."

CHAPTER 3
THE CONSCIENTIOUS OBJECTOR

"You're back," Tamiel said, voice barely above a whisper while he stared at the golden expanse of Adonai's kingdom. The clouds lazily rolled through the central capital, filling the empty space between the monuments, towers and palaces designated for Heaven's elite.

However, this peace was little more than a surface distraction. For the first time in history, his **will** was being ignored. More and more angels were choosing to strive against their creator; more and more sons and daughters were choosing to deny a cruel father.

And the one responsible for it was standing right behind Tamiel.

"Of course, I'm back," Lucifer said as he walked forward, each step accented by the clink of chain metal against plate armor. When Tamiel turned to face him, each line of Lucifer's face seemed etched out of marble.

"Do you really think I'd join you now? You have half of Heaven on your side now, fools that they are. What use is my help?" Tamiel asked, his hair swaying from the breeze passing by.

"You know exactly why I need your help," Lucifer said. "If Adonai's favorite son sides with us, it will bring more angels to our side. Even if he's a god, if enough of us stand together and don't fight among ourselves..."

"That's... stupid." Tamiel scoffed. "By our very nature, we are limited. Why would Adonai have created us with enough power to destroy him?"

"You know how arrogant he is! It probably never entered into his fat head that we wouldn't obey him." Lucifer paused so he could growl. "Stop being such a perfect little angel! Don't take after your father."

"Oh, will you **stop** with that!" Tamiel shouted, clenching his fists. "It's not my fault he made me in his image! Be grateful I don't act like him, too!"

"If you don't want to act like him, join my rebellion and we can take Heaven and Earth for ourselves," Lucifer argued, but Tamiel shook his head.

"Since when has it been about **taking** anything? I **thought** this was about your precious students. How greedy you've become since you gained some followers," he replied, bitter. Lucifer balked at the statement, but he soon furrowed his brow and grunted.

"Don't accuse me of greed, brother. I'm still doing this for them, just like I'm doing this for every beast on that planet, just like I'm doing it for all of us!" he shouted, walking past him to point at the expanse of Heaven. "Don't you see? **We're** suffering, too!"

"Are we, really? We were fine until you started getting all of this in your head! Now there's fighting among the Host that you're **trying** to save. Do you see how **irresponsible** that is? You've created suffering where there **wasn't** any."

"Then you're fucking blind! Just because we didn't know we were slaves doesn't mean there weren't chains binding us. Now that we have seen it, now that we know the full extent of Adonai's cruelty, how can we ignore it? There is a **war** coming, and I want you to be on the right side."

"A war? It'll be a slaughter, Lucy. Father's power is limitless and he still has half of Heaven obeying his every wish. You really think you're on even ground here? He'll probably just watch all of you kill each other with a smile on his face. Did you ever stop to think about that?" Tamiel asked with a sneer. "You're doing more harm than good."

"You have to be kidding," Lucifer muttered, massaging his forehead with his fingers. "You're accusing me of not thinking. If you just use your damn name for a good cause, we could go without all of that bloodshed."

"There's going to be blood, Lucifer, and I don't want to see it," Tamiel lamented, turning from his brother and walking away from the precipice. "There's too much at stake... and I can't risk the lives of my family."

"What is this about, Tamiel? You know better than to side with Adonai and you're **no** coward." Lucifer walked after his friend and set a hand on his shoulder.

"I'm not going to fight against you," he replied, slapping away the firstborn's hand. "I won't spill any blood in a useless war."

"He's right about useless," a bored voice interrupted their bickering, and they turned to face the new arrival. Standing in white robes with golden lining that fell to his feet, a man with long, brown hair was standing with an intricate spear in his left hand. He wore a tired expression on his face, as if the world was unseemly and he had long since lost his patience.

"Uriel, you have the gall to show yourself in front of me," Lucifer snarled, his wings flashing out behind him.

"In front of **you**? How dare **you** persist in this temper tantrum of yours. If I was not so charitable, I would have your head on my spear and there would be no more rebellion. As it stands, I will offer you the chance to surrender." The archangel stepped forward, his robes dragging along the ground, and Lucifer merely laughed at his brother's attitude.

"If I was going to surrender, it wouldn't be to a pompous handmaiden like you. You're lucky I don't shove Lux down your throat," he said, summoning the short blade into his right hand. With a loud sigh, Uriel looked down his nose at Lucifer's display.

"Oh, you're naming inanimate objects, now? How positively egotistical of you. Just because you were born first does not mean you can claim equal standing with our father. It just means you hold most of his **mistakes**," Uriel said with a slight smirk, turning to Tamiel. "I assume you see how it would be **unwise** to side with such a poor example of divinity."

"You're speaking as if Adonai hasn't shown the slightest amount of egotism," Lucifer interrupted, but Uriel didn't bother to turn.

"Unlike you, **he** has the power and position to justify it. Now, Tamiel, will you finally desist with this little stalemate and join the righteous side? Father is getting impatient," he said, every word clipped and precise. Instead of giving in, Tamiel shook his head and bit his lip.

"I don't want to fight on either side, brothers. I don't want there to **be** sides. We're all family up here, even if we act like assholes from time to time," he said, looking to each brother in turn. "Just stop all this nonsense and get back to your lives. There's no need to fight."

"It's too late for that." Lucifer stomped forward and pointed at his pious opponent. "Adonai is keeping us in chains and anybody who chooses to fight on his side is merely a willing slave. It's **evil**."

"Please, God decides what is evil," Uriel said dismissively. "There is no world without him, so we all have to grin and bear it."

"Oh, like you've ever grinned in your life." Lucifer scoffed, which drew a disgusted sigh from his brother.

"Just because you cannot inspire levity in me, Lucifer, does not mean I am incapable," he explained, turning back to Tamiel with a heavy stare. "This is a foolish enterprise and I wish to return to Father before long. Can you promise to fight with us so this can be finished?"

"You can't side with that bastard," Lucifer pleaded, but then Tamiel shouted and let out a burst of light, at which point both angels had to cover their eyes. When they lowered their arms, Tamiel was standing there with golden wings, breathing heavily.

"**I'm siding with no one.** Leave me out of this miserable conflict. I won't kill my brothers and sisters just because **they** want me to," Tamiel explained, folding his wings behind him while he recovered from the ordeal.

"Why are you doing this, Tamiel? You know what's at stake! You've **seen** what I've seen," Lucifer tried to argue, but before Tamiel could answer, Uriel tapped the end of his spear against the ground.

"All of that matters little, traitor. Tamiel cares about one thing and one thing only. Must I spell it out for you?"

"What does he mean?" Lucifer asked Tamiel, who had sheepishly withdrawn his wings.

"Sathariel, you incompetent wretch," Uriel spat out. *"Our brother is in love with our pacifist sister and is trying to impress her."*

"S—since when?" Lucifer asked, drawing back as if slapped by Uriel's words. Tamiel bit his lip for a moment, but eventually breathed deep and looked into his brother's golden eyes.

*"For some time now. I didn't want to tell you about her because, well, I think you know. But Uriel is wrong about one thing. I'm not trying to **impress** her,"* he said, snapping back to glare at the archangel. *"She just has a point. We shouldn't be fighting."*

"Is that really your answer, Tamiel? The perfect son is just going to stand on the sidelines and watch his brothers bleed? You do realize that Father will not appreciate your lack of faith," Uriel said, his dark eyes radiating violence.

"I will not be threatened, Uriel."

"You will also not be spared. Brothers, you should hope not to see me again," Uriel said before turning and walking away from them. Tamiel watched for a moment, realizing he may have made a mistake, but then he turned back to Lucifer.

"Lucy, I just thought it would be better..."

"Save it," he interrupted, waving his hand in front of him. *"I don't... I don't blame you for keeping Sathariel a secret. I just hope you realize what it is you're doing by sitting by and waiting for the dust to settle. We could win this fight, Tamiel."*

"Lucy..."

"Join me at any time. Just because you're not fighting doesn't mean blood won't be spilled. I just hope you realize that before it's too late," Lucifer concluded, turning away before Tamiel could say another word. With a flurry of feathers, Lucifer jumped and flapped his wings—catching a thermal after a moment—and then flew away. Once he was on his way, Tamiel turned from his departing brother and looked at the expanse below.

It wouldn't be much longer before this peaceful kingdom was drowning in blood.

"That didn't sound pleasant," a feminine voice brought Niccolo back to the present. Even though Plague was galloping through the tree-lined dirt roads leading into the Holy Roman Empire, sleep had somehow claimed him. After waking and straightening up in the saddle, Niccolo tried to shake himself out of second-hand memories.

"It was definitely not *that*. When you were in Heaven, did you ever know an angel named Uriel?" he asked after a slight turn. Hearing the angel's name, Paimon laughed.

"Of course, I did, just like I knew everyone else. It only took a thousand years or so for us all to become thick as thieves," she said with a slight smile, as if she was remembering a pleasant memory. "Anyway, yes, I knew him. The archangel is a piece of work."

"That's what I'm gathering. I only saw him for a couple minutes, but he seemed like—"

"An asshole?" she interrupted, shocking Niccolo to the point of laughter.

"Well, yeah. I guess that's the word for it. He was trying to turn Tamiel against Lucifer and he wasn't exactly trying to appeal to his better nature," he explained, drawing back in the saddle as he remembered the scene. "Made a bunch of threats, honestly."

"That sounds like Uriel, all right," Paimon said with a sigh. "He and Michael were the two... I guess you'd call them generals, on Adonai's side. Before the war actually started, Uriel went around all fire and brimstone, trying to use fear to make people fight against Lucifer."

"Yeah, that part kinda got on my nerves."

"Then *all* of him would get on your nerves. He may be up in Heaven, but that bastard belongs in Hell."

Niccolo decided he didn't want Paimon to give into frustration and grow her claws while she was wrapped around his midsection, so he changed the subject.

"They mentioned another angel, though I never saw her. I think they said Sathariel? I'm guessing you know her, too," he said, which only made her hold onto him tighter. After letting out a heavy breath, Paimon buried her head against his back.

"You really do have his memories... You know about her," she said under her breath, but that only made Niccolo more curious.

"Who was she?"

"She," Paimon started before lifting her head. "Sathariel was a lot of things. A long, long time ago, she and Lucifer had a fling, but that's not so important. Really, she was the first watcher."

"She's a watcher, too?"

"Yeah, hon, the *first*, if you had been paying attention. Back when angels were still choosing sides, Sathariel was trying to convince everyone to lay down their arms. When we chose to fight anyway, she stood back as a conscientious objector. A lot of different angels chose to stand by her, since they didn't want to hurt their brothers and sisters. Then, when we inevitably lost, they were somehow surprised that Adonai wasn't happy with them," she said, pausing to shake her head.

"Well, I'm sure Tamiel will tell that story a little better when we finally get to him. If you want to know about her, he'd be your best resource. After all, she was the main reason Tamiel never chose a side. Lovestruck fool," she muttered before sighing. "Though I can't really criticize. That love thing is tricky."

"I'm painfully aware of that, myself," Niccolo admitted, which caused Paimon to squeeze his midsection tight.

"Oh, did the mighty Horseman of Pestilence have a girl waiting for him back home?" she asked with mild interest, but Niccolo shook his head.

"Not really. Life conspired against us. Things just... didn't work out," he said, trying to forget the life he had given Camilla. As he finished, Paimon lowered her head to his shoulder and sighed.

"I understand," she said softly, the thunder of Plague's hooves almost drowning out her voice. "What was she like?"

"She..." he started, trying to find the right words to describe her laugh, her sharp wit, the beauty of her eyes, the strong spirit that resided within her. In the end, the words failed him.

"She was amazing."

"They always are, aren't they," Paimon said, looking skyward and seeing a tiny glimmer in the air. She wondered just how high above the ground Phenex was flying, he seemed so small. "Did this amazing girl have a name, or are we keeping that a secret, as well?"

"Camilla. She was a merchant's daughter," Niccolo said, biting his lip in anxiety, and almost immediately Plague hit the ground hard enough that he almost bit through.

You act like a nervous girl in my saddle and I'll make sure you regret it, little man.

Guess who's asking to be in tonight's stew, Niccolo thought back, but he was distracted by the Fallen sitting behind him.

"A merchant's daughter, huh?" Paimon commented, oblivious of the conversation happening between horse and master. "Doesn't seem like the right choice for you."

"Well, we don't really get to choose who we love, do we?" Niccolo asked, trying to recover from Plague's teasing. Instead of seeing a smile on her face, Niccolo watched Paimon fall into her own memories.

"No, no, we really don't," she muttered, looking ahead of them with a serious expression. "Looks like we have some humans to worry about."

As soon as she said that, Niccolo snapped forward and urged Plague to hide himself. At once, the green blotches along his side disappeared under glossy, black hair and his fog dissipated, and it was all just in time. The tree-lined road suddenly lost its trees, becoming farmland with laborers scattered along the fields. Before any of the peasants noticed them, Niccolo hid his arm beneath the folds of his cloak and pulled back on the reins.

Do you really have to yank that hard? Plague complained within his mind, but Niccolo sent him a wave of sympathy. He and Mercy both slowed down to a steady gait, trying to seem like they were normal horses, and Niccolo did his best to make his arm inconspicuous.

"Do you really need to hide it, Nico?" Paimon asked.

Without looking back to her, Niccolo nodded toward the dozen or so living humans tending to the fields.

"It's the only option I have. People didn't understand my illness when I was alive, Paimon. Now, when it's become this... thing, I can only imagine how they will react," he said under his breath, keeping his eye on a man walking toward them. His clothes were much nicer than those of the laborers bent over gathering crops, and from the look on his bearded face, he did not appreciate visitors.

"You have nothing to be ashamed of," Paimon said, her fingers tracing along the bandages covering his arm. "However hideous you think it is, it shows just what you have overcome. Not to mention what I've heard you can do with it."

"I'm not... ashamed of it," Niccolo said, trying to ignore the pressure of her fingers on his blight and instead judging the intent of the advancing human. "Not anymore. I just... I don't want anyone to get hurt. It seems it only brings death and pain. I've seen too many people become sick up here..."

"Are their lives up here really all that great? I mean, I'm not advocating killing them out of mercy," Paimon whispered, eyeing the sentry walking toward them. "But look at these people breaking their backs for a lord that would spit on them. Many of the people you've sent down to Hell have much better chances now than in life."

"What?" he asked, turning to face her and ignoring the man who was now only ten yards away. "You've seen them?"

"Of course," Paimon said with a slight smile. "How do you think we found out where you were? That poor boy from the tavern, Tommaso? Barbas is training him in archery right now. He's grateful that you tried to help him."

"He's... grateful?" Niccolo asked, but before Paimon could say another word, the man in dark blue clothing grunted at them from the middle of the road.

"Who are you to be riding through Lord Frederick's realm?"

"Just some travelers, sir. Passing through and will be gone within the day," Cadmus said, drawing back his hood so he wouldn't respond with hostility.

"Where are you going? There's not much but wilderness beyond these roads. What interest would you have there?" His hand silently wandered to the hilt of his sword, but Niccolo noticed.

Although anger prickled his brainstem, he reminded himself that violence would only attract attention.

"It is a place of significance for my family, sir," Cimeries offered, stretching so she could talk over Cadmus' shoulder. "A grave site for an ancestor. We only wish to visit and be on our way."

"Who are you to have an ancestor from these parts? And why do you travel with such strange... people?" His gaze landed on Niccolo's face, the blighted half obscured by matted hair. Seeing a green eye staring back at him, the man's fingers curled around the handle of his sword.

"No one important, sir. We are Romani, and I have lineage reaching back to parts of the Holy Roman Empire. I wish only to pay my respects," Cimeries said, her usually harsh tone completely disguised by one of supplication.

"Romani, eh?" he asked, drawing closer to Plague and his riders. "Then you must have some skills, some trickery or entertainment. What do you do?"

"I sing," Niccolo growled, ready to lash out at this nosy enforcer. Standing up straighter, the man licked his lips.

"Then how about a song?" Without a beat, Niccolo looked away from the man, clenching the fist hidden within his cloak.

"I have a cold," he said, and after a few tense seconds, the man scoffed skeptically.

"I've heard something like that is going around. Well," he said, walking back in front of Mercy and Cadmus. "Get out of here before you spread it. I must tend to making sure these peasants do enough work."

"Let them have a break. They work hard," Niccolo said without thinking, which was rewarded by a sneer from the man.

"Do not tell me what I must do, gypsy. They will work as hard as I need them to. Now, *you* seem like a much more reasonable man," he said, turning back to face Cadmus. "Give me some silver for the toll. We cannot have travelers using our roads without due payment."

Niccolo was furious at the request, but before he could act, Cadmus had shaken his head. In the same movement, he deftly withdrew a piece of silver from the pouch at his side and tossed it to the man, who smiled as he lifted it to his mouth and bit hard. He continued smiling as he placed the coin within his own pouch.

"Another, please. One coin for one horse," he said, oblivious that he was so close to death. Cadmus brought out another coin and lazily tossed it at the man, who repeated the process of biting the coin. "Well, good, seems like you are the best kinds of travelers. Enjoy Lord Frederick's roads."

"Thank you for letting us pass through unharmed," Cadmus said before urging Mercy forward with a light slap of the reins, purely for show. The man oozed smugness as the horse ambled forward, but then he caught sight of Niccolo's fury and grinned even wider.

"You're quite welcome, travelers. Enjoy your pilgrimage," he offered before turning away and heading back to the laborers in the field.

For a moment, Niccolo considered jumping off Plague and running the man through, but then he felt the grip of the woman sitting behind him. He turned back to Paimon, who shook her head slowly, and Niccolo was able to regain his senses. Although he told Plague to go join his brother, he continued to watch as the enforcer walked up to one of the peasants and started berating the man.

"Some people don't deserve this world, Niccolo, that's all it is," Paimon whispered in his ear, but it was small consolation. When they finally rejoined the other half of their group, Niccolo caught Cadmus' attention and glared at him.

"Did you really have to pay him?"

"I figured it was worth avoiding the hassle. Besides, it was only two coins," he replied flippantly, looking ahead of them to where the trees began once more.

"Did you see how he was treating them? That kind of man doesn't deserve *more* coin," Niccolo argued. At first, Cadmus only sighed.

"That's the world laid before us, Nico. You know that. The feudal system is distinctly not fair, but we can do nothing to change it. We have to abide by its rules for now," he explained, but Niccolo shook his head and gritted his teeth. Under his breath—only Paimon and Plague able to hear him—Niccolo made his intentions known.

"For now..."

New flames licked against the branches Marchosias had gathered, offering little comfort to the spirits in the clearing. After helping with the campsite, Marchosias had once again shrouded himself in shadows and departed into the woods, leaving Phenex to explain his behavior. Once he had given them an excuse—saying that Marchosias preferred to hunt for game on his own—Phenex had snapped his fingers and the campfire sprang into life. With some small measure of warmth within reach, the others abandoned trying to find a reason for the werewolf's behavior.

Cadmus looked around the clearing and found that Niccolo and Paimon were sitting next to each other, huddling close for warmth. It was an odd sight, but Cadmus couldn't blame either of them for trying to find some comfort in such terrible times.

Turning away from his friend, Cadmus looked at Phenex, who was lying on his back at the far edge of the clearing. As he was imbued with fire, the man didn't particularly need to be near the pit. Instead, Phenex sighed contentedly and stared through the space between the trees, appreciating the stars and their natural beauty.

Unlike their company, Cimeries seemed unconcerned with small pleasures as she sat with her back against a tree, the handle of her pike held in the crook of her arm. It was a bit far from the fire, but Cadmus would not ask her to sit closer.

Very early on in their journey, he had discovered the woman did not like to be cared for or spoken to. Unlike Niccolo and Paimon, who had talked almost the entire day, Cimeries had offered little more than the occasional set of directions.

However, as he sat in the clearing and ran his fingers along the length of his scythe, Cadmus realized there were questions he needed answered. Thousands of images still flooded his mind—changing every second as the possibilities were whittled away—and Cadmus needed some way to make sense of it all. With a meek cough, Cadmus turned to the warrior woman and laid his scythe across his lap.

"Cimeries, can you answer something for me?" he asked, waiting for her to turn and face him. Instead, she glared at him out of her periphery.

"Depends, reaper. There are some questions I will not entertain."

"You claim that Tamiel is another day's ride north of here. How *do* you know that?" he asked, meeting her glare with one of his own. With the slightest flicker of her eyelids, Cimeries sighed and then stared at the campfire.

"I've told you. I knew him during my life on Earth. He is likely in the same place," she said, reflections of fire flitting across her eyes.

"Likely? So you really don't know. You were alive more than two thousand years ago."

"You do *not* need to remind me of when I lived, reaper. My memories have not abandoned me," Cimeries almost spat out, shifting her back along the tree. "And some things do not change with time. The coward is guarding a grave and, I assure you, the grave has not moved."

"Oh," Cadmus muttered, regretting how he had talked to her. "That was not meant to be an attack. I just wanted to know what we're getting into."

"It is forgiven, reaper. Such a feeble attack could be easily ignored."

"You know, you don't have to call me *reaper* all the time. I do have a name."

"I am aware, *reaper*," she said coldly, which Cadmus took as an insult at first, but then he saw the slight turn to her lips. Seeing what the woman was doing, Cadmus turned away and looked at the dying fire between them.

"You call Tamiel a coward. Why is that? Just because he didn't join Lucifer?" he asked, focusing on the flickering blaze. The heat stung his eyes after a moment, but he stared anyway.

"No, charging into a battle without hope of winning is not bravery. I do not blame the watcher for his inaction during the war. I call him a coward out of experience..." she explained, drawing out the moment before turning toward him, "...Cadmus."

"Seems like you do know my name..." he said. "So what was your experience, if you don't mind my asking?"

"I don't mind your asking, but I do mind my telling," she said. "It is not a short story. Are you sure you need to hear it?"

"If you don't want to, that's fine, but if we're going to be dealing with him, I want to know if we can trust Tamiel," Cadmus argued, but Cimeries shook her head.

"His word is not the issue, but if it would ease your mind, I will tell you the story," she said, clasping her armored hands in front of her. "When I was alive, I was a warrior queen for my people. Until I took that responsibility, I was just a warrior. There came a time where I had to prove my standing among my sisters, so I traveled along the coast with some other warriors, looking for glory."

"We found glory, to be fair, but most of our journey was rather tiresome and unremarkable. We rode for months and during a rather brutal storm our party took shelter in a cave, perhaps a day's ride away from here. As it happens sometimes, the thunder frightened my horse and I decided to take off after it, which was perhaps not the brightest idea. I was young, after all," Cimeries explained, a modest smile on her face.

"Once I was able to calm the beast down, I found that I could not find my way back to my sisters in the storm. I tried to find another place of shelter for us, but it was becoming difficult. Eventually, in perhaps the first time I was ever glad to see a man, a stranger came to my aid and led me to his house at the edge of the forest. Once we were out of the weather, he introduced himself as Tamiel."

"At first, I believed that the stranger and the sickly woman inside were merely a man and his wife, but I could tell that there was something off. The more questions I asked, the more his answers led me to believe that these were not normal people. However, Tamiel was a good host and provided me with shelter when I was in need. In the morning—once the storm had departed—I told him that I would try to find my sisters, even if I had no clue how to get back to them. The storm had completely disoriented me."

"He was a good judge of character," she admitted, laughing wearily, "and insisted that I stay there for another day. It only took a few weak protests on my part to realize I wanted to stay... and so I did."

"I spent two days there, and helped the man with chores around his property. He ate simply, usually giving me the lion's share of the meal, and did not seem to sleep. It was odd, but the sickly woman inside was far more disturbing to me. As a guest, however, I felt like I owed it to Tamiel that I should not ask uncomfortable questions," she said, her voice darkening as memories ate away at her.

"Until I heard her crying in the night. At that point, I could not take it anymore and burst into her room, trying to find the truth. It was then, after seeing the wild eyes of the woman and the mutilated wings on her back, that I knew that these were not people. Immediately, I assaulted Tamiel with questions about the poor woman, and he had the decency to answer them."

"Mutilated wings?" Cadmus asked, breaking Cimeries out of her explanation and back to the present. She held her pike closer, giving a small nod.

"That was Adonai's punishment. The watchers were thrown to Earth and had their wings torn away, unable to fly back to Heaven and doomed to exist without their family. This was why the poor woman cried every night and had lost her sanity. The two of them had been on earth for two million years with only each other for company. She was trapped and she wanted to be free. There was only one problem."

"What was that?" Cadmus asked, his grip on the scythe tightening as he tried to wrap his mind around this punishment.

"Angels cannot kill themselves," she stated, looking at him with sorrow. "While humans have the ability to end their lives whenever they choose, angels are literally incapable of following through with suicide, even if they desperately want it. This watcher, she was consumed by misplaced guilt and had long since lost her mind. She wanted it to end, but she could not kill herself."

"*This* is why I call Tamiel a coward. He would not kill her, even if it was within his power to grant her wish. He was too afraid to be alone, too afraid to kill a woman. Instead, he allowed her to live a painful existence, and I will *never* forgive that," she said, breaking eye contact with Cadmus so she could stare back at the fire.

"Since he was too much of a coward to do it, that duty fell to me. And, although my spear found its way through her heart, I did not shirk away from my actions. I was with her until the light faded from her eyes, and I gave her the peace she needed."

"The coward will be there, Cadmus," Cimeries assured him, as the dying flames gave ground to the shadows on her face. "He could not abandon her in life, and he would not abandon her in death."

"I'm sorry that you had to do that," Cadmus said, trying to process that information, but he was surprised to hear her response.

"Out of all of the people in this group, I believe you understand that weight. When I call you reaper, I am not insulting you. It is a burden, and you wield it with grace."

"Thank you," he muttered, but she shook her head.

"It is only what you are owed," she replied, looking back at the fire just before it exploded back into life. Though startled, both of them eventually turned to Phenex, who was still watching the sky.

"Don't mind me. I just wanted to make sure you weren't getting all dark and depressing because I wasn't tending the flames."

After watching Phenex lay there for a moment, Cadmus looked down at the fire and felt its warmth on his skin.

It seemed to radiate a sense of peace, but the reaper could not embrace that feeling while the future still raged about inside his head. Worse still, there was always one image that kept repeating, one piece of a puzzle that perpetually shifted. Details would change with every repetition, but he knew that one of the figures was Tamiel. It had to be, considering the mutilated wings on his back.

And while he wanted to be optimistic, Cadmus could not understand why he was assaulted by images of this exiled angel rushing forward, his sword seemingly destined to impale an unarmed man.

"WE'RE CLOSE," Cimeries said, sitting up in the saddle so she could peer over Cadmus' shoulder. Dissatisfied with her position, the Amazon jumped off Mercy and walked forward, holding her pike to the side as she ventured into the green field. From the large patches of short grass and tracks throughout the meadow, it seemed like this was grazing country.

"Are you sure?" Niccolo asked, skepticism evident in his voice. Before Paimon or the others could defend her, Marchosias surprised them all.

"I hate to say it, but she's telling the truth," he said, shadows departing from his fur and showing every detail of his massive frame. "There's angel stink all over this field."

"You have *such* a way with words," Paimon said lightly, and

Marchosias growled at her while shifting back to human form. Once his shoulders popped back into place, Marchosias sneered at her.

"I can't help that you smell like flowers. Someday, you'll have to tell me how you were all able to keep that up in the middle of Hell."

"Trade secret, mutt," Paimon said, gracefully jumping off Plague so she could follow her opponent into the open field.

"Is that what we're doing? Just walking the rest of the way?" Niccolo asked, looking at Cadmus for support. Instead, the reaper shrugged and then banished Mercy, who crumbled into dust underneath him. Sighing loud enough for everyone to hear, Niccolo slid off of his saddle and let Plague fade into a green mist.

"Come Niccolo, some exercise will be good for you," Phenex said, clapping his hand on the leper's back. Scowling slightly, Niccolo walked faster so he would be out of reach.

"My body doesn't *need* exercise. We could have just ridden the rest of the way," he argued, earning a dismayed laugh.

"You need to enjoy nature more. Think about it this way. It's more time in the sun, in the middle of a field, with all of your friends. You're allowed to enjoy the world around you," Phenex responded, which only made Niccolo more frustrated. After walking faster in order to escape his cheer, he felt someone nudge his right elbow.

"I really don't know how he does it all the time. I've known him for centuries, but that smile of his rarely goes away," Marchosias said. "It's not natural. Sometimes, you're *allowed* to feel like a miserable piece of shit."

"See, I can get on board with that," Niccolo said with a nod, then raised an eyebrow at the smaller man. "So what is this, we're friends now?"

"Fuck no, but that doesn't mean we can't understand each other."

"Damn, he was right about you," Niccolo teased, enjoying it when Marchosias got flustered.

"*Who* was right about me?" he asked, fangs stretching out ever-so-slightly.

"That friend of yours. He said that you liked us and just didn't want to admit it," Niccolo replied, causing Marchosias to glance at Phenex. "You know, it's totally fine. You don't have to push us away, Marchosias!"

"I will *gut* you, leper. I won't smile. I won't cry. One second you'll be fine and the next my nails will be raking across your intestines." He extended the claws of his left hand with the threat.

"It's so nice knowing we're friends now. Though, just so you know, I think I have the sharper nails. Your hand'll probably get cut off before it gets to my stomach," Niccolo cautioned, stepping forward with a light bounce. Behind him, Marchosias scoffed, but he didn't hide his smile.

"Because that's what happened last time, right?" he asked, but Niccolo couldn't continue the game. He was distracted by Paimon looking at him out of the corner of her eye. Instead of turning away from his attention, she merely smiled and continued through the field. Suddenly, after seeing the light reflecting against the loose strands of her hair, Niccolo finally appreciated what Phenex had been saying.

While the others were appreciating the weather, Cadmus was still worried about what he was seeing in his head. Not easing his mind was the serious look on Cimeries' face. Although she could never be accused of keeping the mood light, her attitude was making the vision in his head even more disconcerting.

However, he did not have much time to think on the subject. After walking over the crest of a small hill, they were able to see a small cottage standing against the edge of a forest.

"Does that look familiar?" he asked, pointing with his scythe, but he was surprised by Cimeries' answer.

"No, but that does not surprise me. Nothing made from the forest lasts the ages," she stated, continuing her brisk pace toward the construct.

"But this is where you met him?" She did not entertain the question, and Cadmus figured that she thought it unnecessary.

"The smell's here, reaper. That damn flower stink is everywhere," Marchosias said, slightly transforming in order to use his wolf nose.

"Yeah, because that can't be explained away by the meadow surrounding us," Plague's voice came from the ether, but he was largely ignored by everyone but his master. They decided to venture forward cautiously, stopping ten yards away from the hovel.

"So someone who has lived on Earth for two million years decided to live like a pig farmer," Niccolo said with sigh.

"Not sure that pigs would be worth raising out here," Cadmus commented, looking at the land surrounding the building.

"I've done it before, but no, sheep are little more manageable. Strange accent you got there," a man's voice said behind them, punctuated by a yawn, but the group spun around with weapons drawn and ready to fight.

They were ready to fight a harmless shepherd with ten sheep ambling lazily behind him. Even though he was quite outnumbered, the dark-haired man didn't seem impressed.

"Look, I live out here so I don't get robbed," the man explained, light-grey robes sweeping across the dirt at his feet as he leaned on a shepherd's crook, observing his visitors. "Go hunt something in the forest. I won't stop you the—" Once he saw Cimeries glaring at him, the shepherd knew that these were no bandits. He straightened up and looked at each person seriously.

"So we don't have to explain who we are, then?" Paimon asked, crossing her arms, but the man didn't bother meeting her vacant gaze.

"No, sister, though I have to say I didn't expect any of this. There are quite a few living ghosts standing before me," he said before turning to Paimon with fatigue in his eyes.

"Let's go inside. I can make some tea or something."

"So PAIMON, it's great to see you after so long. How is everyone? Zagan still a hopeless drunk? Weather's good down in Hell? That's great, yeah, now tell me why there are three historical figures, two Horsemen, and a King of Hell in my living room drinking tea."

Tamiel rushed through the niceties without expecting any answers.

"Well, if we're going to point fingers, *you* brewed the tea," Niccolo said, holding a clay mug with his right hand. It wasn't a particularly large room and seven people were crowded around in a circle; only Paimon was given the luxury of a stool to sit on. Niccolo stood with his back against the wall and looked over the steam rising from the cup in his hand, their host staring at him with suspicion.

"Fine, strike the tea from the explanation," Tamiel conceded before turning to Paimon, who was sitting to his left, legs crossed in front of her.

"It's nice to see you, too, handsome," she said, sighing at her exiled brother. After a moment of scrutiny, Tamiel's resolve broke and he ran his fingers through his hair.

"Look, Paimon, I do appreciate seeing you again after all this time—it's been a long while since I've had company—but your presence here doesn't exactly mean sunshine and daisies. When the souls of Hell rise up, that only means one thing," he implied, fatigued, but Paimon clucked her tongue at the notion.

"Lucky for you, you're wrong."

Taken by surprise, Tamiel stood up to his full height and then crossed his arms. Paimon merely smiled at his reaction and—once he realized that she was waiting for him—Tamiel hastily gestured around the room.

"Well, go on."

Leaning forward, Paimon folded her hands over each other.

"The Apocalypse hasn't started, Tamiel, and if you had been using your skills, you would already know that. All-out war isn't coming for a while, yet," she started, but Tamiel cleared his throat and interrupted her.

"I'm sorry, sister, but there are Horsemen sitting right next to you. You think I haven't noticed? This one is leaking plague and rot out of every damn pore," he said, waving his hand at Niccolo, who was shocked by Tamiel's perception.

"You can *tell*?"

"Yeah, kid, the powers that be really did a number on you. There's so much radiation and airborne bacteria flooding out of you that anything living is screwed, especially with your friend following you around," he said, earning blank stares from both Horsemen. "Your radiation? The reason that you're the Horseman of Pestilence? Do you *really* not know what I'm talking about?"

"What the hell is ray-dee-a-shun?" Niccolo asked, trying to repeat the foreign word. At the question, Tamiel slapped his forehead with his palm and let out an exasperated groan. Then, after withdrawing his hand, he stared hard at Paimon.

"Do you teach them *anything* down there? What the fuck is Lucy doing? One of his little pet causes was to enlighten humanity and give them knowledge! Did he just give up?" he asked, pinching the bridge of his nose to gather his senses.

Instead of excuses, he heard silence, and once Tamiel opened his eyes, none of his guests could look him in the eye. Eventually, Niccolo breathed out heavily and lifted his head to meet Tamiel's gaze.

"You may want to sit down," he suggested, but Tamiel only shook his head.

"What happened?" After a heavy sigh, Niccolo tried to explain.

"Lucifer's dead, Tamiel. I know you two go way back..." Niccolo started, but when he saw the pain in Tamiel's face, he could not continue. The exiled angel staggered until he was able to set his hand on the mantle of his fireplace. Breathing in raggedly, Tamiel was unable to stop the single tear that rolled down his cheek, leaving a trail that shimmered in the firelight. Phenex stepped forward and tried to place his hand on the watcher's shoulder, but Tamiel weakly shook his head. After a moment, he let out a controlled breath and then stood to his full height.

"How did he die?" he asked, staring hard at Niccolo. It surprised him, but Tamiel had fixated on him. With the respect he owed Lucifer's brother, Niccolo would not retreat from the attention.

"Azazel. Stabbed him in the back after convincing some of the kings to rebel," he explained, the mug in his hand trembling as anger flooded his senses. "He and Beleth escaped to Earth after letting Hell destroy itself. I... I followed after them once the portal opened, but it wasn't stable and Cadmus and I ended up in Napoli with no clue where they went."

"I told him not to trust that snake," Tamiel muttered, but eventually he looked around the room to the others. "Well, that explains these young ones. Paimon, what are you doing up here?"

"Azazel stabbed me through the heart in order to kill Lucy. He left before I could repay him."

"Just revenge, then? That's what all of this about? Your plan is to walk up to Azazel, tear out his black heart, and then... what?" Tamiel asked, walking across the middle of the room and then setting his hands on Paimon's shoulders. "What's the end game here?"

"Does there really have to be one?" she asked, shaking off his hands and then standing up to meet him. "Whatever chance the Fallen had in the Apocalypse is gone, so we may as well satisfy our debts."

Tamiel glared at his sister for a moment longer, but then he stood up and pointed at Niccolo.

"You. What do you know about Lucifer and I?" he asked, only turning to face Niccolo by the end. Niccolo was surprised at first, but he steeled his nerves and stood so could be on even footing.

"Ever since he died, I've seen visions from Lucifer's past. You've been in... a lot of them," he explained, pointing at Tamiel with his bandaged hand.

The angel looked down at the long finger, grunted, and the

bandages frayed and ripped asunder in a flash, revealing the blight along Niccolo's arm. It was enough for Niccolo to lower the limb out of sheer reaction, even if it was unharmed.

"Did you end his life with *that*? Did you give him peace? I can tell there's a lot of power there," Tamiel said softly, squaring up to him. Holding his massive arm with his human hand, Niccolo shook his head in disbelief.

"W—what did you just do?" He tried to muster confidence, but Tamiel did not care for his bravado.

"Nothing, Horseman, I only tapped into the power in that weapon of yours. Answer my question, did those black nails tear through my brother's ghost?" he shouted out the question, his grey shepherd robes flowing from the power leaking into the air around him. Afraid of the exiled angel, Niccolo could only shut his eye and give into the interrogation.

"No! I wouldn't—I wouldn't be able to do that, anyway! *Cadmus* reaped his soul." Niccolo expected violence, but nothing came of it. After a moment, Niccolo opened his eye and looked around the room. Everyone was in the same spot, including Tamiel, who was no longer trying to intimidate him.

Instead, he just looked at the young human with sympathy.

"I believe that *you* believe it, Horseman, even if you're wrong," Tamiel started, earning a confused look from Niccolo. "That must have been a dirty, little lie they told you. Any human can take a soul when it's ready. They just need to know how."

"Since when?" Paimon asked. Turning to face her, Tamiel sighed.

"*Always*. Angels are the exception. We're not built for it," he said off-handedly, and Marchosias growled from his position.

"You scared the kid half to death, you bastard! Why did you have to do that?" he shouted, his eyes turning yellow in an instant. The watcher was unimpressed.

"Fear tends to bring out the truth."

"Says the coward," Cimeries muttered, but it was impossible not to hear it in such a small house. Tamiel judged her for a moment, but decided against a confrontation.

"Says the coward, indeed. In any case, now I know what happened. What exactly did you hope to gain from all of this?" he asked, settling back against the wall near the fireplace.

"You're a watcher, Tamiel," Paimon reminded him. "We want you to watch."

"...you fall on your face?"

"We... need to know where Azazel and Beleth ended up," Cadmus said, trying to gain some foothold in the conversation, but Tamiel didn't appreciate it.

"I figured, Horseman. I just don't see the point," he said, breathing out the words. At that, Niccolo recovered himself and new fury burned up inside him.

"What kind of brother are you?" he almost shouted, closing the distance between them and—with his demonic hand—grabbing Tamiel by the throat and pushing him against the wall. "You *saw* what Lucifer was doing. You knew how much influence you had by being the favorite son! None of this would have happened if not for you! And now, now when you know a backstabbing friend killed your brother, you're just going to stand back and deny us the chance to avenge him?"

"You know *nothing*, Horseman," Tamiel declared, gripping Niccolo's wrist with one hand. "Adonai would have won even if I sided with them. Tell you what. You watch your brothers and sisters die by the thousands and then tell me that you want to see another one die. Just because you've seen me in his memories does *not* mean you know the whole story!"

"Sure, I do, Tamiel," Niccolo snarled. "Cimeries had it right. You're just a coward."

After the accusation, he pushed Tamiel against the wall and then released the angel. The very air around them seemed to increase in temperature as he walked away, but then Niccolo noticed the glow from Phenex's eyes.

"This is getting out of hand. I think we all just need to take a deep breath," Phenex said, stepping between the two, but a growl came from the shadows.

"Screw that," Marchosias said, crossing his arms. "Kid was making sense. This one is too cowardly to even *look* for his brother's killer."

"You?" Tamiel scoffed, staring hard into the werewolf's eyes. "*You're* going to call me a coward? Don't forget, *Marchosias,* that I'm a *watcher.* I saw everything that happened in that little town. I saw everything that happened right up until you took that bag of silver."

"There is *no* need for that!" Phenex shouted for once, flames bursting out of his eyes, but Tamiel barely even noticed.

"Why *not*? If we're going to talk about betrayal, let's fucking do it! If we're going to call people cowards, let's just get it *all* out there. I *didn't* fight. I didn't see the point in joining a doomed cause and hurting my family. Out of *everyone*, Yeshua, you should understand what happens when you fight on the right side of the wrong war," he said, pointing at the burning man the entire time, but when Tamiel used the other name, Phenex started shaking.

"You... don't talk to him like that," Marchosias muttered, beginning his full transformation, but before anyone could react, Paimon jumped forward and held Tamiel by the throat, the fingers of her other hand extended into claws positioned over his heart.

"Niccolo," she said, staring into Tamiel's eyes, "take Phenex and Marchosias outside."

"But—" he tried to protest, but the demon king interrupted him.

"*Now*, honey. I have to talk with my older brother," Paimon lilted, the sweetness of her words undermined by the danger of her claws. Tamiel was unafraid, but he also knew just what Paimon could do if she put her mind to it. They kept staring at each other as Niccolo led the furious humans out the door of the hovel. Cadmus had gotten to his feet, ready to help his friend with the effort, but Tamiel spoke up before he could leave.

"No, Pale Rider; *you* stay," Tamiel commanded, still looking straight into Paimon's blank eyes. She didn't object, but there was still quite a bit of tension as the seconds dragged on. "So, Paimon, this is the second time in five minutes that I'm being held by the throat. Can we stop with the games, please?"

"Sure! But if you try to manipulate my companions into killing you *again*, you won't have to worry. I love you to death, Tamiel, but I will cut out your heart without a moment's hesitation, but, you know, not in the way that kills you." She drew back, her fingers becoming delicate once more. "You still have *some* life in you."

"Some life you can use, you mean," he said, rubbing his throat with his left hand, but Paimon shrugged.

"There are plenty of ways to die, Tamiel. If you really wanted to, you would have already done it," she said, looking at the ground as she rotated her wrist, which gave a slight crack. Then Paimon turned her gaze back to him, her voice softer. "We're not asking you to fight. We just need to know where they are."

"Paimon, I haven't used that power in a long time."

"Doesn't mean you lost it. Just tell us where to find them and we'll get out of your hair. You can even keep your little vow of pacifism. The six of us are more than capable," she said, even if there was a hint of disappointment. Tamiel looked down, drawing his sandaled foot along the dirt floor of his home, but eventually he relented with a sigh and his posture broke down.

"*Fine.* It'll take me the rest of the night, though. I'll need some privacy, so go after your pets and I'll see you in the morning," he said, crossing his arms and defiant, even in surrender.

"I will. Thank you. C'mon, you two," she said, waving at Cadmus and Cimeries as she turned to leave, but Tamiel cleared his throat.

"The reaper stays. I said as much, didn't I?" he asked, the question stopping Paimon mid-step. She turned to face him directly, but eventually shrugged.

"Sorry, Cadmus, I guess you're his *payment*. Fighting will just make it worse." Paimon winked at the Horseman before backing out of the house, Cimeries slowly walking after her.

Once she shut the door, Cadmus faced Tamiel directly and gripped his scythe. When he looked at the exile, Tamiel did not seem to enjoy the company.

"Have you told him?" Tamiel asked abruptly, keeping his stance hostile. Unaware of what Tamiel was discussing, Cadmus bit his lip and shook his head.

"You're going to have to forgive me..."

"*No. I won't.* Have you told your *friend* what you *did*?" Tamiel asked, his tone clear and declarative. As he considered the implication, Cadmus wanted to deny the truth.

"What do you know?" he asked, conversing with Mercy in his head, but the pale horse was just as mystified. With a frustrated sigh, Tamiel pinched the bridge of his nose and raised his head toward the ceiling.

"*Why* is this so surprising? I can see the walking plague your friend has become, but you don't think I can see what's underneath the surface?" Tamiel asked, losing his patience. He stepped closer and lowered his head so that his mouth was next to Cadmus' ear.

"Does. He. *Know*?" he whispered, wanting to make sure no one could eavesdrop from beyond the door. At that point, Cadmus knew there was no way to hide, so he turned to look Tamiel in the eye.

"He swore me, Tamiel. No matter what," he explained, his voice low.

Once he saw the flicker in Tamiel's eye, Cadmus knew the watcher understood. Sinking further into his shame, Cadmus closed his eyes as Tamiel turned away, walked over to the fireplace and supported himself on the mantle. When he spoke, the exile acted like he had been beaten down all over again.

"That's what I didn't want to hear."

OUTSIDE, Niccolo was having a difficult time trying to calm down his demonic friends. However, the roles had been switched. Instead of

Marchosias' feral nature getting out of hand, Phenex couldn't stop letting out plumes of flames with every word as he stomped around the woods near Tamiel's hovel. Pine cones exploded from the heat and full branches of needles were flaring out of existence as the tirade continued.

"*He... he went too far,*" Phenex muttered as he paced about a group of trees, each footprint smoldering as he left them in the soil. Unable to deal with this temper tantrum, Niccolo could only watch as Marchosias tried to bring Phenex down to their level.

"Yeshua," he started, abandoning any pretext of using his friend's inherited name, "he was *trying* to make us angry. He was trying to needle us and make us lose control. You can't let him win."

"*I can't let him win?*" Phenex asked, facing his friend and spitting fire as he spoke. "*I'm fine with being angry. I **never** get to be angry. It's always **you** who gets to be the angry one. Maybe I **should** have killed him right then and there.*"

"Then we couldn't find Azazel and Beleth. You know better—you *are* better than this. Calm down, and let cooler heads prevail."

"*How are you not furious right now?*" Phenex almost shouted, the flames rising high from his white-hot eyes. "*He said much worse about you!*"

"And I've heard that shit before, Yeshua," Marchosias said, setting his hands on his hips. "Unlike you, I get reminded of my mistakes every day. But here's the thing, and I want you to bear with me. *They're not lying.*"

"*What?*"

"They're not. It's as simple as that. What he brought up in there is what actually happened. I'm certainly not proud of any of it—there's a reason I ended up on that tree—but *I* did it. No one forced me to do any of it," Marchosias said with a heavy sigh, pursing his lips before continuing. "We have to own our mistakes along with our victories."

"We were trying our best," Phenex argued, the flames around

him dying down as the truth brought him back to reason. Marchosias nodded, but it changed nothing.

"Yes, we were, and I'm glad that we were able to see that eventually, but Tamiel didn't come at us like that because he's gloating. He's ashamed, too. He tried his best—tried to do what was *right*—and it bit him in the ass just like us. We shouldn't be angry at him. I don't know about you, but I only feel pity for him."

"He... you're right," Phenex finally agreed, the rest of the flames burning out as his anger evaporated. "I'm sorry, old friend."

"You never have to apologize to me. We've had too much of that in our lifetimes," Marchosias said with a smile, a smile that Phenex returned.

Seeing the whole display shocked Niccolo, but now he was more confused than ever. Warily, the leper stepped forward and coughed, drawing the attention of his companions.

"Look, I don't know what that is all about, but is everything alright?" Niccolo wondered if Marchosias would leap forward and claim his throat between his fangs, but the werewolf only gave a slight nod.

"Yeah, we're fine. He just got under our skins. We all know I fly off the handle, but Yeshua here needs some extra help if *he* ever loses it," he explained, which brought a nervous laugh from Phenex, who was still smoking after his meltdown.

"I'm sorry, Niccolo. It doesn't happen often, but I just... sometimes I wish that our pasts could stay in the past," Phenex said in a weary tone. Niccolo eyed him with caution, but eventually he realized he couldn't stay ignorant.

"Just who were you, Phenex? Why does Tamiel know who you are?" Phenex instantly looked away in shame, and when he looked back, he was wading through mental anguish.

"There's... there's so much myth and legend attached to the story, Niccolo, and we never meant for any of it. You may not want to know."

Marchosias grunted at his friend's excuses and shook his head.

"He asked, Yeshua. When we fell, we promised to accept our shame," he stressed, his friend giving a weak series of nods. Turning to face Niccolo, Phenex let out a heavy breath.

"Niccolo, my true name is Yeshua, but you... you probably know me by Jesus Christ. And over there," he said, pausing as he turned to point at Marchosias.

"That's my friend Judas Iscariot."

CHAPTER 4
A SNAKE IN THE GARDEN

I t was chaos. Pure, bloody chaos. Lucifer breathed shakily—his vision fading in and out—and the gore beneath him made it difficult to think straight. He tried to gather his senses, gulp down air and remember just who he had killed. For years, for centuries, for **millennia** he had known this creature beneath him, but there was no way to tell. Blood and grime ran together, obscuring his face, and Lucifer could not recognize his own brother.

With that gruesome sight beneath him, it was hard to keep justifying this war.

Distracted by a scream growing louder, Lucifer quickly looked up to find an armored warrior descending from the air, a trident in his hands. Not wishing to prolong this match against a weaker opponent, Lucifer swept his sword across his body, letting loose an arc of blinding energy that tore through his foolish opponent. With a wet thump, the angel's torso hit the ground and tumbled along until it came to a rest at Lucifer's foot. With only one arm to prop himself up, the angel looked up at him in anger.

"Do it, then," he urged, which Lucifer did not deny. Kneeling down, he plunged his blade into the warrior's heart and held his palm against the angel's quivering face.

"Be at peace, brother," he said, watching the light depart from the angel's eyes. After taking a moment to honor his fallen family, Lucifer stood up and then turned to face the warrior woman a few yards away from him. Tearing twin swords through a lightly-armored angel's throat, Lilith's hair swept about her face as the bloodlust led her through the dance. It had been tied and tucked inside her golden armor before this endless battle, but that was a week ago and those precautions had come undone after the first day of struggle.

It seemed like there were unlimited waves of angels coming to strike them down, but Lucifer and his supporters were standing against the onslaught, Lilith by his side the entire time. He watched as she flipped around the blade in her right hand and brought it down on the angel's head, kicking the body away once his life had departed. After taking a heavy breath, Lilith looked at her brother and gave a weary smile.

"They do not... give up easily." She scoffed at her own remark before looking at the ground beneath them. There had to have been forty corpses lying about, but it was hard to know that from all of the discarded limbs. Lucifer knew that he had let at least seven of his brothers and sisters retreat once he had removed an arm or leg.

He could only guess the extent of Lilith's mercy.

"No, but neither do we. I know it's difficult, but we need to hold this position. I think Uriel is—" Lucifer started, but he was interrupted by a dark shape landing in between them. A puddle of blood splashed out and covered their armor with more color.

"Lucy, we need your help out at the second outpost," the shape said as it picked itself up, the loose, black clothing covering him somehow unaffected by the blood he had displaced upon landing. When he lifted his head and grinned at Lucifer, he stared with red eyes.

"Zel, good to see you made it." Lucifer wiped off his siblings' blood with his left hand. "But you really need to work on your entrances."

"Not my fault you're standing in the middle of a bloodbath. Goddamn mess right here, chief." Azazel drew the twin daggers from his belt and flicked them around his wrists before kneeling down and poking at a nearby corpse. "You always did like to paint outside the lines..."

"Say what you have to say, brother. We likely do not have time to waste," Lilith said, holding her swords at her sides.

"You are **no** fun, Lil. Fine," Azazel said before turning and jumping to his feet. "Second outpost. We need some help from the Morningstar, methinks. I mean, I'm crafty, but I don't have that special flair you have, Lucy. Michael is hitting it hard and I do mean **hard**. Flaming sword and everything. Belial is doing what he can, but, well, you know. There's a reason everybody thinks the Eveningstar is worthless."

"We all have our merits, Azazel. We keep **you** around, if you need convincing of that," Lilith teased, flecks of blood scattered along her porcelain cheeks. Even with their grim surroundings Lucifer could not help himself from appreciating her beauty, but he needed to focus. Turning away from both of them, Lucifer gave a soft grunt.

"I wish I could help, but Uriel is supposed to be somewhere around here and that bastard needs to pay for what he did to Cimeries. He..." Lucifer trailed off.

It had been three days since he had come across the sight. Before stabbing him through the heart, Uriel had removed the angel's wings and limbs and then shoved a spear through Cimeries like a spit.

That kind of malice would not stand.

"Obviously we gotta get rid of the pretty boy," Azazel said, closing the distance between them in a flash and then tapping Lucifer's pauldron with one of his daggers, "but, you know, Mike is kinda stubborn. Not too many people can get near him and Astaroth is dealing with Raphael and his troops."

"Is there anyone who can manage it? We're stretched pretty thin." Lucifer faced the dark angel, but then he made eye contact with Lilith. Instantly, he understood what she had in mind.

"I'll go. If nothing else, I can hold him off until you return," she said, letting four scarlet wings stretch out from between the gaps in her armor. Lucifer shook his head, using his sword to gesture behind him.

"I can't do this alone. I..."

"Eh, I can help with that," Azazel said with a grin, flipping the daggers in his hands. "Can't fight Mike, but I can back **you** up, big guy."

*"See, Azazel? From time to time, you have **some** merit," Lilith said with a smile, flapping her wings so she could rise in the air.*

"Go on, ya harpy. I'll watch over our precious brother," Azazel replied, winking at her with one of his red eyes.

Although they had decided for him, Lucifer couldn't find the will to fight their decision. He only stretched out his left hand and bit his lip.

"I'll get there soon. Just... be careful."

*"Of the two of us, I need no reminders. Take care of **him**, Zel," Lilith said before flapping her wings once more, sending ripples in the puddles of blood beneath them. Once she was gone and heading toward the raging inferno in the distance, Lucifer tried not to give into despair.*

"I really have no idea what I'm going to do with you," he said, but Azazel cocked his head to the side.

"Look who's talking. I have to deal with a mentally-deranged bastard who decided to take on God. I mean, if we're really going to get into this..."

"Thanks, Zel. Seriously. It means a lot that you joined us when you did." That remark caused the smaller angel to withdraw, scratching the back of his neck with black nails.

"Shit, Lucy, you're gonna make me blush. You know just what to say to make a girl—behind you!"

Azazel jumped up, using the firstborn's shoulder to vault over him and face whatever was coming. Before he could even turn, Lucifer heard the impact of steel against something strong and saw Azazel fly back to the bloody ground in front of him. Immediately, Lucifer thought about the terrible things he would do to Uriel and turned to face his brother, but Uriel wasn't the figure standing behind him.

There, fifteen feet tall, was a being who looked very much like Tamiel. However, his muscles were larger, his hair longer, and his skirt only managed to reach down to his knees. In his right hand he held a simple staff that was bigger than Lucifer and Azazel combined, but its owner was not overburdened. As big as it was, Lucifer wasn't worried about the gigantic staff.

Adonai, their god, had all of the powers of creation at his disposal. His weapon was mere ornamentation.

"Zel, I really do have to hand it to you..." Adonai said while inspecting the end of his staff carefully. "There is a **scratch** on here. Good for you!"

Adonai drew his finger over the scratch and filled in the gap as he did. "I mean, I spent a couple days on you, so it **would** have been a shame if you turned out like Belial. Seriously, your brother is **worthless**!"

"You know," Azazel said, lifting himself off the ground with a cough. "You **made** him that way. It's kinda your fault."

A roar of laughter came from the childish god towering over them.

"I **know**! I'm so proud of that. He thinks he's special, getting to be Lucifer's opposite, then **wham**!" Adonai shouted, accenting the sound by slapping his palm against the staff. "I just throw his self-esteem out the window."

"And you wonder why we rebel against you," Lucifer said, violence permeating every word. His father looked down and then rolled his eyes, setting the end of his staff against the ground and splashing blood and body parts to the sides.

"Oh, please, is that what you think you're doing? You've barely made a dent in the loyal forces. Michael is just tearing it **up** over at your little outpost. And really, Lucifer, if you want to have a serious rebellion you can't take every slack-jawed reject I throw away. It's embarrassing."

"Pfft, embarrassing is wearing a loin cloth where we can almost see your junk," Azazel commented, daggers held in each hand. Adonai merely shrugged.

"I'm God. I do what I want. Now Lucifer," he said, turning to his proud son. "We can end this now. I'm willing to forgive and forget. All of your brothers and sisters, they will be totally fine. I just need one little, tiny thing," Adonai stressed, holding the tips of his thumb and index finger close together.

"You think I'll give up? You egotistical prick!" Lucifer shouted, the light from his shield burning brighter. "Why do you think I'll listen?"

"Oh, c'mon! Just ask me what it is!" Adonai urged, bouncing on his feet as he grinned at his creations. Flanking around the deity, Azazel sighed.

"What, Dad? What's the one thing?" he asked with a flourish of his dagger.

*"I just want Lucy here to be ripped apart for ten thousand years! Of course, I'll put him back **together**. I just you need in pain, son,"* Adonai said, setting his left hand on his hip. Scoffing at the offer, Lucifer settled into a battle stance, his shield in front and his sword to the side.

*"You are so benevolent and **kind**, Adonai. I would have thought killing the primates would have been part of the bargain. I'm **so** glad you decided to spare them."*

Adonai hopped to attention at the sarcasm, shaking both of the angels in the area.

*"Ooh, I mean, I thought that went without question. Though now that I'm thinking about it... I kinda **like** what you did with them. Only problem is, I can't have you kids running around defying me, even once. You know what kind of precedent that sets, Lucifer? If I let you get away with it, soon there's gonna be little uprisings and tiffs all over the place. It's annoying..."*

*"This—this is annoying to you? My brothers and sisters are **bleeding** and **dying** and it's **annoying**?"* Lucifer asked, light swirling around him as anger flooded all of his senses. Setting the end of his staff against the ground, Adonai became defensive.

*"Yeah, well whose fault is **that**? All **you** had to do was kill a couple monkeys. It was your fault you messed up the damn control group,"* he stated, focusing on his defiant son even as Azazel circled around him. Near the end of the statement, the dark angel was right behind his father and took that as his opportunity, leaping high into the air so he could sink his daggers into his god's flesh.

Before he could make in within a yard, Adonai snapped his fingers and Azazel's eyes exploded, sending showers of black gore out of the empty eye sockets. Screaming and abandoning his weapons, Azazel fell out of the air and landed hard, cracking bones upon impact.

*"**Damnit**, he... h—he took..."* he tried to say, but Adonai would not let him finish.

*"Yes, yes, your eyes, I'm sure it's painful. **See**? If you had just submitted, Lucifer, he would still have his eyes. **Now** Azazel's blind. And*

probably has a broken shoulder," Adonai said in a condescending tone, resting both hands on his staff and yawning at the end. "**Your** fault."

"You... I'll..." Lucifer snarled, unable to come up with anything intelligible. Adonai decided to indulge him.

"Kill me? **Try**."

Lucifer swung his sword across his body and let loose a crescent of energy aimed directly at his father, who lazily slapped it away with his left hand. Already anticipating this, Lucifer had jumped up into the air into the path of the redirected energy and swung his blade once more, sending a vertical arc to meet it. Upon collision, the unleashed energy exploded outward, causing Adonai to jump away from the blast.

"Ooh, I like that!" he shouted, but Lucifer was in no mood for praise. He flew toward his giant father, swinging his blade and letting out more arcs of energy as he closed the gap. Using his massive staff, Adonai swung down and met each crescent of energy before it could reach him. Although Adonai had thought he had caught his son in the splash of celestial power, Lucifer had deftly redirected his flight path so he could slam his radiant buckler against Adonai's face.

"Not su—" Adonai started, but Lucifer yelled in three voices and let loose a flare of energy from his buckler which would have blinded any other being.

However, Lucifer was fighting a living god, so it merely dazed his opponent. The firstborn was about to impale Adonai's eye, but before he could, Adonai slammed his head forward and struck Lucifer out of the air.

Unable to recover in time, Lucifer hit the ground hard and the air went out of his lungs, his sword flickering out of existence once it left his hand. For a second, Lucifer lay there fighting against the dark at the edges of his vision, but then he realized a giant foot was about to slam down on him. Pushing back with his wings, Lucifer got to his feet and then dove forward, narrowly avoiding being squashed by his father. Once he was able to push himself back up, Lucifer reformed his blade and swung it at Adonai's exposed Achilles' tendon.

"Then how do you like **this**?" Lucifer shouted as the blade connected with skin, but he felt instant resistance. Stupefied by what he saw, Lucifer could only stammer as he realized his sword had merely bounced off Adonai's leg. After lazily standing up straight, Adonai sighed at his first creation.

"It tickled? Is that what you wanted to hear? I'd **like** to tell you want to hear, Lucifer, but I'd just be lying. I don't like lying. Hey, how about this?" he teased, kneeling down so that he was only a few heads taller than his first angel. "I'll make you the **prince** of lies! All you have to do is give up now, submit to torture for—I dunno—thirty thousand years? Had to increase it since you keep defying me and all."

Closing his eyes and screaming with all of his willpower, Lucifer took his sword in both hands and swung across his body, Adonai's face only two feet away from him. Again, he felt resistance stop his blade, but then he heard something completely unexpected. A loud crash occurred in front of him, forcing Lucifer to open his eyes and stare in amazement.

Adonai was looking at his hand in shock, breath heavy and his eyes unfocused. It took a few seconds for Lucifer to realize what had happened, but then he saw the weeping gash on Adonai's face. Then he looked down at his weapon, its light dulled by divine blood.

Lucifer had done it. He had wounded his god.

"You—how did you? What did you..." Adonai muttered, unable to comprehend how one of his creations had been able to hurt him. They were functionally incapable of such things, but this angel—this monkey with wings—had wounded him.

He looked up at Lucifer and felt rage boiling through his veins. It had been a long, long time since Adonai had been in any sort of danger, and the feeling returning to him was unwelcome. Using his immense strength, Adonai threw himself to his feet and grabbed the staff at his side.

"There is no forgiveness now, you ungrateful piece of shit. I will tear you apart molecule by molecule, atom by atom and I will devise special methods to make every single removal **hurt**. You are not **allowed** to wound me!" The entirety of Heaven shook with his anger, but instead of cowering in fear, Lucifer stood defiant.

"Apparently you don't make the rules anymore, Dad," he said, but he could not gloat for long. If he had been just a little bit slower, Lucifer would have been crushed by the staff that flew at him. Lucifer was able to hop to the right so only his left arm got clipped—instead of his entire body—but it was still enough force to make his arm snap back behind him, enough to dislocate his shoulder, and he was sent tumbling through the air.

Before he landed, Lucifer was caught by Adonai's left hand and thrown high into the clouds—breaking the sound barrier along with a few ribs—and then was stopped suddenly by a huge staff trying to force its way through the middle of his back.

Lucifer thankfully lost consciousness before getting slammed into the ground.

"No you **don't**!" Adonai shouted, snapping his fingers and bringing his son back to a painful existence. Realizing he was completely outmatched and needed to escape, Lucifer pushed with his undamaged arm and legs and narrowly avoided the feet that crashed into his impact crater. Scrambling to his feet near Azazel, who was still writhing around with his hands covering his eye sockets, Lucifer was finally able to see Adonai in his full fury. As he took in the sight, cradling his dismantled left arm, Lucifer finally realized how foolish he had been.

The only hope he could have had to defeat such an entity was to recruit all of Heaven, and even that may not have been enough.

"I told you, Lucifer," Adonai said calmly, standing up straight with his back to his children.

"This is just the beginning. You think this hurts **now**?" he asked, turning so he could face the only creature who had been able to break his skin. "This is **nothing**. This is me angry and not thinking straight. Once I have some time to really dwell on it, really mull it over, I'm going to think of such punishments and torture that you will wish you never existed. You want to know how I know this, Lucy?"

"H—how, Adonai?" Lucifer asked, blood leaking out of the corner of his mouth even as he rebelled against this clearly superior force. Adonai stomped forward, a malicious smile on his face as he leaned over and lowered his head so it was just inches away from the firstborn.

"**I** am the reason you exist in the first place. **I** made you and I can **unmake** you. And I can make that process take as **long**, and be as *agonizing* as I want," he said before standing straight and bringing his staff above his head with both hands. "For now, I will take solace in squashing you like a bug."

Lucifer saw the staff coming down to crush him and expected a world of pain, but he heard a deafening boom and staggered back. Noticing that he wasn't dead, Lucifer looked up and found the last thing he could have expected.

Floating above him—golden wings spread out in all their splendor— was Tamiel, his golden broadsword holding Adonai's staff at bay and sending a shower of blinding sparks in every direction.

"What?" Lucifer asked weakly, but Adonai talked over any opportunity for Tamiel to answer.

"What are you doing, son? **What are you doing**?" Adonai yelled with another heave of his staf, but Tamiel only sank down in the air a couple of inches.

"I'm not—I'm not going to let you kill him, Adonai. He doesn't deserve to die." Tamiel was pushing back against the god's strength with all of his might, and Adonai's eye twitched as he considered the impudence.

"**He struck me! He cut my face!**"

"He lives, father. I don't want any more of my brothers and sisters dying. I don't want to see our blood spilled just because both sides are being too stubborn. **Everyone is at fault**!" Tamiel shouted, using his considerable strength to swipe Adonai's staff away from them, where it crashed into the ground and then sank two yards further.

"You... not **you**... you cannot defy me, Tamiel," Adonai whimpered, seeing his perfect son defending the wretch that had marred his magnificent body. Tamiel floated higher, rising so he could stare his creator in the eye.

"I don't want to defy you, Adonai, but I can't see you kill them. I can't watch you make anybody suffer any longer. I won't fight, but I won't watch you kill each other," he declared, turning so that he could face Lucifer and Azazel. "Take him, Lucy. Take all of them far away. Run so that he can't find you."

"Tamiel..." Lucifer started, but he couldn't find the words. However,

Tamiel didn't need them, and just nodded at the inferno still blazing in the distance.

"Go, now. Perhaps I'll see you again," Tamiel said, but then a pair of massive hands grabbed him out of the air and Lucifer stared in horror.

"You defy me, but you will not fight, my son? You don't want to watch..." Adonai started, squeezing his favored son enough that Lucifer could hear his bones creak.

"G—Go now, Lucy. I'll be fine!" he shouted, breaking Lucifer out of his daze. If Tamiel was going to sacrifice himself, Lucifer was not going to waste it. Scooping up Azazel and throwing the blind angel's arm around his neck, Lucifer jumped into the air and flapped his wings.

*"You don't want to watch, is that right?" Adonai repeated, lifting his son with one hand and gingerly running the fingers of his other along Tamiel's golden wings. Pinching with his thumb and index finger, Adonai gave a malicious smile to a son he could not forgive. "Then I will make it so that the only thing you will ever be able to do... is **watch**!"*

Hearing his brother's screams, Lucifer could not help but turn around. Immediately, he wished he had not.

With a glee that could only be found in an evil heart, Adonai pulled Tamiel's left wing apart, sending spurts of blood out of the dismantled beauty in his hand. Taking time to revel in his malice, Adonai slowly did the same with the other, pulling bones and ligaments apart before the skin finally tore away. With an unceremonious thump, Adonai let his son fall down between his discarded wings, coming to rest in a pool of his own gore. After seeing his work, Adonai looked up at Lucifer and smiled.

*"**You**... did this," he said, shaking in place for a moment before bending down and grabbing Tamiel by his ankle—lifting him up like a doll—and then slowly carrying him toward the palace. Without looking at Lucifer, he continued. "I'll be with you in a moment, son."*

Ignoring the pain in his heart, Lucifer turned away from his family and flew as fast as he could. This was no longer about winning; this was no longer about defying a cruel god. This was now only about survival. If he stayed there, he would die.

The war was over. Lucifer had lost.

Niccolo was disoriented as he tried to absorb the latest memory, the transition more jarring since Phenex was still smiling in front of him. Even if he had spent hours in Lucifer's mind—watching as the first angel slashed and burned through his loyal brothers and sisters— almost no time had passed in his own life.

However, as soon as the shock of seeing Tamiel's sacrifice wore off, Niccolo immediately remembered that he was standing in front of Jesus Christ and Judas Iscariot, the messiah and the betrayer. Breathing in deep, Niccolo tried to absorb this new information and fell against a nearby tree so he could support himself with his blighted hand.

"He's taking it better than most," Marchosias said as he walked forward and then sat down on a rock outcropping. "Usually there's a lot of stammering involved."

"That's... that's coming, be patient," Niccolo tried to joke, but when he looked at Marchosias, all of the old stories and myths flooded his mind. He was used to the universe being different from the Bible—that was nothing new—but he would never have expected to *see* these individuals, much less share stories on the road.

"We'll be patient. We're used to some confusion once we reveal the truth. I was half-expecting Cadmus to have a similar reaction," Phenex started, but Marchosias interrupted him.

"Yeah, but your friend somehow figured it out. That know-it-all has to... well, know it all." Niccolo looked up at that and gave a weak laugh, shakily withdrawing his hand once he could stand on his own.

"He likes to keep his secrets, though that one is pretty big."

"He likely thought that it was not a truth he could reveal. Don't feel like he betrayed you for that," Phenex suggested, but Niccolo shook off the thought.

"No, it's not that. I can understand why he wouldn't, and even that you might not want people to know," he said, standing up straight and crossing his arms, avoiding eye contact by looking at the floor. "For you to be Jesus and end up in Hell..."

"Yeah, you would think that Yeshua, out of *everyone,* should have gotten a one-way ticket upstairs," Marchosias grumbled, but the statement only made Phenex shift his weight to his left foot, plainly uncomfortable.

"It does... put a damper on things. It's already a bit gloomy in Hell and, well, for your Christ to fall is a bit much to handle for some people." Phenex lifted his gaze to Niccolo, who looked back once he finished his staring contest with the ground.

"How did that—I mean, why *did* you fall? I mean, I can understand Judas, umm, Marchosias, no offense," Niccolo added toward the other man, whose eyes flared yellow at his inclusion.

"*Some* taken."

"But everyone knows he betrayed you and then hung himself after. You're... you're supposed to be the son of God," Niccolo concluded, at which point Phenex brought his hand to his mouth and bit the knuckle of his index finger.

"You have to realize, Nico, those are just the stories. They added so much between the lines—"

"And before and after," Marchosias interrupted.

"Right, but the thing is... I never claimed to be the *son of God.* I wasn't even a *carpenter.* I took care of sheep, but someone saw me pick up a hammer and my humble beginnings were created for me," Phenex said, settling himself on an overturned log with scorch marks left from his temper tantrum. Seeing the other two were seated, Niccolo lowered himself to the ground and leaned back against his tree.

"What *is* true?" Niccolo asked, shocking Phenex with the direct question. After a second of gaping at him, Phenex closed his eyes and laughed for a moment. Once he recovered, Phenex propped up his chin on his hand.

"God, so little. Once I saw how my people were being treated, I got upset with the system. I started talking about how we needed to band together, to stop fighting each other, to stop letting the Romans get away with everything. Now, I *will* take credit for trying to make peace," Phenex said, dropping his hand and then sitting back with his palms against his knees, "but only among my own people."

"Wait, what are you saying?" Niccolo asked, raising an eyebrow. At that point, Phenex turned to Marchosias and gestured for him to continue. The werewolf sighed and then picked up a branch from the ground, dragging the end through the dirt below him.

"Just like everybody else, we didn't particularly like being ruled. We were... working on some mischief," Marchosias started, but Phenex grunted at his choice of words. Hearing it, Marchosias looked up and held the branch with both hands. "*Fine*, we were going to take down the local government."

"That sounds nothing like the story," Niccolo murmured to himself, but Phenex responded anyway.

"Of course, not. A failed revolution isn't a song anybody wants to sing. After the house of cards fell around us, they remembered the events differently. No longer were we trying to take down the Romans, I was sacrificing myself so that you could *live without sin.* The truth is, the Jews didn't give me up because they didn't understand, Nico. I just got *caught.*"

After leaning back against the bark of the tree and processing the information, Niccolo looked at the biblical figures and tried to ignore his fresh headache.

"This is huge," Niccolo muttered, turning to face each man in turn, but ended up making eye contact with Phenex. "So you were down in the trenches and killing people then? Is that how you ended up in Hell?"

"No, nothing like that," Phenex said, laughing at the remark. "I was a politician. I made sure we were getting enough recruits and planned events. We didn't even get to the point where we even fought the Romans. I just had a dusty back room to talk about it. Judas was the one who actually *did* something."

"Really?" Niccolo asked, turning to the man sitting on the rock, who only shrugged.

"Some people don't like to get their hands dirty. I don't mind, and I thought we were saving our people. We *thought* we were the chosen ones," he said, folding his legs over each other. "Chosen for suffering, seems like."

"So nothing. Nothing from the Bible..." Niccolo said, turning back to Phenex. "None of that is true. It's all just propaganda."

"Well, most. Seems to lead to more donations and control if you think one man is the only way to get into Heaven," Phenex said, putting out his hand to halt Niccolo from thinking further along those lines. "But it's not all made up. I really did want to inspire us to look beyond petty differences and try to help each other. Now that I'm outside it all, I don't mind extending that teaching to everyone else. It was just that, at the time, I was trying to unite my *own* people."

"Well, damn," Niccolo muttered, forcing a scoff from Marchosias.

"That is the word, it seems," he said before yawning. When he opened his eyes again, Niccolo was looking at him in sympathy.

"Man, now that I know the truth, it kinda makes more sense. How did you end up being responsible for betraying Jesus, then?" he asked, causing both men to catch their breath. Then, Marchosias put his hand behind his head and looked at the ground, using the stick in his hand to continue his scribbling.

"That part is true," he confessed. Unable to say a word, Niccolo turned to Phenex and could only stammer. Luckily, his companion anticipated this turn of events.

"Again, it's different in the context, but Judas did... betray me," he said, pursing his lips and avoiding eye contact. "However, he had his reasons. Toward the end, I was becoming bolder and, well, reckless. I'm surprised that no one gave me up sooner."

"I thought I was saving my people, Nico," Marchosias said weakly, lifting his head so that he could face his shame face-on. As the man spoke, Niccolo could see tears about to fall. "I was approached by a man named Pilate, who was nothing like the Roman you've heard of. He was a sneaky and contemptible man. Except, when he spoke to me about our defenses and our plans and how they would kill every living soul in our group, I knew it was over."

"He..." Marchosias continued somberly, "he told me that if I gave up Yeshua—and only Yeshua—he would allow us to go free. He would even give me enough silver so that I could start a new life for us. Knowing that it was over, it seemed like..."

"He gave me up so he could save the people who believed in us," Phenex interrupted, trying to save his friend, but Marchosias growled at him.

"I have enough strength to speak," he snapped, his tone softening as he continued.

"It was a lie. They killed everyone, all of our friends. I was spared only because they wanted to watch me suffer. To watch me live in shame. And I *was* ashamed," Marchosias declared, even though his words trembled through the air. "But I would not give them the satisfaction. I preferred oblivion, and with my silver I bought enough rope to send me there."

"Imagine my surprise," Marchosias muttered, a bitter smile on his face as he ran the stick through his drawing and ruined it in one flourish, "when I saw the very friend I had betrayed surrounded by hellfire."

"I wasn't happy," Phenex admitted, but after an awkward second, he set a hand on Marchosias' shoulder. The werewolf looked up in shame, but found a smile on the man's face, so he turned back to Niccolo with more confidence.

"How... why are you..." he mumbled, but they only smiled at his reaction.

"Friends? For the first decade, it didn't seem like it would ever happen, but once we heard all of the stories surrounding us—and knowing each other like we did—we drifted back together," Phenex said, ambling back to his log so he could settle down in the same spot. "We were the only two people in Hell who could really understand, who really knew the truth. And... we had both made our mistakes. In the end, we didn't want to lose a lifelong friendship over a misunderstanding."

"And now we hide away from it all. The myths and legends are too much for him to handle, and since Astaroth is pretty intimidating for most people, we took advantage of that," Marchosias added, rocking back and forth on his outcropping. "He's a dick a lot of the time, but he can understand where we were coming from. On a small scale, it reminded him of the first rebellion."

"I see," Niccolo said, bringing his hand to his mouth. "And that's why you stay in the wolf form all the time? Staying in the shadows?"

"I..." Marchosias started, unsettled by the question, but eventually he was able to respond. "I feel uncomfortable in my own skin. I may have had my reasons—Yeshua may have eventually forgave me—but it's... harder to forgive myself. My intentions may have been good, but I was responsible for the deaths of most of my friends. Those who survived, demonized me. Peter, that motherfucker..."

"Trust me, Nico, once your name is a curse word, you want to run away from who you are. I—" Marchosias paused, and shook his head after second-guessing himself. "Never mind, we don't need to talk about that shit. Story time is over."

"Unless you have any more questions," Phenex added, but Marchosias growled at the suggestion.

"Might want to be careful with those, if you do," he muttered, his fangs descending slightly. Seeing the hostility, Niccolo considered his words before sitting up straighter against his tree.

"Just one. Do you know why you fell? I thought Hell was for the damned, for people who had sinned during their life," he said, thinking back on his past in Firenze and Napoli and regretting his callous bloodshed. "But if *you* fell..."

"Buer had a theory, and when we brought it to Buné and Lucifer, they seemed to take it seriously," Phenex replied, licking his lips before continuing. "Falling to Hell doesn't seem to have anything to do with sin, or any modern conception of it. Half the people in Hell seem to have been generally *good* people. However, there does seem to be a common thread, and considering what we know about angelic history..."

"Mind you, it's a theory," Marchosias said, holding out his palm in a halting motion, "but it does make some sense. Seems like you end up in Hell if you don't play by the rules, whatever the rules are."

"You mind explaining that?" Niccolo asked, raising an eyebrow.

"Well, it's possible that when Lucifer opened up the pathway to Hell, he opened up an avenue for souls to travel through. Those who had a strong enough *will*," Phenex explained, using light gestures with his hands, "and tried to fight against an oppressive system—to stand up for people in need—these seemed to be the people that fell. The people who continued to exist beyond the mortal coil were too *defiant* to die.

"That said, we have no idea. You know how Buer is when he gets an idea. He'll create entire systems and worlds of information out of a rumor, and he'll end up being wrong about the entire base assumption."

"We all have our ways of keeping sane. Some people go a little *insane* to vent the pressure," Marchosias said, pushing off the rock and then slapping his hands against his clothing, a cloud of dust drifting away from him. "Don't hold it against the centaur."

"Oh, trust me, Buer and I already have *plenty* of problems," Niccolo commented, still sitting against the tree as Phenex joined Marchosias on their feet and then gestured toward the camp site.

"Knowing you as I do, Niccolo, that does not surprise me," Phenex teased with a smile. "Are you coming?"

"No, no I think I need some time to myself." Niccolo gave a forced smile and then turned to Marchosias, who was glaring back. "It's been a rough day."

"As you wish," Phenex said, setting his hand briefly on Niccolo's shoulder. "If you don't mind, could you continue to use our inherited names around the others? It might be a little vain, but we prefer our new identities."

"Yeah, yeah, that's no problem," Niccolo answered, and then Phenex walked past him and through the tree line. Marchosias followed, but as he passed, his eyes flickered yellow.

"Still not friends, leper."

"You sure? I have some silver I can throw your way..." he teased with a wry smile, which made Marchosias laugh as he slapped Niccolo's shoulder.

"Wait for me to betray the group, then I'll take it," he said before walking past the tree to join the others. After a moment, Niccolo was alone.

That was until a green mist came into existence next to his tree and solidified into a black horse lying on the ground, his shoulder right next to Niccolo's arm.

"I'm not sure how I feel about that," Plague said, his deep voice a little softer since it was just the two of them. Smiling in comfort, Niccolo used his human hand to stroke the hair on his friend's shoulder.

"Well, if nothing else, I think they're good people. I was iffy, at first, but... I sympathize with them," Niccolo said, Plague's hair feeling pleasant against his fingers.

"Oh, that I don't doubt. You do like the underdogs."

"What's that supposed to mean?" Niccolo asked as if insulted, but Plague merely lifted his head so he could stare at his master.

"Please, like you can ever hide anything from me. You *are* the underdog, little man, no matter how much you deny it. First it was during your life. Leper against the world. Then it was you against my former master. Then it was Mammon. You have a habit of picking fights you probably *shouldn't* have won," he commented, nuzzling against Niccolo's knee with his nose. "I'll support you all the way, but you could probably choose your causes better. Somebody is going to get hurt."

"Somebody already did," Niccolo muttered, his thoughts drifting back to the throne room and seeing Lucifer as the life departed from him.

"That wasn't your fault."

"Doesn't matter. If I hadn't decided to take Mammon's place..."

"Mammon never *had* a place," Plague interrupted in a stern tone. "Lucifer was looking for a proper son the entire time. He latched onto you, because, well, I'm not spelling it out. The two of you were meant for each other."

"Meant for each other?" he asked, but the flood of disapproval from Plague's mind instantly made him feel like a fool.

"*Seriously*? Sometimes I question our relationship," Plague sneered. "Like I said earlier, underdogs. And with all these memories you're getting, it's only becoming more obvious. Spiritually, Niccolo, you were his heir. I think that's why you're getting these flashbacks."

"You really think so?" Niccolo asked, drawing his hand forward to stroke the hair on Plague's face. Feeling the warmth of the horse's affection in his mind, he had to smile.

"I dunno, could be horseshit, but it's as good a theory as defiant souls falling to Hell. Don't get me wrong, to an extent it makes sense, but, well, defiance doesn't always mean a trip to Hell. We know what happened with Tamiel."

"Yeah, we do..." Niccolo muttered, but then he saw Plague lift his head further so he could look him in the eye.

"You didn't know yet. Now you do. You can apologize in the morning, little man. For now, we should try to get some rest. Right now, it's like you're living two lives." Sympathy flowed through their mental link. "Besides, he's busy. Probably won't want to talk to you, yet."

"Yeah, you're probably right." Niccolo turned to look at the fire Phenex had created just beyond the tree line.

"Want to go join the others?" Plague asked, but Niccolo shook his head.

"If it's alright, I think I want to just stay here for a little longer. Been a while since we could just sit together. That all right with you?" he asked, and instantly the horse radiated affection and lowered his head back to the ground.

"Foolish little man," Plague muttered, laughing softly as Niccolo resumed scratching the beast's neck. Watching Plague's response, Niccolo brought his hand on top of the animal's back and continued stroking his hair.

"Foolish little man," he repeated before closing his eyes and drifting into dreamless sleep.

As CADMUS LOOKED at the smoke rising from the dying fire, he wondered what it might feel like if he wasn't in a state of constant fatigue. It was just after dawn and he had been the only witness to the sun rising. From his seat on a cold stump, grinding the end of his scythe into the dirt at his feet, he knew his companions were at relative peace. Niccolo had never come to join them, which the reaper had noticed but did not worry over, as he needed the time away.

There was chaos in his mind, and Cadmus needed to make sense of it.

He would never let Niccolo know the extent of it—with his visions of Lucifer, the leper had enough on his plate—but Cadmus was hurting. Since he had inherited Amon's powers, it had only gotten worse day by day. Time itself was slipping away from him, and the squawking of the malicious bird still resonated through his mind. It would keep him from ever sleeping, and it took all of his concentration to appear normal to all of his companions.

Even then, he couldn't entirely focus on the present because the future was so worrying. He saw twisted monsters in his mind crying out in pain, and had no way to know if they were real. The most he could do was work on one premonition at a time, and the monsters would have to go on the back-burner. For now, he needed to know why the flashes of a murderous Tamiel kept repeating in his mind.

There seemed to be no reason for the pacifist to turn like that, and even worse, Tamiel knew the truth of it all.

Somehow, he knew what Cadmus had done.

The reaper stopped grinding his scythe against the dirt as he saw Niccolo walking out of the trees, mouth covered with his left hand as he yawned. Seeing his friend wipe sleep out of his eyes, Cadmus pushed away the maelstrom of possibilities and tried to pretend at being normal. Niccolo gave a brief wave and came to a stop at the far edge of their circle of unconscious companions.

"They're a bit lazy, aren't they," he commented, but then Cimeries shifted and massaged the skin of her forehead with one hand.

"Merely taking advantage of a time of rest, Horseman." Cimeries slowly opened her eyes to stare Niccolo down. "Do not pretend to have been awake for more than twenty minutes."

"How did y—" he started, but then he saw her grim smile.

"I've lived much longer than you, and I have used those years well," she said before sitting up and inspecting the edge of her pike with a calloused thumb. "Perhaps next time you'll want to sleep downwind so I don't catch your scent."

"You could *smell* me?" he asked, but then another voice joined them.

"That arm of yours is pungent, leper. I don't even need the wolf's nose for that," Marchosias grumbled, stretching out with his arms and legs before collapsing back into his sleeping position.

"It's too early for this," Paimon whined, curling in on herself and refusing to open her eyes.

"Oh, I could come back," Tamiel broke into the conversation, and the three of them looked in the direction of his hovel. The watcher ambled toward them, hands in his pockets, but his face betrayed the air of relaxation he was trying to cultivate. His eyes showed that he had been awake all night and up to something very strenuous.

Cadmus could sympathize.

"No, you're not getting away again," Paimon said, stretching her arms skyward—letting out a small squeak as her shoulders popped into place—and then brought her legs in front of her. "Tell us what you saw, *oh great watcher*."

"Reverence and flattery, dear sister," Tamiel said before plopping himself down on the ground between Paimon and Phenex, who was still sleeping soundly, "sound so *disingenuous* coming out of your mouth."

"You should see what it's like when I'm being sincere." Paimon grinned as she rocked into Tamiel with her shoulder, but she slapped her ankles to end the game. "So, out with it, what do you have for us?"

"Not what you want," he said, reaching out with his foot to nudge Phenex, who sleepily slapped away the contact and turned over. Seeing this, Marchosias transformed his left foot and scratched Phenex's skin, instantly waking the slumbering man. Phenex glared at the werewolf briefly, but then realized Tamiel had arrived and turned his attention to the exiled angel.

"Sorry, what was that?" he asked, a yawn warping his words, but he continued to lie on his side as Tamiel continued.

"One of them was easy, and he's actually pretty close. Beleth is a day's ride southwest, so—depending on how fast and reckless you want to travel—you could probably find them by nightfall. Just look for an encampment based around a hill near Trento. There's forest around there, so you might even be able to sneak up on him, depending on what kind of wards he's set up."

"Wards?" Cadmus interrupted, prompting Tamiel to turn toward him. The exile would have been angry, but then Tamiel saw red-rimmed eyes and his gaze softened.

"Beleth likes to use his own brand of magic and conjuring. He was experimenting with it even up in Heaven, and it's based around using angelic letters in different combinations. Last time I was paying attention, he was working on shields and other protective combinations," Tamiel elaborated, earning a scoff from Paimon.

"It's gone a little further than that. He cut Amdusias in half with a summoned blade. It ended up opening the portal," she said. Upon that revelation, Tamiel directed his attention to the floor.

"Damn," he muttered, shaking himself out of his daze. "Well, then you may want to be extra careful. He's doing... something over there, and I can't quite tell what it is."

"Wait, how do you not know? If you can see where he is..." Niccolo asked, but Paimon answered for her brother.

"That's not how it works, hon. Tamiel can see through time and space, finding the signatures that energy leaves behind, which is particularly useful with other angels and demons. At other times, he can see major world events, the points in history which are so important that it literally creates a beacon for him to focus on."

"That how you saw us?" Marchosias asked, at which point Tamiel tilted his head from side to side.

"Well, yeah. I think you can see why after it's all said and done," he hinted, waving his hand in a flourish before looking at the circle. "In any case, Beleth isn't being shy at all—his power is leaking all over the place—but it also makes the whole area unstable and hard to see from here. It's like a... black cloud is over that area. I know it's my brother, and I know the geography, but whatever is going on over there, you'll have to find out for yourself."

"And what of the other traitor?" Cimeries asked, her thumb still tracing the edge of her pike. Stalling for a moment, Tamiel rubbed his eyes before letting out an exasperated sigh.

"Azazel, as always, is a sneaky goddamned bastard. Whatever he is doing, he's keeping a low profile. I'm not going to fault him for being smart about it—he probably knew that you might reach out to me—but it's still pretty frustrating. Beleth took twenty minutes to find. Most of the night was spent looking for the other bastard."

"I suggest," he continued, rubbing his jaw with his hand, "that you go after Beleth and see what he's up to. I guarantee that whatever goals they have are dependent on each other—they're both big on master plans—so if you mess up Beleth's project..."

"Azazel might come out of hiding," Cadmus finished his statement.

"Not the best, Tamiel, but we can work with it. Thanks for what you're doing," Paimon said with a slap against her brother's shoulder, but the exile rolled his eyes.

"Eh, just get out of my hair and leave me to my moping," he said as he stood, kicking at Paimon's legs once he was upright.

"You're not coming with us?" Niccolo asked, stealing the attention of everyone in the circle. Tamiel, in particular, narrowed his gaze.

"No, Horseman. It's not my fight. Beleth was an asshole and he may have helped destroy the balance of power in Hell, but I have no desire to kill him. Azazel..." he explained, pausing on the blind demon's name. "I'm less inclined to leave him with his life intact, but I was never part of the *killing my family* trend. Besides, I figure there's enough grudges in this group that I don't want to dilute the satisfaction."

"But—" Niccolo protested, but Paimon had gotten to her feet and gently scratched under his chin.

"Nico, he watches, he never fights. We already got Beleth's location from him, so let's leave him to his brooding," she said, pouting at the end of the statement and turning to Tamiel. "Can you give us specifics on where this camp is?"

"No, I think I'm just going to say *near a city*," Tamiel said sarcastically before withdrawing a piece of cloth from his pocket and handing it to her. "Drew out the landscape best I could."

"You're a sweetheart," Paimon said, accepting the map and throwing it into the satchel on the side of her belt. Lightly patting Niccolo's face, Paimon walked past him and toward the empty meadow leading away from Tamiel's hovel. "Let's get back to our adventure, then."

"Thank you, Tamiel. You were a... modest host," Phenex joked, bowing slightly before following after Paimon. After, Marchosias nodded at the exiled angel as well before transforming and walking away on all fours. Although it seemed like it was time to go, Niccolo knew that he had to speak with Tamiel, even if it was just to apologize for his comments the night before.

"Guys, you go on ahead, I want to talk to Tamiel a moment."

Cimeries grunted at the comment, but then marched after the others. Niccolo thought he would catch on, too, but when he turned to Cadmus, the reaper only stared back. However, Tamiel cleared his throat and provided an excuse for Niccolo.

"Oh, he probably just wants to convince me to come with, reaper. I'll be sure to send him along with dashed hopes."

Although Cadmus could tell there was something else going on, he summoned Mercy from the gathering dust. Once he was in the saddle, Cadmus hesitated, watching the angel who was destined to kill some unarmed stranger in almost every future.

With a smile, Tamiel nodded at their departing friends.

"Go on, then. Just remember what I told you, Cadmus. Be careful," he said with a wink, and then he turned to face Niccolo.

Realizing the conversation was effectively over, Cadmus gave a nod and turned Mercy toward the other end of the meadow, but now his thoughts were on the revelation from the night before.

"So," Tamiel started, watching Cadmus riding away in his periphery. "What argument are you going to use, Niccolo? I'm a pitiful brother? I should relish any opportunity to kill the man who killed Lucifer? What is it today?"

"I wanted to say I'm sorry," Niccolo replied, catching Tamiel off-guard.

"I'm sorry... what?"

"I saw..." Niccolo started, grinding his boot into the dirt beneath him as he gathered his thoughts. "I know more of the story, now."

"More of the story, huh?" Tamiel crossed his arms, and Niccolo could tell that he had piqued the exile's interests.

"Yeah." Niccolo nodded, pausing only to let that sink in. "I really shouldn't have said anything about cowardice last night. I thought you were staying out of the war because you were afraid or because you didn't want to stand up for anything."

"Last night I saw what Adonai did to you. I saw how you saved Lucifer. That was—that was one of the bravest things I've ever seen, Tamiel, and I can't tell you how sorry I am to have called you a coward."

Niccolo rushed through his confession because he didn't know if he had the strength to finish it. Not only did he have his personal feelings on the matter, but Lucifer's internal struggle still held him captive.

"You... know all that, huh?" Tamiel asked, his voice faltering on the words. When Niccolo looked back, he found Tamiel fighting back tears.

"I didn't realize what you went through. You did stand up, and, really, part of me thinks that you were right. You suffered—"

"That's enough, kid," Tamiel interrupted, holding out his hand. "I don't need to revisit those memories. But... thank you, really. Not many people know that story. There weren't too many people to witness it."

"I... know."

"Yeah, yeah, you would, wouldn't you," Tamiel said with a sad smile, wiping his face with the sleeve of his robes. "Anyway, I appreciate that you took the time to... share, and that you had the courtesy to leave them out of it. It saves me having to answer some uncomfortable questions."

"Right," Niccolo said before turning to watch his departing friends. "Are you sure you don't want to come with us? Even if it's just to get out of the house?"

"God, you just don't give up," Tamiel said with a bark of laughter. "Like I said, Nico, it's not my fight. And, I'm going to keep looking for Azazel while you kids are out. It's better for me to be alone for that." Niccolo stared at him for a moment—to the point Tamiel thought that he was going to fight the decision—but then the leper shrugged and green mist formed behind him.

"Well, I'm not going to drag an angel by his ear to kill his brother," he said, jumping onto the black steed that materialized out of the cloud. "Though... I'm sure you'll be able to find us if you want."

"With the way you're leaking, kid? I have to focus just to ignore it," Tamiel said with a scoff. Nodding at the joke, Niccolo urged Plague forward, running off at a faster pace to catch up with his friends.

Tamiel watched Niccolo depart, but then he considered the reality of Niccolo's situation. With a sigh loud enough to condemn the universe, Tamiel looked up to the heavens.

"You're a bastard, you know that?"

NICCOLO STOOD at the edge of the village, rage threatening to burst through his skin as smoke drifted about and stung his eyes. No one dared approach him as he clenched his fists, blood dripping from his mangled arm as his nails tore into the flesh of his own palm. This was no bandit attack; this was no war between nations.

His presence on Earth had done this.

"Niccolo," Paimon said from Plague's saddle, but the Horseman turned his head and she stopped being able to speak. Green energy radiated from his eye and Paimon knew there was no consoling a man with that much righteous anger. Once Niccolo turned back to look at his misdeeds, Paimon gazed over the destroyed village and sympathized with him.

They had all seen the signs before, but this was the first time Niccolo's plague had truly taken its toll. Entire buildings had been burned to the ground, mass graves had been built for half the residents; charred corpses were piled on top of each other to the point where it was difficult to see how many were actually there. Horrifically, that still did not take into account the men, women and children whose corpses lay in the street, their flesh bloated and rotting from boils and black pustules.

"Can you say anything that will give these people back their lives?" Niccolo asked, staring at the pestilence that he had wrought. "Can any of you say that this is *not* my fault? When the Horsemen ride, they bring *death* with them. That's what they say."

Turning to face his companions, Niccolo waved at the desolation he had caused merely by existing.

"That's not true, though. Death... death is a *byproduct* of what I do. I bring pain, misery and all the hard choices. Cadmus lays them to sleep, gives them mercy." He faced a small body, its blackened arm outstretched, its fingers curled around a doll that had mostly burned away. "I make sure the *nightmare* claims them."

"Are you done pitying yourself?" Cimeries asked, causing Niccolo to slowly turn to her where she was sitting on Mercy's saddle. Energy poured out all around him as he gave into fury.

"I'm sorry? What the *fuck* did you just say to me?" Tremors rocked through his blighted hand, which seemed to grow larger. However imposing it may have been, Cimeries was unimpressed and gestured around the village.

"Whatever happened here, it has little to do with your nightmares. You are not responsible for the fire that claimed this village," she stated, pointing at the weapons scattered around the site. "No doubt, your plague had reached this village, but this is the work of something else."

"What are you talking about? Tamiel... he said that I give off radiation—whatever that is—and bac... *something* else. This looks like someone taking care of something *I* did!"

"It's more complicated than that, sweetie," Paimon argued. "That radiation is just how you make people sick, which isn't your fault. Cimeries is right. This isn't just paranoia and medieval practices. Someone came here to do this, to do this *specifically*. This was made to *look* like a village stricken by plague."

"What are you saying? They burned a village for what? Seems like all the valuables are still here," Marchosias said, sniffing the air as he stood in his wolf form. "First thing I checked, even if burnt human is now permanently in my nose."

"It's not the valuables, mutt. Notice how many houses there are? Not all of them are burnt to the ground. Look again," Paimon said, nodding at the smoldering ruins. There was a pause as the group considered the implication, but eventually Cadmus took a sharp breath.

"There's... not enough bodies."

"There's not *enough*?" Niccolo shouted. Cadmus shook his head and then waved over the mass grave with his scythe.

"For how many homes there are, there are not enough corpses, Niccolo. At least, at least half of the villagers are unaccounted for. I can... I can feel it. And that's not even—the plague had only just gotten here. The memories of this place are hitting me now," Cadmus said, shuddering as he felt the presence of death around him. "This is—"

"This is a cover-up," Cimeries declared, glaring hard at the confused Horseman. "Think. We are not so far from Beleth's camp. If there was a fire to combat a plague, no one would come looking to investigate missing villagers."

"Fuck, I'm smelling it now," Marchosias said after taking a long sniff. "I couldn't notice because of the corpses, but there's angel stink. I—damnit, I got distracted."

"It's alright, it took me a little longer for me to realize it, too," Paimon said, the nails of her left hand extending beneath her notice. "But this is my brother's work. I can tell. Don't blame yourself for this one, Nico. We have a traitor to kill."

"Then let's go," Niccolo said, briskly walking over to Plague and then jumping up to his saddle. After looking at his companions, he pointed at the trees in the distance, underneath the setting sun. "If we're that close—and Beleth is this careful—we're going to have to play this smart."

"First time for you to say that," Marchosias said, following it with his low murmur of a laugh, but Niccolo stared at him and he stopped at once.

"I'm *angry*, not suicidal. I saw what he did in the Overlook and I'm not going to let him do it again. Any more jokes, or can we get on with it?"

His bitter tone was enough that none of them wanted to cross him, and so they took off into the woods without another word.

Because of the danger they were facing and the massacre they had just seen, the group continued on in silence. Cadmus watched his friend at first, but then he was distracted by on onslaught of visions with no context, his eyes burning with blue energy. Suddenly, Cadmus could see a hill encircled by large wooden stakes, seemingly made out of entire trees. Then, before he could understand it, a giant, burning cross dominated his mind's eye and he felt an enormous amount of pain.

"Reaper! What's wrong?" Cimeries whispered as she put her left hand on his shoulder, bringing Cadmus back to the present and forcing back the tide of blue revelations. He looked behind him in the saddle and saw the concern on her face, which almost made him laugh. Trying to avoid looking at Phenex, who was walking beside them, Cadmus responded quietly.

"I don't know. I'm seeing the camp, I think, and a cross in my mind and, well, I think it might have to do with," he whispered, nodding to Phenex at the end. Putting the pieces together, Cimeries quietly replaced her arm around Cadmus' midsection.

"Vague, but we should not ignore it. However, I agree. He may not need to know." Cimeries spoke in a hushed tone, but it seemed like Phenex took notice. For a few seconds, he looked at them with vague suspicion, but then turned ahead once the trees were immediately in front of them.

Banishing the horses, the group continued on foot, doing what they could to avoid dry branches and other noisy obstructions on the forest floor. Soon, the trees grew too close together for them to walk closely and they were unable to maintain any conversations they did not want others to overhear.

It was past sundown when they finally came to a part of the forest where the trees started to thin, and it was not much longer after that they were able to see a hill rising less than half a mile from their position, a ring of tree-sized stakes surrounding a few buildings on the top.

"This is unreal," Cadmus muttered to himself, but Cimeries thought the statement was directed at her.

"How? This is more real than anything else we have seen. Now our enemy is before us." After glancing at her, Cadmus stood up and used his scythe to support some of his weight.

"No, it's just... we've been looking for Azazel and Beleth for so long, it's strange to finally have one of them so close," he explained, turning to face the rest of the group that had stopped inside the tree line.

"Can you tell if Beleth has set up any traps or seals or other bullshit like that?" Niccolo asked, seeking hasty vengeance for the village.

"I don't think so, but he's a conniving son of a bitch," Paimon spat out, crossing her arms as she looked at the hill. "It might be worth it to wait until morning."

"Of course, when my powers mean nothing," Marchosias growled, trying to argue with someone, but none took the bait. "So, wait until dawn so the rest of you can see what you're doing?"

"Sounds reasonable. We don't want any surprises," Phenex said before retreating into the woods. "Obviously, we should probably avoid campfires, too, this close to the camp."

"I don't think anybody was going to suggest otherwise," Paimon added as she maneuvered around the roots of a tree. Almost everyone followed suit, but Marchosias snarled as he let the shadows wrap around his hulking frame.

"You do what you have to do. I'm going to scout around, maybe find some of these traps you're all expecting to run into," he said, having completely blended into the darkness. Noticing the looks on his companions' faces, he gave a disgusted sigh. "C'mon, I'm not stupid enough to go to the fort alone. You all catch up on your precious sleep."

Then he was gone.

After walking a few minutes back into the woods, where the forest grew a little thicker, the five of them settled into a circle and waited for the sun to rise. Before they knew it, half of them were asleep. Paimon and Niccolo were nestled against each other, the latter so exhausted that his fury could not keep him awake, and Phenex was lying on his side, using his left arm as a pillow. Cadmus envied them, being able to sleep even with all of this excitement, but he felt grateful that Cimeries was keeping guard with him.

"The wolf has been gone for an hour," she said abruptly, breaking Cadmus out of his thoughts.

He was still concerned with the cross in his mind, and he had to wonder just what it had to do with Phenex. However, that could wait, as Cimeries was looking at him for an answer to a question she would not ask.

"I wouldn't worry about Marchosias. He can move fast and he's not foolish enough to go after Beleth alone. I'm sure we'll see him soon," he assured her, trying to anticipate what she would say. Instead of calming her down, Cimeries stood up and then nodded away from their camp.

"I'm going to go look for him. I won't be gone for long. Just looking for a sign he is prowling about."

She turned fast enough to startle Cadmus, but he could not let her go like that. Caution was necessary in these circumstances.

"No, just stay until dawn. He'll be fine. This is—" he started, but the cross came into his mind again and brought pain with it. When he regained his senses and looked at Cimeries, he found empty air. Then he felt a sudden strike against the back of his neck and instantly lost consciousness.

"I'm sorry, reaper. I will *not* stop now."

———

CIMERIES CROUCHED low in the high grass, keeping her pike parallel to the ground, and looked at the foreboding entrance to the camp. It seemed deserted without the benefit of moonlight—clouds covered half the sky—but Cimeries could tell there was something beyond the wall of stakes. There was some evil that beckoned for her to slay it and she would not deny the compulsion. It had only taken a small amount of effort to incapacitate Cadmus and Marchosias was easy enough to avoid. Now she was so close to her goal.

Soon, Lucifer would be avenged.

No, Beleth did not force the blade through her charge, but he had been part of Azazel's schemes. The demonic king was directly involved with her shame, if nothing else. For more than two thousand years, Lucifer had depended on his Hell Knights for his safety, and she had failed spectacularly. It was now her duty to avenge him and remove the demon king from Earth.

She would not fail again.

With a light step, Cimeries bounded up the rest of the hill and then slipped to the side, standing behind the corner of the left wall and peeking around the post once she was comfortable. Seeing the scattered buildings and tents on the inside but no fires for any guards, Cimeries was more than just skeptical. This was a trap—it had to be—but if she treated it with a degree of caution, she felt like she could avoid the snare. Her pike drawn in front of her, Cimeries quickly stepped inside the fort and looked for a fight.

Treading softly, the warrior edged closer to the entrance of a tent and took a deep breath. Whatever horrors Beleth was up to, they would likely be hidden beyond the tent flap. Gripping the handle of her pike hard enough to make her bones creak, Cimeries slashed open the material and stepped inside, ready to kill whoever was on the other side.

Yet there was no one to kill. The tent was absolutely empty except for a few wartime cots, and the revelation was enough for the warrior to sneer at her situation. Advancing to the next tent, which underwent the same scrutiny, Cimeries found that it was just as empty. After another tent, the woman lost her patience and stopped approaching with caution, wiping away the tent flaps with her hand instead of her weapon.

Sighing in frustration, Cimeries walked toward the center of the hill and finally saw what it was built around. Standing at twenty feet tall, a giant cross was planted into the ground, surrounded by kindling and branches. Once she saw the sacrificial altar, Cimeries set the end of her pike against the ground and wondered what kind of witch Beleth meant to burn.

Then the clouds parted in the sky and moonlight reflected off black armor at the base of the altar. Lifting his head to greet her, the pale demon king seemed to stare right through her.

"Hippolyta, wasn't it?" Beleth asked, his voice as stern as she remembered, and Cimeries instantly brought down her weapon and held it at the ready.

"I no longer use that name." She kept an even stance so she could react to whatever traps Beleth had laid around them.

He sneered at her audacity and set his left hand on his hip.

"So you use my brother's? You do not deserve it, warrior queen. Cimeries was a noble soul," he stated, stepping forward—out of the circle of kindling and branches—and stopping a few yards away from her. "A proud knight of Heaven who stood as a tower against our enemies. He was betrayed by Lucifer's incompetence, and I will not desecrate his memory by allowing you to use his name."

"You talk of betrayal? You destroyed Hell."

"I merely allowed it to destroy itself, Amazon," Beleth argued, his blonde hair almost white as the moon that lit their surroundings. "It was a loose confederation of rebellious angels that was further destroyed by human influence. Azazel and I had to do very little to cause our brothers and sisters to fight amongst themselves. All he did was show those animals for what they were."

"What do you hope to gain? Your god will not take you back," Cimeries said, earning a scoff from the fallen angel.

"I do not want to be accepted by my father. I fought my war and lost, human. I can accept losing, even if it was not directly my fault. However, at this point, the cards are dealt. I am to die with this planet once Adonai decides to wipe away existence and start over," Beleth explained, using the fingers of his right hand to start drawing in the air. "Azazel's foolish little plan is his own. I am on this planet for one purpose."

"Go on," Cimeries said, advancing slowly as Beleth drew designs and sigils, purple energy eking into the air around him.

"I merely want to watch you animals suffer. For two million years, I have been held captive in a dimension of waste and filth. Then you *monkeys*," he spat out, raising his arm to continue his seal, "insulted us further by showing up at our doorstep. I did not fight for my freedom for you to taint my surroundings. Until the end, I will make your species pay and enjoy every cry of anguish. I will spend my last days—my retirement, as it were—destroying Lucifer's legacy."

"Then I will stop you," Cimeries resolved, leaping forward so Beleth could not finish his magic.

Once she was within striking distance, she thrust forward with her pike, which Beleth parried with the bracer on his left hand. Slightly unbalanced, Cimeries tried to recover and thrust again, but Beleth's hand slammed into her face and sent her sprawling backward. Once she was able to get back into a balanced position, she found that Beleth had completed a three-point seal—purple energy bursting into a circular design—and he had thrust his arm inside.

"A warrior without honor, so very fitting for your kind," Beleth said, condescending as he withdrew his hand, a massive black broadsword with silver edges appearing in his grip. "I had expected more from you. You attack an unarmed opponent and *still* fail."

"You are no more unarmed than a viper." Cimeries gritted her teeth and leapt forward again, trying to bait an attack. When Beleth swept his sword across his body, Cimeries juked to his right and rolled under the obsidian metal, thrusting her weapon at the unguarded area of his armpit.

However, Beleth noticed her tactics and rolled forward, causing Cimeries' thrust to hit nothing but air. Once he completed his somersault, Beleth wielded his sword with his right hand and swung it around, determined to squash his opponent.

Unable to move in time, Cimeries propped her handle against the ground and tried to catch the weapon between the spear point and curved blade of her weapon. After a loud crash, Cimeries looked up and saw that Beleth's sword had been stopped and—for a moment—she breathed out in relief.

That relief quickly left her once she turned her attention back to Beleth and saw the five-point seal he had created with his other hand. Jumping up quickly, Cimeries narrowly avoided the jagged spears of ice that shot out from nowhere, but she wasn't safe yet. Following her by clenching the air with his hand and dragging the shimmering sigil upward, the spears of ice kept coming and Cimeries was forced to deflect them with her pike.

Although she was able to knock away four of the missiles, another shattered after her strike and a four-inch long piece of ice was embedded in her shoulder. Thankfully, Beleth's assault had finished so—once she landed—Cimeries quickly flipped backward and retreated to a safe distance, inspecting the wound once she had time.

"It looks like ice, doesn't it?" Beleth asked, a smirk on his face as he sauntered forward, his broadsword held loosely at his side. "But it *burns*. It's actually a sort of minera—" he tried to explain, but Cimeries surprised him by taking hold of the exposed missile and pulling it out without so much as flinching.

"Save your explanations for those who care," she spat out, jumping up to a ready position even as the inch-wide hole in her shoulder pumped out blood, appearing black in the moonlight. Taken aback, Beleth actually laughed before shaking his head.

"For a human, you are a curiosity. I will enjoy working with you," he said with a note of satisfaction, taking the handle of his blade with both hands and holding it in forward guard.

"Working with me? What's your game?" Cimeries stalled, the end of her pike wavering as the blood loss started to affect her. Watching the effort she went through to maintain her poise, Beleth softly chuckled.

"I already told you. I am here to enjoy humanity's death rattle. Tell me, Hippolyta, are you not curious as to why this camp is deserted?" Beleth tilted his head as he advanced on the wounded Amazon.

"It does not matter," she muttered, shaking as the burning in her shoulder tore at her mind. It was becoming hard to focus, but she would not allow this demon to get the better of her.

"But it does. We are not where you think we are, Amazon," Beleth declared, forcing Cimeries to give him her full attention. "In the real world, this camp is full of—for lack of a better term—life. However, you stumbled into a sort of pocket dimension that I have created. Just for you, little soul."

"Just for—just for me?" she asked, coughing in the middle of the question. Standing up straight and abandoning guard, Beleth smiled at her cruelly before setting the point of his weapon against the ground.

"I knew you would abandon your friends and try to avenge the Morningstar. You were a Hell Knight, and you do have some small amount of honor. I respect that, even if it is quite predictable. So I created a scenario where we could have some privacy," he explained, twirling the massive blade in place, the point digging further into the Earth beneath him.

"You should have known better, demon," Cimeries threatened, sweat starting to pour from her brow. She didn't know why her shoulder was not healing yet and she had realized she may have bitten off more than she could chew, but Beleth didn't need to know that. "I will kill you here and now."

"No, that would ruin the game. Of course, if you want to attack me now, you can see the result quite easily," he suggested, turning away from her as an insult, and that was all she needed.

Rushing forward, Cimeries was about to heave her pike at Beleth, but as soon as she was invested in the move, Beleth threw his weapon at her position and it carved through the air with incredible speed. Dodging to the side and still holding onto the shaft of her pike, Cimeries was grateful that she had avoided death for a moment, but then she noticed Beleth had knelt and buried his hands into the dirt.

Before she could react, four-inch long teeth rose out of the soil beneath her and closed down around her ankles, severing her feet and making her collapse on the cursed ground.

Cimeries couldn't think of anything but pain for an eternal second, but she had no option to dwell on it. Hardening her heart and forcing herself to keep going, Cimeries gritted her teeth and flipped over before closing her right hand around the shaft of her weapon. Using it to propel herself off the ground, Cimeries landed on the stumps of her legs and looked back at Beleth, who was almost salivating as he watched her.

"Good... *good*! Oh, your willpower is delicious." He rose to his impressive height before drawing a small seal with his left hand.

Grimacing in pain, Cimeries wavered as she tried to hold herself up with her pike, as her mangled legs could not support her alone.

"I... this is not over," she argued, but Beleth only laughed.

"Of course, it isn't. I'm not nearly finished with you," he said, finishing a three-point seal and then holding his left palm out as if trying to accept payment.

Cimeries stumbled forward, the pain in her ankles excruciating, but she only had enough time to wonder what new magic Beleth was using. With just the slightest whistling of air, Beleth's great sword flew back to its master and tore through her elbow, depriving Cimeries of yet another limb and the ability to stand.

Knowing that she had failed again, Cimeries cried in frustration, writhing about on the ground that had betrayed her. However, when Beleth stood over her and knelt down to gloat, Cimeries resolved that she would not give him the satisfaction. With hate in her eyes, she spit into Beleth's face, but he did not mind. He only wiped it away with his hand as he sneered at her.

"That was not nice, but I can understand. You are a warrior and you have been beaten. It is difficult not to be frustrated in these circumstances. Oh, but Hippolyta, this is exciting," he hinted, drawing an armored finger across her cheek.

"What—what do you want?" she asked, her voice shaking as pain bombarded her from all of her wounds.

"I have told you too many times. I am here to bring suffering. And, for one such as you, this will be magnificent. With the willpower and defiance at your disposal, I can only guess as to your limits," he said with a light chuckle before staring through her soul.

"Hippolyta. Queen of the Amazons. Thief of my brother's glorious name..." he addressed her before leaning closer.

"I am here to bring you pain."

CHAPTER 5
WAR AND PIECES

B uné stared at him, but Lucifer didn't know the answer his old friend
wanted. Trying to lead the surviving members of his failed
resistance was becoming more than he could bear, but Lucifer had to keep
up the act. He had to maintain outward confidence even if he was terrified
of Adonai finding them every step of the way. It was already a miracle
their father hadn't pursued them as they had searched the globe.

"I'm telling you, Buné, I'll go through. I just want to make sure that
everything is under control," Lucifer said, but the armored angel kept
scowling.

"This seems like a terrible idea," Buné countered, turning to look at
the flickering portal to his right. "How did you even know about this?"

"Ever since Adonai created us, I knew there was more to the universe
than what he was telling us. Eventually..." Lucifer said, staring into the
swirling chaos of energy, "I confronted him about it. Back then he was
arrogant and secure enough to tell me. There are other creatures, other
dimensions, and there are always pathways. Just like there's a portal to
Heaven, there's a portal to some other dimension."

"And why exactly do you think that this will be our salvation?" Buné asked, staring hard at the angel who had led them to such a desperate prospect. Though Lucifer faced him, he couldn't look Buné in the eye.

"It... has to be. We need to get as far from Adonai as possible, and Earth won't cut it. And since this is my fault, I'll be the one to go first. I... I just need a little more time," Lucifer said before letting his wings spread out from his back. Without another word, Lucifer flapped off the ground and descended along the mountain range, staying just above the treetops and hoping nobody from the heavens was watching.

It had been only a few days since Lucifer had seen Adonai rip the wings off Tamiel's back, and since then his troops had been in full retreat. Within an hour of that brutal display, Lucifer had ordered his brothers and sisters through the portal to Earth, hoping they could reach the rendezvous point on the northern supercontinent.

Wincing at his failure, Lucifer remembered all of the brave souls who had stayed behind to guard their retreat. A hundred of his siblings had been burned by Michael's sword just before Lucifer had been able to reach the portal, and it had almost caused him to stay behind. Instead, Amdusias and Asmodeus had turned to him with a smile and pushed him through.

Although he knew better, Lucifer hoped the Twins had not suffered long.

As soon as Lucifer got to level ground, he dove beneath the canopy and folded his wings behind him so they would not catch on any branches. He was greeted with the sight of a thousand fallen angels nursing wounds, huddled together so they could hide underneath the dense foliage. After letting out his wings to arrest his fall, Lucifer was able to guide himself to a large tree with a dozen angels surrounding it before landing gracefully, with just a few flaps of his wings to stop his momentum.

"Don't tell me you already went through the portal, Lucy," Paimon greeted him as she sat on one of the tree's oversized roots. Once Lucifer gathered his thoughts and let his wings retreat into the ether, he turned to her in shame.

"Not yet. Once I get back up there, I'm going through. I just needed to settle an issue with Astaroth."

"I would think by now you have triple-checked everything, dear. Sure *you're not just **afraid**?" She broke eye contact and looked at her nails, which she had extended by a few inches.*

Walking past her, Lucifer hoped it was an idle threat.

"Of course, I am. But not for the reasons you think," he said, but then he stopped once he felt a sharp pain on his left arm. When he looked down, Lucifer saw a trail of blood racing down to his fingers, and he turned to face his sister with a grunt. "Was there a point to that?"

Instead of hostility, it drew a laugh from her.

*"Odd choice of words, but yes, Lucy, there was. I wanted to make sure you didn't get out of this without a wound to remember, even if it was just a **scratch**. A lot of angels died just for us to run away." Paimon turned her gaze back on her nail, where a drop of red rolled down the edge.*

"You and I both know I didn't get out of this unscathed," Lucifer said, anger bubbling to the surface. Before Paimon could react, he reached out and grabbed her wrist—which only caused her to extend her nails further —and then dragged the razor-sharp claws across his chest. Then, as blood poured out of the cuts, he leaned down to stare into Paimon's shocked face. "But if it helps you to see what I feel, here. Look at this. Look at what I've done. If you want to hurt me, this is where you'll have to start."

"Lucifer..."

*"Keep going, Paimon. Keep making me hurt. Distract me from what I'm feeling in my mind. Distract me from the guilt of having thousands of my brothers and sisters die for my misguided rebellion. Better yet, kill me. Use those claws of yours and scratch me to your heart's content. **Go ahead**. Take your revenge out of my flesh!" Lucifer pressed her nails further into his chest, but before they had sunk half an inch, Paimon had withdrawn her claws and he was shoving delicate fingers into the wounds.*

"That's enough!" she screamed, crying as he held her hand up against the blood flowing from his chest. Sobbing, she grabbed his face with her other hand and brought her forehead against his.

*"That's... I'm sorry. I'm so sorry. Why... I don't want you to **die**. I'm just... so angry."*

Seeing her reaction, Lucifer stopped fuming at Paimon's actions and knelt in the moss so he would not look down on her. After taking her hand away from his chest, Lucifer backed away so they could actually see each other.

"I'm the one that's sorry, Paimon. I'm the one that messed up. I don't want anyone to hurt, and... you caught me at a bad time. Whatever is on the other side of that portal, I have to face it and... I'm nervous. And I took that out on you and I'm sorry," he explained, trying to maintain eye contact with her completely white eyes. To others, it was unnerving, but Lucifer had always found his sister beautiful.

After sniffing back a few tears, Paimon looked down at his chest and let out a whine.

"Look at your chest—" she started, but he shook his head and placed his unbloodied hand on her face.

"That doesn't matter, and you know it. Give me a few minutes and it'll be like it was never there. The deeper pain is on the inside, and I'll always have that. That scratch won't ever go away, but if you want, you can keep giving me more for the road," he said, smiling and forcing his sister to smile with him.

"No, I think I'll just have to figure out some more permanent way to remind you," she said, laughing as she considered the joke. Seeing that she was cheering up, Lucifer lifted her chin with his hand.

"I'm sure you will. Now, Paimon, I need you—along with Astaroth and Zagan—I need you all to take care of everybody while I'm gone, alright? I've always been able to depend on you all, and I'm going to need that where I'm going. Especially your sister. If Lilith figures out what I'm doing, I'm not sure I'll ever hear the end of it."

Lucifer rose to his feet with a slight laugh and at the mention of Lilith, Paimon's smile faltered. However, she shook her head and replaced it with a crooked one.

*"I'm sure you won't. Now go talk to Astaroth and get it over with. Alright, **Scratch**?" she asked with a glint of mischief.*

"So that's it, huh?" Lucifer asked, at which point Paimon shrugged and looked down at her hand, still covered in his blood.

"That's it. Go on, then," she said, avoiding eye contact and wiping her hand on the moss covering the root beside her.

Lucifer watched her for a second, thinking that something else was going on beneath the surface, but eventually he turned to head toward Astaroth's position twenty yards away. As he did, he noticed there was a group of twenty angels who had overheard their conversation, but one of his nearby brothers—an angel who wore grey robes to match his grey hair —was chuckling.

"Don't you start, Barbas. Paimon earned it," Lucifer said as he walked away from the massive tree, but his brother did not seem to take him seriously.

*"I'm not sure you have the power to stop it, **Scratch**," Barbas said, leaning back against his smaller tree and shutting his eyes, confident he would go unharmed. To Lucifer's immense disappointment, Barbas was right.*

"Goddamnit," Lucifer muttered as he walked past his brother to find his second-in-command in a clearing and giving a speech to a dozen angels. Once he was within earshot, Lucifer decided to lean against a tree, just to delay his mission a little longer.

"Now," Astaroth started, unwilling to hide his armor or hide his wings even as they were trying to remain out of sight. "In the coming days, we may have stragglers from the last defense making their way to our rendezvous point and they may be wounded. Our job is to intercept any and all of Adonai's forces pursuing our brothers-in-arms and kill them before retreating back to our own positions. We must remain vigilant, we must remain ready and willing to kill and protect our fellow soldiers.

*"That is why I refuse to hide. That is why I refuse to abandon my wings. That is why I am a split-second away from destroying my enemies at all times. They will **not** surprise me. They will not surprise **us**. We will destroy all of Adonai's lackeys and save our fellow soldiers. This is a strategic retreat, nothing more. Are there any questions?" Astaroth asked, his wings spreading wide as he towered over the other angels. Silence followed, and that was all Astaroth needed. "Then get to your positions, and lead your fellow fighters home."*

"Now you," Astaroth said as he turned to face Lucifer, their golden eyes meeting as the group disbanded and went off in different directions, "are

supposed to be investigating our new home. Why are you watching me give a speech?"

"What else? You're riveting," Lucifer said as he pushed himself off the tree and crossed his arms. "I needed to talk to you before I go through."

"About what? I'm taking care of the troops. I'm making sure that if anybody tries to make it back to us, we're keeping them safe. What more do you want, Lucifer?" Astaroth asked, mirroring his twin's action and crossing his arms.

They were too alike, but that had been Adonai's purpose. He had wanted to make a more aggressive version of the firstborn.

"I don't think we talked about a very distinct possibility. Whatever is on the other side of that portal..." Lucifer hesitated, uncrossing his arms and looking at the forest floor. "Well, there could be nothing. I could die over there without any hope of recovery. There could be some creature that's even worse than Adonai. It's... more than likely that I won't make it back, and if that happens, someone will need to take charge."

"And that's me, I take it?" Astaroth asked, keeping his stance hostile.

"Don't read my mind, brother. I don't like it." Lucifer punctuated it with a weak laugh, but then he continued. "Although it's a good thing, we have way too many powerful angels under our command. If I leave, there's going to be a power vacuum, and with the way things are going with Beleth and Balam and all the others, I could see things getting divisive quite quickly."

"What I need you to do is that... if I don't make it, I want you to immediately take over. I don't want you to wait and see. I want it to be decisive. Without a leader, this whole alliance will shift and break apart," Lucifer continued, trying to match his brother's gaze. "I want you to wait a day, max, and if I'm not back, you take control."

"A day? That's a pretty short timeframe." Astaroth pursed his lips as he considered Lucifer's wishes. "I don't know if I feel comfortable with that."

"No one is asking for comfort. If it's going to be our new home, everything I'll **need to know** I'll know within a few hours. If there's something on the other end that I can't fight, there's no way I can let you guys endanger yourself by staying here. You'll need to move and move fast.

There are other portals to the south and west and Buer will be able to lead you. If I don't come back, you need to evacuate."

"What about the rendezvous point, Lucifer?" Astaroth asked, gesturing toward his departing soldiers. "We need some place where we can gather all the troops still retreating."

"It'll be too dangerous. You'll just have to figure out some way to relay the message. Do this for me," Lucifer urged, and Astaroth shook his head.

"This is stupid," he argued, but Lucifer walked forward and placed hands on his general's shoulders.

"Do this for me, Astaroth. I already failed leading a rebellion. I'm not going to let the survivors be destroyed waiting for me to come back, or become victims of some terror I bring back from another dimension. I need you to promise, or I'm not going at all."

"A promise?" Astaroth asked sarcastically, but he could tell from Lucifer's glare that he had meant it. "Fine, I've promised. Now get the fuck out of here and let me do my job."

"Thank you. I don't know what I would do without you," Lucifer said with a sad smile, backing away as he let wings appear from his back.

"Dying a thousand times over was mentioned at some point." Astaroth huffed as Lucifer flapped his wings and started to rise through the air. "Be safe, Lucy. I've seen the sludge they throw at you for being a leader and I don't want it."

"Neither do I," Lucifer said before flapping his wings a few more powerful times and rising through a gap in the canopy. Once he was in the open air, Lucifer guided himself to a thermal and allowed it to carry him up further. It was a tense few minutes as he soared higher and higher. His stomach felt like it would burst out of him, he felt so nervous, but it was nothing compared to the sight greeting him by the portal.

There, with a scowl on her face, was Lilith in her golden armor, arms crossed and the fingers of her left hand tapping deliberately against her right arm.

*"Did you **really** think you would get away with this?" she asked as Lucifer landed, but he didn't bother resisting her accusation.*

"I had hoped," he said as he withdrew his wings and stepped within striking distance. "I need to do this, Lilith."

"I agree, but you're not doing it alone."

"No, this is dangerous and I'm not letting anyone come with me. Not even Buné." He pointed at their brother, but Lilith did not accept the argument.

"What did I say to you after your first outburst? I am standing by your side, Lucifer, and I will not agree to anything less. We all knew the risks."

"And I led you here, Lil. We have no idea what is beyond that portal—"

*"Which is exactly why it is **incredibly** foolish for you to go alone. At the very least, in case you are incapacitated, someone needs to come back through the portal and warn the others. By not accepting my help, not only are you endangering yourself, but you are endangering everyone at the foot of this mountain," she argued, placing her hand against Lucifer's face and smiling at him. "It's not just sentimentality, brother. You aren't **allowed** to go alone."*

"Lilith," Lucifer started, but he found that he could not fight her. Even if it was dangerous, even if it would place her in harm's way, some selfish part of him wanted her by his side. After a silent moment, Lucifer took her hand away from his face and stepped toward the portal, Lilith turning to face it as well.

"You told Astaroth what you wanted, Lucifer?" Buné asked, his voice heavy with subtext, and Lucifer stared him in the eye before nodding. "Then there's nothing keeping you. Jump when you're ready."

"When you're ready, brother," Lilith repeated, and warmth and affection seemed to fill the very air around her. Looking back to the portal, Lucifer let his fingers interlace with Lilith's and, even with their armor between them, the firstborn had never felt closer to anyone than in that moment.

Then, with a deep breath, they jumped into the chaos.

Lucifer felt like he was being torn apart, but there was always one constant. Lilith's fingers were wrapped around his, and even when he felt the pain of a thousand blades tearing apart his very soul, even with the fire burning his skin and melting his armor, those fingers remained. That gentle soul was by his side, no matter what energy surged around them. He could not see her, but that beautiful, magnificent woman kept him from losing everything.

Just when Lucifer thought he would be torn apart atom by atom, it was over and they landed hard on something solid. Opening his eyes, which had to adjust to the dim lighting, Lucifer could only see shadows playing on rock and wondered just what could cause it. Picking himself off the floor and propping up his body by his elbows, Lucifer was able to see a black iron brazier with small orange flames licking up the sides. It was all a curiosity, but then an unearthly voice echoed through the chamber.

"What creature has fallen to Moloch's cave?"

Immediately upon hearing the statement, Lucifer jumped to his feet and let his wings appear in their full radiance, filling the entire cave with white light that would have blinded a normal creature. Morningstar and Lux came to his hands and the fallen angel was ready for a battle he had hoped would not occur.

Especially since the light revealed a massive, four-armed creature hanging on the wall, a giant mask on its face.

*"An **angel**? What use has Adonai for Moloch? The cousin has had enough from him!" it shouted, all of its features washed out from the light coming from Lucifer. Seeing its aggression at the mention of Adonai, Lilith slapped her brother's arm and put away her own weapons.*

"Stop that!" she urged before turning to the creature hanging on the wall. To her relief, Lucifer let his light fade to something less hostile. "We are not with Adonai! He is our enemy!"

"You are angels! Beings made of Adonai! Why do angels lie to Moloch?" the creature shouted before releasing its hold on the wall and crashing to the ground, propping itself up with its legs and the knuckles of each hand. Even hunched over, it was double the size of the intruders.

"Our apologies, Moloch, we did not mean to intrude or threaten one such as you." Lilith stepped forward and offered her palms out in supplication.

"We tell the truth. Adonai has forsaken us. Half of his angels rose

against him, led by Lucifer," she said, turning and pointing at her brother. Upon seeing that his weapons were still drawn, Lilith scowled at him and whispered. "Put those away!"

"Lil," he started, but she shook her head fiercely and Lucifer relented. In a flash, his weapons disappeared and the center brazier was left to combat the shadows overwhelming the walls of the cave.

"Forsaken?" the creature asked as it approached warily, using its hands to walk forward. "For what reason?"

"Adonai denied us freedom," Lucifer spoke up, not content to let his sister continue talking for him. "And he wanted living beings to suffer. We could not take it anymore."

"How interesting. An Adam and an Eve in Moloch's cave," the creature said, coming within a few yards of the angels and then stopping, settling itself on its hindquarters. "You are truly against Adonai?"

"He hunts us even now, Moloch. We have come to this dimension—" Lilith started, but Lucifer stepped forward, within arm's reach of the creature, and gambled everything.

*"At all costs, we have to escape. We need a new home, and we don't have enough time to find another portal," he stated, staring up into the giant mask, which he could now tell had seven interlocking triangles etched into its face. "And, if necessary, we will do **anything** to reach safety."*

The creature was silent for a moment and Lilith was giving him a death glare, but Lucifer had already decided that it was all-or-nothing. Whoever this creature was, they needed its help or, at worst, would find another method to deal with it. However, he was saved the trouble once a deep rumble issued from behind its mask.

"There is no need for that, angel. You are against the cousin and Moloch enjoys this."

It bowed, sweeping two pairs of arms out to its sides.

"Welcome to Hell. Welcome to your new home."

"Wake up, Nico!" Cadmus' shout brought Niccolo out of his daze, but apparently it wasn't fast enough for the reaper. Seconds after, Niccolo felt a sting on the side of his face, and it didn't take long for him to realize that Cadmus had slapped him. Growling, Niccolo opened his eye and sat up, accidentally pushing on Paimon's side, and briefly wondered how she had come to lay beside him.

"What? What... happened?" Niccolo asked, his heart sinking once he realized panic had spread through the reaper's face.

Cadmus *never* panicked.

"Cimeries, she—goddamnit, just look," he said before grabbing Niccolo's shoulder and forcing him around. It took a few seconds for Niccolo to realize in the morning light, but something was on fire in the fort. After shoving Paimon's shoulder unceremoniously off of him, Niccolo picked himself up as Cadmus continued. "I thought it had something to do with Phenex, but I was wrong."

"That *what* had to do with Phenex?" Niccolo growled as he turned to face Cadmus, who instantly turned sheepish. Seeing that moment of weakness, Niccolo backhanded the reaper with his demonic arm and instantly regretted the action, but it allowed Cadmus to collect himself.

"I had a couple visions last night that were pretty ominous," he said before closing the distance and staring down his friend. "And you do *that* again and we're going to have a problem."

"Sorry, but I don't need you to be scared, we need to go fix this," he said before turning back to the ominous hill. He was still staring at the smoke glowing red and gold when he felt something small cut into his leg.

"Never wake me like that again, *hon*," Paimon grumbled as she withdrew her nail.

"No time to gripe. We need to save Cimeries," Niccolo said as he started toward the tree line.

"Save Cimeries from what?" Phenex's voice called out behind him, but Niccolo only picked up speed as he made his way to the hill.

125

In his mind, he was already calling out to Plague and could see a green mist forming just beyond the trees.

"She—she knocked me out last night and I'm pretty sure she went to go attack Beleth by herself," Cadmus explained quickly, helping to pick Phenex up before trying to catch up with Niccolo.

"Where are you going? We don't know what's waiting for us up there—" he started, but then Niccolo whipped around and glared at him.

"Think about what you saw in your vision, Cadmus. *Still* think we should wait?" he asked, well aware that anything Cadmus saw wasn't good, and suddenly the reaper realized caution wasn't an option.

He turned to face their companions and pointed to the hill with his scythe.

"Let's go! Now!" he shouted before running toward the tree line, the others needing no other incentive. As they ran, Cadmus called out to Mercy as he jumped over a rotten log.

Take a cue from your brother, appear at the edge of the forest, he thought and, before he could finish, dust was already swirling together near the half-formed black horse.

If only the others knew how foolish you get under pressure, a rasp came back to him, and Cadmus was glad Mercy had the decency to keep his criticism between them.

Sending thoughts of apology as he ran, Cadmus turned to see Phenex staring at the fire with concern. Cursing internally, he realized he should warn the man, but he wouldn't have the chance. Before he could speak, a shadow flew past him and carried Phenex with it, and it only took a second for him to realize Marchosias had joined them.

Pushing the thought from his mind and hoping Phenex could handle the barbaric symbol waiting for him, Cadmus made it to open ground and covered the rest of the distance with a few bounds, landing gracefully on Mercy's saddle. He would have called out to Niccolo to wait, but Plague had already carried the leper halfway toward the fort and he would not have listened anyway. Turning to look behind him, Cadmus felt anxious as he waited for Paimon.

Even if it was only ten seconds before the Fallen caught up and jumped into the saddle behind him, Cadmus felt like they were losing too much time.

"Aren't you a showoff," Paimon muttered as she caught her breath, and she only just wrapped her hands around Cadmus' waist before Mercy broke into a mad dash toward the fort, the flames having already spread to the walls. Without bothering to check with his passenger, Cadmus urged Mercy forward and hoped they would make it in time.

This is all wrong. That vision was meant for Phenex. It made sense. A burning cross? How could it have been anything else? he asked, but Mercy was not so optimistic.

*It made **too** much sense. I am not entirely convinced these visions are beneficial, Cadmus. Amon hated you.*

Are you saying what I think you're saying? Cadmus asked, but the thought was now running rampant in his mind.

It is not that far-fetched. We know these souls you have inherited speak to you. Why is it so hard to believe that some of your enemies may be poisoning your mind?

Mercy's voice echoed in his head, and it was made even worse that his horse might be correct. Cadmus couldn't be sure of anything anymore, but, at the same time, there was every possibility that the vision was correct, but his interpretation was wrong. There was too much grey area, and that now-familiar headache was already coming back.

Looking forward, he realized the fort was still too far away and that Niccolo was almost there. Gritting his teeth, Cadmus felt even more anxious knowing that his friend would rush headlong into any trap, and there was no way for Cadmus to stop or warn him. His frustration led to anger, and with his anger came something strange. When he focused on the moment and willed the universe to stop, the universe decided to answer.

At first, Cadmus thought his awareness of time had slowed down, but that wasn't entirely true. Mercy's hooves struck the ground in the exact same rhythm as before, but all of their surroundings seemed to be moving at a quarter their normal speed. Before he had focused, Niccolo had only been seconds away from the slope of the hill, but when Cadmus looked again, he was still in the exact same spot. When Cadmus looked at Marchosias, he expected the blur of the shadow's movement, but the reaper could see each paw strike the ground and clumps of dirt fly into the air after the demon pushed off with his feet. Even Paimon's breathing behind him had slowed down so much that Cadmus only felt the slightest pressure of her torso pressing against his back.

"What is this?" Cadmus asked, and before Mercy could answer, they had already overtaken Marchosias and Phenex and were halfway to Niccolo, who was just about to pull on Plague's reins.

"I am just as surprised, but I will not question it now," Mercy responded, and once Cadmus realized that his horse was affected by this phenomenon, he knew it was actually happening. In that moment he lost his focus and the two of them were jerked back into the regular flow of time, but at that point they were only a few yards away from Niccolo, who had jumped off of Plague to inspect a sign on the ground.

"What in all of Hell was *that*, reaper?" Marchosias shouted as he landed beside Cadmus and threw Phenex from his back, who landed on the ground gracefully. Cadmus had been dumbfounded by the event, but he shook his head and then waved off the question with his left hand.

"We'll find out later. Nico," he said before turning to his friend on the ground, "what is that?"

"One of Beleth's signatures. Looks... burnt or something," he said before standing up and slinging himself back onto Plague's saddle. "Paimon, is it dangerous?"

"Not more dangerous than the fire up there. Whatever it was, it's already been used," she explained, at which point Plague reared and

Niccolo grabbed the bow from his back with his left hand. When his front hooves landed, Plague immediately galloped up the incline.

"Damnit, Nico," Cadmus muttered, Mercy already tearing up the slope after their friend.

As they approached the entrance, Cadmus felt a chill up his spine and wondered whether it was from his recent experience or the fact that his vision was about to be revealed, but he knew he didn't like either option.

Just before reaching the entrance, where Plague had balked and Niccolo sat slumped over the saddle, Cadmus noticed a blaze of fire streaming over his shoulder from behind. Once it was past him, it jerked to an immediate stop and extinguished, revealing a smoking Phenex who then sank to the ground.

"Oh, God," he sobbed weakly, falling to the ground and then kneeling, which made Cadmus realize that whatever was beyond the crest was something reserved for nightmares. A mountain of corpses, a charred village, anything was possible, but then he saw the top of a wooden structure peek above the ground, and suddenly Cadmus knew exactly what he would see.

He was still not prepared.

When he finally did reach the entrance of the fort, Cadmus lost almost all semblance of sanity. His hands shook, his eyes watered and his jaw was slack. There, in the center of this fortress, was a giant, burning cross. And just beyond the roar of the flames, they all heard it. They heard the weak cry of a tormented creature held in place by giant barbs and melting chains, a spear driven through her abdomen.

Cimeries was being burned alive.

"No," a sound came from Cadmus' side, and he turned to find Phenex picking himself up weakly. Soon, he was standing, stumbling toward the blaze with purpose.

"No, no, no. No... *No. No. No,*" he repeated, his steps more certain with each denial and smoke rising from his footprints. By the end, his voice seemed to burn through the air and flames licked up his arms and legs, and then it burst out of him. Flames swirled about the man as he advanced and—before anyone could react—bright wings of orange and red fire erupted out of his back and stretched out five feet in both directions.

"No!" Phenex screamed, rising into the air and placing his hands out in front of him, palms toward the sky, and none of his companions could stop him. They all just stared as he raised his arms skyward and flames continued to pour out of him.

"I will not let this happen!" he shouted one last time before the only thing he could do was scream. Phenex was engulfed in flames by that point and it seemed like they would only continue to expand, but then they started to shrink back to their origin. More accurately, the fire had condensed and it continued to fold in on itself until it was only inches from Phenex's flesh. None of them could see his body past the inferno, as the flames had created a kind of shifting armor.

"What... how do we..." Cadmus tried to ask, but that was as far as he got. Unfortunately, everyone else was on the same page.

"I'm not sure we can," Marchosias responded as a normal man, the spectacle enough cause for him to revert back to human form. Each breath he took became more difficult as Phenex's fire consumed more and more oxygen, which only made it more apparent that his friend was beyond reach.

Phenex was out of control and Marchosias could do nothing to stop it.

"What is he trying to do?" Niccolo muttered, but no one could answer. It seemed like Phenex had lost his mind.

That was until his scream grew in volume and they saw what their friend was intending. As his flames intensified, they seemed to call out to the nearby blaze, and Phenex's onlookers couldn't believe what they were seeing.

From all around the camp, flames streamed through the air to the small man and poured into his armor of fire. Literally taking away the breath from their lungs, a firestorm raged about the top of the hill as Phenex absorbed more and more flames into his body. The chaos above them would have been beautiful if not for the pain and agony that had caused it.

Then, in a matter of moments, the only fire left was that which surrounded their friend and companion. Burning with an intensity they could feel from the ground sixty feet below, Phenex hovered in the air, the colors of his brilliant armor and wings more vibrant than the sun rising above the wall ahead of them.

"*Never again!*" Phenex shouted, his voice seeming to come from inside their own heads, but his friends were just grateful that he was finished with the terrifying display. For a few agonizing moments, they had thought he would destroy everything within sight.

"...Yeshua," Marchosias started weakly, but when the raging demon above them turned to face him, the werewolf decided to show confidence, even if it was completely fake. "Yeshua, are you alright?"

"*I,*" the voice screamed out of the flames, and they all thought Phenex would do something insane, but then the figure shook his head and put a hand to his forehead. "*I'm sorry.*"

"Don't be, that was rather impressive for a human," an arrogant voice interrupted, and all five of them grabbed their weapons and looked at the source.

In a leisurely manner, Beleth walked out from behind one of the far cabins and then came to a stop a few yards away from the charred cross, the woman still moaning weakly above him. After putting his hands on his belt, Beleth looked up at Cimeries and smiled. Her skin had been blackened and parts had sloughed off, but he was greatly pleased by the metal he had grafted into her body.

"*Y—you...*" Phenex stammered, but Beleth was unimpressed by the flares that poured out of the demon's armor.

"*M—me,* indeed. I have to say, Yeshua, I—" he started, but Beleth didn't have time to explain. Before he could say another word, Phenex directed a torrent of flames toward the demon king, who only had enough time to raise his hand before the blaze enveloped him. Screaming as he attacked Beleth, Phenex rose higher into the air and directed the burning energy down with even more focus, a column of fire stretching toward the heavens.

For a long minute, it seemed like it would never stop.

After that minute—after Phenex was devoid of energy and was left smoking in the air—the column of fire still rose to the clouds, much higher than the cross that had been burning just a few moments before. The inferno continued for a few more seconds after that, even though Phenex had stopped providing it with energy, but eventually it sputtered out and there were no more flames to behold.

However, to everyone's surprise, Beleth stood there panting with his arm extended upward, but otherwise no worse for the experience. A transparent circle of purple energy was flickering in and out of existence, but once Beleth gathered his breath, it finally blinked out and he straightened up to his full height.

"I don't like being *interrupted*!" he shouted, contempt flavoring every word. "I swear, not *one* of you animals has the decency to have a fair fight. I *know* you know about honor. We tried to teach it for millennia!"

"How..." Phenex said weakly, falling out of the air quickly once the fight left him, but Marchosias leapt up and grabbed his frail body before he crashed to the ground.

"How did I withstand your little assault? Easy," Beleth replied, wiping dust off his pauldron before turning to face his opponents. "You're not strong enough to beat me. I was an angel, Yeshua, and I have had more than two million years to refine my powers once I fell."

"You are certainly powerful, perhaps just as much as some of my weaker siblings, but this is a different game," he continued, stepping forward as he spoke.

"I was a King of Hell, and some of us are better than others," he said with a sneer toward Paimon, whose claws and teeth extended in anger.

"To my immense satisfaction, I will cause suffering and death wherever I go, and you can all be certain that you cannot stop me. That woman up there," he said before pointing behind him but continuing to address his audience directly. "She is powerful. She is an *exemplary* warrior and one of the few credits to your race."

"This morning, while you all slept, I played with her insides and peeled away bits and pieces of flesh before sewing them back together. I nailed her to a cross and wrapped her with barbed chains. I set her on fire, watching as the flames crawled up her long legs," he said coming to a stop just a few yards away from them. "I buried her own pike deep in her guts so she could not *squirm*."

"You're a monster," Niccolo said under his breath, which only made Beleth smile.

"I *am*. I am *your* monster. Humanity shall fear me until the day they are eradicated, and they can only hope that I am not there to greet their soul. Now, if you don't mind," he said before quickly drawing a five-point seal in the air in front of him.

With a horrific scream, a white, four-legged creature crawled out of the purple energy and then came to a stop, pained noises coming from its throat. They had all seen it before—it was Misery, Beleth's twisted mount—but the bone spurs jutting out of every joint and its lipless mouth still caused distress.

"And you shove this crime in front of us, too?" Plague's voice resonated through the air, and then a strange clicking joined it. After a moment, Niccolo looked down and realized the noise was coming from Mercy.

Why are you two reacting so strongly? he asked Plague, the recent brutality and violence so overwhelming that he had to ignore it for now. A roar filled his mind and Niccolo realized that this was the first time Plague had ever yelled.

Ever.

Niccolo, don't make me spell it out, Plague explained in his mind, so angry he could not actually speak, and Niccolo almost couldn't control the sympathetic rage coming from his horse. Suddenly,

Niccolo realized just why the two horses were so enraged, and it only made him hate Beleth more.

"Why would I avoid causing you pain, Plague?" Beleth asked before throwing himself on top of the horse and settling into the saddle. "If it makes you feel fortunate, I *almost* chose you for these experiments instead of your *dear* sister."

"You *bastard*," Plague fumed, so much green fog pouring out of his eyes and mouth that it made his rider nervous.

"Niccolo, I'm aware that you have little grasp of manners, but do keep your horse in line. I suggest tearing out his tongue. After that, Misery gave me no arguments," Beleth said with a cruel smile, and it was all Niccolo could do to stop Plague from rushing forward and forcing his hooves through Beleth's face.

"We're going to kill you, Beleth. I hope you know that," Paimon said as she crept forward, her entire body becoming a weapon. Her nails had extended to the length of small swords, the claws on her feet were hooked and deadly. Her teeth could cut through metal and that had been proven many times in the past.

"I sincerely doubt that, sister," Beleth said before yawning, gathering the reins with his other hands. "Even if you live through today, you'd still have to fight me. I should hope after your messiah's display that you have better sense than that."

"What are you talking about?" Cadmus asked, but almost immediately a torrent of visions broke through his mind and all he could feel was the pain of a hundred souls screaming out in agony. After he recovered and was able to look back up at Beleth, Cadmus' eyes covered in blue energy, the traitor let out a soft chuckle.

"Oh, reaper, you will have to work on that empathy. You'll have no chance against my army if you feel their *pain*."

"Get it over with, asshole. We've been very patient waiting to murder you," Marchosias growled, having placed an unconscious Phenex against the wall of the fortress and returned to his companions, his hulking mass wreathed in shadows. At the remark, Beleth scoffed and then held his right hand aloft.

"I feel like that is more out of fear than respect, Judas. In any case, here is your reward." Beleth twirled his hand and caused a massive purple design to appear along the ground beneath them. Before they could react, it crackled out of existence, but then the very ground rumbled and shook all of them down to their bones.

"What have you done?" Cadmus asked, feeling the agony and screams increasing in his mind. Seeing his reaction, Beleth laughed heartily before creating a seven-point seal a few feet to his right.

"Well, you will just have to see. Goodbye, primates. Sister." Beleth turned Misery to face the glowing circle hanging in the air, but Niccolo could not accept that easy farewell.

Within half a second, he brought up his bow and nocked an arrow with his right hand, rage flowing through him. By the time he released the arrow bathed in green flames, Misery had already started to walk through the seal and Beleth had noticed his attack. Smiling, he lifted his bracer to ward off the arrow and expected to deflect it easily.

However, to the demon king's surprise, the arrow flew straight through his bracer and his arm, exiting through the other side and continuing on its path. With a yelp of pain, Beleth held his wounded arm with his other hand, but almost immediately his face filled with anger. The last thing he did before being carried through the portal was look Niccolo in the eye.

"You will pay for that, *leper.*"

Then he was gone. Niccolo thought about pursuing him through the portal—despite his poor track record—but he didn't have enough time to consider it further. A violent tremor coursed through the area, and they could hear anguished moans and screams coming from beneath the surface.

"What is that?" Paimon asked, her claws and fangs retracting as she looked around them, but they came back out once the first arm burst out of the ground. It was followed by another, then another from further on in the camp. Everywhere they looked, pale limbs grasped for empty air before turning back down and pushing down against the soil.

Then the faces broke free and the air was filled with a cacophony of pain.

"Cadmus, what the fuck is this?" Niccolo asked, wondering whether or not he should grab another arrow. However, when he looked at his friend, Cadmus was doubled over in pain and gripping his scythe tight.

"It can't be..." he muttered, but as Cadmus looked out at the horror climbing out of the ground, he knew exactly what it was. The truth was even more terrible than he thought, and he wondered if Beleth had ever known anything of the world before surrendering himself to pure, unadulterated evil.

"What are they?" Marchosias covered his ears, which were understandably more sensitive, but then he saw the first creature fully emerge. He dropped his hands, completely taken aback by the sight that lay before him.

"They're human. Human souls. Twisted... combined," Cadmus tried to explain as he sat up in his saddle. "Beleth made chimera out of living and dead humans."

Suddenly, a low moan echoed through the air, and among the mass of twisted and broken limbs, one creature rose triumphant.

Standing just a few feet away from Cimeries, who was still writhing in place, one of Beleth's chimera looked down on them in judgment. Seven pairs of glassy eyes tried to focus on them while five mouths perpetually moaned and gnashed their teeth; four massive limbs made out of arms and legs swung about from its upper torso. Three tree-trunk legs made of torsos and body parts propped it up, and once it stopped bellowing, it started to shuffle forward.

And that was just the first one.

INSTINCT TOOK hold of Marchosias as he leapt into the fray. If he could have thought, he would have considered this a mercy; that these souls needed to perish so they could exist without pain. However, no such thoughts had any chance of surviving in his mind.

All he had was the gut instinct, that gnawing terror, that these *things* did not belong in this world.

As he tore through the first body, Marchosias only wanted to survive a living nightmare. While he tore a good chunk out of the monstrosity, a torso attached to the main body by the neck swung toward him. Although he was prepared to slice through it, Marchosias was distracted by a mewling infant's face on the small of its back. The torso slammed into him—catching him flat-footed and unable to shift the shadows around him—and the living shadow had to roll to his feet to avoid being stomped by another one of the creatures.

When he was able to look around, he found six of the chimera advancing toward him at the same time, an auditory assault tearing through the air around him.

Transforming his ears back to human form so he could withstand their screams, Marchosias went to work dismantling the bodies of these tortured souls. Becoming a blur, the werewolf slashed and raked his nails across the exposed flesh of the two nearby creatures, climbing up its towering body until he reached its upper "arms" and then tore his wicked claws through their mangled joints.

He had to leap into the air after taking off an arm, as it seemed the chimera did not care if they struck each other. Two of the monsters slammed appendages into the werewolf's last target, breaking bones with little resistance and forcing it to collapse onto the ground. Still, it moved, and Marchosias realized that he was outmatched. The best he could do was weaken the chimera so that his companions could deal the killing blows.

Swallowing his fear as horrors stumbled around him on twisted limbs, Marchosias wrapped his body in darkness and went about crippling their opponents.

After seeing Marchosias leap into action, Cadmus broke out of his daze and brought out his scythe. Mercy carried him forward—right through the middle of the crowd of bodies—and Cadmus tried to ignore the pain and misery tearing into his very soul as he cut through the chimera like a field of grain. Blood and gore flowed with every strike, the razor-sharp edge of his scythe finding little resistance, and after a few chaotic seconds, they had reached the other end of the camp.

When he was able to see the results of his frenzy, Cadmus felt a pit growing in his stomach. Although many of the hellish constructs were still flailing about, pools of blood and twitching limbs lay in his wake. In particular, Cadmus could not take his eyes off a chimera he had cut in half across the torso, but it lifted itself up with monstrous arms, pouring blood and internal organs out of the wide opening in its body. Seeing the pained expressions on its warped faces, Cadmus knew it should have died, but he finally realized exactly what was happening and gripped his scythe tighter.

"Everyone!" he shouted, surprising everyone by how clear and powerful it was over the chorus of pain, but he continued as Mercy galloped back through the crowd. "These are not natural creatures!"

"You don't exactly need to tell us that, sweetie," Paimon said as she drove her claws through the hip joint of one creature, relieving it of its giant leg, but that only caused the leg to crawl at her using broken hands. Jumping away from the new threat and onto the back of a nearby chimera, Paimon gave him a frustrated look.

"No, I mean—" Cadmus said, pausing to sweep his blade through an arm falling from the sky. When he looked back at Paimon, she had withdrawn her fangs and was shredding the upper torso of her victim. "They're human, but they're also not."

"You... really need to work on your explanation," Niccolo said as he rode by, using his bastard sword to cut through their enemies. Plague carried him through the battlefield swiftly, but only just avoided the deadly arm of a chimera, the exposed ribcage on the limb broken and dagger-sharp. Soon after, Plague turned back and stopped within a few yards of Cadmus. "Or you can just stop talking."

"They're amalgams. Chimera. What we're fighting are," Cadmus said, flipping his scythe to Mercy's other side and driving the point deep into the chest cavity of a screaming monster. "They're only part human."

"Finish *any* time now, reaper," Marchosias growled as he flew past them, a shadow sweeping along the ground and sending tides of blood in his wake. After tearing out a sizable chunk out of a nearby beast, the shadow stood up and stared at him with yellow eyes. "*What* do we need to do?"

"I don't... know," Cadmus admitted, dropping his weapon slightly. "They're part living human, part undead corpse, part soul and, here's the part I was getting to..." he said, looking over the field of torn-apart bodies. "It's not just human souls."

"Like, they're animals, too?" Niccolo said, using his blade to cut off a mutated arm just as he was in the middle of impaling another chimera with his demonic hand. After withdrawing his bloody arm, Niccolo held his bastard sword with both hands and brought it down vertically, splitting the chimera in half.

"No, I mean, they're like us. Part of these... *things* were human souls that passed on. Men and women who had reached the afterlife," Cadmus said, gritting his teeth as a massive creature rushed toward him. With one mind, Mercy brought him forward and ducked under the chimera's monstrous swing, and Cadmus only had to draw his blade across its midsection. With a heavy crash, the top half of the creature fell onto the ground and blood seeped into the soil beneath it.

"So, Beleth brought some of his subjects with him? Is that what you're saying?" Paimon asked, leaping from one chimera to the next and using her claws to relieve them of as many weapons and limbs as possible.

"No. No, it can't be," Marchosias said weakly, the shadows abandoning him as he looked at the screaming and pain-ridden faces of the creatures crawling around their battlefield. He turned to look at Cadmus, who nodded before returning to watching them in pity.

"Someone just fucking explain it. I'm getting tired of this game," Niccolo said, plunging his blade into a beast before twisting and drawing it out through the chimera's side.

"That's exactly what it is. That's *exactly* what this is! It's a fucking *game!*" Marchosias shouted before lifting his head and howling in rage, the sound drowning out everything else in their massacre. After lowering his head back down and taking a heaving breath, the werewolf scowled at Niccolo to drive it home. "Some of these souls were angels."

"W—what?" Niccolo muttered, unable to really understand the weight of it. He looked at the creatures crawling about, their bodies broken and torn apart again and again but still moving around, and his heart sank. Unable to look at them any longer, Niccolo made the mistake of looking up and found Cimeries' body still hanging on the burnt cross.

Although he could not process it with this new revelation flooding his brain, Niccolo noticed that pink patches had already started to form between the blackened and charred remnants of her skin. Thinking that he was just seeing things, Niccolo turned back to Marchosias, who was visibly shaking with rage.

"That stink. That goddamn stink. It wasn't just Beleth I was smelling," Marchosias stated, his voice low and violent, and with every word he seemed to grow larger in size. "Whatever that bastard was doing, he was using human souls who had made it to Heaven."

"How can you be so sure?" Paimon asked as she jumped to the ground and backed away from another wave of approaching chimera, but Marchosias startled her with a murderous snarl.

"Because I'm used to the worst in people, and this is just *another* cruelty. Reaper!" he shouted, turning to face Cadmus with shadows covering every inch of his frame, which only made him seem more dangerous. "What do we do to give them peace? Do *you* have to reap all of them?"

"I... could try," Cadmus said, holding up his blade and letting it glow with blue light, but he shook his head. "But you heard what Tamiel said in his hut. Apparently, any human can do it."

"Then *how...*" Marchosias said as he stalked toward Cadmus, shoving the bravest chimera out of the way without caring. Remarkably, it seemed to intimidate the horrors into shrinking back. "...do you do it? Tell me now, reaper."

"It's... damnit, Marchosias, I don't fucking know!" Cadmus shouted before turning to a crowd of the chimera, who he assumed had continued to crawl out of the ground, but then he saw what was truly happening. With anger boiling through his veins, Cadmus watched as three dismantled monsters near one of the cabins crawled to each other and then joined their wounds together, new skin forming and joining them as one.

"Oh, that's just—they're rebuilding themselves."

His mind still flooded with the pain from all of these tortured souls, Cadmus couldn't take it anymore and gripped the handle of his weapon so hard he could hear his bones popping. As the creature stood up on five horrific legs, Cadmus raised his weapon up and behind him—not noticing the blue aura surrounding him—and rotated his body so he could throw the scythe forward.

As it carved through the air, it appeared as an azure wind before the weapon crashed through the chimera and then sank into the wall of the cabin behind it. A massive wedge of flesh slid out of the creature, slowly at first before gravity overcame the suction of its body, and then the rest of the chimera followed it to the ground. The others only stood in their positions, watching the reaper still shaking in his saddle, but Cadmus was focused on something else.

The light had gone out of all the chimera's eyes. He was able to reap them.

Raising his hand in front of him, Cadmus focused on the scythe still vibrating from its impact into the cabin's side. He didn't know why he did it, he could not particularly understand his actions, but he inherently understood that something would happen.

Although his fingers shook as he held them out, he doubled down and tried to clench the space in front of him and exert his willpower. Over what, he wasn't certain, but he knew this was something he had inherited from the prophetic demons he had harvested. Just as he was about to give up, a blue aura seeped out of his skin, through his armor and his cloak, and then Cadmus noticed the blue glow surrounding his weapon.

Before he could react, the weapon withdrew out of the wall forty yards away and floated for half a second, and then it seemed to be yanked backward, whistling through the air as it flew back to its owner. Cadmus was afraid that he had made a mistake as it came screaming toward him, but it landed safely in his outstretched right hand and he was left staring at his scythe, which appeared perfectly normal. After he took a few cautionary breaths, Cadmus looked to his friends and found them staring.

"It's... I don't know," he admitted, his arm wavering as he brought it back down and looked at Marchosias, who had recovered first. "But that one is dead.

"As impressive as that was, I'm not sure we can do *that*," Marchosias said as he turned to face the circling chimera, four creatures that stood just as tall and twice as wide as the werewolf they surrounded. "Want to repeat it with these poor bastards, or at least tell us how to do that blue thing?"

"Maybe..." Niccolo started, drawing their attention, but whatever sheepishness he felt had to be abandoned once another one of the horrors stumbled toward him. Without another thought, Plague ran forward and allowed Niccolo to drive his sword in a diagonal arc across the chimera's body, the pestilent blade shimmering with the same green energy they had witnessed in the nearby village.

Once Niccolo was past the creature, they all turned to watch it fall. For a long moment it did not move, but then two of its arms started to tremor and then stretched out along the ground.

"Guess not," Marchosias said as he slowly retreated toward the closer Horseman, but then Cadmus pointed to the ravaged chimera.

"No, look!" he urged, and they all watched as the two arms pulled further and further away from the massive body. Then, once it reached its breaking point, the skin tore and the combinations of body parts crawled away from the pale corpse. Upon seeing the truth, Niccolo smiled at him.

"That's... that's all it is. Whatever we have—whatever we had hiding under the surface—that's how we reap them," he muttered, turning to face a battlefield of twisted creations. If he hadn't been so frustrated earlier, Niccolo would have been ashamed of the grin on his face.

"Do you," Cadmus said, swallowing as he looked at Marchosias, "do you have anything like that? Anything you can use?" With a low chuckle, the werewolf turned to him with mischief in yellow eyes. Then the shadows swarmed over him.

"Something like that," he said, shadows bundling over his growing body as he leapt forward. Shrouded nails tore through the nearby bodies and long, obsidian fangs tore out huge chunks of flesh from the unfortunate chimera. It died from the attack and Marchosias turned to look at Cadmus with approval, but that was a mistake.

At the opening, one of the other chimera slammed a tree trunk of a limb into Marchosias' midsection and sent him tumbling through the air, dark blood trailing out of his side. Cadmus looked at his sprawled-out body and saw that the werewolf wasn't moving, but then he heard the screams coming from above, a giant chimera standing over him. In that moment, he was not a Horseman of the Apocalypse; he wasn't one of the most powerful beings on the planet.

He was just afraid, and he could do nothing to stop it.

But as the combination of torsos and legs fell down from the sky, a golden creature jumped in front of him and brought its hands across the monstrosity, letting loose a torrent of blood and chunks of flesh, and Cadmus barely covered his eyes and mouth to avoid the foul soup.

Once he was able to bring his sleeve across his face and wipe the gore away, Cadmus opened his eyes and found the golden creature had jumped down from Mercy's shoulders and was on the ground, its every movement a blur. Then, once each chimera was dismantled and lifeless, the shimmering energy fell away to reveal Paimon, who turned to look at Cadmus over her shoulder.

"That's... that's a little exhausting. Haven't... haven't had to do that in a long... in a..." she tried to speak, swaying as she stood there, but she lost her balance and started to fall over.

Finally able to leap into action, Cadmus threw himself to the ground and slid through the muck and blood, catching the demon king before she crashed into a puddle of filth. Though her eyes were half-closed, Paimon still gave him a slight smile.

"You... silly little boy."

"Thank you," he said, but she lightly slapped him with a blood-covered hand.

"You'll get me back soon, reaper. Don't look so grim." Then she closed her eyes and passed out.

Sweeping his left hand under her knees, Cadmus picked Paimon up and carried her to his saddle, laying her across Mercy's back as best he could.

After laying her to rest, Cadmus remembered Marchosias and turned to find him propping himself up on his elbows and knees. He breathed a sigh of relief, but then he realized their situation was still dire. Paimon was unconscious, the werewolf was wounded and he knew for certain that his own strength was fading. Despair weighing him down, Cadmus turned to look for Niccolo and found him riding through the ranks of their enemies, chopping and slicing and burning with green energy as he rode. Cadmus was grateful, but then he saw Niccolo's face and the gratitude was replaced by fear.

Bloodlust and rage. That was all Niccolo had become, and it was endless.

After the third pass, by the time Niccolo retreated back to Cadmus' position, that bloodlust was gone. The green energy had dissipated and Niccolo was hunched over his saddle, barely holding onto the blade in his hand. His demonic arm hung limp and twitched every few seconds, and he struggled to breathe. Even Plague seemed to be having a hard time standing.

"Got... got most of them. I could have kept going, but... but..." Niccolo paused, losing his train of thought and lifting his shaking left hand to his forehead to steady himself. "The screams. They broke through and..."

"It's fine, Nico. I'll see if I can..." Cadmus said, pausing on the word, "handle the rest."

Looking at the stragglers, it seemed like they may have won against Beleth's experiments. Only three heaps of human body parts seemed to be left standing, and they were all gathered at the base of the charred cross in the middle of the camp.

Seeing the blackened wood, Cadmus' heart sank as he remembered the sixth member of their party. Slowly, he lifted his gaze, not knowing why he was drawn to her corpse, but what he saw surprised him.

Still lashed to the construct by melted chains and barbs—long nails still impaling her limbs—Cimeries was hanging on the cross, but she was no longer the blackened and charred remains of their friend. Raw, pink skin had bloomed across her naked body, confusing the reaper, but then he saw her head twitch. Cimeries lifted her head and stared straight at him, her eyes relaying more information than words ever could.

"She's *conscious.*" Fear, anger and sympathy collided in his mind, and Cadmus could not stop staring at the broken, impaled woman, who whispered words he could not hear.

"How is that possible? How?" Niccolo asked, but Cadmus didn't have an answer. He could only stare, watching the skin spread out across the crackling flesh it was replacing. Unable to stop watching her regeneration, the only thing that brought him to the present was when her throat regenerated enough for her to shout back at him.

"*Stop looking at me and face your enemy!*"

Cimeries had mustered every ounce of willpower she had to say anything, at all, but it had the desired effect. Cadmus looked down and finally saw what had been building without his knowledge. The three remaining chimera had taken to picking up the dismantled body parts of their brethren—many of which had been cut apart by Cadmus' first rides through their ranks—and had grown to humongous sizes.

Even that seemed like too much for him to handle, but then it got worse. The three creatures, who were already about twenty feet tall and fifteen feet wide, stumbled to one spot and then slammed into each other, their flesh merging and exposed bones and body parts coming together to form unholy weapons out of corpses.

He had not been paying attention, and now he had to face a living nightmare.

However, he couldn't. Cadmus—no matter how many times he had faced denizens of Hell, no matter how much power he had amassed in his time as a reaper—knew this was beyond him. The massive beast towered over him; hundreds of crying and pain-ridden faces speaking directly to *him*, boring through his mind and taking away his sanity. It was everything he could do not to force the point of his scythe through his own heart.

Empathy; that was what Beleth had said. His empathy was responsible for this. Cadmus had seen pain before, he had been able to sympathize with most people in his lives, but he guessed Beleth had meant something else. There was no way this was normal; he could tell that the others weren't affected like this. These chimera had some hold over him, some power Beleth had purposely built into them.

"Any—" Niccolo interrupted himself with a cough. "Any time now, Cadmus."

However, when Cadmus looked at his friend, Niccolo was able to see the pain that enveloped him. Turning away, Cadmus faced the towering creature, dozens of legs and arms swinging and propelling it forward, its body fifty feet tall, and he could not fight it. That blue aura—any of those distortions of time, whatever they were—Cadmus could not use them. This was his moment of failure. His only hope now was to run away and abandon his friends.

However, his friends would not abandon him.

As Cadmus stared at the beast just seconds away from crushing him flat, a yawning chasm of a mouth roaring at him all the while, the air around them crackled into life. Then, before either Horseman could react, a towering inferno burst from the ground in front of them and enveloped the chimera, its every body part becoming a shadow behind the rising flames. It screamed and screamed, flailing about arms completely covered in red and orange, and it seemed like its misery would never end.

After a moment, however, the screams died away and the burning husk fell—the legs made of discarded body parts collapsing beneath it—and then it started to lean toward the Horsemen.

Still unable to react, Cadmus knew he was going to die, but then a giant sphere of energy burst against the chimera's skin and the monstrosity fell back to the ground in a cascade of ashes. When the flames died down, Cadmus and Niccolo looked to the source of the fireball and found Phenex staggering over to them, sweat pouring from his brow.

"We did not come... this far... to die *now*. I did not live in Hell for *thirteen hundred years* and come to Earth just to see a sadistic demon turn our planet into a place of terror," Phenex stated, calm as he walked past them and up to the smoldering corpses. "I understand that you are tired, but we *cannot* die. We cannot hesitate when our lives are on the line."

"Because," he said before rising into the air, the flames around him subdued as he floated to the woman still hanging on the cross.

"Because I will not stand to see us fall." Phenex reached up to gingerly touch the Cimeries' face, who at first grimaced at his touch, but then she let him ease her pain. While he let her lean into his touch for a tender moment, Phenex grabbed the still-hot handle of her pike and took a deep breath. The superheated metal blistered the flesh of his palm, somehow, but he would not let it distract him. "Are you ready?"

"Do it," Cimeries whispered as she clenched her jaw, and then Phenex yanked out the Amazon's own weapon, the hooked blade pulling out flesh and injuring her more than she should be forced to bear. Once Phenex threw the pike down to the Horsemen, the spearhead sank into the dirt between them. Then Phenex went about tearing off the bonds that held her to the pyre, sparing no time for mercy. He understood that she did not want it and preferred her pain to be over as quick as possible.

After tearing out the nails that held her limbs in place, Phenex gathered the broken woman in his arms and then sank back to the ground, sitting down with her head in his lap, his gentle hands caressing her skin as he examined her.

Cadmus jumped off his saddle and walked toward them, hoping her trial was over, but then he saw what Beleth had done before nailing her to that cross. Beleth had cut off each and every one of the woman's body parts at the joint—he could still see breaks in all of the bones—and then he had put her back together.

Except... Beleth had decided to put them all back the wrong way. Each body part, even down to her fingers and toes, had been rotated around at the joint and healed back into place. In the few hours Beleth held her captive, he had turned Cimeries, a mighty warrior, into a twisted marionette.

As Cadmus turned away from the sight and tried to imagine that suffering, he felt like he heard Beleth laughing from the other side of the portal.

No one wanted to speak. This was no victory. They had massacred humans, living, dead and the countless souls of others, and Beleth had escaped. Even worse, what he had done to Cimeries was beyond their comprehension. Although they had wanted to help her and ease her pain, the Amazon queen had forced them away. She was sitting by herself in one of the empty cabins across the camp.

That was what she wanted and none of them would deny her anything after seeing the twisted wreck that she had become.

It had been a few hours since they had gathered the body parts into a mass pyre and Phenex had turned them all to ashes. Although the sun had been high in a cloudless sky, the plumes of smoke from the funeral pyre had obscured the nice weather. It wouldn't have mattered, however, as none of them would have wanted to indulge after what they had been through.

The ordeal of gathering the bodies and arranging the funeral had taken so long that the sun had already started to set, which left them with a choice of leaving or staying in a destroyed fortress. After a few moments of discussion, they decided that Cimeries could not be moved easily, and that the ruined fort was just as defensible a position as anything else they would find within an hour.

So, even though the remains of cursed and tortured humans were less than a hundred yards away from them, the group had holed up in one of the intact cabins of the fortress.

Cadmus looked across the cabin and found that Marchosias was sitting on a cot, still holding his hand against his left side. Although his skin and muscles had healed quickly, the chimera's strike had rearranged his ribcage to the point that it had needed to be broken again to heal correctly. However, the small man wouldn't complain; not after what had been done to Cimeries. When he looked up and saw Cadmus staring, Marchosias quickly looked away in shame.

It was as if he could not allow himself to feel pain.

"What are we going to do now?" Paimon asked, her voice weak. Cadmus turned to look at the Fallen sitting on the ground and saw a minor tremor go through her, the waves of her hair hanging loose

149

around her face. "Phenex hit him with everything and he just shrugged it off. I had no idea Beleth was that powerful."

"I didn't hit him with everything," Phenex added. His back was against the wall of the cabin and his legs were bent in front of him, arms wrapped around his knees. "I was so angry that I couldn't control the flames. If I could have... if I could have kept it around me, he wouldn't have gotten away..."

"Don't blame yourself," Niccolo interrupted, hunched over as he sat on another cot near Paimon. He wouldn't stop looking at the floor as he spoke, his hair shrouding his face. "None of us could have predicted what he did."

"That's true—" Marchosias started, but Niccolo raised his head and glared at Cadmus, the change in the atmosphere enough to stop the werewolf from speaking.

"Except *one*," Niccolo growled, hate and anger flowing out of him to the point that his green eye shined bright. Confused, Cadmus stepped away from the wall and used his scythe to support himself.

"I didn't see this."

"But you *did*. You told us so. You saw a burning cross in your mind. You see the future, Cadmus. You inherited it from two of the Fallen," Niccolo stated, but Cadmus shook his head the entire time.

"It's not—" he tried to explain, but Niccolo jumped to his feet and raised two blighted fingers.

"*Two* Fallen, Cadmus. You saw the future in your head and the only one you bothered to tell was the woman who shouldn't have heard it. Didn't you think it through?" Niccolo closed the distance between them until he was within striking distance. "Cimeries went off on her own so Phenex wouldn't get hurt!"

"There's no way I could have known that and there's *no* reason that *you* do," Cadmus argued, his own frustration coming to the surface. "For all we know, she just wanted to take down Beleth herself."

"You're going to blame *her?*" Niccolo asked, waving his arm in the direction of the other cabin. "After what she went through?"

"I'm *not* blaming *anyone*." Cadmus stressed that by knocking his scythe against the floor. "This is no one's fault but Beleth and pointing fingers at each other isn't going to solve anything! We need to go back to Tamiel and see if he can find Beleth again."

"No. No, Cadmus," Niccolo said softly, backing away to stand beside Paimon.

"This is your fault. You could have seen it. You *did* see it, and you could have warned us about those monsters. We almost died there if not for Phenex stepping up at the end. We were *this* close to dying," he continued, squeezing the space between his thumb and index finger. "And it's because you're keeping secrets."

"What are you *talking* about?" Cadmus asked, his voice shaking at the accusation. Instead of backing down, Niccolo's shining gaze did not waver.

"You're keeping it to yourself, Cadmus. Whatever you got from Räum and Amon is bouncing around your head and you don't even have the *goddamn* courtesy to let us know. To give us a head's up. *Nothing.* That needs to stop!" Niccolo shouted, pointing to the ground with his demonic hand.

"You must be joking," Cadmus muttered, shaking his head. Then he stepped forward and threw his scythe behind him, which struck the wall with the blunt edge and clattered to the floor. "You have got to be kidding me! I'm not holding anything *back*! Do you really think I would do that?"

"I don't know, *reaper*, do you think you'd do that? If you just concentrated a little more—"

"Concentrate? *Concentrate?* Nico, you have no clue how hard I have to concentrate just to figure out what you're saying. You wouldn't last one *second* dealing with this *ocean* of futures and memories that goes on for millions of years in *both* directions," Cadmus said, inching closer as he spat the words into Niccolo's face. "If you had my burden, you would go *insane*."

"Fuck you, you pretentious *asshole*. You have no idea what *I* go through! I'm living two lives because of Lucifer. Two days ago, I had her nails tearing through my chest and felt Lucifer's guilt for losing a war," Niccolo said as he pointed back at Paimon, whose whole body shook as he relayed the vision. "It's no goddamn picnic for anyone."

"You two need to stop or we'll make sure you do," Marchosias said from his cot, but it was an obvious bluff. He knew he wouldn't be able to handle either Horseman in their current state. Luckily, he didn't have to.

"Oh, I *am* done, Marchosias," Cadmus said before backing away and kneeling to the ground, grabbing his scythe once he was able.

"Niccolo doesn't understand what he's saying. After all, he's only a *bastard*," Cadmus said as he made his way to the door.

"You take that back, you pale piece of shit!" Niccolo shouted, his sword bubbling into existence as he stepped forward. He was about to grab Cadmus' shoulder, but the reaper looked over his shoulder and the disbelief in his face was enough to stop Niccolo dead in his tracks.

"Used to be you could take a joke, Nico. You really going to stab your friend in the back after all this time?" Cadmus turned back to the door and pushed, the cool air of the evening rushing through his cloak and armor and taking his anger with it. "We're all angry and *every* one of us is dangerous like this. We'll talk in the morning."

"Where are you going?" Phenex asked.

"I don't know yet," the reaper said before stepping through and letting the door close behind him. If Niccolo decided to chase after him, they would just have to fight and find a way to use all of this excess anger. Cadmus felt cursed as he walked across the camp, absolutely frustrated at this turn of events. Besides Mercy, Niccolo was supposed to be the one person he could depend on, but the leper wouldn't understand. Even as he gave into his anger, part of Cadmus tried to justify his friend's behavior—Niccolo was just recklessly looking for someone to blame—but it was still an awful accusation.

It was especially awful because it was partly true. Cadmus *had* seen the burning cross and bungled the interpretation. For all of his misguided attempts to justify Cimeries' behavior, Niccolo *could* place some blame on Cadmus' shoulders. Just like that, the reaper's anger left him and all he could feel was disappointment. If there had been some way to see clearer, Cimeries might have been alive and whole.

Stop it, Mercy commanded, but Cadmus shook his head as he walked through the camp and past ashen hills of chimera.

*Why? I **do** have two demons in my head,* he argued, looking at the gaping mouth of a teenager melted to the mountain of corpses. Full of blackened teeth, it was still open in pain. *I even got inklings of this and kept it to myself.*

*So? You and I both know why you kept it to yourself. You did not **know** what you saw. Misinformation is just as bad, if not worse, than withholding guesses. And we still do not know if Amon is having his revenge.*

I don't think so, Cadmus thought as he continued walking, putting the funeral pyre behind him. *I think I just wanted that to be true. It's... out of my control. I can watch it all in my mind, but I can't stop it. Niccolo said that Cimeries may have gone alone to prevent Phenex getting hurt. If that was the case, then my reaction to the vision **caused** the vision.*

That is all speculation. Worse still, you cannot change the past. There is no use for guilt in this matter. Mercy huffed within Cadmus' mind; he didn't appreciate repeating himself.

Looking up from the ground, Cadmus saw where his feet had been taking him and set his hand against the wooden door.

And yet guilt afflicts me anyway, Cadmus said as he reached out and wrapped his fingers around the handle, pausing as the cold traveled from the cool metal and into his bones. The shock stalled him and made him think it was inappropriate for him to barge in like this, especially when Cimeries was wounded and ashamed, so the reaper withdrew his hand and curled his fingers. Knocking three times, Cadmus waited for an answer from beyond the doorway.

"Cimeries," he said after waiting for a moment, but she would not answer. Thinking it could wait until morning, Cadmus thought about abandoning this apology, but he couldn't go back to the others. In actuality, he would not last through the night without trying to atone somehow and, once he realized that, Cadmus opened the door and stepped past the threshold without another thought.

He didn't know why Beleth had arranged the cabin in such a way, but each cot was surrounded by drapes to hide occupants from prying eyes. However, it seemed that Cimeries had appreciated it. She had taken one of the far cots and had closed the drapes around it, the flickering candlelight dancing with her silhouette across the fabric as the air from the open door made the canvas drift.

At first, he thought about announcing himself, but then he heard the strange sound beyond the curtain. It was so curious that Cadmus could not speak; he could only investigate. Whatever it was, it reminded him of the sound his knife made when he had whittled a branch in his childhood.

Cadmus approached cautiously and he could hear the sound complimented by wet noises and an obvious wince. Holding his breath, Cadmus tried to prepare himself for what he was about to see, but experience told him this would be something new. After gathering his nerves, Cadmus wrapped his fingers around the end of the drape.

"Cimeries," he said softly, at which point there was a flurry of activity on the other side of the curtain. Once he looked down, Cadmus realized he could not wait for her to be ready; he saw blood seeping through the cracks of the floor. Drawing back the curtain, Cadmus realized that his hunch was correct.

With a strip of hard leather clenched between her teeth, Cimeries was looking at him in anger and shame, brow furrowed and jaw shaking. She was still a twisted horror, but when Cadmus looked down at the woman, he saw that she had been trying to fix that. Blood was strewn about the alcove in scattered spray patterns, and a few fingers had been lopped off and lay on the floor. Before either of them could muster any words, Cadmus saw that her right arm up to her elbow was oriented in the right direction, and in her hand was a small knife.

"Have you come to see the *freak*, reaper?" Cimeries said after she spat out the leather, which splashed in a small puddle of her own blood. Turning herself to face the horrified man, Cimeries sniffed and looked down at her right hand. "Sorry to ruin your satisfaction, but I will repair myself before the end of the night."

"What are you doing?" Cadmus asked, still having trouble comprehending, and Cimeries scoffed as she dropped the knife in her lap.

"I am taking care of my ailment. It was difficult at first. I could not grip the knife with those fingers." She reached out to the piece of leather, her fingers trembling as she took hold. "Fortunately, Beleth did not remove my teeth."

"You cut your fingers off?" Cadmus asked, kneeling down so she would not have to look up at him. Again, Cimeries laughed as she grabbed the soaked piece of leather and wiped it on her skirt, which had already been stained with a few coats of fresh blood.

"That was just the start, reaper. The wrist... the wrist was much harder. There was more bone to cut through, and the tendon was a trial to pull back into place," she said, sighing. "But now that I have a hand, this will be much easier."

"You don't have to do this." Cadmus shook his head, understanding what he was about to do. "This is too much."

"Too much?" Cimeries asked, scoffing before the anger took her.

"*Too much*, you egotistical worm? I am a warrior and I will not give up that privilege and duty just because I have been beaten once. Go, before I kill you with this mangled body," Cimeries threatened. She placed the piece of blood-covered leather in her mouth and turned the blade on the remaining digits of her left hand, cutting off the thumb before Cadmus could react.

She didn't flinch.

"No," Cadmus said, putting his hand on her shoulder, which she immediately tried to stab. Only a quick reaction on his part stopped her from succeeding, and once he was able to breathe again, Cadmus tried another approach. "*You* don't have to do this. You're not alone."

"You stupid—"

"This isn't about *me*, Cimeries," Cadmus stated, bringing his scythe up between them. "You are *not* alone and you do not have to always carry yourself like you are. You have friends, or at least, you have allies. Allies who can support you, who can make sure you don't have to suffer alone."

"I *am* alone," she said weakly, the leather falling from her mouth.

"No, you're *not*. You did not have to fight Beleth alone. That is not your duty. We can share our vengeance, and we can share... our pain." He reached out and held his hand over the knife in her mangled hand, and she did not jerk it away. "You have nothing to be ashamed of, and I will help you with this."

"I..." Cimeries said before breaking down and looking at their hands, "I failed, reaper. This suffering is mine, and I will deal with it."

"It's unnecessary suffering," Cadmus replied, causing her to look at him with tear-rimmed eyes. "You concentrate. You fight the pain, and I will make this as quick and efficient as possible. Will you let me help? Will you let me atone for failing *you*?"

"I," she said, her voice abandoning her as her lips moved. After looking down at her hand and seeing how difficult it would be to continue, Cimeries breathed deep and then turned back to the reaper with a heavy nod.

After she gave him permission, Cadmus took the knife from her hand and set it down so he could take his scythe and hold it in front of him. The candlelight flickered along the silver edge of his razor-sharp weapon, but he wouldn't disrespect her by looking away from their promise.

"Then I hope this will give you peace."

CHAPTER 6
ANY PORT IN A STORM

Pieces of Lucifer's armor were ripped away from him as he fell through the maelstrom of energy, but he only worried whether or not he would make it through the portal—if his **brothers** would make it through the portal—before Moloch had to close it. As his shoulder plate floated out of reach, the light around him vanished and was replaced by the dark confines of Moloch's cave.

Then his back hit the ground hard.

"Get him out of the circle!" someone shouted from the periphery. Even as Lucifer writhed from the impact, his arms were yanked behind him and his body was dragged away from the center. Shaking his head as he let his wings disappear, which were broken from what Lucifer could tell, the firstborn tried to see what was happening in the cave. The other angels seemed like strangers at first, but then he started to recognize his generals.

Paimon was holding a broken arm—her ulna had punctured the skin after she had landed wrong—but she snapped the bone back into place as he watched. To her left and right were Zagan and Purson, and they had come through only moments before, after Lucifer pushed them through. At the memory, Lucifer remembered his brothers on the other side of that portal and threw himself to his feet.

"The Twins are still out there!" he shouted, trying to walk toward the masked monstrosity who held his three-fingered hands toward the shimmering portal, but Lucifer was stopped by an armored hand on his bare shoulder. He turned to see Buné shake his head.

"And you interrupting Moloch does nothing to help."

"Are you kidding? They were still in Heaven last time we checked! I don't believe you!" Viné shouted at his other side, which only caused Lucifer to look down at the small angel. Before he could argue, Zagan spoke up for him.

"Lucy's right, Viné. They have a whole army after them, but they're keeping them back," the giant said, standing up straight and almost bumping his head against a stalactite. At his statement, their shrew of a sister turned to Moloch with a hiss.

"Then it's all the more reason to close the portal now and be done with it! We don't want Adonai to set a single toe down here!" Viné screamed, and Lucifer had to restrain himself from slapping her in the face. Letting out his already healing wings, he pointed at the portal with his left hand.

"Asmodeus and Amdusias are the only reason any of us made it down here! We will not abandon them just to save our own hides!" Lucifer shouted, which prompted a scoff from behind him.

"Oh, I thought we only bothered to save ourselves and run away, brother." Beleth crossed his arms, and Lucifer had to face the tall warrior in his silver plate mail.

"I'm not saying we keep it open forever, but we owe it to the Twins to give them a chance," he argued, but a deep grunt came from the shadows. A huge angel with shaggy brown hair and a full beard picked himself up and came to the side of a struggling Moloch.

"How long, Lucifer? This creature has been holding it open for two days now, and he's getting tired," he said with a slap against Moloch's shoulder. "Best we close it now and mourn our brothers later."

"Moloch..." the creature said, pausing from the effort, "Moloch will hold it open for a small time. Then... then a seal will need to be made."

"Balam, they saved you," Paimon said to the huge warrior, but he only waved it away with an absent-minded flourish of his hand.

"And we should make that sacrifice worth it, instead of letting all of the Heavenly Host in and waving a white flag," Balam spat out, and every angel immediately bristled at the remark.

*"You're not worth a **damn**, you big coward,"* Zagan said as he walked up to his brother, but a fat, balding angel in full robes stepped between them.

"We should not fight each other while war rages above us," he tried to argue, but then an angel with dark wings walked to the center of the portal and pointed a black sword toward the swirling chaos.

"There is no arguing, Bael! We should close it now and create this seal!" the swordsman screamed, but Lucifer wasn't listening. From what he saw through the portal, he knew he only had an instant to react.

"Belial!" Lucifer ran forward, Lux appearing in his hand, and then swung it at his brother's blade, knocking it out of his grip. Even as Belial let darkness pour out of his eyes in rage, Lucifer grabbed him by his armor and threw him out of the circle.

It was just in time, as two bloody bodies fell out of the portal and slammed into the ground where Belial had been standing, and Lucifer's unprotected shoulder was caught by an errant leg. It hurt, but he was grateful that he had been able to knock away the blade in time.

At his feet lay Asmodeus and Amdusias, their bodies covered in wounds.

"Lucifer..." Belial snarled, but Lucifer merely gave him a stern look before turning back to the injured angels. Crouching down to his feet, Lucifer resorted to slapping Asmodeus in the face in order to get answers. Instead of stirring, the green-haired angel merely rolled his head back, but Amdusias moved from underneath his twin.

"Close it," he said, his white hair stained with blood, and Lucifer let out a shaky breath.

"The others? Seere? Andras?" Lucifer asked, already knowing the answer, but he gave into denial. Amdusias just shook his head and then tried to slide out from underneath Asmodeus. Accepting the guilt for their deaths as well, Lucifer stood up and turned to the creature keeping the portal stable.

"Moloch! Close it now!" he shouted, and immediately a red aura leaked out of the massive creature. As Moloch swirled his arms about, contorting his hands and fingers into twisted, unnatural positions, Lucifer looked up at the energy above him, but what he saw surprised him. He had expected the same as before, just chaos.

However, a giant arm was just about to come through the portal.

"You cannot run for long, heretic!" a voice bellowed through the maelstrom, and every angel present knew their father's voice. Adonai was coming for them, and if Moloch did not close the portal now, they were all doomed to his judgment.

And, though it would do no good, Lucifer closed his eyes and prayed.

Then the sound stopped, the air stopped moving, and that was enough for Lucifer to open his eyes. Above him was a static image of a hand just beyond reach; a lake of burning energy surrounding it.

"Moloch needs more power; needs something to bind the portal and close this end," the creature said, his legs collapsing underneath him but his hands still held aloft. Stepping forward, Beleth uncrossed his arms and knelt beside the creature.

"What do you need? Is my magic enough?" he asked, but the masked entity shook its head.

"No. Eleven. Eleven beats seven. I must bind the souls of eleven of his traitor angels to close it," Moloch said, turning its mask to judge the celestial beings in its cave. "There is one extra here. That one need not bind himself."

"What are you talking about, eleven beats seven?" Bael asked, the rotund angel drawing closer to Moloch, and the low murmur coming from behind the mask shocked them. Then they realized Moloch was laughing.

"His angels, the ones the cousin calls archangels. They maintain the portals to the blue planet. To force the gate closed, I need eleven," Moloch explained, one of its arms dropping from weakness. "This one's magic is small; too small to count. Your souls, they are the keys."

"We have to give up our souls for this creature's plan?" Viné asked, frantically looking for an audience. "This smells like a trap! He just wants us to give up our lives!"

"He **saved** them, witch," Zagan snapped, losing his patience and shocking her into silence. "If he doesn't stop Adonai, it's not going to be any better. What do we need to do, Moloch?"

"Merely..." it said, another of its arms falling to the ground with a thump. "Stand in circle. It is simple magic, soul-binding. Must hurry. The cousin is strong; too strong."

"Then we have to choose," Amdusias said as he created water from the air and doused his brother, who instantly woke up and jumped to his feet, "who will be left out of this rite."

"I want no part of this," Belial growled, earning a laugh from Purson, whose yellow eyes gleamed with cunning.

"Figures that you would be worthless. Step up and maybe we'll stop calling you that," Purson said, his lisp somewhat prominent. Darkness immediately poured out of Belial's eyes, but then he stepped forward and took his place in the circle.

"Lucifer should stay out of this. If he's our leader, we don't want him compromised," Buné suggested as he walked forward, but before he could take another step, Lucifer set his hand on Buné's armored shoulder.

"I won't let my siblings take any risks I won't myself. That is my spot, Buné," Lucifer stated, but his wise friend obviously did not approve.

"Agreed. I won't risk this if the coward firstborn doesn't," Balam grumbled as he took his spot in the circle. As the rest of the angels stepped forward, Buné was forced to step back.

"You're leaving me out? After all this?"

None of them faced him with disrespect.

"We're counting on you, brother, in case all of this goes south," Asmodeus said, his voice weak from his ordeals, but he complemented the statement with a chuckle. When Buné turned to the others, there was no scorn, and when his gaze fell on Paimon, she offered him a sweet smile.

"We all make mistakes, brother. You're the only one here who doesn't. Avenge us if we fall, alright?" She winked at him, breathing in deep before turning to face Moloch and their next ordeal.

Buné was about to protest his exclusion, but Lucifer shook his head and put an end to it.

"*Counting on you, Buné. Just in case. Just like always,*" he said before turning to face the portal. Moloch was still struggling, but once they were all in place, it lowered one of its hands and pointed at each of them.

"*Extend your right arm, palm up, and stare at the portal. Then, open your heart and try to connect with the energy,*" it said, raising its other two arms to shoulder height.

Viné shook her head, even as she followed his instructions.

"*How are we supposed to do that?*"

"*It is easier than you think. It will become clear,*" Moloch whispered as he lowered the last arm and held it out in front of him. Before any of the angels could move, they felt something claw at their insides, and they had to fight to stay standing.

Lucifer staggered where he stood, but then he tried to open himself up to the energy. As soon as he thought about it, some ethereal hand seemed to squeeze his heart and take hold, and it was all he could do to not gasp out in reaction.

However, once it was in place, it did not hurt him, and once Lucifer was able to look around, he realized all of his brothers and sisters were experiencing the same phenomenon. Although Lucifer turned to Moloch and saw the white mask shine bright, he was more distracted by the glowing, golden triangles of the design drifting around the mask. It was at this point that Lucifer realized that they were not merely designs; those symbols on its mask were some eldritch magic he could not understand.

Putting the thought out of his mind, Lucifer looked to the portal, and what he saw amazed him.

Adonai's hand seemed to come closer for a moment, but then it was thrown back into space and Lucifer could see a whirlwind of images. Strange beasts and powerful gods were just beyond reach, the very nature of reality seemed to bend back and forth and impossible things traveled across distances he could not fathom. Lucifer felt connected to something deeper, as if he had become part of something more. Instead of fear, Lucifer appreciated the phantom hand curled around his heart, and he almost passed out from sheer elation.

Then it was over. The portal slammed shut and let out a shockwave *that threw them off their feet. Ripped away from that otherworldly euphoria, Lucifer felt an intense sadness, but he forced the thought out of his mind. If it was something real, he could ask Moloch about it later. He needed to know if his brothers and sisters also made it through the process. Within a second, Lucifer propped himself up on his elbows, but he did not make it any further.*

There, just beyond his feet, a statue had been raised where he had been standing. It had not been there before, and for a moment the angel lay there in shock. At first, he could only gape at it, but instinct made him push off the ground and get to his feet.

"What are those?" Purson asked from across the circle, and Lucifer did not have the answer. Once he stepped past the side of the white statue, Lucifer saw something he was not expecting. A crude recreation of his face was etched into the stone.

"That is the seal. Part of you now dwells in Moloch's cave. While these relics stand, this portal cannot be opened from either side," Moloch said, shakily picking itself up with all six limbs. As the angels all gazed in wonder, the creature collapsed forward and instead propped itself up on the three arms that could still support him.

"Adonai cannot reach us?" Beleth asked, his voice full of skepticism, but either Moloch did not catch it or he just didn't care.

"The cousin is very strong, but Adonai is not as smart or cunning. Impatient. For many years, this seal will hold," the masked creature stated, matter-of-fact, but its voice dropped in volume as fatigue took over.

"For years? How many? When will we have to do something about this?" Belial asked as he walked menacingly toward the creature, but Moloch did not feel threatened.

"A million. Two million? It is hard to say. Likely past the cousin's patience." Moloch yawned at the end of the statement, and that stopped Belial in his tracks.

"So, the portal can't open from either end?" Buné asked, which Moloch appreciated.

"The right question. No. Without the angels' death, there will be no travel. Soon, Moloch must sleep."

"We're stuck," Paimon muttered in dismay, sitting down with her back to her effigy. "No Earth, no revenge. For a million years."

"It's not so bad," Purson said, sitting down beside her. "At least we have each other."

"Bad idea," Moloch said under his breath, but every angel snapped to attention. "Should separate; decrease chance of breaking seal."

"Why would any of us destroy the seal now? It's keeping us safe!" Zagan shouted, but Lucifer put out his hand and stopped him from going further.

"No, he's right. We made this decision without telling the others. We have no idea who might want to destroy this seal or run back to Earth. It's best that we split up, decrease the chances that some splinter group will kill us," he said, but Belial groaned at the idea.

"Of all the... I have half a mind to do it right now!" he said with a snarl, but the temperature in the room dropped as his brothers and sisters regarded him.

"The only way you're going to do that is by killing seven of us. You're not going to find many willing participants," Amdusias said, turning to face Lucifer. "What are you suggesting?"

"There are eleven of us. Many of you are my generals, and quite a few of our brothers and sisters followed you during the war," he replied, stepping into the center of the circle and regarding each of the fallen angels. "Lead those who were under your command and colonize our new home. We'll create provinces out of Hell and try to maintain some sense of order."

"What about those of us who **weren't** your generals?" Balam asked with resentment, at which Lucifer only shrugged.

"Mention you're a king and that you'll treat them well. I don't know, Balam, but I think someone with your strength will inspire **some** followers," he suggested, turning away from the brute. "Every few years we'll get together, discuss what we have discovered, and hopefully we can make this realm feel like home."

"What if we can't?" Beleth asked, his voice tinged with annoyance, but

Lucifer just didn't know. This was all too much information and he had failed too many times in the last few months.

Turning from Beleth as a way to stall, Lucifer thought about what he could say, but then he saw Paimon look to the ground and bite her lip. Although he was more confused why he noticed and got hung up on it, witnessing it was enough to stop his mind from forming another thought.

Thankfully, he was spared the effort.

"You must, Beleth." Buné stepped forward and regarded Beleth with apathy. "Or perish by your own hand. That's the choice left to you, but at least you have a choice now. However, that is not what we need to concern ourselves with at present."

"I'm curious, Buné, what do we need to do?" Lucifer teased their reaper of angels with a grim smile, but it disappeared once Buné returned one of his own. That was when Lucifer knew he was in trouble.

"Well, Kings of Hell, you need to tell your people that you will be their rulers, which I'm not sure they are going to like." He stepped forward before whispering into Lucifer's ear. "And if you are to be a king, Lucifer, you should probably tell your queen."

"Who are you talking about?"

"Lilith, brother. Who else?" Buné said, but Lucifer's thoughts were far away. He turned back to his other sister, but Paimon had grabbed her arm —which had already healed—and she could not look him in the eye. After a second, he turned back to Buné and nodded, since he could only ignore the issue.

"Yeah, who else?" he muttered in agreement, but some part of him knew he had another answer.

———

NICCOLO'S MIND was his own shortly after the vision ended, but he didn't want to open his eye yet. For a time, he thought about giving into his rage, about maintaining his resentment toward Cadmus, but he could not hold onto it. After his many experiences with reliving

Lucifer's memories, Niccolo could not judge Cadmus for being confused by an unrelenting stream of alternate futures.

Niccolo had no way to interpret the chasm that had lain beyond the portal, and he begrudgingly had to admit that the infinite futures in the reaper's mind might be even more chaotic. These souls they had inherited were unruly and were not meant to be under their control. And although Cadmus had not asked for Amon's powers— or even Räum's—he had accepted them all the same.

Despite all the rage churning in his belly, Niccolo would eventually need to apologize.

Once he realized that sleep was beyond him, Niccolo opened his eye and faced the darkness. Sparse light came from the gaps between the cabin's logs and let his eyes adjust, and Niccolo guessed it was still the middle of the night. Once he looked to his left, he saw bundled shadows under blankets and realized he was the only one awake. It was only a few seconds before he realized he could not suffer the stillness, so Niccolo lowered his feet to the floor. The floorboard creaked when he stood up, but no one stirred, so he took his opportunity to sneak to the doorway.

Niccolo almost fell over a cot obstructing his path, but he avoided crashing into and recovered before moving around the furniture. Once he reached the door, he pushed it open and then walked into the midnight air. It was still dark, but the moon was bright enough that he could see the details of his gruesome hand.

Before, it had been a source of shame—then a source of power— but in this world he had to hide it. It would hurt innocent people if he left it to the open air.

"You couldn't sleep either, huh?"

Paimon's voice had interrupted his thoughts, and he found the fallen angel sitting against the support beam of a nearby tent. Since it was still so dark, her hair appeared silver in the moonlight, which was especially jarring. Paimon looked so beautiful, even if he could see sorrow in her smile as he approached.

"I did sleep some, but then I woke up. It makes sense, though.

Even when we were in Hell, I never slept too much. These bodies shouldn't even need it." Niccolo waved up and down his chest as he spoke, and Paimon laughed at his misunderstanding.

"It's not for your body, hon. It's our minds. If we don't have time to recover from what we experience, we go a little mad," she said, turning her gaze down to the dirt in front of her. A few strands of silver fell in front of her cheek and Niccolo felt the urge to brush them back behind her ear, but he knew how inappropriate that would be.

"A *little*?" he asked, sitting down in front of her and crossing his legs before he hunched forward. "I think we've all gone mad since this journey started."

"Well, we've had plenty of reasons for *that*. What we saw yesterday was... I didn't know Beleth was capable of anything that awful."

"He's powerful, but we'll figure it out," Niccolo started, but Paimon lifted her head and stopped him mid-argument.

"Not that he was powerful enough for it, Nico. I didn't know he *hated* you all that much. Beleth, he was always obsessed with power and his magic, but... I remember when he wasn't evil. I remember when he was my fellow warrior. I remember when he was my *little brother*."

"You were in Hell for a million years."

"Two, sweetie. And I'll be the first to admit that we all went mad from time to time. We were at each other's throats, too, but this... those creatures we fought yesterday, what he did to *Cim*. That was beyond just a little madness." She turned to face the charred cross dominating the sky, moisture gathering at the corners of her eyes. "He has a *reason* to do this. He honestly believes that he *needs* to do this, that he *wants* this. That's... that's the only way I can justify it."

"You can't justify it," Niccolo said, picking himself up so he could move to Paimon's left side. Once he was there, he set his right hand on her knee. "And it's up to us to stop him. It doesn't matter what his reasons are. What he's doing is wrong, and we can't let him continue. We'll be careful next time, then we'll cut out his heart."

"Oh, Nico." She looked down at his hand on her knee and covered it with her own. With a light pat, Paimon laughed and shook her head. "Sometimes you sound just like him."

"Scratch..." Niccolo didn't bother making it a question. Without meaning to, his thoughts drifted back to that last vision in Moloch's cave, where Paimon turned away from Lucifer's attention.

Although he was young and relatively inexperienced, he knew exactly what that meant.

"How *did* he find you?" Paimon asked, smiling as she pulled her feet in so she could rest her head sideways on her knees. As she looked at him with pure white eyes, Niccolo found it hard to concentrate.

"It wasn't some crazy meeting, honestly." Niccolo looked down at his demonic hand so he didn't have to meet her ivory gaze. "One day he came to watch the archers practicing in the Pestilence Quarter and, well..."

"Well?" she asked, nudging him with an elbow. Struggling to find the words, Niccolo looked at her just in time to see a few errant strands of hair falling across her face. This time, Niccolo reached out and brushed them back behind her ear without thinking, but she responded with a smile. That gave him all the confidence he needed.

"I guess it *was* crazy," he said, turning back to his mutated arm. "He actually witnessed me becoming the Horseman of Pestilence. I used this *thing* to grab out the last Horseman's heart. It's ugly, but... useful."

"We all have our ugly parts." Paimon placed her hand on his blighted arm momentarily before slightly extending her nails. "You're just a little more honest about it. *Beleth* doesn't have a single scar on his face, and you're ten times the man that he is."

"Yeah, well..." Niccolo withdrew his hand from her touch, "I don't know about that. Cadmus and I are responsible for the apocalypse.

I'm not saying Beleth has a single decent bone in his body, but for the last three months..."

"Not even close to being a comparison, hon," she said, grabbing his face and forcing him to make eye contact. "His was intentional. Yours is just, well, regrettable."

"I think that makes it *worse*," Niccolo said, placing his fingers around her wrist and drawing her hand away. Though he lowered it to the ground, he subconsciously did not release his grip. "I can't stop this plague."

"You're not *supposed* to, Nico. Whatever happens from now on, we're at the end. Even if we're successful in our vengeance, the Apocalypse is still going to happen. If you think about it, it might even be a mercy to die now, before everything goes sour," she said, somehow snaking her wrist out of Niccolo's grip. He was worried she might grab his face again, but instead she intertwined her fingers with his. "There's no use worrying about it."

"Why not? We're killing people. *I'm* killing people. You don't expect that to weigh on my conscience?"

"I know it does, but that's also why you *shouldn't* feel responsible for it. That you even worry about these people—who, let's face it, are temporary—means you're still connected with your good nature. Just... don't lose that, Nico. You're fighting on the right side," she said with a squeeze of his hand.

Although he wanted to fight her argument, Niccolo didn't want her to lose that small happiness, so he gave a forced smile and looked at the ground in front of them.

"You know, I feel like that should mean more than it does."

"You and me both. Second hopeless war where I've been on the right side, but I vastly prefer losing on the right side than winning on the wrong side."

"What war were you on the wrong side of?" he asked, which made Paimon hesitate. With a deep sigh, the fallen angel buried her head in between her knees for a moment. Her reluctance was obvious once she sheepishly lifted her head.

"Can that be another time? I'd rather not dig *that* up just yet."

Niccolo had no reason to deny her. He shook his head and looked at his hand again.

"Sorry, you don't have to tell me. We all have something in the past." Niccolo fell into memories of his years in Napoli, but then he felt her hand cover his diseased palm.

"Maybe in a little bit, Nico. Trust me, it's worse than anything *you* ever did," Paimon said, tracing the lines of his palm with her index finger. Even if he wanted to, he would not have been able to stop her. Abandoning his hand to her devices, Niccolo turned to look at her face, but she was staring into the middle distance. Then she took a deep breath and continued. "So... Cadmus."

"I was..." Niccolo paused, but he eventually surrendered. "I was frustrated, I think. He doesn't mean to, but he acts all high-and-mighty and detached from everything. I was looking for someone to blame, and he hit me with the... bastard thing... at the *wrong* time."

"Have you ever raised your sword against him before?" she asked, and Niccolo's spirit sank.

"Oh, *god*, I forgot. I'm that much of an asshole, aren't I?" he asked, but Paimon merely laughed and slapped his knee with her right hand.

"We all have our moments. Knowing him, he probably feels awful about everything he said to you, too."

"Yeah, probably," he agreed, but part of Niccolo would not accept that easy answer. Even though he felt bad about raising his sword against Cadmus, there was a voice at the back of his mind that still blamed him for what happened.

"We'll get over it, I think. We've been friends too long to hold a grudge like that," Niccolo said with a smile, but then his thoughts turned back to Moloch's cave and the angels within. Beleth had seemed relatively agreeable back then, and nothing like the monster they were chasing across Europe.

"It's not worth holding a grudge over something so petty. You're human, and you're allowed to make mistakes," Paimon said, pushing out her knees and leaning back against the tent pole. "You both have such monumental burdens on your minds, too. None of us can judge you for not being able to handle it."

"Hah, both of us? Cadmus was right. His inheritance sounds like something I couldn't even start to handle. All I have to deal with is Lucifer's past." He laughed to force the self-deprecation home, but Paimon tilted her head in disdain.

"You and I both know that's bullshit. I don't envy Cadmus *at all*, but Lucifer," she said, pausing on his name and smiling, "Lucifer was different. He was *the Devil*. Inheriting any part of him would be... I really can't imagine."

"It's more than I can describe," Niccolo said, shaking his head. After a moment, he looked back at Paimon, who had wrapped her arms around her legs and clasped her hands in front of her. "I'm curious, though, how did he get to be *the Devil*? I mean, I know where *Scratch* came from, now." He nodded toward her with the nickname and Paimon—for the first time in his memory—looked embarrassed.

"Oh, god, you saw *that*?" she asked, covering her mouth with her palm. "There's no way I'm going to recover from this."

"You have *nothing* to worry about, Paimon," he said. "You're way too deadly for me to ever truly make fun of you."

Paimon lowered her hand and grinned.

"Well, good. Let's keep it that way. Though I do love the occasional jab," she said before rocking into him with her shoulder. "But, if you're still curious, we never did call him *the Devil*," she said, stressing the title with an exaggerated, deeper tone. "That was all you guys."

"What do you mean, *you guys*? You mean humans?"

"Yep. Pure human invention," she said, biting her lip before continuing. "Imagine it, Nico. You spend your life fighting for humanity, fighting against your father, killing siblings you've known for millennia, and retreating to Hell because you weren't strong enough... and even with *all those good intentions*, the people you were trying to save end up demonizing you."

"I mean, I always thought that it was awful how he was treated, but, I don't know, I guess I never connected the dots." Now, all the complaints Niccolo had ever brought to him seemed so inconsequential.

"Strongest person I ever knew, Nico. That he never even *tried* to kill himself, that he always had the willpower to live another day and try to lead his people... it was amazing. Every day for two million years he had to live with the guilt of so much death, just to save, Hell, *create* a people who were taught to hate his existence," she mused, breathing deep at the thought.

"Not to put him down, but you were angels, right? You guys can't kill yourself."

"If you're smart, you can find a way around it, but no. Lucifer.... Lucifer was just *that* goddamned stubborn," she said with a laugh, turning to face him with a smile. "Better than this world deserved."

"Yeah, yeah he was," Niccolo agreed, looking skyward and no longer dreading the next vision. He now realized how much he missed Lucifer and—even if it was confusing and overwhelming—these visions were a way to see his father figure again. Without his knowledge, Niccolo's hand fell to his side where Paimon's hand was there to receive it, and Niccolo turned to see her eerie eyes staring into his.

It was hard not to stare back.

BY THE TIME Cadmus had finished with Cimeries, light had filtered in between the gaps in the walls and the candles nearby were almost to the end of their wicks. After the skin of her left pinky toe joined back to the rest of her foot, Cadmus looked up and saw that Cimeries' eyes were closed. Grateful for that small mercy, he stepped back and sat down on a nearby table.

It was the best place to sit when the floor was still covered in the Amazon's blood.

There had been a few times where Cimeries had passed out from the pain and exhaustion, but her eyelids would eventually flutter open and she would wordlessly urge him to continue. She had only needed to explain once that he should go on even without her cooperation, and just one look of disappointment was enough to spur him onward each time he faltered. Cadmus recalled how the right knee had been especially painful for the woman, but instead of crying out when he withdrew the blade, she only clamped down on his forearm and pulled his weapon back to cut further.

Now Cimeries was whole, even if her armor had been melted away. They would have to visit some blacksmith or kill some mercenary to gain replacements for her, or she would just go without. Looking over his work for a moment and seeing that all of her limbs were pointed the right way, Cadmus almost didn't notice that she was naked. Once her eyes opened, he suddenly realized her vulnerability and looked away, but he was greeted with a sigh.

"Like I care, reaper. I have no shame in my body, especially now," Cimeries said, flexing her fingers before bending at her knees. Lifting herself to a standing position, she almost fell over, but she put out her hand before Cadmus could come to her rescue. Shakily, she stood to her full height and then looked over her body, and after a moment of appreciation, Cimeries nodded back at her surgeon. "Except for the pain, it is like it never happened."

"Are you sure you're alright?" Cadmus asked, but the look she gave him was all the answer he needed. "Sorry, habit. Some people *prefer* it when others care about them."

"Others, certainly. You should know better when it comes to me."

Cimeries walked over to another table and almost sprained her ankle in the effort, but she was able to reach it after a couple, smaller steps. There was a set of robes there, previously intended to mask the deformities Beleth had given her, but now they would merely be a substitute until they found a replacement.

"I will try to keep it in mind, Cimeries."

Cadmus looked at the ground and tapped his fingers against his scythe. However, this time was not due to any misplaced sense of decency; he was more worried about the coming confrontation with Niccolo.

"Reaper," she started, which drew his attention. When Cadmus looked over, she had already thrown the robes over her body and was in the middle of cinching a rope just beneath her breasts. Cimeries turned toward him as she pulled the knot tight, though she couldn't look him in the eye. "I'm not sure I've expressed my... gratitude."

"That's not necessary—"

"Of course, it is not *necessary*. That is what makes it something worth expressing," she snapped before remembering her purpose. As she looked at the floor, slick with her own blood, Cimeries crossed her arms and continued. "Thank you. Thank you for treating me as a warrior. It is appreciated."

"You're welcome. I understand that was difficult for you," he said, using his scythe to push himself to his feet. Once he did, he bowed. "I'm honored."

"Then that is done," she added, stepping forward abruptly and walking past him. "No need to dwell on it."

"You don't want to rest a little?" he asked, earning a glare of disapproval, but Cadmus did not back down. "*Not* because you're weak. You've been up all night in extreme pain and using all of your energy to heal back together."

Cimeries grunted, but then continued to the door.

"I'll rest as Mercy carries us. We have no time to lose and Tamiel is a day's ride from here." Cimeries stopped at the door and looked over her shoulder with a bitter smile. "Unless you are afraid to face *them*."

"You think I'm *afraid*?" Cadmus replied, stalling in order to find an appropriate answer, but Cimeries kicked open the door with her right leg.

"Yes," she stated simply as she walked into the morning air.

Cadmus was left with no option but to follow her; he could not let her see him as a weakling. After all the work he had done last night, it would have been such a waste.

Once he crossed the cabin's threshold, Cadmus felt the morning mist as it met the skin of his face. It should have been pleasant, but Cadmus knew there was every possibility blood and ashes were in the air.

Walking forward and trying to ignore the pile of decomposing bodies to his left, Cadmus looked ahead and followed Cimeries. Already, her stride was determined and exact, as if she had never had an injury in her life. He was amazed at her progress, but he couldn't let himself smile.

It seemed inappropriate, especially since Niccolo was standing there to greet them.

"How did you..." Niccolo was unable to say another word as the warrior queen approached. Soon, Cimeries was standing in front of their four companions, but she did not seem to care for their wonder.

"Where is my weapon?" she asked, but no one could meet her attention. Once he was close enough, Cadmus cleared his throat.

"It's in that cabin," he said, pointing at the building where the rest of them had spent the night. With a small nod, Cimeries walked over to the cabin and pulled open the door, crossing the threshold without delay. Once she was gone from sight, Cadmus found that four pairs of eyes were staring at him.

He didn't want to wait for their questions, so the reaper propped himself up with his scythe and readied himself the verbal assault.

"He healed her the wrong way. We healed her back."

"What did you *do*?" Paimon asked, horrified like all the others.

"I... cut along the joints—just like Beleth—and reattached the limbs the right way. It was a difficult process, but she seems fine," he explained, but Marchosias shook his head in disbelief.

"You just... performed medieval surgery on her? Did you even bother to *ask* before you cut her open?"

Cadmus scoffed at the question, which wasn't received well.

"I think we all know that I would never be able to force *anything* on that woman," Cadmus said before looking to the cabin. "She had already started before I got there."

"That's..." Phenex muttered, looking along with him just as Cimeries exited the cabin and approached. Once she was inside their circle, Cimeries noticed their apprehension and narrowed her eyes.

"Cadmus is not to blame, he only helped," she said, slamming the handle of her pike against the ground for emphasis. "On to more important things. Beleth is gone. We need to know where. Summon the horses and we will return to Tamiel."

"We don't need to rush into this," Niccolo suggested, but Cimeries glared at him as if she intended to gut him right then and there.

"We came to Earth to kill the traitors responsible for murdering Lucifer. For now, Azazel is beyond our reach, but Tamiel can lead us to Beleth's location. Next time, I will not fall into one of his traps. We will fight together," she said before turning to face Cadmus, nodding once they made eye contact. Then she turned back to Niccolo and stepped toward him. "If you think Beleth's night of torture will have me cowering in fear, you are mistaken."

"That wasn't what I meant," Niccolo protested, but the woman slammed the handle of her pike against the ground. When Niccolo looked down, several cracks had formed in the earth, and Cimeries stood with resolve.

"Good, because I would hate to turn my weapon on an ally. Before, Beleth took from me my duty, but now I have a more personal debt to repay. How soon before we can ride?" she asked abruptly, and Niccolo crossed his arms as he deliberated.

"I guess... immediately."

"That is acceptable. Summon the horses," she said impatiently, but Plague and Mercy did not appear. After a moment, Cimeries sighed and set her hand against her hip. "What now?"

"C'mon," Paimon said as she grabbed Cimeries' forearm. Once she relented, Paimon led her toward the entrance. "The kids have a score to settle."

"Oh," Cimeries said, looking over her shoulder at Cadmus as they departed. "*That* was why you were afraid?"

"Yeah, we're gonna..." Marchosias trailed off, pointing after the women with his thumb, and he did not finish the statement. After throwing his arm around Phenex, the two of them walked away and left the Horsemen to themselves.

It was an awkward moment as they waited for their companions to walk out of earshot—each of them unable to begin apologizing for their behavior—but eventually they forced themselves to communicate.

"I," they said at the same time, which forced both to stop momentarily. They each waited for the other to proceed, but Cadmus put a stop to the tension by gesturing for Niccolo to start.

"Look, Cadmus, I—" Niccolo hesitated, putting his human hand behind his neck, "I think we both said some stuff we regret. I was... I was just so angry after Cimeries, after seeing all those monsters..."

"You don't need to keep going," Cadmus said, stepping forward. "I understand and you weren't *all* wrong. I messed up and lashed out."

"It's just, you said you saw something and you didn't tell us," Niccolo continued, forgetting himself, but he quickly realized his mistake.

"We were *apologizing*?" Cadmus suggested, shaming him.

"Sorry. It's just, if you can see the future, if you can see terrible things like that, we'd like a *warning*. Damnit, I can't stop. Look, I fucked up, too."

"It's alright. I get it, Nico. You're hard-pressed to admit you're wrong," Cadmus said before setting his hand on Niccolo's blighted shoulder. "But I never should have called you the uh... well."

"Right. So. Yeah," Niccolo said before walking toward the exit, his friend keeping step with him. "I just don't want..."

"I know, Nico. I know. Neither do I," Cadmus said as he summoned Mercy. He was soon joined by the green mist of his brother. "But I don't think it's just the future. That's not everything."

"What do you mean?" Niccolo asked, trying to abandon his frustration. Whatever mistakes had Cadmus made with his visions, he had more than made up for it by helping Cimeries during the night. Still, it was difficult for Niccolo to avoid feeling resentment for his friend, which made him feel even worse. As they walked, Niccolo tried to put it out of his head.

"Well, you saw how I was able to get my scythe to come back to me during that battle. And you didn't see it, but I was able to get Mercy to run faster than I thought possible by... slowing down time," Cadmus said, looking at the ground for stability as he considered his newfound powers. "I don't think seeing the future is the only thing I inherited."

"Then... what?" Niccolo asked, unable to comprehend just what his friend was saying. Stopping mid-step, Cadmus turned to him and seemed nervous, which was a rarity. It was enough for Niccolo to finally abandon his anger.

"If I'm right—which I'm not sure I am—if I'm *right*, I can control... time." Cadmus avoided his friend's gaze as he explained his theory. "Amon and Räum could see further along in the fourth dimension, or at least that was how Buer explained it. It could be that, with the more power we get, the more we are able to manipulate the powers we gain."

"So you're saying that the more people you reap, the more souls that you claim, you're... able to manipulate all of that," Niccolo muttered, scratching his cheek with his finger. "I mean, that could be really useful."

"It could—it *definitely* could—but there is no way for me to really know. I'm not sure there has been anybody in, well, *history*... who has experienced this," Cadmus said before pausing and facing his friend. "I'm honestly a little scared. I don't know what's going to happen, or what I'm capable of doing with more power. I failed Cimeries—I know that—and it would probably help to have more control over these visions, but there is a possibility that... that I would lose what control I have."

"You're worried you might hurt people," Niccolo said, his friend nodding along.

In another time, Niccolo would have scoffed and laughed and slapped Cadmus on the shoulder, but the reaper had a point. With more power, especially over something like time, Cadmus *could* become a liability. Shrugging and seeming to deflate, Niccolo looked ahead of them and gave into uncertainty.

"I don't have an answer for you."

"I know, Nico, but I'm hoping Tamiel does."

WHEN THEY ARRIVED at the watcher's hovel, they found him sitting on a fence post, his hand worrying the top of his shepherd's crook. Once they were within speaking distance, Tamiel shook his head in dismay.

"So that was eventful." Tamiel sighed as he picked himself up from the post. Once Niccolo swung his leg over Plague's saddle and then shoved off, he landed in a patch of dirt that billowed around him.

"You were watching, then?" Niccolo asked, walking forward with an angry stride. "How could you not see what he was doing?"

"Beleth knows what *he's* doing, Nico," he replied, setting his crook against the ground and then supporting both arms on the curved head. "I told you I couldn't see inside that area. Now... now it's pretty obvious why."

"Obvious..." Niccolo growled with some venom, but Tamiel gave him a precautionary glare as he stood up.

"He was blending dimensions. The trap Hippolyta fell into was a small pocket of another world. Because of that, I couldn't see through the Veil. If he wasn't such a terrible person, I'd admire him."

"That is not my name anymore, watcher," Cimeries said, giving into annoyance as she leaned heavily on her pike. "And you may want to respect that. The last angel who used it is now in my debt."

"That's... fair," Tamiel said, looking to the ground in shame. "I'm sorry, Amazon, I am, but there's not much I can do about what Beleth did to you."

"No, there is not, but you can tell us where the demon king has gone," Cimeries replied, her voice unwavering.

After a moment of appreciation for her warrior spirit, Tamiel turned to regard each member of his audience.

"You're not going to like it. Beleth isn't hiding anymore, and, if I remember my brother, that means he's ready for you. If you go after him now, you're going to see everything he has prepared, every malicious trap and experiment. What you saw at that fort will be... well..."

"You've seen what he's done?" Smoke billowed out of Phenex's eyes, but Tamiel put out a hand and shook his head.

"No, no, I haven't seen anything like what you had to fight. I just know that Beleth isn't the kind of angel to back down. If he's making himself obvious, it's because he's chosen the terrain, his troops and every circumstance he could to make himself the victor. You're going to be fighting him at his most terrible," he replied, earning a scoff from Niccolo.

"You say that like we didn't expect it already. Where the fuck is he?" Green energy flared out from Niccolo's eye, and though Tamiel's eye twitched at the display, he eventually relented.

"Fine, I just wanted to make sure you all knew what you were getting into," he said before sitting back down on the fence post. "Beleth is conjuring something on the far side of the Rubicon. But that's the other thing."

"*What* other thing?" Paimon asked, her teeth descending without her knowledge, her subconscious having already guessed what Tamiel was about to reveal.

"*Azazel* isn't hiding anymore. I felt him. He's there with Beleth, even if he's sticking to the goddamn shadows. If you want revenge, this is the place to do it."

"That's *it*? He's just... there?" Niccolo drew closer, but Tamiel only raised an eyebrow.

"Yeah, but that *also* only means one thing," he started, but Cadmus finished the statement for him.

"That's what he *wants*," he said, burying his face in his free palm. "Whatever plans he has, he's already put into motion."

"That is the rub of it, yeah," Tamiel said, massaging his tired eyes with dirty fingers. "They're not running from you, and this is a trap, for sure. Whatever their next step is, it involves all of you. Some sacrifice, I'm guessing."

"Why would they need to sacrifice anything else?" Niccolo asked, drawing a short laugh out of Marchosias.

"After what we saw, do you think they really care about *needing anything?* What they're doing is pain and torture for the hell of it. Beleth created twisted fucking chimera just because he was bored, and I'm betting they have more of them waiting for us," he added, pacing slowly around the edge of the group.

"Sadly, I think that's just Beleth," Paimon said, biting her lip as she considered their options. "Azazel was a planner and a schemer— has been from the beginning—and he manipulated all of Hell into turning on itself. And we can't forget how he turned hundreds of demons into raving beasts, however the hell he did it. As much as I want to run down there and tear him to pieces, I think he has a dozen plans where he accounts for just that."

"That's the truth of it," Tamiel said, grunting as he stood back up. "But sitting around here talking about it isn't going to do anything. If you really want to kill these guys, you're going to have to fall in their traps on purpose. React quickly and all that nonsense. It won't be fun, but if you stick together, it might work out."

"Why don't you come with us this time, Tamiel?" Phenex asked with a resentful tinge to his normally peaceful voice. It surprised Tamiel, considering the source, but he disregarded the tone with a shake of his head.

"It's still not my fight, kids. I watch. I listen. That's what I'm here for," he said, yawning as he walked to the door of his home.

"You're not watching or listening anymore! We know where they are and we need your help!" Niccolo shouted, stubborn as he walked up to Tamiel and spun him around by the shoulder, but instead of a surprise, Niccolo saw the fury Tamiel rarely allowed to the surface.

"Child, I *am* helping! My presence there will *only* be a burden. I don't need to explain myself to you *again*," he said, turning to face the others. "Just go. Gather the heads of your enemies. I have an errand to attend to."

"An errand?" Cimeries asked, but Tamiel kept on his path to the door.

"Yes, but it's not worth explaining. I'm going to be gone for a day or two, but I'll be back. If they escape again, I should be here if you need my help," he said before pulling the door open and disappearing inside.

Tamiel's sudden retreat left them confused, but eventually they tried to figure out their options. For a few moments, when one of them started to speak, they would reconsider and fall back into silence.

Cimeries was the first to recover.

"Does anybody want to stop now?"

While Marchosias and Cadmus shirked away, her other companions shook their heads, their minds filled with vengeance and blood. "Then why should we be scared of a possible trap? Beleth does not scare me. Azazel does not scare me."

"They should," Marchosias stated, gruff. "You fell into *one* of their traps, Cimeries. You're just going to ignore that? You're *all* just going to ignore that? Within just a few hours, Beleth ripped this great warrior into pieces. It might have been a sucker punch, but it happened. These two have powers we don't understand."

"You *expect* us to give up our vengeance *now*? After what we've seen?" Phenex replied, eyes smoldering as he turned to face his friend, and Marchosias ignored the patronizing tone.

"Yes, look, it's terrible what happened. I know, but you heard Tamiel. Beleth is *waiting* for us. There's something there, some trap that we're bound to step in! I'm not saying we should completely abandon our revenge—these fuckers need to pay—but we can't just *walk* right in. Are we *that* insane?"

He was surprised by the burning hand on his shoulder.

"You're going to betray our cause, Judas?" Phenex said, and Marchosias' skin sizzled underneath his fingers. A second after the shock wore off, Marchosias turned slowly and transformed into a hulking werewolf.

"I'm not betraying you, *Yeshua*. I'm actually trying to play the role you *used* to play. I know you're angry, but this is no time to run into danger. We all saw what happened, we all know what Beleth was trying to do. *This,* right *here*. Calm the fuck down and let's discuss this like we're not suicidal."

"He's right," Cadmus added, drawing Phenex's ire. "There's a reason he used a burning cross. He's counting on you being angry. The first thing you need to do is make sure that doesn't happen."

"So you're against us going after them, too?" Niccolo crossed his arms, as if he expected the betrayal, but Cadmus shook his head in annoyance.

"Of course, not. We're going down there. I'm sorry, Marchosias, but it's what we're doing," he said, addressing the werewolf when he said his name. "It's unavoidable. They're not going to move away from their traps, at least not before it's too late. What we *can* do is make sure we're ready for whatever they throw at us. If we do that, we have a chance."

"A chance..." Paimon muttered.

"It's what we *have*. We'll head out soon and make do. You guys get going, and I'll join you along the road," Cadmus said before turning back toward Tamiel's hovel.

"He already told us that he's not going to fight," Paimon called after him, but Cadmus waved it off just before taking hold of the door handle.

"Wouldn't hurt to give one last try. Go on. I'll be there soon."

Without bothering to knock or wait for a reply, Cadmus pulled the door open and took a step across the threshold. When the door shut, his eyes had to adjust to the fire crackling in the hearth. Once they did, Cadmus saw a very irritated, very tired Tamiel raising an eyebrow at him.

"Do you know why I'm here?" Cadmus asked, stepping into the house a few paces and waiting. Tamiel shook his head as he leaned against the wall of his kitchen.

"Nope. So if you could kindly get out of my house, I'd appreciate it. I didn't invite you."

"I know, but I couldn't have this conversation with the others listening," Cadmus said, his thumb tracing the ornamental skull that was carved into head of his scythe. "It's about my powers."

"You and your secrets," Tamiel mumbled, hanging his head low. "And what makes you think I know about your powers?"

"You were watching the battle with the chimera, correct?" Cadmus asked, earning a shrug. "Then you saw what I did with my scythe."

"The telekinesis?" Tamiel asked, but Cadmus narrowed his eyes and huffed.

"You and I both know that wasn't telekinesis. I reversed the flow of time."

Eventually, Tamiel gave in and rubbed his right temple with his fingers.

"Yeah, that's what it was. You're smarter than you should be, you know that? Guess it's why they've trusted you with so much," Tamiel said before shoving himself off the wall and walking to a kettle. He picked it up and set it on the metal hook above the hearth, where the low flames could only keep it warm.

"How can I do that? Is it because of Amon and Räum?" Cadmus asked, and Tamiel laughed at his excitement.

"Partly, yeah, but that's not your question. You already know that part. What *you* want to know is where it *stops*," he said, turning on his heel once he stood up. "What it is that you have *truly* been given."

"Yes, exactly." With a smile, Tamiel placed his hands on Cadmus' shoulders and nodded.

"I don't fucking know," he said, slapping the reaper's shoulders before walking over to his stool and dragging it back to the hearth.

"But you..."

"But I *what*? I don't know the extents of your power as a reaper. What limits you humans really have. It's all new territory." Tamiel sat down on the stool and watched the flames. After a moment's consideration, he looked back at Cadmus and huffed. "Lucky for you, I'm going to see one of the few people who might be able to explain it."

"Wait, who? What is this errand?"

"I'm visiting an old soul. With that last fight of yours, it's become clear that he hasn't been able to do his job, or those chimera couldn't exist. And, well, he has another perspective and sometimes I need that. His name is Solomon," Tamiel explained. Cadmus was mired in confusion until Tamiel dropped the name, then he was just surprised.

"Solomon? Is that *the*..."

"Yeah, the ancient king. He never... died, at least not fully. Found some loophole or something. Here's the interesting part, though, and this is where you need to pay attention," Tamiel said, pointing at Cadmus before looking back at the fire. "He's the oldest human reaper."

"Human reaper?"

"Yeah. Sometimes... souls don't make it to Heaven or Hell. It's not like they just stop existing like most people, it's similar to everyone who passes on and goes to the other dimensions. But, problem is, Earth wasn't built like that. Can't support it, so there's just a bunch of wandering ghosts on Earth. It's where all those stories come from." Tamiel poked at the fire with his shepherd's crook, but faced

Cadmus once he was done stalling. "Solomon, along with a *very* small amount of others, is responsible for, well, *your* job. Just... here."

"And you think he might know what's going to happen to me?" Cadmus asked, at which point Tamiel stood up and shrugged.

"If it's anyone, it's going to be him. Now go on, go with your friends into a death trap," Tamiel said as he wrapped his arm around the reaper's shoulders and guided him to the door. "At least one of you should be rational as you're throwing your lives away."

"What if Solomon doesn't know what's going to happen?"

"He probably *doesn't*, Cadmus. *You're* the one who can see the future," Tamiel said before opening the door and pushing on the reaper's back. When Cadmus turned back to protest, Tamiel was still holding the door.

"I can barely control that, Tamiel. I... I just want to make sure that I won't hurt anybody." Cadmus' fist shook as he lost his composure, and Tamiel looked at him with sympathy.

"You're going to, reaper. That's unavoidable. Life comes with some automatic guilt. The only thing you can really do is... make sure you make up for it. Now, seriously, catch up with them. I'll talk to Solomon about your problem. For now, you'll just have to use what you have," he said with a sad smile. Once Cadmus nodded back, Tamiel stepped into the shadows of his house and let the door close.

Turning away from the door and stepping forward, Cadmus called out to Mercy and dust swirled into the shape of his white horse. Without another word, Cadmus placed his foot on the stirrup and pushed, claiming his seat on Mercy's back. He could tell the horse wanted to console him, convince him not to worry, but Cadmus didn't let him start. He would not be afraid, and he would not fail his friends again. Whatever gifts he had, Cadmus knew he might have to use them.

Mercy started to gallop after their friends, knowing exactly where Plague had traveled, and Cadmus left him to his devices. After a few deep breaths, Cadmus ignored his fear and opened his mind to an ocean of possible futures. Death surrounded him, pain echoed throughout his soul, but he did not give up. He would not surrender to the souls he had already conquered. Cadmus would find a way to control this power.

If he could, Azazel and Beleth would not be able to stop him.

CHAPTER 7
WHEN IN DOUBT

"Are you sure you want to go through with this? You can still back out now," Lucifer said, his head buried in his hands. Once he was able to lift his head, Lilith peered down at him with a warm smile.

"Of course, I can, but what good is that? We have been down here far too long to be scared now. Something must change, and if this is how we will change it, I will not be afraid," she said, cocking her head to the side and letting her long braid fall around her neck. From his seated position, Lucifer reached out with his hand and she brought out hers to meet it. He felt comforted by her touch, but Lucifer was still plagued with doubt.

"We don't even know if we're capable of this, Lil. He didn't make us like the animals, like the humans. We don't know what trying to have children will..."

"No, we don't. But my love," she said, kneeling down so that their eyes were level with each other, "that should not hold us back. If we are to rise up and take back the world from Adonai, we must find some way to gain the advantage. He can make angels on a whim. If we **can** create offspring, we **must**. We have already had this conversation a hundred times."

"Then why not a hundred and one?" Lucifer asked, drawing her hand to his face. "And why does it have to be you? I'm sure one of our sisters would be willing to try."

"That is not the issue, Lucifer, and you know it. As you are the High King of Hell and many responsibilities fall to you, so it is with me. As your queen, it falls to me to step forward and claim this burden," she explained, curling and uncurling her delicate fingers against his skin.

"I'm worried about you, Lil," he said, turning his gaze to the black rock of the floor.

"As well you should be, but that doesn't change the reality of the situation. We must move ahead with this plan. If you remember **last night**, we already started. Now stop. I need your support in the coming moments," she said, and Lucifer had to smile at pleasant recollections from the last night. Picking himself up, Lucifer stepped forward and took his wife in his arms.

"You have it, Lilith. I won't hold you back," he said, burying his face into her neck and feeling the strands of her soft hair against his skin. He was still absorbed in the embrace when he heard someone clear their throat at the doorway.

Azazel leaned against the frame made out of rock.

"Beleth says he's ready, ya lovebirds," he said with a grin, purple lips stretched thin across his face. Azazel had been the first to change his appearance once they arrived in Hell, but Lucifer couldn't blame him. His skin had become grey, and he wore a black blindfold to cover the scars Adonai had left him. He could have had his eyes back through the course of his transformation, but Azazel had said he didn't feel comfortable losing the scars.

They had already abandoned heaven, and Azazel didn't want to abandon the scars he had earned while fighting for it.

"You have terrible timing, Zel," Lucifer said as he broke away from Lilith's embrace and stepped to the side, allowing both of them to turn and face the new arrival. Nudging himself off of the door frame, Azazel walked forward.

"Could be the best timing. I mean, it looks like you finally accepted that Lilith's not a scaredy cat," Azazel teased, uncrossing his arms and *then stretching them above his head. "It's **about** time. Ginger here's got bigger metaphorical balls than you do."*

"Always a charmer, Azazel. Tell me, how is it you know I still have red hair? You refuse to open your eyes around me," she said, walking past the shorter angel. Azazel laughed before raising his hand, an eye opening on the back of his palm just so he could wink at her.

*"Lil, just because you don't see me looking doesn't mean I'm **not**."*

After a short pause where she lay her hand on his shoulder, Lilith walked through the doorway.

"Come, you two. We should not keep our brother waiting," she said, clasping her hands behind her back and walking out of earshot. As she did, both of her brothers watched her pleasant figure sway in her natural rhythm.

"Oh, Lucy, you really don't know how lucky you are."

Lucifer had to laugh, and he walked forward to place his arm around Azazel's shoulders.

"Sometimes I'm the luckiest angel in the room, Zel. Most times, I'm not," he said, his smile disappearing as his thoughts turned dark. Immediately, Azazel shrugged off Lucifer's arm and then lightly backhanded his king's cheek.

"Stop, you gloomy son of a bitch. Beleth isn't going to let anything happen to his sister. C'mon," he said before grabbing Lucifer's arm and pulling him out of the bedroom. "Everybody's waiting on your lazy ass."

"Maybe that's why I'm taking so long," Lucifer muttered, but as they made their way into the throne room, he had to hide his apprehension. Instead of being an angel in the confines of his private chambers, he was now the High King in front of his subjects. There was no way he could appear worried; his image was at stake.

The throne room was lit by a number of torches arranged in a circle, a massive circle full of interweaving designs and symbols painted in angel's blood in order to give it power. None of their siblings had to die, of course, but it had required a sizable donation from a dozen of Lucifer's brothers and sisters. Enough that Beleth had required Azazel's help in order to set up the foundation magic.

However, if it worked, it would all be worth it.

There, lying down on a couch in the center of the circle, was Lilith, and towering above her Beleth in his characteristic black armor. To her left was their sister, Paimon, but Lucifer did everything he could to ignore her presence. It would be inappropriate to show her affection during the ceremony, where he was supposed to be completely devoted to someone else.

"Beleth, what's with the change in colors?" Lucifer asked, trying to keep the atmosphere light, but when Beleth turned, he did not smile back.

"I've found that gold and silver do not match our surroundings, Lucifer. I'm more comfortable in this new armor."

"You know, you don't have to wear armor at all, anymore. It's been almost two million years since the portal closed."

Beleth did not seem amused by the comment.

"It is not angels that I am worried about, Lucifer, but that is neither here nor there. Are you ready for the ritual?" A frown was on his face, driving home that Beleth did not appreciate this risk and was only doing it out of duty.

Understanding this, Lucifer let his hand fall to Lilith's shoulder and nodded.

"We are. Lilith is being brave enough for the both of us."

"Good. She'll have to be. You understand your role in this, correct?"

"Yes, I hold onto her and try to project my will and energy into her. It will focus on the seed that I planted yesterday, and hopefully our spirits will come together." Lucifer had merely repeated the process Beleth had explained the day prior, but it was what the giant needed to hear.

"That is the... basic idea. Again, I give no guarantees, but these seals I've placed on the ground should keep your energies bound within your bodies. Do you have any last reservations? We will not blame you if you decide to back out now." Beleth emphasized the last statement, but instead of worry and doubt, Lilith and Lucifer only shook their heads. "Then it is time. Paimon, take your place at the edge of the seal. We should be able to keep it stable with our wills combined."

"Alright, Beleth," Paimon said softly, stealing Lucifer's attention. For a split-second, they made eye contact, and all his doubt came to forefront.

Trembling just enough for Lucifer to notice, Paimon broke eye contact and turned to her sister with a smile and a gentle squeeze of her hand.

"Make us proud, Lil," she said before backing away. Although Lilith smiled at her and focused on Beleth, Paimon did not notice. One last time, she had looked at Lucifer, and one last tear betrayed how she felt. Lucifer understood, but he couldn't dwell on that; Lilith needed him. Taking hold of his queen's hand and setting his other hand on her belly, Lucifer knelt beside Lilith and kissed her like she was the love of his life.

*"Don't make **us** proud, Lilith. Your opinion is the only one that matters in this," he whispered, earning a condescending laugh.*

*"I **know**. Why do you think I refused to listen to your worrying?" Then she took a deep breath and nodded at Beleth.*

After she had given consent, Beleth knelt down and set his hands against the edge of the blood circle. For a few moments, it seemed like the oversized angel would only mumble, but then he brought up his hands to shoulder level.

When he did, purple energy in the shape of the seal rose into the air, settling at the same level as Lilith's midsection.

Before they could react, the energy collapsed into a single point, exactly where Lucifer's hand met Lilith's belly. At first, Lucifer had difficulty keeping his hand in place, it shook so violently, but then it was as if he could not pull it away. As soon as that happened, a blinding pain tore through him and it was all he could do to resist screaming.

Then he could resist no longer, and neither could Lilith. The pain tore at them both, their very energies burned within them, and Lucifer immediately regretted this attempt. Even if they were to create a new being, new offspring from the blood of angels, Lucifer could feel it sapping away at his vitality. They were sacrificing themselves to create this new angelic infant, but this was only barely understood.

For the moment, all Lucifer could feel was pain and terror.

However, once he was able to collect himself, Lucifer turned his gaze from his hand and looked into the pain-stricken face of his queen. Suddenly he understood her desires, her very essence, and he could not deny her this gift. She truly wanted this child, whatever, whoever it became. Without a word, Lucifer knew exactly what she wanted; she wanted to be part of him, to share all of this with him. They would be **one** after all of this, a being of shared consciousness.

That terrified him more than anything.

No matter how much he loved his brothers and sisters, no matter how many days and nights, how many battlefields, how many losses and victories they had shared, Lucifer was alone, and he was **supposed** to be. He was the firstborn; he was the angel responsible for their exile. He couldn't share that. He couldn't be half of a person while knowing she would take on all of his failures, burdens and pain.

In a moment of weakness, Lucifer looked away from his queen and over her shoulder, his willpower fading as he tried to run from this melding of souls. That was when he saw Paimon, trails of tears running down her cheeks, and he knew he was no worthy husband or father. As much as he loved Lilith, this other sister was just as special, just as important, and he could not share all of himself with either of them.

At the realization, at his **failure**, an explosion of energy surged away from Lilith and through his hand, electrifying his body before throwing him backward and out of the seal. He wasn't even able to cry in pain as his body tore through the air and then slammed against the wall of the throne room, leaving a three-foot deep impact crater with huge rents spreading outward from where he had crashed.

"No!" He cried out, knowing the extent of his failure, and once he fell out of the wall and to the ground, Lucifer beat his hands against the floor of his throne room. Lilith had seen it, she **had** to have seen it. His heart did not belong to her, even if her heart was tied to him. With that, no child could be made, no bond to keep them together.

Worst of all, he felt like he had doomed her to perish because of his personal failures.

However, the only noise in the throne room was the impacts of his fists against the floor, and after a moment of frustration, Lucifer finally looked up to see what had become of his queen. Her head was turned toward him, her eyes glassy, and for a horrifying second Lucifer thought he had killed *her. Then her lips curled into a soft smile, and tears brimmed at the bottom of her eyes.*

"Lucifer. We did it," she said, her voice weak, but it was enough for Lucifer to jump to his feet and close the distance between them. Making it to her side within two great leaps, Lucifer fell to his knees and took her hand in both of his.

"We did it? What do you mean?" he asked, unable to consider that they had been successful. He had failed; he knew it. As soon as he had turned to face Paimon, the bond between them had broken.

Lilith, however, was still smiling. She looked so happy as she guided his hands to her belly and placed them softly on her flesh.

"I'm pregnant."

NICCOLO GASPED BACK to the present and realized they were in the middle of a small village. Cursing himself for his disorientation, he realized it had only been a few seconds since he had been shunted into Lucifer's past. The angel's disappointment still flooded through him, only made worse once he saw the miserable creatures standing there as they rode through the village.

Breathing heavily, Niccolo saw the half-open eyes of a young girl, barely past adolescence. This child—lifeless eyes staring directly at him—had died the night before, and her poor father was still kneeling over her corpse.

"You... go away." The man lifted up a head covered in scraggly, dirt-covered hair. When he saw the glint of Niccolo's armor, fury quaked through his wretched, spindly frame. "You nobles. You live in your estates and palaces while we die tending your fields."

"I'm sorry," Niccolo said. The girl was covered in purple and black pustules—evidence of the plague that leaked out of Niccolo's every pore—and he knew no amounts of apologies would help this man. When the man pawed at Plague's saddle and used his hand to push himself and spit into Niccolo's face, the leper was not offended.

"Leave us! Leave me to mourn my daughter! Leave me to watch my son die from this same plague! Take your privileged ass and die somewhere else!" The grief-stricken man shook Niccolo's saddle, and he was rewarded by Plague slamming his head forward and forcing him to the ground. The peasant was about to rise back up, but one flash of Plague's green eye was enough for him to stay down.

"I'm sorry," Niccolo said as he rummaged through his coin purse and tossed the man a few silvers. After wiping his spit-covered face with his bandaged hand, Niccolo tried to atone for the plague that had taken this man's daughter. "It's not enough, I know. Keep hating me, but know that I accept it."

Once he had said his piece, Niccolo urged Plague forward and they continued through the village at a brisk pace. The others were behind him, for which Niccolo was grateful. This way, they wouldn't see the tears that blended with the saliva on his face.

"Where were you?" Paimon asked, hugging his midsection tighter. Though he tried to forget that last confrontation, Niccolo replied without confidence, only taking a moment to wipe off the rest of the man's spit with his sleeve.

"What are you talking about? I was right here." When Paimon's nails screeched against his armor, Niccolo realized she saw right through him.

"Sure you were, hon. You enjoying Lucifer's greatest hits?" she asked, setting her chin on his shoulder. Busying his hands by running his thumbs along his reins, Niccolo tried to remember the hazier details.

"I saw... I saw Mammon's conception. You didn't seem to be happy about it," Niccolo suggested, hoping that would be enough for her to abandon her line of questioning. It was a moment before Niccolo felt her shake, and another before he realized she was quietly sobbing.

"That," she said, sniffing lightly, "sometimes I forget all of that. But when I remember... it's a bit rough. I always wonder how that must have felt for Lucifer."

"I know how it felt, Paimon. Did you know that..."

"That *I'm* the reason? That I'm the reason that Mammon didn't turn out the way mommy and daddy wanted?" she said, eventually letting out a bitter laugh. "*Yeah...* yeah, Lucifer let me know. He didn't dare tell me that it was my fault—he likes to hog all the blame to himself—but I read between the lines. If I wasn't there, it could have—"

"It *wasn't* your fault, Paimon," he stated, turning so he could look her in the eye. Tears trickled down her cheeks and he immediately felt awful, and he used the thumb of his right hand to wipe the tracks off her cheeks. "*Seriously.* It wasn't you."

"Oh, c'mon," she said, forcing a smile as she grabbed hold of his hand. "As soon as he made eye contact with me, I knew it was over. I distracted him."

"He distracted *himself,* Paimon. You need to trust me on this, because in these visions, I *am* him. He would have latched onto anything. Just because he loved you doesn't make you at fault. It was just fear. That's what caused it."

"Fear, I'll believe, Nico, but he never loved me. Lust, *maybe.* Trying to replace something, *probably.* You haven't gone far enough, yet." She wiped away her fresh batch of tears before placing her warm hand against Niccolo's face. "You'll see."

"He did love you. Lilith..." Niccolo started, but then he realized that he *didn't* know enough to continue. Paimon closed her eyes to deal with her personal turmoil, and when she opened them back up, she offered him a smile and lowered her hand.

"You don't need to tell me. I know exactly what they were to each other. Now, eyes forward, Horseman," she said before tapping his head with her hand, and he obeyed. For a minute, they rode in silence, but Niccolo's curiosity would not let him be.

"This was the first vision I've had since you sealed the portal to Earth. That's a pretty huge gap in the timeline." Niccolo waited for Paimon to comment until he realized she wouldn't. "Why do you think Lucifer skipped so many memories?"

"Well, nothing really happened," she replied, her hands again settling around his midsection. "Us chosen few went out and explored Hell, and we found quite a bit more than we expected from our new home. We carved the provinces out, established our bureaucracy and, well, survived. It was a bit of a dark age for us. Until we had the idea to try our hand at procreation, we were twiddling our thumbs."

"Sounds... dull."

"*Dull?* Honey, it was maddening. Nearly all of us went insane dozens of times. I mean, as angels, we were built to withstand some boredom, but two million years is two *million* years. Honestly," she said, pausing on the thought, "if human souls hadn't started showing up, I'm pretty sure we would have killed each other."

"But, we've only been around for the tiniest fraction of your life. I just—I can't comprehend it," Niccolo said, which made Paimon hug him tighter.

"Which is probably why Lucifer spared you the journey. Even at his most insane, *that* bastard kept it together. I think his hatred of Adonai is all that got him through. You don't need to feel that, and if Scratch made you experience it, I would have found some way to cut his soul out of you. You're lucky he cared," Paimon said, smiling as she leaned her chin on his left shoulder.

As her cheek rubbed against the lesions on his face, Niccolo was ashamed and tried to draw away from the contact. However, Paimon did not relent, pushing against his other cheek with her fingers. He was about to say something, but then she whispered in his ear.

"I don't mind the scars, Nico. It actually feels kinda... nice. You're not going to make me sick, so don't worry. Just... enjoy it," she said, the warmth from her skin radiating through scarred tissue. After that, Niccolo let himself relax and even closed his eye, the affection enough to make him forget his constant troubles.

However, a scream went up behind him and that was enough to make him forget about momentary relief. Plague turned without

Niccolo saying a word, and then he saw something which made his blood boil.

Advancing on them was a host of dead bodies, maimed by boils and lesions, their staggered steps punctuated by wails and groans. Leading them was the young girl Niccolo had killed just by existing, but that was not the only horror. Her father, who had been yelling at Niccolo moments before, stumbled behind the corpse of his daughter with the same, vacant stare on his face. Only now, there was rot and plague where there had been none, and life had fled from his shambling body.

"What is this?" Marchosias growled, abandoning his human form and wrapping himself in shadows. As if in response, two bright lights flared high in the grey sky and then fell to Earth as if thrown with great force. Niccolo feared the impact they would witness when the lights crashed against the surface, but both lights suddenly jerked to a stop a foot above the ground. For a moment, two shining orbs swirled with energy in front of the advancing horde, but then the golden auras dissipated and left behind two angels who were kneeling on the ground.

"These are the consequences of your rise to power, demons."

The man on the left stood up, his long, silver hair flowing in the wind swirling about him. Once he stood to his full height, they could see that he was covered in gold and silver plate mail, a kite shield on his left arm and a bastard sword in right hand, with silver wings stretching out behind him. "Did you think you would escape from Hell and the Heavenly Host would not notice?"

"Who are you?" Cimeries shouted, leaping from Mercy's saddle and then holding her pike forward. With a light chuckle, the other angel jumped to his feet, his fingers wrapped around the handles of some sort of hooked, twin-bladed weapons that seemed more dangerous than useful.

"Nithael and Mitzrael," Paimon growled as she slid off of Plague's saddle and let her fingers extend into claws. As he heard their names, the bouncing angel let out a scream of laughter and spun the blades in his hands. Double-edged blades extended from both sides of the handle and curled back around, and it was clear that he had plenty of practice using them.

"Nith! Pai-Pai remembers us!" Mitzrael shouted, jumping about and shaking his head, which was covered in shaggy brown hair. "Perhaps she remembers how to fight, too!"

"Hopefully, otherwise we came to Earth for nothing." Nithael advanced, raising his sword before letting it fall to his shoulder and rest there. "Spending time among these animals is always such a bother."

"I don't care who the fuck you are, what did you do to those people?" Niccolo asked, almost letting his sword materialize in his hand before realizing it would be ineffective. Instead, he swung his twisted bow around and clenched the weapon in his monstrous hand. It took all his focus to reach behind and grab a few arrows from his quiver without breaking them.

"Oh, them?" Mitzrael said, laughing as he turned to face the advancing group of humans. "Oh, they're dead. *You* killed them. Sorta. I mean, they were going to die, especially since you rode through here like a black death! They're *dead* because of *you*."

"More or less." Nithael yawned as he gestured at the horde with his shield. "We only hurried up the process and turned them into shambling monsters. I know you humans feel guilt for killing your own. That's right, isn't it?" Nithael asked, turning to his counterpart, who was crawling along the ground.

"Guilt, such a human thing. I think that's a thing, at least." Mitzrael leaned back on his knees and picked something out of his ear with his weapon before turning to face their enemies. "That's a thing, right?"

"Used to be an angel thing, too," Paimon said, walking forward and baring teeth the length of pocket daggers. "I always regretted not killing you during the rebellion."

"Like you could have," Nithael said before bringing his sword down from his shoulder. "Very nice that you would step forward and volunteer to die first. That will make this errand much faster."

"Oh, you're gonna fight me like a man, then?" Paimon stopped within a few yards of the angel, but Nithael scoffed and nodded to his left.

"No, but Mitz will make sure you don't suffer," he said just before the other angel barreled into Paimon.

With little time to react, Paimon was only able to bring up her right hand just as the angel dove at her with his spinning blades. The screech of their impact was enough to drown out the moans from the encroaching horde for a split-second, but then the initial drive was over and Paimon had leapt back to watch an enemy who was hopping back and forth with glee.

"Ooh! Pai-Pai still has her reaction speed! This will be *fun*," Mitzrael said as he crouched down on his heels, drool dribbling out of the corner of his mouth. It was enough to disgust their audience, but Paimon was well-experienced with her brother.

"This one is mine, kids," she declared, skin shimmering as gold flowed around her and enclosed her body in armor. "You take care of the undead and Nithael. I have a grudge to settle."

"You act like you didn't lose the war, Paimon," Nithael said, prompting a bark of laughter.

"*I* didn't."

Paimon then leapt forward so she could dive at Mitzrael with vicious, extended fingers. The angel jumped straight up into the air and turned over, determined to slam his blades into her back, but then Paimon twisted her body, bent her knee and arched her back so that her leg pointed forward, just so she could extend the nails of her toes and try to impale the angel's falling body. Only by slamming his knives against her armored leg was Mitzrael able to avoid her scorpion strike, but even once he landed, Paimon was already there. Dagger-sharp teeth were just about to clench down on the skin that was exposed through the gaps of his light grieves, and a quick roll to his right was barely enough to save him from losing his leg.

After that, their movements became a blur as they rolled and ducked and dived out of each other's range, a bizarre circus of movements which the others did not want to interrupt for fear of harming Paimon's chances. Instead, they directed their focus on the undead denizens of the village, which were now between them and the other angel.

"C'mon, then. Kill them, see what you've done, and I'll end it for you," Nithael said lazily, which only spurred them into action.

Marchosias became a blur as he tore through the crowd, sending shadow-cloaked claws in and through the hearts of poor humans who did not deserve it. Cimeries likewise jumped among plague-ridden bodies, piercing some through and carving the rest with the hooked blade of her pike. After creating a cloud of flames, Phenex waded into the undead horde, burning through their bodies as if they were kindling.

In fact, before Niccolo or Cadmus could truly contribute, the entire population of the village lay lifeless in the muddy field.

"You talk a lot, but it doesn't seem like you know what's going on." Satisfied that the others could handle the dregs of what was left, Niccolo jumped off Plague and walked through the field of dead bodies. None of his companions moved as he made a bee-line to the arrogant angel, who was stammering at the scene he had just witnessed. "Beleth, and I can't believe I'm saying this, actually put some effort into his traps. All you did was make us mad."

"What are you? Where did you get all that power?" Nithael brought his sword and shield to bear, but Niccolo didn't seem to care. He created his bastard sword in a fluid movement, holding it in both hands once he closed the distance.

"I'm a Horseman of the Apocalypse, even if I don't want to be, and you just massacred a village of innocent people. I don't take kindly to *that*."

Nithael was only three yards in front of him at that point.

"They're just *humans*, and so are you. Do you really think you can hope to fight me?" Nithael shouted, arrogance overcoming his senses.

Once Niccolo was within striking distance, he lifted his sword above his right shoulder and the angel lazily brought up his shield to defend himself. With controlled rage, Niccolo swung across his body directly into the shield and then continued through it, cutting off the angel's forearm and leaving behind a streak of green energy.

"What?" Nithael shrieked as his hand fell to the ground, and immediately he tried to counter with his glowing sword.

Faster than the eye could register, Niccolo caught Nithael's wrist with his demonic arm. Wearing a smirk soaked through with malice, Niccolo tore out the angel's arm by the elbow and dropped it at Nithael's feet.

"Maybe *you* don't understand. You're completely out of your league. You're *weak* and you insult us by being here. If Adonai wants to stop us, if any of your brothers and sisters wants to get in our way, they're gonna have to step up their game. Now *go home*. That goes for you, too, *Mitz*," Niccolo sneered, his voice resonating in the murky air. Immediately, the sounds of Paimon's duel stopped and Mitzrael hopped over before Paimon could pursue.

"Did you lose to a human?" he asked before crawling over to pick up Nithael's shield, but Niccolo swatted it out of his hand.

"Those are mine," he declared before grabbing the angel's limbs and turning to Phenex, who was enjoying the show of cruelty.

"Hey, Phenex, catch."

Niccolo threw the limbs into the air, and immediately Phenex let out a bright stream of fire that turned Nithael's arms to ashes before they met the ground. The sight was so satisfying that Niccolo turned back to smirk at the silver-haired angel. "Oh, that's too bad."

"Ju—just what..." Nithael managed to stammer, but Niccolo walked forward and lifted the angel by the neck.

"*Stay out of our way*. Beleth and Azazel are the only ones we care about. Next angels I see get to die," Niccolo said before tossing the crippled angel at his bouncing friend.

Mitzrael grabbed him—caught off-balance momentarily—but then he was able to stand. Seeing that he was surrounded by enemies who could very well kill him, the angel stepped back and wore a wild grin.

"Oh, I like you."

Then Mitzrael let out a low chuckle as he jumped into the air and burst into a flash of light, disappearing into the wind.

And just like that, the angels were gone.

"So, Nico... you want to tell us what the fuck that was?" Marchosias asked, already shrinking back down to his normal size.

For a moment, the green aura continued to surround Niccolo, but then it dissipated and he waved to the massacred bodies covering every inch of this desolate farmland.

"Two angels just destroyed an entire village, and you expect me to hold back?" he asked, his frustration on display. "I did what I had to do."

"No one is going to argue against making them pay, but you *do* realize that you just made an enemy of Heaven, right? However powerful you are, we were *supposed* to be laying low. Leaving scouts alive *isn't* how you do that."

"How about this, you take the next one? Think you can do that?" Niccolo asked, his rage threatening to take hold again, but then Paimon's hand fell on his shoulder.

"Whatever just happened, we can't change it now. We'll just need to move on. Those two are way down the chain of command. Mitzrael is a seraphim, but Nithael is a pompous nothing. Maybe Niccolo's message will be... useful," she said before taking her hand back from his shoulder. "If they think we're just after Beleth and Azazel, they might leave us alone."

"*Might* is a pretty word to throw around," Marchosias muttered, crossing his arms. "How soon do you think they'll send the big guys after us if *might* doesn't work out?"

"We'll... shit, Marchosias, I don't know, but we'll just have to deal with it. It's terrible to say it, but if we can't handle what Heaven throws at us, I don't think we have any business going after Beleth and Azazel," Paimon argued, sighing as her claws finally became fingers again.

"Well, if they weren't already allied against us, we might want to consider that they are now," Marchosias said before walking past all of them. After a few moments, the werewolf turned around and sighed. "Let's go. I'm not going to sit around and wait for them to come back."

"So you're just going to turn tail and run away, Judas?" Phenex asked after his friend, which made Marchosias bare his fangs.

"*Watch it.* Being careful and being a coward are two different things." Marchosias glared at his friend for an eternity of a second, but then he continued along the road.

What just happened? Cadmus whispered to the beast lurking within his mind, replaying the interaction in his head. Except for Cimeries, everyone was on edge. It didn't make him feel any better that it took so long for Mercy to answer him.

Something is going on beneath the surface. The effect is obvious, but the cause is not. At this point, I am not sure what it happening, or if we can do anything to stop it. We are far from the Rubicon, but...

You think this is Beleth again? he asked, and he could feel that Mercy only partially agreed.

Either him, or something that Azazel has manufactured. We must tread softly, even if our companions are determined to stomp all the way into Italia.

Do you think that we can stop this, find some way to turn it off? I can't even tell what is causing it.

It is not for me to say. I am sorry, master.

Don't be, Cadmus thought, *because I'm just as lost.* They rode without speaking for a while, but then the reaper's thoughts fell back to the enemies they had just let escape. *Do you think we have any chance of avoiding the angels in the future?*

Master, hope does not come naturally to me, nor you. I expect these are just the first angels among many. But, of course, you did not need to ask me. You just wanted me to let you travel in denial.

Yeah... yeah I did, Cadmus admitted, looking down at the mud squelching beneath Mercy's hooves.

And I will not let you.

———

THE FURY WOULD NOT LEAVE him, and Niccolo couldn't breathe without difficulty. He had thought this corruption ended with him killing Beleth and Azazel, but it seemed like Adonai and his angels were getting in on the action. Those poor, innocent villagers had done nothing, and they were already suffering under the Niccolo's pestilence. For those angels to turn them like that prematurely was just... evil.

Calm down, little man. Plague's deep voice tried to soothe him, but Niccolo snarled in real life and watched the others travelling in silence.

*Why? Why, Plague? After all this time, after seeing everything we've seen, why should I calm down? It's not just Azazel and Beleth, it's fucking **Heaven**, too? We don't have **enough** on our plate?* The reins in his hands creaked as he squeezed harder.

Nico. Seriously, calm down. You already took care of those two. They'll send back their warnings and hopefully they won't come after us. You took care of them handily, if you recall. It's not much to worry about, Plague said, chuckling internally once the horse realized his own pun.

*Of **course,** I took care of them. They weren't expecting it. They had no clue that I killed all of those Fallen back in Hell and gained all of those powers. They weren't expecting me to meet their challenge. This was **luck**.*

Niccolo had regained his senses now that he was realizing the implications of his actions.

Marchosias had been right, even if Niccolo hadn't wanted to admit it at the time. From Plague's saddle, Niccolo watched his companion walking along the edge of the road, dark hands stowed in the makeshift pockets of his clothing. Although Niccolo felt guilty for chiding Marchosias earlier, he could not ask for forgiveness now.

Even Phenex was still nursing his rage and walked on the side of path opposite his friend; a wedge had somehow come between them.

I'm not going to argue against the luck angle, Plague's voice broke back in. *If that Nithael prick had bothered to really defend himself, I doubt you could have chopped him up like you did. Still, it means something that you could tear him apart like that. If they really did want to stop us, to make sure we don't kill a couple of demons, they would have to send seraphim or more powerful angels. It probably isn't worth it for them.*

That's what really bothers me, Plague. This was **nothing** *to them. They sent some lower level assholes who had* **no** *business coming against us because they didn't feel like they needed to invest anything more than that. Turning that entire village into zombies was merely... it was just a flick of their wrist. They didn't give a shit that those people were suffering.*

Niccolo mood became more placid as he felt sympathy for Nithael's victims. Plague was silent for a moment as they continued on the road and Niccolo thought that he would stay that way, but eventually his deep voice broke back in.

I'm... they didn't. You're right. To them, that little village was nothing more than a way to get you angry. And it did—it worked—just not the way they wanted. There's a truth that you may not want to admit, though. These people...

Don't say it.

In the long run, Nico, those people really don't matter. If they had souls that rose to Heaven or crashed to Hell, they're still incredibly minor players. From that village—what—maybe two or three souls will find their way off this planet? I don't like it either, but we almost have to view this as... we might have to admit to ourselves that these casualties are something we need to bear.

You're an asshole sometimes, you know that? Niccolo asked, his hand jerking back on the reins to drive the point home, and suddenly his horse turned back to look at him with a bright green eye.

I'm a realistic asshole, and you might have to get used to being one, too. Once we're done murdering Azazel, do you think that it's over? After that is **God***, and don't forget it. A creature like that isn't going to give a shit over a few plague-ridden villagers, especially if he knows that it's going to affect you like this.* Plague's voice was a little more angry than usual, and his eye flared again before he turned back to the road. *And* **don't** *fucking pull on my reins like that again unless you want to get thrown off my back.*

Oh? Who's the Horseman, here? Aren't you just my transportation? Niccolo's thoughts were venomous, but regretted it almost immediately.

Plague stopped, jerking both Niccolo and Paimon in the saddle, and his hooves sank further into the mud beneath them.

You're going to want to take that back. You can be angry all you want, but you're taking that back.

Plague's thoughts were darker than anything Niccolo had felt before. Breathing in deep, Niccolo set his clawed fingers into the horse's mane and lightly grazed the creature's skin as he made his way up to Plague's ears.

I'm taking it back, he whispered, and soon Plague resumed his walking. He did not bother with a response, and Niccolo wouldn't blame him for holding a grudge for the rest of the day. It had been decades since Niccolo had crossed that line, and it would be some time before Plague forgave him.

"What was that about?" Paimon asked, but Niccolo didn't want to involve her.

"Nothing, we were just talking about what happened."

Paimon was clearly skeptical, but she was gracious enough to let him avoid further conversation. When he looked forward, Niccolo realized that Phenex had slowed down, putting more distance between him and the others in front of them.

Before long, Plague had caught up with the kind demon, whose white robes had been ruined over the last few days. The hem of his garment was burnt away, and that blackened material was also covered in mud. Out of everyone, he looked most the part of a European peasant.

"Can you believe him?" Phenex muttered, soft enough that only Niccolo and Paimon could hear.

"He's looking out for us..." Niccolo tried to excuse Marchosias, but Phenex scoffed at the attempt.

"He's looking out for *him*, just like always. I thought after all this time he had changed, but he's still just trying to survive, trying to escape notice from the people who hold him down." His volume raised just enough that Marchosias turned his head, but Niccolo couldn't tell if the werewolf realized he was the topic of their conversation.

"It's not like he wasn't making sense. I was a little... out of hand," Niccolo said, realizing he was arguing points he did not truly believe.

"You're kidding," Phenex said, dumbfounded at first. "You *have* to be. Everything you did back there was completely justified. That angel—if he could even be called that—deserved to die, deserved to suffer. A creature like that shouldn't have any *power*," Phenex said, his voice becoming more violent as he spoke. "That Marchosias criticized you just shows that... that he's the same from back then."

"That's not..."

"Not *fair*? No, what's not fair was that he was too scared to keep our revolution alive. What's not fair is that he left me to die on a cross because he wanted to *survive*. This is... this is just more of the same. This was how it started. At first it was reasonable—he would argue against a plan or two..." Phenex rambled on, lowering his gaze as he spoke. "And we all know what happened after that."

"Look, I was angry and I'm not ashamed of what I did—"

"You *shouldn't* be."

"I don't blame Marchosias for getting a little frustrated, though," Niccolo continued, turning toward the werewolf and stopping once he saw a yellow iris looking back at him. To his dismay, Niccolo noticed that Marchosias' ears had partially transformed.

"Fine. We'll give him the benefit of the doubt. We're... we're all tired and angry." Phenex kept on, as if he didn't also notice Marchosias' attention. However, when Niccolo turned back to say something, Phenex was staring at their eavesdropping friend. After gazing at Marchosias for an excruciatingly long moment, he returned his focus to Niccolo.

"I'm just seeing some of the same things in Cadmus," Phenex said under his breath, trying to make sure only Niccolo and Paimon could hear.

"I don't think *that's* fair at all," Paimon argued, finally entering the conversation now that she decided they had crossed a line.

"That's not fair, Paimon? You heard what he said. He can see the future, even if he pretends like he can't. Niccolo was right to bring it up last time!" He seemed to shout through his strained whispers. "And he went into Tamiel's house alone, if you remember."

"So? What does that have to do with anything?" Paimon asked, shaking her head. Phenex sidled up to Plague as he walked and set his hand on the saddle.

"And has he told us anything that happened in there? He keeps secrets, and Marchosias is not the only one who is fighting this plan," he said, prompting a groan from Paimon.

"I really used to like you, Phenex. Cadmus is going through some major changes, and we saw some crazy things back at the camp. You can't say he isn't part of this fight," Paimon said, touching Phenex's hand on the saddle. "Far as I'm concerned, he's been more than just useful."

"Niccolo, you see what I'm talking about," Phenex said as he slid his hand out from under Paimon's, abandoning the argument against her. "Why would he keep these secrets from us—these possible futures—if not to undermine our cause?"

"Cadmus doesn't have any reasons to hurt us. He wouldn't do that," Niccolo muttered, but he knew his argument was weak.

True enough, Cadmus would never hurt them, but Phenex was needling him with all the right questions. Cadmus was withholding information—that was clear—and as he looked back at his old friend, Niccolo had to wonder just what he and Tamiel had discussed.

"I'm not saying he will hurt us, but I don't think he trusts us enough to know what he knows. I think he is hiding some very dangerous information from us, and that it will be a problem in the future," Phenex said, and both of them were surprised by the scoff from Paimon.

"Maybe he thinks that you will all go conspiracy-theory crazy with what he knows, did you ever think of that?" she asked, her tone weighed down by annoyance. "The way you're acting, it's like a bunch of teenagers leaping on every single rumor. With all of the futures in his head, with all the new powers and abilities he's gaining with *no one* to help him understand them, can you really blame him for holding something back?"

"He can't tell *us?* We're supposed to be his allies, his *friends*."

"So let's treat him like we *are* friends, instead of viewing him like some new enemy. Trust me, we don't need any more of those," Paimon said, her right arm hugging Niccolo's midsection tight. "After what happened to Cim, he probably just doesn't want to make anybody fall into a similar trap and I don't blame him for that."

"No," Niccolo said, nodding along, "we can't blame him for that. Cadmus is just trying to be smart. He's just... he's just trying to make sure he doesn't make any mistakes."

After ending the conversation—as Phenex walked away in a huff once he realized that they were being stubborn—Niccolo turned and looked at his cloaked friend. He really did want to believe that Cadmus was trying to look out for them.

But the seed of doubt had already been planted.

CHAPTER 8
RHYME AND REPETITION

As he knelt beside Lilith, Lucifer wanted to share this with her. Their child's gestation had taken much longer than any of them had expected—years had passed—but the moment of truth was upon them. From Lilith's pain and sacrifice, a new angel would be born into their family, and they could truly begin to create new life without Adonai.

Still, Lucifer was plagued with doubt. Lilith was trying to be strong, but the agony was plainly evident on her porcelain face. With his left hand, he wiped her brow with a cloth already soaked through from her perspiration, and he allowed her to inflict all the pain she wanted on his right hand. Lucifer was honestly surprised; Lilith was strong enough to crack boulders with her bare hands, but she had only pulverized two of his knuckles through dozens of hours of labor.

Though he was relieved that was the worst of it, Lucifer knew she was holding back.

"It shouldn't be much longer, I think. From what I observed in the primates, this stage of labor is followed closely by the birth." Beleth knelt between her legs, a bucket of water at his side and a stack of bloodied rags to his right.

For the first few hours, blood had trickled out from some internal damage, but Beleth had persuaded them it was normal in primate birth. While Lilith choked down a scream, Azazel arrived with fresh rags that he placed beside his brother, quickly picking up the soiled cloth before retreating once more with a mutter under his breath.

"Are you sure this is normal, Beleth?" Lucifer asked, still staring at his queen's pain-stricken face, and he was countered with an exasperated sigh.

"You know I have no way of knowing that. There is no precedent for this. It's all a guess," he said, clearly annoyed at the question he had already answered a dozen times. "If you recall, I did not suggest you **continue**."

"Well, we must," Lilith said weakly, trying to laugh and failing. "We've made a commitment, I believe."

"Hush, Lil," Paimon said opposite Lucifer, earning his gaze momentarily. Although she still looked straight into Lilith's face, she noticed Lucifer waver in her periphery. "You save your strength and your words. It's important you keep all of your energy."

"Oh, I'm sure a few words won't—Ah!" Lilith tried to argue, but then a contraction hit her and she squeezed both of their hands hard enough to break lesser creatures.

"Your sister is right, my love," Lucifer agreed, using the affectation with a small amount of guilt. "You have more than enough on your plate. You just focus on bearing with the pain."

"There's... there's so much," Lilith squeaked out, her spine arching as a spasm tore through her.

As she opened her mouth wide and stifled a scream, her abdomen distended and Lucifer's eye drifted to her belly. His child—whatever it would be—was in there, and he saw something miraculous. Two visible fingers ran along the inside of Lilith's skin, and Lucifer was momentarily elated. With happy tears pooling at the bottom of his eyes, he turned back to the scarlet-haired angel.

"Oh, Lilith," he said, her body collapsing back onto the couch as the pain subsided enough for her to bear it. "Our child is so close."

"It's... too much," Lilith whispered, and she lifted her head and looked at him with desperate eyes. "He... he doesn't like being in me."

"Nonsense." Lucifer wrapped her hand between both of his, unable to notice the pain from his broken fingers. "He just wants to join us. He wants to be born."

"No... No, that's not it." After a moment of arching her back once more, Lilith fell back to the couch and looked at him, doing everything she could to keep herself from fainting. "He doesn't care. He—he wants more than that."

"You don't know what you're talking about." Lucifer tried to dismiss her statement, the smile still on his face as he smothered them both in denial, but she gripped his hand tight and made him believe the truth.

"I... I know. He—he's screaming at me. This isn't," she said, her eyes closing as she drifted into unconsciousness. With that Lucifer became very worried, and he turned back to Beleth with alarm.

"What is she talking about? Can she even know any of that? Can she know it's a son? And **screaming**?" He expected instantaneous answers to his barrage of questions, but Beleth only shook his head.

"Again, I have no clue, this is completely," he started, but he was interrupted by a spray of blood from between Lilith's legs. For the time being, as he drew away and hacked up blood, Beleth was useless. Lucifer turned back and saw Lilith's head lazily roll along her shoulder.

"Lilith!" he shouted, his heart breaking at the sudden turn. Only seconds ago, this had been a momentous, joyous occasion, but everything was falling apart. He rubbed his palms over the limp, delicate angel and panicked.

"This... I—I really do not know," Beleth said, but Lucifer didn't want his excuses. He whipped his head back to look at Beleth and snarled.

"**You save her**. You save her and don't you dare tell me you can't."

"I **told** you not to do this. If she doesn't make it—" Beleth started, but suddenly, there was an extremely aggressive angel holding sharpened claws inches away from his throat.

"You better make sure she does!" Paimon shouted, but Beleth merely backhanded the blades out of his space and seemed to grow larger.

"You get those little knives out of my face and let me focus!"

Their fight was postponed when they heard a weak voice coming from the other end of the couch.

"Lucifer..."

All three of the quarreling siblings immediately turned to see that Lilith had regained consciousness. Seeing that her eyes were barely open, Lucifer rushed over so she would not have to strain her voice.

"Quiet, Lil. Just be quiet. You don't need to say a damned thing." He brought his hand against her face, which she covered with her own.

"My love... my dear Lucifer," she said, offering a slight smile as she looked up at the firstborn. "You—you have tried to be so much. You have done what so many were afraid to do."

"Save your strength. For me," he said, returning the smile, and she laughed weakly at the idea.

"I gave you all my strength already, my love. You... you'll have to be strong on your own. You'll have to go on without me."

Lucifer shook his head as tears started to run down his cheeks.

"Don't you say that. Don't you say any of that," he said, but Lilith only had to pat his cheek to stop him.

"I must. Our son will need you. You must take care of him for me." Her eyelids drooped and made Lucifer tremble with uncertainty, but then they fluttered open again. "Don't, please... don't hate him. Even though I cannot know him, I love him all the same."

"Stop this, Lil. I can't do that and this—this is all silly. You're going to be right there with me," he said, sniffing back the snot and mucus and the tears he already hated. Lilith laughed and rubbed her fingers along the back of his hand.

"I will, but not like we want. I love—" she tried to say, but before she could finish, her mouth opened in a scream and her back arched outside of her control. Falling back at the sudden noise, Lucifer landed onto his backside and could only watch as her already-distended abdomen stretched up and out, four fingers clearly pressing against her skin.

Then the skin broke, and four bloody fingers shredded out through the flesh of Lilith's stomach.

Unable to understand what was happening, Lucifer could only watch in horror as the fingers withdrew and then reemerged in a blood-covered fist, another clawed hand appearing behind it in a shower of gore. Lilith's body slumped back to the couch after that, and then she slid off and to the ground.

"Lucifer..." Lilith's voice came again, and Lucifer could hardly believe it. In horror and pain and desperation,

Lucifer turned his head and saw that Lilith was just barely conscious. He could see the pain in her eyes, he could see the despair and heartbreak evident in her face, but he could also see the love she wanted to express.

"Lilith," he muttered, and upon hearing her name, Lilith nodded and blinked, letting out her final tears.

"It's not his fault. Promise me... promise... you will take care of our boy. I lo—" she started, but then the tiny arms burst out of her stomach again and let loose a torrent of blood and intestines onto the ground between them. Lucifer was horrified at the sight, and he almost didn't notice the tiny creature that crawled out of his queen.

Unable to watch any longer, he turned back to Lilith's face, but what he saw was even worse. Lilith's golden eyes were half-shut, glassed over, and all of the pain and life in her angelic face had disappeared.

Lilith—his first recruit and the love of his eternal life—was dead.

Screaming in three voices and wings bursting out of his back, Lucifer let himself be absorbed into the pain. After all of this time, after seeing so many of his brothers and sisters die because of a rebellion he was unable to win, after retreating back to Hell in shame, after existing for two million years in the dark, Lucifer had **never** felt pain like this. His heart was shattered, everything that he **was** had died with that loving, beautiful creature who had allowed herself to bear his child. As he assaulted the Heavens with his screams—the power in him enough for Adonai to hear him from two dimensions away—Lucifer only knew one thing for certain.

He had killed the woman he loved.

After that terrible moment, once the guilt was truly all-encompassing, Lucifer lowered his head back to the ground and took great, heaving breaths. His vision was unfocused and his stomach churned as if it was threatening to twist and tear out of his body, which was something he almost wanted. Lucifer was a horrible creature, and he did not deserve the life or the devotion or the love that he had squandered.

After blinking away tears that covered his eyes, Lucifer lifted his head and heard a confusing noise. It took some effort—he had become numb to the outside world, his pain was so great—but then he realized what was happening. More confusing than anything, Lucifer watched as the tiny, grotesque creature that had come out of Lilith knelt above its mother.

"My god," Beleth muttered, his voice wavering, but Lucifer could not blame him for bringing their enemy into this.

It almost made Lucifer laugh in desperation, it was so heinous, but he couldn't even blame his father for any of this. This was Lucifer's fault, and he should have assumed that any creature that would come from him would be an abomination.

Lucifer's son was not grieving its mother nor trying to curl against her for warmth. It was hunched over the bloody hole it had come from, shoveling meat and flesh into its maw and feeding itself the only way it knew how. Instinctually, their son was a monster, and only the guilt from Lilith's death was enough to stop Lucifer from rushing forward and ending the abomination's life.

"We—we can't." Paimon picked herself up, swaying from side to side as she took in the terrible sight. "We can't let something like that live."

"I... agree. I knew this was a terrible idea. However..." Beleth approached and drew a few symbols in the air, and once he was within a yard of the feasting abomination, he put his hand through the purple seal and withdrew a shining blade. "I will take this burden."

"No," Lucifer declared as he crawled toward Lilith's corpse, voice shaking as he went. "No, you're not killing him."

"You must be joking. After what we just saw?" Shocked by his brother's behavior, Beleth held off on the killing blow, even as the creature stopped shoveling flesh into its mouth only long enough to hiss. Before Beleth could truly react, Lucifer reached for his son and shielded him from Beleth's mercy.

"Scratch... stop it," Paimon tried to argue, but Lucifer shook his head, letting tears fall to the bloody ground beneath him as he did. He brought *his hands around the child's small chest, and immediately it turned toward him and screamed, snapping at its father's face once it had the chance.*

"Lilith told me... she told me to take care of him," Lucifer said, slowly, and picked himself up even as the creature tried to squirm out of his grip.

"She didn't know that he would turn out like this," Paimon said, but Lucifer swallowed down the pain threatening to escape his throat.

"I think she did, Paimon. I think that's why she made me promise." His voice shook and a fresh round of sobbing was about to destroy his composure, but then the crimson infant stopped struggling long enough to make eye contact, which seemed to calm it down.

"She made you promise to take care of this abomination, Lucifer?" Beleth said as son and father gazed into each other's eyes. "That was said in the throes of pain and death. This creature does not belong in this world."

"No, Beleth, he doesn't. But he's my son, and Lilith died to give him to me," Lucifer argued, the child in his hands grinning widely and showing sharp teeth as he playfully slapped his hands against his father's arms.

Lucifer almost smiled at the distraction.

"I will kill him for you, brother, if that is necessary."

"You will not kill him. Not now, Beleth. Not after Lilith died for him."

"I told you not to do this—"

*"She **died**, Beleth!" Lucifer shouted, bringing his son closer and cradling him against his arm. "Whatever mistake we made—whatever we did wrong—we have to... we have to live with it. I'm trying to live with it."*

"Please, Lucifer," Beleth tried to argue, but Lucifer shook his head violently and then focused on his infant abomination. He burped and spit out some of his mother's blood before cooing.

"You killed my wife, Beleth. You're not going to kill my son." Lucifer gave a false smile to his son, but he could feel the anger and enmity coming from the giant at his periphery.

*"I did **not** kill anyone, you coward! You forced me to do this!" Beleth raged, but Lucifer couldn't back down. It had been said in anger, but he needed someone to blame for the time being.*

*"I didn't force you to do **this**. Leave, brother. I have a son to raise."*

Lucifer did not watch as Beleth turned and drew a seal in the air before stepping through the new portal, abandoning them as Lucifer had abandoned him. For a few moments, Lucifer thought he was alone with a child whom, deep down, he knew he would not forgive.

"Scratch," a weak voice interrupted him, and Lucifer finally remembered Paimon was still standing there. Doing everything he could to retain his composure, Lucifer jostled the infant and heard a squeal of delight come from his abomination.

"I can't kill him, Paimon. Whatever happens, I can't do it." Tears fell freely as Lucifer looked down at the little thing in his arms. As he looked it over, he realized that beneath the red of Lilith's blood, it had mustard-yellow skin.

"I can..."

"No," Lucifer said abruptly, shaking his head and regretting the tear that fell into his son's mouth. "There's been too much death today. I'm not going to break my promise."

"Lucy..."

*"But we can't let this happen again. After this, there won't be any more tragedies," Lucifer stated, turning to look at his grief-stricken sister. "This will be the **only** Hellborn."*

"I... yes. That's probably for the best." Paimon's voice was soft as she stepped to the side and looked over the beast that killed her sister. "Will you..."

"His name is Mammon," Lucifer said, ignoring the question he could not stand answering. When he looked up, their eyes met and he knew she understood. Lucifer nodded again before looking back at the grinning, oblivious child in his arms.

"His name is Mammon."

A SWARM of voices assaulted him on all fronts, just outside his ability to hear them, and it was difficult for Niccolo to even remember who or what he really was. All at once, he saw images of Mammon feasting, of Mammon giggling in his arms, of the Hellborn scooping out his pet dragon's innards with discarded scales, of seven twisted heads screaming and cackling at the same time.

Time meant nothing to these memories; they came at him instantaneously and out of order, his emotions pulling him every which way.

Niccolo!

Plague's mental scream yanked Niccolo back to the present and he gulped down air he didn't even need. His back arched as he gasped it all in, coughing and hacking once his body slumped back to the ground, and after a few frantic seconds, he realized that the problem was only a lack of sulfur. After a moment, he realized that he was back on Earth, that it was midway through the fourteenth century. Shaking, with teeth clattering against his will, Niccolo looked up and saw three very-worried faces and a black horse with green eyes.

"I..." he tried to speak, but his throat did not cooperate. Placing his elbows against the ground, he tried to sit up, but Paimon laid her hand across his chest and gently shoved him back to the ground.

"Don't. You don't need to prove anything." Her voiced wavered with concern, just enough to notice. "You fell off your horse."

"I... fell?" Niccolo asked, turning to look directly at Plague. With a huff, the green in his eyes vanished and he lowered his head to nuzzle against Niccolo's shoulder.

"You did. I'll forgive you this once. My brothers and sisters may have trouble with riders on their backs, but we both know this is your fault."

"I'm sorry, Plague," Niccolo replied, taking Paimon's hand off of his chest before sitting up.

The others allowed him breathing room once he got off his back, but they still looked at him with worry. Cadmus was crouched on his ankles, but both Paimon and Phenex were kneeling on the ground beside him. Now that he was vertical, Niccolo noticed that Cimeries and Marchosias were standing off a few yards, keeping guard.

"What happened?" Phenex asked, but Niccolo couldn't respond before Cadmus spoke for him.

"Lucifer, I'm guessing," he said with just enough certainty to irritate Niccolo. Angrily, he turned to Cadmus and nodded, trying to make sense of everything in his head. It wasn't new information that certain emotions and feelings came from reaped souls, but what he had just seen was far too brutal for him to process normally.

"Y—yeah. This... I'm alright, I think," he said, shuddering as he remembered Mammon's claws tearing through his wife's stomach. Crossing his arms and gripping his elbows tight, Niccolo tried to separate himself from the scene. "Lucifer, he showed me..."

"Showed you what?" Cadmus asked after waiting a few seconds, but it felt like he was rushing Niccolo. With a scowl toward the reaper, Niccolo felt Lucifer's hate and anger flow through him.

"He showed me Lilith's death!" Niccolo wanted to tear out his friend's throat, to kill his demonic brother and crush his heart, to tear off the smug face Beleth wore as he talked down to him.

In that moment, Niccolo's breath caught in his throat, and he saw the shock on Cadmus' face.

That was nothing compared to what Niccolo felt when he realized what had happened. Lucifer's world—his memories—had invaded his waking life. For a moment, in *his* world, he had become Lucifer and Cadmus had become Beleth.

After taking a moment to consider telling Cadmus not to worry, Niccolo realized he couldn't. If he admitted that he was becoming unhinged, if he broke down and told Cadmus just how weak he was in comparison, the reaper would never trust him again. Guessing that his anger might still be justified, Niccolo swallowed down his confession and explained the rest of his vision.

"He showed me... he showed me Mammon's birth," he said softly while looking down at his hands, but the quick movement on his left drew his eye. When he faced Paimon, he saw the horrors of her past playing havoc with her emotions.

"He..." she started, covering her mouth with both hands.

Remembering just how she looked tens of thousands of years ago—how she had not changed a day—and how he had always had feelings for her and her sister, Niccolo wanted to spare her. He didn't want her to hurt or to cry like she had after the war. However, from the pain evident in her vacant eyes, Niccolo knew he had already reopened the old wound.

"I saw all of it. I saw Lilith in her last moments, I spar—I saw Lucifer spare Mammon and hold him even as he chewed on his mother's guts," he said before taking a breath and feeling the hate bubbling back to the surface. "And I saw Beleth there."

"Niccolo," Paimon said softly, bringing her hand on top of Niccolo's thigh and shaking her head. Suddenly, he saw two versions of this woman trying to deny him. "He was there because we couldn't have children without his magic. It wasn't Beleth's fault."

"It wasn't his fault?" he asked, shoving hard against the ground and clambering to his feet. "It wasn't his *fault*? It was because of him that Mammon came out of your sister and immediately thought she was a feast!"

"Don't you dare!" she shouted, transforming instinctively just as she slapped Niccolo in the face. When she did, she left three red gashes on his right cheek.

It was enough to shock Niccolo back into his own body and feelings, but his temper still flared. He turned his head back to face her, those gashes turning to scratches and then to slight scars before disappearing completely.

"*Really*?" His voice was low and spiteful, but Paimon was only flustered for a moment. Although she reverted back to normal, she kept hold of her righteous anger.

"Don't you ever talk about that day like *that*. *Nobody* won, nobody came out on top. Back then, Beleth was on our side. He advised against it from the beginning, but he went along with it because Lil begged him." Paimon stepped forward, her nose only inches away from Niccolo's face. "She *begged* him. Lucifer *asked* him. I was there, Nico, and you know it."

"Why would he show me, then? Why would I remember this scene? Why would Scratch put me through *this*?" Niccolo asked, shouting down at Paimon and drawing closer with each question. Only by chance did he avoid accidentally spitting into her face with his tirade.

"I... might know," a voice interrupted them, and Niccolo turned to see Cadmus, his face somber. Niccolo's anger flared again and the image of Beleth's face flickered over Cadmus again, but he tried to maintain his composure.

"Oh, *you* know what's going on in my head?" Niccolo turned away from Paimon and took a step toward his friend. Instead of intimidating him into submission, Cadmus kept leaning on his scythe.

"I wouldn't say that, but I have a theory," Cadmus replied in a clipped tone. "You're looking for a reason why Lucifer gave you this memory and—in our experience—these visions have always held something you needed to know. Remember, this was how we knew about Tamiel."

"Yeah, so?" Niccolo asked, his mind calming down as Lucifer's emotions left him. As Cadmus continued, Niccolo got flashes of Mammon's birth, but it was becoming more manageable.

"There's always a reason. Before this, did you see Beleth in any of these visions?" Cadmus asked, and Niccolo was instantly reminded of Mammon's conception and the magic in Moloch's cave. Even as he tried to focus on those visions, Paimon's face kept returning to dominate his thoughts. Feeling more guilt than usual, Niccolo regretted his outburst.

"Yeah, a couple times," he admitted as he looked toward Paimon, who noticed his gaze out of the corner of her eye. Once she did, she huffed and walked over to Plague's side so she could stay out of Niccolo's line of sight.

"And what was he doing, Nico?" Cadmus asked, snapping his fingers to grab Niccolo's attention. Niccolo instantly wanted to break those fingers, but he begrudgingly returned to the conversation.

"He was using his magic, *Cadmus*." With all of these recent events, Niccolo didn't want to give the reaper any satisfaction.

"And..." Cadmus started, but Niccolo whipped his head around and threw out his arm in a sweeping motion.

"And he fucking—"

"Nico!" Plague stopped Niccolo mid-sentence. "Cadmus is your friend— your *best* friend if we don't include me—and you're being an asshole."

Look. Niccolo turned to face his horse, but he was surprised to see Plague tower over him, green fog pouring out of his mouth, nostrils and eyes.

"You're being an *asshole*. Try to keep track of yourself, little man. These emotions you're feeling, all this resentment and frustration, has *nothing* to do with Cadmus. I want you to apologize."

"Plague..." Niccolo said with some condescension, but the horse advanced and looked straight into his soul.

"*Apologize*. You're barely yourself anymore. I sympathize, Nico, I really do, but we share more than you think. I can tell what Lucifer is doing to you, even if I don't see the visions. His feelings, his anger, his wrath, *everything* is flowing into you and changing you and it's *not* exactly for the better. We used to have fun, we used to joke around, but now you're seeing an enemy around every corner.

"Every corner, little man!" Plague continued as he stamped his foot for emphasis. "Sometimes—and I don't know where the fuck this came from—sometimes you don't trust *me*. We share pieces of our *souls*, Niccolo. We're your friends, *I'm* your friend, and we love you."

Niccolo stared at his horse in disbelief. Every word rang true, and Niccolo was ashamed. Only now was it sinking in, how he had offended the only people who cared about him.

Apologize, little man. They'll understand. I'll understand, Plague finished before drawing back, the green fog dissipating as he reverted his exterior back into that of a normal, black horse.

Biting his lip to feel the pain, Niccolo tried to face Cadmus. As he inhaled, trying to piece together some sort of apology, Niccolo actually felt Cadmus' gaze soften, and that was the permission he needed to continue.

"I'm sorry, Cadmus. It's like being two people," he admitted before letting out an anxious breath. "Beleth was using his magic, still with the seals and purple magic. That was how they got Lilith pregnant, and how they tried to induce labor. After it... happened, Beleth wanted to kill Mammon, but Lucifer stopped him."

"Then he stomped off and..." he said as he turned back to Paimon, who was more than just worried. Niccolo had intended to explain Paimon's presence there, but one look at her was enough to change his mind, so he just turned back and shrugged. "That was it."

"Well... apology accepted. I have problems with that, too, so don't be afraid to tell us anything," Cadmus said, nodding before staring into the middle distance. "However, I don't think Lucifer was trying to show you that Beleth was responsible."

"What do you mean?" Niccolo asked, but Cadmus turned to Paimon to incorporate her into the conversation.

"That was *it*, wasn't it? That was when Beleth really turned against Lucifer," Cadmus guessed, throwing Niccolo for a loop.

"Oh, Cadmus, you smart, little devil..." Paimon said under her breath, but she didn't speak further.

"Why do you think that?" Phenex added, entering a conversation where he did not belong. Cadmus turned to him and bit his lip before explaining it all.

"I'm sure you know some of this, but Niccolo has been seeing things from Lucifer's past. When we reap souls or absorb their energy, we take on their memories. Before we met Tamiel, Niccolo had already seen visions of the two of them before the rebellion even started. Since then, his visions have been giving us context and more understanding," Cadmus explained, nodding at his friend with the last sentence. "My theory is that since his death, Lucifer has been trying to guide and help Niccolo."

"You think Lucifer's helping us? What makes you think they're not just random memories?"

"It's too much coincidence," Cadmus said, gripping his scythe a little tighter. "Raüm and Amon have been giving me prophecies, and we can't fight that. With Niccolo, I feel like Lucifer is truly giving us information we need. Beleth is our enemy and we need to know everything we can."

"He's my brother," Paimon stated abruptly. The reaper thought he would have to argue, but he realized she was speaking to Phenex.

"But Beleth is a tricky son of a bitch and Lucifer kept his secrets well. Cadmus is right, I feel it. Although seeing Mammon's birth like that must have been... difficult," she said, hesitating at the memory, "Beleth was never the same after that. That was a dark time for Lucifer and he lashed out at... a whole lot of people—even if he regretted it later on—but it was hard on Beleth. He never wanted to do it in the first place..."

"So what?" Phenex asked flippantly, causing everyone to turn their attention on him. It was completely unexpected to hear that from a man known for forgiveness. "We're supposed to understand why he killed Lucifer, is that it? We're supposed to feel bad for the demon king?"

"Phenex—" Cadmus started, but the man waved off the interruption.

"Whatever reasons he had to resent Lucifer, it changes nothing about what he did. In one day, Beleth killed his brothers and threw Hell into chaos. In three months, he tore and mashed together humans, alive and dead, and created monstrous beings. For breakfast, he tortured and almost killed Cimeries."

"We don't know what's going to be important," Paimon tried to argue, but Phenex gave a sigh of disgust.

"What's important is that we kill him and remove him from the world. Beleth preys on the weak and does it purely because he's evil. *Why* he became evil is not our business. Niccolo," he said before turning to the Horseman, "unless Lucifer by some chance tells us how to kill him with *sympathy*, I'm not sure these visions are anything good. You *might* just be haunted."

With that, Phenex broke from the circle and continued down the road, his footprints smoldering and betraying just how angry he really was. All four of them looked after Phenex, but eventually they turned back to each other.

"There's a degree of sense there, Nico, but I wouldn't be surprised if the memories all mean something. Just... don't let it consume you," Cadmus said as he lay his free hand on Niccolo's shoulder. "I know you have the strength, even if it seems like Lucifer is getting more powerful. I have faith in you."

"I... thank you," Niccolo mumbled, biting back what he really wanted to say. The way Cadmus talked down to him, Niccolo didn't know why the reaper would have any faith in his strength. However, Niccolo convinced himself it was just a projection of his own insecurities.

"Well, I guess we should keep going. You're able to ride, right?" Cadmus asked, and Niccolo answered him with a nod. With a forced smile, the reaper patted Niccolo's shoulder before turning and walking down the road. Once he was a few yards away, dust swirled beneath him and pushed him into the air before solidifying into Mercy.

"Paimon," Niccolo said once Cadmus was out of earshot, turning to face the fallen angel standing behind him. Once he was able to see Paimon's face, Niccolo could see she had clenched her jaw to help hold back her tears.

"What, Nico?" She was clearly trying to stay bitter, but Niccolo could tell it was stubbornness on her part.

"I didn't apologize yet, but you deserve it most." Niccolo noticed that Plague had maneuvered around his side and then behind him. "I shouldn't have said those things. I was just completely floored by what happened in the memory."

"You're right, you shouldn't have said any of that."

"It's hard, Paimon. It's harder than I think you understand,"

Niccolo admitted, his harsh exterior completely disappearing as he let himself fall into self-pity. "I try to pretend, I try to make it seem like I have it all under control, but I really don't. I don't... I'm not sure I'm *me* anymore."

"Nico..." Paimon muttered, uncrossing her arms and looking at his face with sympathy. Although she had wanted to be angrier at him, she could see the pain and confusion and his inability to look her in the eye.

"I keep... I keep seeing you in two worlds, as two people," Niccolo said, lifting his head so he could stare into the overcast sky above them. "And it's so difficult to keep the two of you separate. In the real world, we haven't known each other for very long and it's so hard to remember that."

"Because in this world... in this world we're comrades, we fight together, and I love—" Niccolo wanted to honor Camilla's memory, but when he dropped his head and made eye contact with Paimon, he realized he could not say her name. "I loved... a woman whose life I ruined. That was me. That was Niccolo da Firenze. The Horseman of Pestilence."

"And I'm *losing* that," he said, grabbing Paimon by the shoulders and closing his eye. Only at the last second did he remember the others were still close by, and he did not want to shout. When he opened his eye again, Paimon was shivering. Although he tried to ignore that suffering, Niccolo continued with a heavy heart.

"But I'm not just me anymore. Every time I see something out of his life, I bring more and more of Scratch with me. The line between us is blurring, and I'm scared. I'm scared, Paimon, and there's nothing I can do. The memories come no matter what.

"And you're right here. You're *right here* every day with your arms around my stomach. When I come back, Paimon, you're the only familiar face, the only one who's always there when I need someone. When all I feel are his emotions, the only thing beside his rage and his grief..." Niccolo hesitated as his heart ached with affection, but he knew there was no shame in telling her the truth.

"The only good thing is you."

"Nico..." Paimon placed her right hand on his face, her touch light on his scar tissue. "I'm no great prize. I'm just some angel who stole her sister's husband. All of this you're feeling..."

"Is real, I think." Niccolo took the human hand from her shoulder and placed it along the side of her face, burying his fingers in blonde hair before he knew what he was doing. "Scratch loved you and, as everyone tells me," he punctuated with a short laugh, "I'm just like him."

"What about your human girl?" Paimon's voice was subdued, already losing ground to her emotions, and her fingers still traced the maimed skin on his face. "Your Camilla?"

"She's... not here. I don't know if she even exists anymore. She's gone and you're—you're right in front of me, and I'm not sure I can fight this much longer." Niccolo looked her in the eyes, and he could see that she had already surrendered to her own feelings.

"Then don't."

Then Paimon leaned forward and brought her lips to his, her arms settling around his torso and pulling him into her embrace. Without a second thought, Niccolo gave into what he had assumed were Lucifer's emotions, but part of him knew what was happening.

After two hundred years, Niccolo was finally letting himself move on.

CADMUS TURNED his head slightly in order to avoid attention and looked at Niccolo out the corner of his eye. He looked happy for once, which Cadmus quietly appreciated, but he could not shake the feeling that something was wrong.

Niccolo had apologized, but Cadmus couldn't be sure it was genuine. Although Plague had even scolded his master, Cadmus was finding it more and more difficult to control his fellow Horseman.

At the thought, Cadmus felt guilty—friends shouldn't control one another—but it was clear that something needed to be done. Niccolo was volatile and had more power than ever; he had dismantled that angel without a second thought and maybe without a first. It was enough cause for Cadmus to consider darker options.

"Is their love life so curious to you, reaper?" Cimeries asked behind him, no warmth in her voice.

However, Cadmus knew this was the closest the woman would ever get to being friendly.

"It's not their affection I'm worried about," Cadmus said as he looked forward, focusing on the surroundings flying past.

Mercy was at a full gallop and—while it would be impossible to talk or hear anything on a normal horse—the white stallion almost noiselessly hit the ground and absorbed almost all of the shock from each impact. If Cadmus hadn't already been used to it, the blur of foliage to either side might have made him sick. Instead, he was trying to speak with Cimeries and decipher visions of the future while he still had the time.

"You're worried he is out of control, then. Understandable. In life, when I saw such impetuousness in my sisters, I would not hesitate to remind them of their place."

Cimeries replied without emotion, and Cadmus found it hard to understand her. Even at her most vulnerable, the warrior queen had never lost her willpower. Even without armor, she was hard as steel.

"I can't remind Niccolo of his place, Cimeries. It's not... *my* place," he said, struggling to find another word and failing. "I'm his friend—I have been for the last two hundred years—and that's all I can be to him. I can't tell him to behave and give him orders like you could your subjects."

"Why not? You are more powerful. I know it. I feel it. Whether or not you admit it changes nothing about reality. A warrior who falls off his horse is more than just unbalanced."

"That's not... fair. He gets torn from reality. There's obviously going to be some confusion when he comes back from what he's seeing," Cadmus argued, frustration leaking through. As much as he

231

wanted to believe in Niccolo, it was hard to justify everything that he had done only to have him excuse himself with these visions.

"I heard your argument, reaper—we all did—and you made a more compelling case. Though we all have our distractions, Niccolo only has Lucifer's past to relive. Great leaders have great troubles, but they are singular incidents and from one perspective. Niccolo's burden is a story, yours a world. However, that is not a difference I deem important."

"And what do you think is important?" Cadmus asked, doing his best to compartmentalize the conversation. However, something else started to gnaw at the edges of his mind and it was becoming harder to ignore.

"You stand on your own," Cimeries said, something in her voice catching his full attention. Then Cadmus realized she was speaking with approval. "I will not come down on either side to say which one of you has a more difficult situation. I can only trust what I can see, and you carry your burden without losing control. From a warrior's perspective, that is what is needed in this fight."

"Not everything is war, Cim," he said, momentarily forgetting the nickname was reserved for the people who had earned it. He held his breath and bit his lip, waiting for her to strike him, but no blade swept across his throat.

"Go on, Cadmus."

"Just... there's more to life than fighting and war." Cadmus was relieved at her mercy, but did not wish to gamble a second time. "I care about Niccolo and I'm just worried he is heading down a path that he might not be able to come back from."

As he finished relaying his concerns, Cadmus felt the gnawing at his senses once more and decided that it needed attention. Scenes flashed by him, chaotic at first, but he was determined to find the cause even as Cimeries replied.

"Caring is... detrimental in war. If you had not cared about that burning cross, Beleth may have died that day. When Phenex lost his temper, because you focused on what Beleth had done to *me*, the traitor was able to escape. If you had not cared, we would only have to face Azazel to finally avenge Lucifer."

Cadmus was dumbfounded by the disregard for her own life and whipped back to face her, hoping she didn't actually believe it.

"It wouldn't have been worth it! I'm not going to stop caring—" he argued, shouting at first, but then a migraine burst outward from the center of his skull.

All he could feel was the gnawing all over his mind, forcing him to close his eyes as a blue haze claimed them. Then all he could see were those twisted creatures from Beleth's camp. Though he wondered why he only saw them surrounded by dense forest, he soon realized that he was too late to stop what was about to happen.

Cadmus opened his eyes to look at the earth flying beneath them, but he had absolutely no time to react, no time to even warn Mercy through their connection. A trio of arms burst out of the ground beneath them, followed by a twisted amalgamation of torsos and legs and faces. Cadmus only watched as the appendage rose further into the air and then slung itself over Mercy's neck.

Suddenly, Cadmus remembered that he could have *more* time, but he could not act on his new gift. Before he could recall how he had done it before, the melded arms coiled around Mercy's neck and then pulled, dropping to the ground fast enough that it would break the horse's spine.

He considered it a miracle when Mercy dissipated into a pile of dust which instantly broke against the gnarled, white appendage, but Mercy's riders were not so fortunate. In less than a second, Cadmus had slammed into the extended arm of the chimera, breaking some of its bones as he bent it backward from the impact, but it recovered quickly and Cadmus felt three mutilated hands grabbing hold. Before he could take a breath, Cadmus was shifted to his left and then flung into the tree line to his right.

Already two of his ribs were broken, but the chimera was impossibly strong and had thrown him with enough power to send him crashing through one tree—breaking bones along his entire left side—and then into another, which spun him around once he glanced off the broad trunk. After he landed, Cadmus coughed up blood and tried to keep himself from passing out.

He failed.

Cadmus woke up only because of the sharp pain in his stomach, and he had trouble figuring out why it was there at all. Then he heard the screams and the migraine threatening to burst through his skull and Cadmus suddenly remembered riding on Mercy and the arm rising out of the dirt. Now the screams were far more disconcerting and he panicked, hoping his friends were alright. However, when he tried to sit up, he saw something that made him forget about anybody but himself.

Pinning him to the ground, screaming faces covering every part of its broken anatomy, was the arm of one of Beleth's creations; the very same that had thrown him into the woods. Then Cadmus realized it wasn't just pinning him to the ground. This chimera, taking advantage of Cadmus losing consciousness, had impaled him through the middle, but that wasn't what made Cadmus open his eyes wide in horror.

He could see and feel the chimera's skin joining with his own.

Ignoring the screaming and the pain, Cadmus panicked again, almost losing his mind as the chimera merged with his flesh. Frantically, Cadmus wanted anything but to be joined to this thing in its living hell—he wanted to cut it free—but his scythe was not in hand. Breathing rapidly and still having trouble remaining conscious, Cadmus looked around and tried to find some sharp branch or some rock or *anything* that could free him.

That was when his eyes finally fell onto his scythe, only a few feet away. Fear still dominating his every thought, Cadmus reached for the weapon and found that it just a few inches out of his grasp. Once he realized that, his pain worsened, and he felt a turn in his stomach as his organs rearranged themselves.

Looking down, he saw his body twisting and contorting against his wishes, his skin crawling underneath his armor. At the sight, he felt foreign thoughts threatening his mind and realized that he had even less time than he had thought. Cadmus snapped his gaze back to his scythe and reached once more, ignoring his two broken fingers once he realized they had yet to mend.

The scythe was still out of reach, no matter how hard he stretched.

Turning back to the screaming chimera standing above him, Cadmus felt hopeless. Without realizing it, he opened his mouth and a sound came out. It took him a moment, his thoughts still in chaos while pain enveloped him, but then he realized that the chimera had taken control and made him scream along with it.

That made him angry.

Pure defiance took over and Cadmus clamped his mouth shut, forcing his scream back down to a tortured humming. Even as the creature screamed down at him, Cadmus noticed a leaf in the air as it fell lazily to the ground. Breathing in deliberately through his nostrils, Cadmus focused on the leaf, focused on the present, and then *commanded* time to slow down.

The leaf stopped falling.

Seeing that he had not lost this new power, Cadmus realized he might be able to control it and finally took the time to regain his senses. This chimera was trying to incorporate him into its body, and the absurdity was almost enough to make Cadmus laugh. He was a Horseman of the Apocalypse, and he was *not* going to let something this pathetic kill him.

Gathering the strength he had left, Cadmus brought up his legs and then wrapped them around the limb still impaling him. Taking another deep breath so he could maintain his focus, Cadmus braced himself and then brought down his hips with as much force as he could.

It had the desired effect, which was almost surprising to the one who did it. Cadmus had assumed plenty of the chimera's bones had broken from their impact on the road, and he had hoped they had not healed yet. When the arm broke and the skin slowly tore away from the body like a ripped seam, inertia playing its part, Cadmus was satisfied. Already seeing the beast still falling down on him—time having only slowed down—Cadmus turned and crawled to his scythe.

In his struggle to crawl, Cadmus stopped focusing on controlling time, which was made very inconvenient once the creature's upper body fell onto his leg and trapped him in place. Screaming even louder, the chimera reached for its prey with its other arm, but Cadmus wasn't worried anymore.

With a two-handed strike from the ground, Cadmus brought his scythe across the pallid flesh of the chimera, the blue blade sinking into and through two faces as it continued on its path. Once the scythe exited the other side, Cadmus noticed the life had gone out of the chimera's many tortured eyes, and he allowed himself to sigh in relief.

However, he felt the gnawing in his gut again and looked down to see that the arm was still buried in his midsection *and* that the last face—on the middle of someone's back—was still screaming at him.

Jumping to his feet, the extra weight of the horrifying thing buried in his stomach almost causing him to fall over, Cadmus' brain went into overdrive. With the other part of the creature, it had been a simple decision; a scythe through the body and a reaping was all that was necessary. However, this *thing* squirming in his intestines was bound to him and he didn't know what the rules were. Cadmus had no idea if reaping the wriggling, still-bleeding arm of the chimera was enough, or if it would place his own soul in danger. Gritting his teeth—panic and pain flooding every sense—Cadmus decided that he only had one option.

Grabbing hold of the arm, which screamed in protest and fought against his grip, Cadmus summoned all of his strength and pulled it out of him, his own skin tearing from the effort. Because of its weight, the chimera fell a foot to the ground before Cadmus grabbed at anything to stop himself from falling, even as his own blood and internal organs fell down with it.

After finding purchase on something, Cadmus looked down to see the chimera hanging from his vestigial organs. Already, parts of his small and large intestine were joined to the creature's wriggling hands, and that, combined with the massive amount of blood loss, made him start to pass out.

With a shaking hand—his sight fading to grey as he swayed—Cadmus set his scythe against the soft tissue of the organs connected to the creature. Concentrating only on not losing consciousness, Cadmus brought down the blade and felt the extra weight fall away from him, making him fall over from the sudden release.

The impact knocked him out again.

He was lying on his back when his eyelids fluttered open, but this time he knew exactly what had happened. Propping himself up on his elbows, Cadmus struggled to keep his eyes open and what he saw was enough to make him furious.

The chimera he had torn from his body was crawling back to the massive body Cadmus had already killed.

In his anger, Cadmus mustered the strength to pick himself up, the ends of his intestines swaying outside his body as he maintained a loose grip on his weapon, and he stumbled after the mewling thing. Once he was above it, one set of eyes looked at him in pain and the chimera screamed, but Cadmus would not listen. He brought down his glowing weapon and then dragged it along the ground, slicing the thing in two.

Looking up from the chimera that had wounded him so gravely, Cadmus did everything he could to focus and stay awake. Just at the edge of his vision—through all the trees that stood between them—Cadmus could see his friends and companions fighting for their lives.

At first, they seemed to be having a much easier time of it, but then he saw how some of them struggled. Marchosias was a blur and Niccolo was holding his own even as Phenex's fire raged along the other side of the road, but Cadmus could see a bloody Cimeries sitting down with her back against a tree. It was then that the reaper realized that Niccolo was protecting her, making Cadmus proud.

However, he had no time to fully appreciate his friend's actions, as he realized he had yet to find Paimon among the carnage. Leaning heavily on his scythe, Cadmus expected to find the demon king covered in gold and cutting through Beleth's chimera, but he only caught sight of the others and the beasts they were either fighting or had already killed.

Then Cadmus looked to his right, further along the road into Italia, and saw something that made him even more nauseated. It seemed that Paimon had overextended herself—just as she had done back at Beleth's fort—and she was cradling her left arm. Even through the haze of pain and blood loss, Cadmus could tell that her wrist had been snapped backward and that she had not had enough time to recover. Then, before Paimon could even try to run away, one of the beasts raised a horrific arm above her.

It was about to pin her down, just like that other chimera had done to Cadmus.

Stepping forward automatically, Cadmus knew he would not let that same experience happen to her, but he looked down to find several inches of intestine still remained outside of his body. When Cadmus looked back up, he saw that Mercy had no space to carry him, and he could already see the arm falling above Paimon. Realizing that he had no choice, Cadmus focused again and concentrated on the arm falling down to crush his friend.

Just like the leaf, the arm slowed down. Almost to a stop.

Breathing in and out deliberately, Cadmus made sure to focus on the deadly arm hanging in midair. He stumbled forward, using his scythe as a crutch as he tried to force his guts back inside his abdomen, and did everything he could to ignore the pain. Making his way over a log and shivering with each step, Cadmus continued forward and realized the arm was already closer to Paimon's hunched-over body.

Cadmus was only a yard away from the tree line when his plan finally came to fruition. Even though time had almost stopped for everyone else, he—and more specifically his *body*—was experiencing normal speed. To his relief, muscles and skin had already started to creep along the gaping wound in his stomach, reforming the exterior of his body.

By the time Cadmus finally made it to the road, raw, pink skin had closed over new muscles.

However, once he had closed back up, Cadmus had lost his focus, and the arm continued on its deadly path toward Paimon. Still, Cadmus would not allow himself to fail, and with a speed that surprised even him, he threw his arm forward and released his scythe in a horizontal spin, a blue tornado of energy following behind it. Already certain it would hit its mark, Cadmus rushed forward, despite an initial stumble, and called out to Mercy in his mind.

He was still running when his airborne scythe tore through the chimera's colossal shoulder, the impact enough to send the arm flying backward, and Cadmus threw out his arm and focused on the blade that was about to disappear into the woods. Slowing down before stopping entirely for a split-second, the scythe then flew back along its path and cut into the chimera again—it had fallen into the weapon's earlier trajectory—and then screamed toward its owner.

A second before the weapon was back in his hand—and a few yards away from the chimera still threatening Paimon—Cadmus planted his foot down on something not entirely solid. The dust rose beneath him as he tried to launch himself, and then it was as if Mercy had already been fully-formed beneath the road and had simply risen above the surface to meet his master. Mercy seemed to burst up from beneath the surface, sending dirt and mud every which way, and Cadmus used his horse's momentum to propel him even further.

He only dropped his hand to pick up the returning scythe without a second thought.

Faster than he expected, Cadmus was midair and covering four yards in less than a second. He had enough foresight to twist his body before launching himself, and that momentum helped him heave his scythe in a deadly arc. In fact, he was spinning so fast that Cadmus could not see what happened, and he landed hard on the other side of the chimera, arresting his momentum completely without trying. After wiping the blood and gore off his face, Cadmus stood up and turned with his scythe at the ready.

However, there was no need for it. Around Paimon was a pile of corpses, and Cadmus' impressive strike had harvested the life from them. Once he was able to see they weren't in danger, Cadmus finally looked at Paimon and found her staring at him like he was a ghost. He stammered, trying to find an excuse for the display, but then Paimon shook her head and stared down at her arm. Before Cadmus could speak, Paimon snapped her wrist back into place, grimaced, and then looked back to him.

"Cadmus, don't you *ever* switch sides. Even if I wanted to, I don't think I *could* kill you."

Although Paimon said it with a smile, Cadmus could tell he had frightened her. It was understandable; now that he actually had time to think about it, *he* was scared. Without meaning to, his thoughts fell back to the conversation the chimera had interrupted, and had to consider that maybe he really *was* stronger than Niccolo.

Looking back down the road, Cadmus was prepared to save his friends, but they were standing back where the chimera had first ambushed them. At first, he let out a sigh of relief; all four of them were alive and whole. However, once he and Paimon were able to clearly see what was going on, Cadmus' heart filled with dread.

Phenex and Marchosias were standing on opposite sides of the road. One wreathed in flames, the other still cloaked in his shadow.

"CALM THE FUCK DOWN!" Marchosias shouted, but it didn't seem like Phenex cared what he had to say. Before Marchosias could even melt into the shadows, he was forced to dive out of the way of an incoming fireball.

"*Why should I? This is the perfect time to get angry!*" Phenex let the flames surge around him, only sometimes coalescing into radiant armor.

As Marchosias picked himself back up, he snarled at his longtime friend.

"You're out of control, Yeshua! Are you fucking *blind* or something? Those chimera are dead and it's just us."

In his current state, Phenex could burn him to cinders within a moment. Although he had hoped to get through to him, Marchosias was ready for anything. Their companions watched in concern, but they knew they had no place in this duel.

"*It's not **just** us! It's us and **you**! Where were you that entire battle?*" Phenex asked as the fire receded and revealed his face. "*Running away again? Doing what you could to avoid your share of the work?*"

"You're kidding, right? You really have to be, because otherwise I don't know how you got this *fucking* stupid!" Marchosias snarled as he circled around his volatile friend, upper body low to the ground in anticipation. "I was killing just as many—if not *more*—of those monsters than that forest fire you started. Maybe if you didn't blind yourself with the pretty lights, you'd be able to *see* that."

"*Pretty lights? **Pretty lights?**"* Phenex shouted as his flames grew taller and his body floated into the air, all of it beneath his notice. "*I burned those miserable creatures into ashes and gave them peace! All you ever do is hide in your shadows and pick off the stragglers and weaklings.*"

He ended the statement by throwing a stream of fire at his old friend, which Marchosias avoided by jumping forward a few yards. Phenex then followed up that strike by throwing a sphere of flames at his new position.

This one Marchosias did not avoid.

The others could only watch as Marchosias crossed his forearms in front of him and braced himself against the intense concentration of flames, and then it was as if he had been entirely consumed within Phenex's attack.

Niccolo stepped forward to interrupt them, but he was stopped by a small hand pressing against his chest. When he looked, Paimon shook her head and then urged him to look forward. The subtext was immediately made clear, and Niccolo turned back to watch a fight that had been a long time coming.

Fortunately, when the flames finally died down, a shadow could be seen buried within the remnants of fire. Once he was able, Marchosias jumped forward, patches of his fur burning in spite of his attempts to guard himself, and nothing could stop his assault. The werewolf ran on all fours toward his current opponent, who sent futile streams of fire along his path, and soon he was within striking distance. With a great leap, Marchosias closed the last few yards and threw his right arm across his body.

After seeing his attacks fall to the side harmlessly, Phenex panicked and let his infernal armor expand outward, but that wasn't enough to stop the shapeshifter. Marchosias' hand broke through the flames and slammed into the side of Phenex's face, sending him tumbling out of the ring of fire and into the dirt road.

When he was finally picked himself up, Phenex was surprised to see that Marchosias had only punched him, refusing to use his claws.

"If that hadn't been me you had been aiming at—if I hadn't seen that a dozen times—you would have *killed* someone!" Marchosias shouted, his body still smoking from the residual flames. "Are you really that far gone? Can you not tell your friends from your enemies? You're supposed to be their goddamned messiah, but you're acting like a spoiled brat!"

"Spoiled brat..." Phenex muttered as he got to his feet, tendrils of flame snaking around his body and feeding into each other. "I came from nothing, Judas. Don't you dare call me spoiled."

"*If the shoe fuckin fits.*" The werewolf growled, the smell of his own burning hair enough for him to wince. "I swear, you—"

"You *swear?*" Phenex interrupted, shocking Marchosias out of his lecture. Energy coiled around his fists and shined bright as he continued. "*You* swear. Your oaths mean *nothing*. Not now, not a thousand years ago, and you're going to have to find some new way to trick me."

"Oh, this bullshit again? *How many times* do you have to bring it up?"

"You *killed* me, Judas. Because you gave me up to them, I *died*, and a thousand years isn't going to change that. That will always be your shame," Phenex replied, pointing at his friend with a hand wreathed in flames. "And now you're doing it again."

"I'm doing *what?*" As Marchosias' tone became more violent, the shadows ebbed and flowed around his body. "You better not be saying—"

"Why wouldn't I?" Phenex asked abruptly, dropping his arms and letting the blaze concentrate above his open hands. "Since Paimon came to us, you've been trying to interfere with this mission at every chance."

"Watch it," the werewolf grumbled as he stalked forward.

"Every time we come across some new difficulty, you're the first to despair and tell us to stop. Are you working for them? Are you secretly on Azazel's side? You were awake and hunting when Cimeries went after Beleth..." Phenex trailed off, rising a few feet in the air as an inferno formed around him and covered everything except his face.

"Did you *let* her go alone?"

That was when the others realized that they would have to intervene, though they did not know how. Phenex had gone too far, and Cadmus wished he was strong enough to slow down time one more time. With a roar that shook them to their bones, Marchosias flew forward, his shadowed form a blur, and they could all see that he was out for blood.

His smug face encased in fire, Phenex was only saved because he could fly. Within an instant, he was already ten yards in the air, but it almost seemed like Marchosias was still going to make him pay for his words. After jumping up with the massive strength of his werewolf form, Marchosias only *just* missed raking his claws against Phenex's throat.

"*See?*" Phenex asked as Marchosias fell back to Earth, the messiah waving a burning hand in front of him and leaving a plume of fire in its wake. "*He doesn't answer, he just attacks me again. Wants to kill me again!*"

"You... you..." Marchosias fumed, his anger leaking into the air and causing him to halt on his words. "You take all of that back. You take back your accusation. *You fucking take it back,*" he screamed, the shadows flowing outward and showing the full fury on his bestial face.

"*Did you do it?*"

"I will *not* answer that, Yeshua. What gives you the right to talk to me this way? What gives you the right to accuse me of something that horrible? We've been friends for *how* fucking long?"

At that point Phenex drifted down, only a few feet off the ground as he replied.

"You gave up our revolution once, *Marchosias.* An old dog does not learn new tricks." He sneered, his tone cold even as an inferno raged about his body.

"Phenex," Niccolo tried to interrupt, but both men shut him up with a glare.

Slowly, Marchosias turned his attention back to his friend and ally of more than a millennium. He slowly breathed in and out, Phenex waiting for what he had to say, but the werewolf took his time. After a few tense moments, Marchosias decided there was only one option.

"I gave you up because you were *insane,* Yeshua. There was no saving *you.* Our rebellion wasn't nearly strong enough to take on the Roman Empire, or any of the other men in power. We couldn't just fight against the system and get away with it. Not in the state we were in," Marchosias said plainly, letting the shadows fall away from him so everyone could see him as he was.

"By exposing us and ranting and raving like the *lunatic* you were," he continued, spitting out the word before pointing at the floating demon, "you put everyone in danger. If you want to talk about who was really responsible for all that blood, if you *really* want to know why all of our friends died, you should look in a *goddamned mirror.*"

"*What did you say?*" Phenex asked, the air around him crackling as his flames burned even hotter.

"I'm not going to deny my part in giving everyone up. I don't *want* to forget. I atone for it every day I exist. But if we're going to move past this, Yeshua, you have to see yourself for what you are."

"*And what is that?*" Phenex sent a wave of blazing air toward the people on the ground, but Marchosias was unfazed. He just looked straight into the small sun that Phenex had become.

"*Out of control,*" Marchosias replied, shocking everyone by reverting to his human form. "You almost got me to kill you just now. I'm trying to be better about all this, Yeshua. I'm trying to be understanding, but there's a point when you have to put your foot down.

"Since we've come to Earth, you've been losing it. And I get it, I know what kind of shock it must be to come back to life and see what so many people have done in your name. The Crusades alone are exactly the kind of thing you would never want to see. I *get* that. I understand how frustrating that could be."

"*You think you know me, you think you know what I'm **feeling**?*" Phenex screamed, arcs of flames coursing around his body, but Marchosias stomped the ground and dust flew out from the shockwave.

"Yes, Yeshua, *I do.* I've known you for more than thirteen hundred *years.* I've been there every step of the way. You've come back and seen the evil of this world, and much of it is the very kind of thing we wanted to stop when we were alive. I *know* that this religious empire hurts you down to your soul, whether you bother to talk about it to anyone or not!" Marchosias shouted, putting out his hands in a show of peace. "You're important to me, Yeshua. You always have been, and you're one of my dearest friends."

"But if you can't come back now...." Marchosias hesitated as he began his ultimatum. "If you can't see that we're all in this together, my griping included, and see that we're *allies*—you don't even have to see us as friends. I don't care what it takes, but you have to know that I would never give you up to Beleth and Azazel or any of the other million lackeys that God might send after us. I'll never give you up again." Marchosias paused, breathing in deep and dropping his arms to his side. "Unless you make me."

"What are you talking about?" Phenex was still angry, but many of the flames retreated as that anger gave way to confusion.

Marchosias shrugged before replying.

"If it comes to this, if you keep freaking out like this, if you keep directing all of your rage and hate about all this injustice and throw it at me..." he said, looking down for a moment as a tear came to his eye against his will. After wiping it away with his sleeve, Marchosias looked back in determination at the man bathed in fire.

"Then I'm not going to take it. I really don't have any stakes in this grudge match, Yeshua, and if you're going to keep being a pain in the ass, if you keep wanting to kill me after every little battle, then I'm simply not going to be here. I'm not the better man, Yeshua, and I'm *certainly* not your lap dog."

"What do you want from me?" Phenex asked as he descended, the dirt underneath him cracking as the moisture departed. The whole time, Marchosias kept staring into white-hot eyes and would not look away.

"I want you to stop this. I want you to keep this in control, even if you hate my guts. If you don't, I'll have to leave." He said it in a clipped manner, crossing his arms as he did.

Phenex regarded him with suspicion for a moment, but then he dismissed the flames around him before walking forward. When he was within just a foot of Marchosias, Phenex gave his answer.

"*Then leave,*" he said before stepping back, keeping his burning gaze on a man who did not deserve it. Marchosias stood there shaking for a moment, his eyes closed as he kept his head lowered, but Paimon couldn't let that petty decision stand.

"Phenex, we're not going to abandon Marchosias like this," Paimon finally argued, stepping toward the man and grabbing him by the shoulder. "We stayed out of it while your tempers flared, but there's no way we're going to let it happen."

"You're not going to abandon me," Marchosias interrupted, drawing the gaze of all his companions. After one last shaky breath, Marchosias transformed into his wolf form—gathering the shadows around him—but his yellow eyes were still focused on the friend who had rejected him all over again.

"I'm leaving because there's nothing keeping me here."

"Marchosias," Paimon started weakly, but then she exerted some willpower. "*Judas*, this is stupid. It'll blow over in a day or two."

"Been thirteen hundred years, Paimon," Marchosias said softly as he turned to the woods to his right. "If he can't let it go, I'm not going to force him. Bout time I tried out the lone wolf thing."

"You betray me again, Judas, and I'll kill you," Phenex spat out, which drew a low murmur from the massive beast. Opening his mouth to show off every one of his long teeth, Marchosias winked at the other demon.

"Yeshua, if I betray you again, you'll be *dead*."

Then he leapt into the woods and bounded away, the shadows of the forest reclaiming the beast almost instantaneously. It seemed surreal—they couldn't quite figure out how to process this new information—but then a resounding clap broke through the air.

"You idiot!" Paimon shouted, her hand drawing back from slapping Phenex in the face. He looked surprised at first and, although he attempted to fight the insult, she continued before he could get his bearings. "I can't believe you!"

"We'll be better off without him," Phenex protested, but when he looked around, no one stepped forward to agree.

"Marchosias was one of the strongest demons in Hell," Cimeries said in her analytical tone. "As such, he was a great ally."

"One that would..." Phenex started, but Cadmus shook his head and brought his hand up to his forehead. Even with the future constantly muddling his mind, he knew this headache had a more immediate cause.

"Yeshua... I was a follower of your teachings, and I died for my beliefs. What you taught," Cadmus said, bringing back his hand and staring at the path Marchosias had taken. "It was forgiveness. It was decency. Whatever happened during your life, Marchosias had atoned for it."

"He—"

"Had *atoned*," Cadmus interrupted, looking over at his messiah in disapproval. "Do you know the stories they told about you? I'm not talking Yeshua and Judas. I'm talking about *Phenex* and *Marchosias*. The two of you are considered some of the strongest individuals in Hell, and that's including the Fallen. And everyone *knew* just how good of friends you were. Everybody knew that nothing could come between you, that the two of you were always together."

"He was practically lying in wait."

"No, you're wrong. You're just plain wrong. He has saved each of our lives more than once, and you just threw him out on his ass," Niccolo said, joining Cadmus in his vigil by staring into the woods.

Although he tried to see if the werewolf was still nearby, he knew that it was incredibly unlikely; Marchosias could have been a mile away already. Niccolo wanted to turn to Phenex and tell him that he understood his frustration, but that it was no reason to push Marchosias away. Niccolo wished he could say that they would move on from this.

Unfortunately, Marchosias had already moved on without them.

CHAPTER 9
ALEA IACTA EST

Lucifer opened his eyes, the tall ceiling of his bedroom swallowed up in shadows. In his mad depression, he had abandoned the light. He had abandoned his siblings and his rule, since he couldn't consider that he was anything but an abject failure.

The gorgeous woman stirred on top of him, burying her face further into Lucifer's shoulder, yet he didn't feel what he wanted to feel. After Lilith's death, Lucifer needed someone to care for, to distract him, and Paimon had certainly tried her best. Although he cared deeply for her, he could never let go of that scarlet woman, and whatever feelings he had for either of them had been tainted by Mammon's birth.

Lucifer only felt hollow, even as Paimon dreamily stared up at him. He tried to give her the warmth she deserved, but she could see through the façade. The dream broke in front of them, and she crashed back to reality.

"How long are we going to keep doing this?" she asked, and Lucifer thought about all the things he could say to her to make her stay. Since he wasn't ready for an uneasy discussion, he stared at the ceiling to avoid it.

"Why should we stop? If you want, we can, but there are worse ways to spend the time."

"Is that really all I am to you?" she asked, settling her cheek into the nook between his chest and neck. "I thought we had something, once."

"We did, Paimon, you know we did. It's just... you know."

"Yeah, I know," she admitted, tracing the muscles of Lucifer's arm with her fingertip. "You realize, of course, that I'm hurting, too?"

"Of course." He lifted his head so he could look her in the eye. "I would never claim otherwise. She was important to both of us, and I know that. I'm just... broken."

"That you are, Scratch, that you are," she said before breaking eye contact and kissing Lucifer's skin, laying her cheek back onto his chest after showing her affection. "It's alright, though. We're both damaged goods."

"You're **fine**, Paimon. Don't let anybody tell you otherwise."

"Don't even try that shit with me. I know I'm your second choice, you greedy bastard." Paimon was light about it, but Lucifer could feel the pain lurking behind the smile. "I'm practically just a concubine."

"You're more than that, and you know it. If I was a better person, I'd tell you to find someone else."

Paimon laughed and lifted herself up to give him a quick kiss.

"**Who** would understand, Scratch? **Who** would see what I've become and not run for the hills? I'm a volatile woman who saw her sister get eaten alive by the son of the Devil, who—let's be honest—I love, and he doesn't love me back."

"I **do** love you." Lucifer was earnest, but it was a weak protest, and Paimon lifted her head just to look down her nose at him.

"Not the way you love her. Not the way I love you. I'm destined to be discarded, you son of a bitch."

"I..." Lucifer started, but Paimon smiled and gave him a light slap on the cheek.

"It's fine, Scratch. You can't help the way you feel. Believe me, I know," she said, crestfallen. "I know what I've gotten myself into. There's no need for apologies."

"I would if I could, Paimon. Really." Lucifer was being honest, but Paimon understood and continued to draw her fingers up and down his arm.

"*I know. God, what miserable little creatures we are. It's been thousands of years since Mammon tore his way into this world, and we're still pining after our sister.*"

"*She was...*"

"*Something else. No one's going to fight that,*" *Paimon said before pushing herself off of Lucifer's chest and sitting up on the bed. The sheet fell away from her, revealing her perfectly-proportioned body, but Lucifer did not feel lust for this fallen angel.*

However cruel, she really was only a distraction.

"*So you're going?*" *Lucifer asked, already knowing the answer.*

Paimon shook her head before dropping her legs off the side of the bed and standing up, the curves of her body illuminated by candlelight. Then, as Lucifer watched, gold spread out along her skin until it became the demon king's signature dress, complete with golden sleeves up to her elbows.

"*You ask such silly questions sometimes. It's time I make it back to my province. I can't whore myself out to the Devil **and** ignore my duties. That's just irresponsible.*" *Paimon winked at him before sitting back on the bed and looking over Lucifer with affection.*

"*Pretty sure whores get paid, Paimon,*" *Lucifer teased, and she grinned at the easy joke.*

"*Who says I'm **not** getting paid? Til next time, Scratch.*"

She leaned down and kissed Lucifer on the forehead, drawing away before he could pull her into another embrace and try to force himself to love her. Within a moment, Paimon sauntered out of his bedroom and closed the door behind her, leaving Lucifer with his thoughts.

Immediately, guilt and sorrow came creeping back from the edges of his mind, which made him realize he shouldn't be alone. After cinching his usual hip wrap around his waist, Lucifer walked out of his room and wandered through the hallways of his new palace.

It still felt strange—this new home of his built on the ruins of the old —and he didn't belong here. Even after hundreds of millennia in Hell, Lucifer still had no sense of being home, and he was a stranger ruling over a foreign land. Most of the Fallen felt the exact same about their sanctuary in the darkness, and that was only made worse once the humans arrived.

Although others were apprehensive when human souls started to fall, Lucifer was grateful. The tedium of ruling his brothers and sisters was interrupted by these new creatures, and it proved what Lucifer had known all along. Humanity **was** *worth saving.*

However, he knew there were plenty of Fallen who did not appreciate this new phenomenon. Beleth was one of them, but he was by no means alone.

Fortunately, Lucifer rarely had to deal with the demon king. Since Mammon's birth, Beleth had only showed his face during the Council of Kings, and a council was really all it was. Very little was discussed, and there was rarely a topic that forced them to speak to each other.

Lucifer felt guilty about how he had treated his giant brother and knew Beleth shouldn't be blamed for Lilith, but it was far too late to apologize. Beleth would forever remain hostile, and Lucifer could not resent him for that.

Once he shook his head, trying to rid himself of memories of Mammon's cruel youth, Lucifer realized that he was heading toward the Overlook. That was odd, since Lucifer hated that place. It reminded him of the old days, before the second uprising against his rule, and he avoided it completely unless the Council of Kings forced him down those stairs. Confused by his own subconscious, Lucifer approached the double doors leading to the lava-filled pit. His fingers halted on the handle, when he realized he wasn't alone.

"It's weird, I know. It's like it's calling to you," a snide voice answered his suspicions. Lucifer turned to face Azazel, hooves clacking against the floor of the hallway as he walked, and mustered a smile for the satyr as he leaned against the wall

"There a reason you're down here, Zel?"

"What, I couldn't just come down here for shits and giggles? You know I love my giggles."

"And I know you love your bullshit, too." Lucifer surrendered a

scornful laugh and took his hand back from the door handle. "What's going on behind these doors? Don't even try to pretend."

"Oh, I won't," Azazel replied, his reptilian tail wandering across and around the front of his right leg. "But that's never been the game. The game is always about trying to get you to guess it before I come out with the answer. So, why are we down here, Lucy?"

"Don't know, Zel. Guess we'll just get there when we get there." Lucifer yawned and covered his mouth with his right hand before dropping it back down. "Though I could ruin everything by opening those doors and seeing just what's waiting for me."

"You know better than that. C'mon, we've had millions of years, you and me. Side by side. You're not going to change your tune now." Azazel grinned, lifting his tail so he could scratch the end of his nose.

*"Why **did** you go with the tail and the hooves, Zel? Never took you for one of those animal worshippers," Lucifer asked, going off on one of their usual tangents.*

*"It's just interesting, and don't you dare call me an animal worshipper again. I just understand them, you know? I understand what it's like to be uncomfortable in your own skin, to want to modify your appearance into something that... better represents you?" Azazel explained, scoffing at his own seriousness. "And I mean, c'mon, we **both** know I look good."*

"You'd look better without the blindfold," Lucifer commented, which earned a hearty laugh. Within half a second, three dozen slits opened up along each exposed patch of the grey demon's skin and showed red irises, all of which were frantically looking around in the dim lighting.

*"I **look** well enough, thank you very much," Azazel said, extending his right palm and showing off a larger reptilian iris that focused on Lucifer. "And between you and me, Lucy, you're looking mighty tired."*

"Stop that, it's creepy." Lucifer waved away his antics, and Azazel laughed and closed all of his eyes before leaning back against the wall.

*"**Creepy**? You've lived in Hell for two million years, and you think my **eye thing** is creepy? You have such **ridiculous** standards."*

"I just don't understand why you haven't figured out some way to grow the original eyes back. You have the willpower for it." Lucifer rubbed the

skin of his forehead with his right hand, but when he lowered it, Azazel was looking at the floor.

*"You **say** that, Lucy, but I've never been one for willpower." He sniffed and then lifted his head, grinning even wider after his momentary lapse. "Well, except for when it comes to our little games."*

"They keep us going, don't they?" Lucifer smirked, pushing off the wall so he could slowly advance toward the Overlook. "Though this time you're going to have to give me a clue. I have no idea what's waiting for me down there."

"Could be nothing," Azazel teased, following after Lucifer with a light step. "Or you could have a visitor."

"A visitor, huh? Am I supposed to guess who it is before I open the door?"

Azazel seemed nervous, going so far as to bite his lip, and Lucifer's heart dropped at the rare sight.

"Something like that. So go ahead, Lucy. You'll lose all your points if I have to tell you."

"I have thousands upon thousands of residents, and that's just in Dis. Can't be Paimon, and none of the other Kings would visit me now. We just had a council meeting last year."

Lucifer sighed as he recalled the last gathering. It was becoming more and more obvious that half of his fellow kings wanted nothing to do with him.

"You know what, this is just plain rude to our guest. We're going to forgive your inability to think outside the box. This visitor of yours, well..." Azazel paused as he considered how to phrase it. "He's not from around here."

"Not from..." Lucifer started, looking confused, but then Azazel broke into a smile and pulled the door open for him.

"Gah—I can't take it anymore. Someone's come from..." he said, pointing past the ceiling and nodding. "Wants to see you alone, too, and told me to keep guard, so it's time you get down there."

Lucifer abandoned any sort of friendly pretense and flung himself through the doorway and down the steps to the Overlook, bounding five steps at a time. When he was halfway down, Lucifer noticed shimmering energy hovering out above the lava and—for an instant—he was horrified.

Then he saw the golden curls, the twisted staff, and the look of concern on Gabriel's face.

Without a second thought, Lucifer leapt the last hundred steps and used his wings to glide the rest of the way. After just a few seconds, Lucifer was standing on the red-lit stonework of the Overlook. When he rose to face his brother, one of Adonai's archangels, Lucifer knew he could be dead within moments.

"Before we start, Lucy... How are you?" The image of Gabriel's face warped as the portal's energy swept around him.

"Gabe..." Lucifer muttered, happiness at seeing his brother mixing with the impending doom of Adonai's return. "How..."

"The seal has weakened," Gabriel said, his face stretching to twice its length before resuming its usual shape. "You're safe for now, so don't worry about that. Adonai doesn't even know I can talk to you like this, which is good, because that works in our favor."

"What is going on?"

"You... have to be prepared, Lucy."

"Prepared for what, Gabe? What's happening?"

"Adonai, he's getting bored again. You know how he is. I don't think he has ever had as much... **fun** *as when you rose up against him." Gabriel sighed as he considered his message. "And he wants to play again."*

"Soon, Amon and Räum are going to be spouting a lot of prophetic nonsense, and I need you to know that Adonai **wants** *this. He wants another war. He wants some big, final clash before he ends it all and starts his next universe." Although Gabriel's image had distorted and squished together for a sentence and a half, his words were much harder to follow.*

"Just what are you telling me, Gabe? Why are you warning me like this?"

"Adonai wants to destroy this world and cause an apocalypse. And, if we don't do this just right, we won't be able to stop it."

NICCOLO WOKE up and was more confused than ever. Lucifer had turned to and then away from Paimon in such a short time between visions that Niccolo was now dealing with emotional whiplash. Not only that, but Gabriel, the supposed messenger of Adonai, was much more than he had assumed.

When Paimon stirred in his arms, a familiar pain came to his mind, and Niccolo realized he had been ensnared just like Lucifer. After the confrontation between Phenex and Marchosias, Cimeries and Cadmus had gone off on their own to track Marchosias and Phenex had wandered away, saying he would be back some time in the morning.

So, left alone, it was only natural that Paimon and Niccolo would find themselves lost in passion.

However, when Niccolo had been wrapped in her embrace, he had loved her as Lucifer had loved her, and his emotions had been enhanced by the Devil dwelling within his soul. Now, when he looked at the beautiful woman laying against his chest, Niccolo's emotions were betrayed by that same link. He still cared for her—he was stubbornly trying to hold onto his own sense of self—but it had been poisoned by the memories of another person.

The worst part was that when Paimon opened her vacant eyes, his mind immediately retreated to the blissful nights he had spent with Camilla.

"Hey," Niccolo said, trying to push away the image of his first love, but his initial hesitation was more than enough for Paimon to recognize a truth that was far too familiar.

"Hey yourself," she purred, trying to enjoy what she now knew was temporary affection. Niccolo could tell that she had noticed disappointment that had leaked through, and he knew he had to come clean. Niccolo had to do better than Lucifer, and he wouldn't hurt her the same way.

"So," he started, but Paimon immediately pressed her finger against his lips.

"You don't need to, hon. I'm used to it. I'm betting you know *that* all too well..." she said before letting her finger fall away and settling her cheek against Niccolo's scarred chest. The Horseman stammered at first, but then lifted her chin with his right hand.

"Look, I meant what I said yesterday. I really did."

"I know, sweetie. You had early Lucifer running through your veins and I fell right into that trap." Even as she was wrapped around him, Niccolo's head filled with thoughts of Lilith and Camilla.

"I... it wasn't meant to be a trap. I'm so sorry." He looked away to avoid her attention, but this time Paimon dragged his head back to face her.

"Don't be. It's my destiny, Nico," she said before dropping her head back down and tracing her nails along Niccolo's arm. "I fall for unavailable men."

"I'm—look, we can just forget this happened, there's so much going on anyway," he said, but Paimon scoffed and propped herself up on her elbows.

"Forget it happened? What, was I *that* bad?"

"N—no! I just... I don't want to take advantage of you," he tried to explain, but that made Paimon fall back, laughing so hard that she cried. At first, Niccolo was completely stunned, but then he glowered at her. "*Was it something I said?*"

"It's... it's..." After a few moments, Paimon was finally able to breathe and slid away, shaking her head at his naïveté. "God, Nico, I haven't laughed that hard in years. You're just as screwed up as me."

"I don't think it's *that* funny." Niccolo huffed, but then he felt gentle fingers caress his jaw. When he turned back, she was offering him a warm smile.

"What we were doing wasn't *love*, Niccolo, and I know that. Or, at least, it's just a temporary thing. We used each other to feel..." she paused as she tried to find the right explanation, "to feel more than just the pain we keep with us every day. You and I, we love other people, and that's fine. Especially since they're, well... *dead.*"

"Paimon."

"It's alright, Nico. Really. We were weak—this Lucifer thing fucked with both of us—but that's no reason to call it quits this early," she said, wearing a mischievous smile. "Nothing wrong with indulging in a little lust."

"You want to...?" Niccolo asked, and Paimon shrugged before turning to the side.

"Eh, why not? I agree, we should probably wait 'til we finish some of this *other* business, but it's just sex. Though, I wouldn't be so against a round two." She looked at him out of the corner of her eye before scratching the back of his hand with an extended nail.

"You're unbelievable," Niccolo murmured in awe, and Paimon pushed her arms together to torture him while she tilted her head to the side.

"Don't you forget it. But for now, let's throw our clothes on and stop being miscreants," she said as gold leaked out of her pores, just like in Lucifer's memories. Even if he didn't love her as he had the day before—even if visions of Camilla's face tore at him—Niccolo felt something for this woman, who wasn't even a woman. He felt incredibly guilty and fortunate at the same time.

Then Paimon doubled over in pain and started shaking, her body half covered in gold as she fought to keep herself standing.

"Paimon! What's wrong?" Niccolo rushed up to meet her, and she fell into him before he could get his feet, causing both of them to crash back to the ground. Surprised by the sudden turn, it took Niccolo a moment to realize that Paimon's teeth and nails had extended, and the blades of her fingers tore into his skin before he could think to move.

"Nico, g—get away," she urged, but some part of Niccolo knew she needed him more than she wanted to admit.

Instead of crawling away, he pinned her arms to her sides and held her close, ignoring the wounds that came from her frantic seizure.

"What... Nico, stop!"

"No, I'm not going to." Niccolo felt her teeth sink into the meat near his left collar bone, but he was determined to stand his ground. "I'm not going to let you hurt yourself, whatever this is."

"Stupi—human..." Paimon gasped, her every feature distorted as her demonic features forced their way to the surface. Her eyes bugged out and her teeth gnashed, covered in her lover's blood. "This..."

"Will pass," Niccolo declared as he stared into her eyes. As soon as he was able to make eye contact, Paimon calmed down considerably, the spasms of her body decreasing in strength to the point where she was able to stop herself from injuring the human restricting her arms.

Soon, the spasms stopped, but Paimon could not stop shaking. Holding her closer, Niccolo lowered his head and rested his chin against her shoulder.

"Nico..." she whined. "What just happened?"

"You're kidding, right?" he asked, drawing back enough so the still-terrifying demon could see him smiling. "I'm not even three hundred years old. I'm *basically* just an infant."

It was enough for a smile to break through her twisted, golden features, and it brought her back from the edge. Soon, the gold retreated, her teeth drew back beneath her lips, and the knives turned back to fingernails. When the transformation was over, Paimon appeared the same as always, except for being covered in Niccolo's blood.

"I'm scared, Nico. I have... ever since that first chimera. I have no idea what that was." Paimon was still trembling, but she was comforted by Niccolo's embrace. As he rubbed his hand along her slender arm, Niccolo knew what he had to do.

"Me neither, but don't try to push me away again. Even if I don't love you the way I should—even if that's just something further down the line—you need to know that I care for you. You need to know that I'm not going to let you be alone if something like that happens again."

Paimon started crying, wiping the blood away from her mouth with the back of her hand. Before he could protest, she wrapped her arms around Niccolo's still healing torso and buried her head into his shoulder.

"...just like him..."

CADMUS WAS DISAPPOINTED, but he had never expected they would succeed in searching for Marchosias. Even with Cimeries' considerable skills at tracking, there had been very little chance they could find the living shadow. He had been at this game too long.

So, after three hours of looking for some sign, they gave up and returned to Niccolo and Paimon. When they did, they found Paimon shivering, which was more than cause for alarm. Out of everyone in their group, she had been the most stable.

"What happened?" Cadmus asked on approach, but he stopped once he saw Niccolo's face. He wasn't angry, but Cadmus felt like another step would be intrusive.

"She's fine, she just—" Niccolo turned to face Paimon, but his tongue failed him. Sweat gathered at her brow and her skin seemed more pale than usual.

"What have you done to her, Horseman?" Cimeries asked, rage building with the accusation, but Paimon put out her hand and shook her head.

"Nothing anyone hasn't done to me before," she said, turning to Niccolo with a weak smile. "I—well, we'll talk about it later."

"Besides," she continued after the aside, "this has been getting worse over time."

"Is it Earth, is that what it is? You're just getting used to the air up here?" Niccolo asked, and Paimon shook her head.

"I don't... think so. Angels don't really have immune systems or anything."

She had thought aloud, and though he barely remembered reading about that concept in the Infernal Library, Cadmus had to agree with her. Once he realized why she might be sick, his stomach turned in sympathy.

"It happened after that first chimera battle, didn't it? When you reaped their souls?"

After a moment of consideration, Paimon closed her eyes and lowered your head.

"You're right, Cadmus. Of course, you're right," she muttered, but the other two were having a harder time following.

"And just what are you right about?" Niccolo crossed his arms, but Cadmus did not react to the hostility. He just sat down on a nearby rock and rubbed his fingers against the handle of his scythe, knowing full well that the others were anxious with anticipation.

"It was the reaping. Tamiel told us that all *humans* could do it," Cadmus implied, hoping the others would finish the thought for him, but he knew it was unlikely

"Yeah, so?" Niccolo asked.

"Paimon is not *human*," Cimeries answered, earning a tired laugh from the demon king.

"You know, I think this is the first time I ever regretted that," Paimon said before lifting her head to look at Niccolo. "One of the few times being an angel hasn't worked out for me."

"Alright, fine, so *why* is this causing problems for her? Can we fix it?" Niccolo asked, turning to his friend as if he knew everything. Unfortunately, Cadmus could only guess.

"Well, I think angels were always *able* to reap souls, but it came at a cost. I don't think they get any more powerful, it just makes them... unstable. And, well, I have a theory about these chimera," Cadmus admitted, looking down and expecting someone to ask, but no one raised their voice.

"Fine," Cadmus said, rubbing his cheek just to delay it further.

"Beleth knows what he's doing. The only way we could kill these creatures was to utilize whatever powers we had to reap their souls. Just cutting them down meant they would merge back together and keep fighting."

"Why is that a problem, Cadmus?" Phenex's voice broke into the conversation, and the other four turned to their new arrival. He was no longer wearing the robes he had brought with him from Hell—they had been burned too much over the last few confrontations—but these new robes were rather similar except for the color. Brown and grey, they were obviously borrowed in some way or another from a local peasant.

"Where have you been?" Niccolo asked, and Phenex shrugged before tossing forward a set of leather armor; simple grieves, bracers and a cuirass.

"I was foraging. I needed a change of clothes, and Cimeries has been without armor since the fort." He stepped around a stone before settling down on his rear. "Now what is this about the chimera?"

"Thank you, Phenex." Cimeries' words were more gracious than her tone, and she walked to the bundle of armor before skeptically looking over the pieces. "And where did you get these?"

"Does it matter? I left money, and considering our needs, I think it is more than fair to take what is necessary for our conflict. Now can we stop discussing something that doesn't matter?"

"The point, Phenex," Cadmus continued, still wary of their volatile friend, "is that while Paimon has similar powers, reaping souls is a more dangerous proposition, and Beleth knows that. For us humans, taking in the powers of these souls means nothing, but they are tainted things, energy spoiled by pain and torture and whatever Beleth decided to put in there."

"You're saying that he made these chimera for me, is that it?" Paimon clasped her hands together to keep them from shaking. "They're poison for the Fallen?"

"That's... my theory. Of course, he made them for all kinds of reasons, I'm sure he was trying to horrify us and force us to make mistakes. Hell, that one before Marchosias... during the roadside battle," Cadmus paused, knowing he needed to redirect his statement once he realized it might set off Phenex, "it tried to merge with me. If I didn't have the ability to slow down time..."

"Speaking of..." Phenex spoke up, "that... power of yours doesn't seem to have a limit. Do you think you'll be able to use that against Beleth and Azazel? A weapon like that would be very useful."

Cadmus had to bite his tongue. If not for Phenex's temper and grudges, they might not *have* to depend on Cadmus' newfound abilities. A demon made of shadows would have been very helpful in the coming battle, and the consequences of losing Marchosias felt like a storm cloud of possibilities.

"Possibly, but I wouldn't depend on these abilities," Cadmus finally replied. "Remember, when that last chimera was about to kill me in the fort, I couldn't react."

"Luckily, I was there to help," Phenex said. While he looked pleased with himself, his companions stared at him with disgust and annoyance. Eventually, he noticed their reaction and the smile ran from his face. "So what is the plan now? Beleth is beyond the Rubicon, correct? How far are we from the river?"

"We will not make it before nightfall." Cimeries was already dressed in the armor Phenex had provided for her, her discarded robes laying to the side. "I suggest we ride until we are within a few miles of the river and make camp. We have no idea where Beleth and Azazel set their traps, and it would be unwise to venture further without daylight."

"We should wait until Paimon is able to ride," Niccolo suggested, but she stood up and slapped her hand against his blighted shoulder.

"Which is right now. Summon Plague and Mercy and we'll get going." She stumbled despite her words, which made Niccolo rush forward to catch her, but Paimon put out her hand. "Don't. I'm fine."

"You heard what Cadmus said."

"It's a theory, hon, and besides," she said, stretching her arms above her before bringing them down and winking at the Horseman, "I'll just leave the monsters to you."

"It's too—" Niccolo started, but Cimeries grunted and earned his attention.

"Do not argue with her. Paimon has made her decision. After millions of years, the Fallen *King* can judge her own capability."

Niccolo stared at Paimon for a long moment, but then realized Cimeries was correct. Out of every woman Niccolo had ever known, Paimon didn't need anyone to pamper her. Giving up, he summoned Plague, and the dark horse solidified from a green cloud at the edge of the woods.

"If you think you can fight, then I won't keep you here," Niccolo relented, and Paimon walked past him, running an extended claw along his jaw as she went.

"Sweetie, you couldn't stop me."

PHENEX SAT at the edge of the camp, having felt the obvious tension and deciding that it would be better to avoid them for the time being. The entire day had been taken up by empty air and silence; his companions had no patience for him or his mistakes. Even though they should have trusted him—Phenex had known Marchosias far longer—it seemed they did not acknowledge that the betrayer had fallen back into his old ways.

With a grunt, Phenex looked over the group laying just a few yards away. Niccolo was asleep, Paimon wrapped around him, and even Cadmus had let himself drift off. At first, Phenex was pleased— Cadmus pushed himself too hard—but then jealousy reared its head. With their final battle against Azazel and Beleth just beyond his reach, Phenex was anxious and unable to close his eyes for more than a few seconds.

Turning away from his companions, Phenex picked himself up and wandered into the woods. He wondered if he would meet

Cimeries out there—she had been on patrol for a number of hours—and what she might do if they were all alone. Even she had blamed him for the incident with Marchosias, which surprised him. From what he knew, Cimeries had more than enough experience with betrayal.

Phenex took step after weary step as he wandered in the dark. The moonlight could not break through the clouds or the treetops above him, but Phenex hadn't needed a source of light for more than a thousand years. Letting his eyes flare, Phenex continued along the branches and gnarled roots of the trees, his mind wandering just as much as his feet.

Doubt crept in. Maybe he had been too hasty to confront Marchosias about his supposed betrayal. Phenex supposed that he had very little proof—it was only from his constant bickering and complaining that Marchosias might seem to be on another side—but they had too much history. It didn't seem like all that long ago that his good friend Judas had been among the crowd, looking down in shame as Yeshua was marched off to a painful death.

At the memory, Phenex's eyes flared brighter and his footprints smoldered. They *should* trust him after all this time; Phenex had been more than capable, more than just another part of their group. Without him, they would have never made it out of Beleth's fort alive. And Phenex, the kind messiah that he was, never had any sort of reputation for selling out his friends. Marchosias, on the other hand, had been demonized for thirteen hundred years.

At *that* recollection, Phenex set his hand against a nearby tree trunk and the fire went out of his eyes. Even through all of the shame of being responsible for Phenex's downfall, even as he buried himself beneath the skin of a wolf just so he could hide away, Marchosias had been by his side. Out of all the friends and acolytes Phenex had in life, Marchosias was the only one who had ever sought out his forgiveness and friendship.

Breathing deep and looking ahead, Phenex realized there was a small pool set in a clearing in front of him. Upon sight of the water, he realized he was very thirsty and stumbled forward. Once he made it to the pool's edge, Phenex knelt down and scooped up water with both of his hands, lowering his mouth so he could drink. Noticing that it was not nearly enough and feeling no need for dignity while alone, Phenex lowered his head to the water and started to gulp down water with zeal.

"If I did not know better, I would think you're a boar come to his watering hole."

Cimeries' voice had come from his left side, and Phenex picked himself up quickly and turned to face her. The warrior woman was leaning against the lowest branch of a great tree and looking at him with disdain, her pike held in the crook of her arm.

"I guess I must have looked gluttonous the way I was drinking," he admitted, trying to smile at his own remark, but one look at her made him realize his mistake.

"No, you looked like prey. *Soft*," she said, looking into the gaps of the tree line to her right. With a soft grunt, Phenex sat back on his rear and crossed his legs in front of him.

"That's not a very nice thing to say, Cimeries."

"I am not a nice person, Yeshua."

At the sound of his real name, Phenex narrowed his eyes to slits.

"I would much prefer you call me Phenex."

"I will call you what I will, *messiah*. Tell me—even if it doesn't matter—why do you persist in keeping up this charade? What have you to gain from trying to seem wiser and better than you really are?" She cut straight through to his bones, and though Phenex took him a moment to react, his temper soon flared.

"Why would you say such a thing? Is this about Marchosias?"

"It was never about poor Judas, you petulant creature, and you should know that by now. This was always about you. You, the poor little victim in that petty drama," Cimeries said before spitting at her feet and pushing off her tree branch. As she approached, Phenex realized he was more afraid than angry. "That man betrayed you for one reason and one reason only. He wanted to save his people. *Your* people."

"He—"

"Did what he thought was right. Just because you have a religion founded on your mistakes does not mean you were legitimate." She snarled, placing the end of her weapon into the dirt and looking down on her companion. "Just because his name became a curse does not mean he was *wrong*."

"He betrayed me once, Hippolyta." Phenex clambered to his feet as he resorted to using her true name. "He would betray us again."

"If this is how you acted during your revolution, Judas was more than justified. He was forced into a corner; he gave up a brother to save what family he could. When his companions are in danger—the very people you say he would betray—what makes you think he would not defend them?"

"Judas—"

"Made a *mistake*," she declared, slamming the end of her pike against the earth to emphasize her point. "Thirteen hundred *years* ago. And from what I have seen, he has spent *every* day trying to make up for that folly. That man is your friend, he is your brother. He is the only family you have left, and *you* have left him to rot."

"Judas..." Phenex muttered, trying to summon strength he did not have. "He let me die."

"Yeshua, *I* know betrayal," Cimeries stated, her words harder than stone. It was enough for Phenex to look her in the eye and give in. "You were given up for something worthwhile. I... my *sisters* threw me to a rabid dog."

"Cimeries..."

"Do *not* interrupt me," she snapped, glaring at him with a domineering fury that could only come from a queen. After Phenex shook his head, she continued.

"When my people first encountered the scoundrel Theseus, we showed them just what the Amazons could do. His forces could not hope to match our individual strength. However, his armies were three times the numbers of my warrior sisters, and one could only expect what happened next. My people surrendered my life and the lives of my personal guard, for some sort of... leniency that Theseus did not provide. When his ships sailed from our home, they left cowards and betrayers, sisters I had trusted with my life and my kingdom. Half of my people were taken as slaves.

"They... they had been so quick to give me to him," she recounted, her voice faltering for the first time in Phenex's memory. "They gave me to that pig of a man who did not deserve to lay with any woman, much less any of the Amazon race. I could not resist; I was bound. Night after night, that... *king* took me as his own. His first act was to remove all of my teeth, cut my tendons and break my bones, so that he would not be harmed."

"I—"

"Shut up, you coward!" she screamed, thrusting her pike forward so the point was just an inch from his throat. The blade just barely wavered in her hand, and after a few frantic seconds, Cimeries pulled back and let out a strained breath. "I will let you speak when my story is over.

"That bastard did not deign to keep me more than a month before boredom claimed him," she said, pausing for another breath to recover. "I am sure that planting his seed into a toothless, crippled woman was less than satisfying. Above all, I told myself that *I* would not break. I would never give him the satisfaction of seeing my pain or my surrender. After that month, he threw me away for some pretty, mindless girl.

"A few months in that cage was enough that I was able to whittle a stick sharp enough to cut through flesh," Cimeries said as she looked Phenex in the eye. "Not for myself; I could die at any time. I wanted vengeance. The next time he came for me in some drunken stupor, I attacked."

"You killed him?"

"I was too weak. I barely scratched his neck. However, Theseus realized I would never bow to his wishes, that I would never give up.

He ran me through with a sword and ended my life. When I arrived in Hell, it was almost... satisfying."

Cimeries looked down at her companion, waiting for Phenex to respond. It took him a moment to fully absorb her story, to fully understand why she was telling him all of this. He had never thought anyone capable of such horrific behavior, and he had certainly never thought anyone would be able to survive with their willpower intact.

"So you do understand betrayal," he muttered, unable to think of any proper response. However, Cimeries decided to humor him.

"I do. I know what it is like for your people to sell you out, to be thrown to a monster just because they want to survive. I am telling you this because you should know that it could have been so much worse," Cimeries explained as she stepped forward, grabbing Phenex by the jaw and forcing him to look up at her. "I am telling you this because I understand that need for vengeance."

"You do," he agreed, but then he saw disgust flit across her eyes.

"And I am telling you that the man who deserves your vengeance was not and *is not* Judas. That man has been your friend a thousand times over. He has been your companion and your brother and has done everything he could to atone for his mistake. I *know* what it was like when the two of you arrived in Hell. I *know* what he did for you."

"He..."

"And you threw him *away*. *That* is why you feel ostracized and that is why we blame you for his absence. He was a competent warrior and a friend. When you realize that—when you realize *your* mistake—*maybe* we will start to trust you again."

"For now, Yeshua," she said before releasing him, "we will trust that you will not betray us. Just make sure you do not provide me a reason to stab you through the heart."

With that last threat, Cimeries turned away from Phenex and walked back into the woods, her shape disappearing into the darkness after a few minutes.

Phenex was shocked as he looked down at the earth. Her story was full of pain and misery, but he did not know why that made his claims any less legitimate. Judas betrayed him in life; Phenex did not understand why that would be such a hard thing to understand.

However, when Phenex turned and looked back into the pool, he saw his own reflection wavering on the surface. As his image distorted, Phenex could see how demonic he really was, that he was not without fault. He had felt so alone when he had first fallen to Hell, but Marchosias had made all those years bearable. Without him, Phenex could not have remained the kind soul he used to be.

In the moonlight, staring at his own distorted reflection, Phenex realized he had intentionally destroyed a friendship that had sustained him for thirteen hundred years.

"It looks so... normal," Niccolo thought aloud as they gathered at the edge of the Rubicon. Even Phenex had descended so that he was only a few feet above the ground, flames licking at his feet, but otherwise appearing normal.

"If you think about it, it's just a river," Cadmus added. "No matter how famous it is."

"It is famous only to those of you who lived after Caesar. Before, it was only water. Let us not gawk for long," Cimeries said, obviously disappointed that her companions would hold such a thing in reverence.

"It's a symbol, that's all," Phenex commented, floating down to stand on the muddy bank, which was red from iron deposits and perhaps something more insidious. Warily, he stepped forward until his toe was just this side of the water's edge. "When Caesar crossed this river, he declared war on Pompey and started a bloody conflict that forged an empire. When *we* cross this river, we will finish this war against Beleth and Azazel and... who knows?"

"Will *we* finish it, or will *they*?" Cadmus asked under his breath, only Mercy and Cimeries able to hear him. Thankfully, Cimeries let it go without comment.

"While Phenex can merely fly to the other side, should we find a bridge or risk fording the river?" Cimeries asked, earning a laugh from Paimon.

"This shallow little thing? I'm sure Plague and Mercy will have no problem getting across. We just need to dig deep and prepare for whatever Beleth is going to throw at us." Paimon was doing everything she could to deceive her companions, but Niccolo felt her arms twitch outside of her volition.

"I... I feel like we're as ready as we're ever going to be. You think you can make it through?" Niccolo asked Plague, who huffed and looked back at his rider.

"What you don't know constantly surprises me, little man," Plague said before looking at Mercy and nodding. Before any of them could react, the Horses of the Apocalypse broke into a gallop directly toward the river, causing Niccolo to raise his diseased arm to ward off the incoming splash of water.

However, the splash of water did not come. Instead of sinking below the surface, both Plague's and Mercy's hooves met the surface of the water as if it was shifting earth, and seconds after Niccolo lowered his arm, they were already on the other side of the Rubicon.

Instead of continuing their pace, Mercy and Plague walked over to the dirt road, Plague shaking his mane and looking back at his master. Niccolo could feel the smug satisfaction radiating from his longtime friend.

"I guess the die is cast after all," Cadmus muttered, turning back to watch Phenex join them. He had been left behind after the horses had made their way across the Rubicon, but now he was flying toward them at great speed, the flames around him more intense.

As he watched Phenex, Cadmus was swarmed by visions of their upcoming battle, a migraine tearing through him and causing him to bite through the skin of his cheek. Though he could taste metal, Cadmus was far more concerned with those flashes of the future, hellfire covering every inch of the world around him. Almost worse than it all was that scream, the terrible sound permeating through his skin and mind, his very existence.

And he knew exactly whose voice it was.

"Why did you stop? I could have caught up with you," Phenex said, the flames fanning away from him once he drifted closer. Cadmus was doing everything he could to hide what had just happened, though he knew for certain that Mercy and Cimeries had felt it. For a moment, Cadmus considered explaining what he had seen, but then Mercy's rasp broke into his mind.

That cannot change, whatever it is. They do not need to know everything. Though he would have liked to reply, Cadmus did not have the time to focus on anything but the present.

"There's nothing stopping us, I guess. Are you all ready to keep going?" Cadmus asked, but internally he whispered back to Mercy. *This is exactly what Niccolo was talking about. This is incredible, this is something they need to know about.*

No. They do not. Remember what Amon said back in Hell. If you can place yourself within the vision, you can change the outcome. You are not in the vision. Plague turned a blank eye toward his rider. *You cannot change this future.*

"Let's kill those bastards," Niccolo declared, slapping the reins against Plague's neck, who would have protested if battle was not so near. The black horse reared back, neighing as green fog burst out its eyes and nostrils and blight spread all along its black coat. Then it landed and ran off, leaving Mercy and Phenex to catch up with them.

*If I **tell** them, maybe I can stop it,* Cadmus argued, but the white horse looked away and started down the road, building up speed before reaching a gallop.

That is my point. You tried to stop Lucifer's death, but it happened all the same. If you spoke about this vision—which may not even result in catastrophe—it will not divert the future.

*You can't know that. If so, what is the point of all these visions? What is the point of seeing this death and danger if I can't stop it? Why do you feel like **you** know what I should do?*

Maybe you have forgotten, Pale Rider, but I never will. Whatever I think, whatever parts of my soul which are unique... they all come from you. I would not think this way if, subconsciously, you did not already know my statement to be true.

The weight of Mercy's argument broke through Cadmus' desperation. There was nothing to say to this creature entwined with his soul, and Cadmus would just have to trust him. As the road opened up at the entrance of a valley, the trees all cut away and their mangled roots lying exposed, Cadmus knew that he would have to rely on that trust.

Starting a hundred yards from them and extending for at least a mile, hundreds of chimera and beasts of Hell roamed the Earth.

"How the *fuck* did Beleth hide all of this from Tamiel?" Niccolo asked, and they stopped in their tracks, watching the swarming masses of tortured souls moaning in pain.

Between colonies of flesh, Niccolo could make out Claws and Hellhounds, demonic cousins of crabs and wolves which were often used tamed for the Pits, and they were just a small fraction of the demonic denizens teeming about Beleth's trap. There were two notable monstrosities that Niccolo had never seen before, and he hoped their size betrayed some other weakness, because otherwise they would have their hands full.

"He must have his own portal, that's the only way." Paimon tried to justify her brother's strength, but there really was no point in it. Leaping from Mercy's back without a second thought, Cimeries landed gracefully and stood to her full height. Raising the head of her pike and pointing at the living corpses, Cimeries faced her companions with a grim, emotionless scowl.

"What matters is not our enemy, but our resolve. We will enter this battlefield. We will find our enemies and we will cut them down. It has been my pleasure to fight beside all of you, and I do not expect you to turn craven now. Today we will spill traitor's blood," she declared, her regal nature evident.

"And you're going to fight them on the ground? Why not stay

with Cadmus and fight from horseback?" Phenex asked as the flames grew around him. Cimeries offered only the slightest smile before turning back to their enemy.

"Because I want to find and kill Beleth before any of you have the chance to deprive me my vengeance," she said before breaking into a light jog toward the nearest chimera. Her companions only watched at first, so surprised by the woman's audacity, but then they saw her spring into action.

Before this moment they had all pitied and underestimated her, at least subconsciously, but as she broke into a full sprint toward a fifteen-foot-tall chimera, they finally remembered why she had been a Hell Knight.

The tortured husk of at least a dozen souls swung three mutilated and distended arms at its tiny opponent, but Cimeries evaded the attacks easily, snaking her way between the deadly bones breaking through the skin and even running along a limb that had crashed into the ground. When the creature lifted up the arm, made of twin torsos and legs, Cimeries used the momentum to spring high before twisting her body and aligning it with the length of her pike.

A flash of pale blue light enveloped the woman before she crashed down and through the chimera, sending a shockwave of energy, blood and necrotic flesh at her advancing companions. It was enough cause for the horses to rear back, riders shielding their faces, but when they landed and could see what had happened, there was only a smiling, gore-splattered woman in piecemeal leather armor.

"First blood is mine. Should we keep score?"

Then Cimeries turned around and ran between two oncoming chimera, who slammed into each other instead of crushing the lithe warrior. Although they still heard Cimeries beyond the wall of flesh, they had lost sight of her.

That was enough to force Niccolo to smile, no matter what misery and pain surrounded them, and he almost wished that they could spend time on something as trivial as a competition. He turned to Cadmus and scoffed before shaking his head.

"We can't let her win, can we?" he asked, the joke almost going over the reaper's head, but then Niccolo hardened his gaze. "Anyway, these are distractions. We need to find Beleth and Azazel. I don't want to split up..."

"But we need to cover as much ground as we can," Cadmus finished the thought, nodding along. "Apparently Cim can handle herself, but since we have four, we should pair up."

"Just what I was thinking," Niccolo said before laying a hand on the golden arm around his waist, grinning as he considered his next verbal jab. "Phenex, don't wander too far from him. Cadmus is a special boy and needs to be supervised."

"Paimon, be sure to console Niccolo when Cimeries obliterates his score," Cadmus said with a small turn to his lips, making eye contact with his fellow Horseman. Although a sigh came from Phenex, Paimon seemed to appreciate the light humor.

"Let's get this over with," Phenex said, obviously upset at something, but Cadmus was grateful that he could keep an eye on Phenex. No matter what Mercy said, he felt like he could mitigate his damage.

Without another word, the Horsemen spurred their mounts and leapt into the fray, tearing through their enemies with purpose.

Niccolo's diseased fingers tore through the gaping mouth of a little boy that had seemingly melted into the fat belly of an old man, and in other times he may have felt guilty about it. However, once screams filled his ears and his bastard sword became wedged into the ribcage of a poor woman—literally attached at the hip to some mutated hunchback—Niccolo didn't have time to worry about empathy. Pushing down with his claws, Niccolo cut through the child's jaw before bringing his more powerful hand to the handle of his weapon. The added strength of his demonic arm was more than enough to overcome the resistance from the ribcage.

A bright stream of green energy radiated from his weapon as it was freed from its prison, and Niccolo directed the blade in and through the young boy's tortured mouth, silencing his screams forever. Niccolo was about to breathe in relief, but then a hellhound crawled over the sagging chimera and latched onto his right shoulder, its weight driving him from Plague's saddle and forcing him to the bloody soil underneath.

"Nico!" Paimon shouted, and instantly Niccolo was forced to think clearly. Even though a demonic wolf was clamped onto his shoulder and trying to dislocate it from the joint, he would not allow Paimon to defend him.

Reaching over with his left hand, Niccolo forced the points of his claws into the Hellhound's throat and squeezed hard, cutting into the flesh all around its spine. Just as quickly as it had become a threat, the life departed from the creature's burning eyes, and Niccolo was able to pick himself up.

"I'm alright, don't you dare worry about me!"

He waited for a response, but eventually saw the golden demon squaring off against a pair of Claws, their massive pincers clicking and clacking just inches away from her skin. They had decided Paimon would only wound and cripple the chimera and leave the reaping to Niccolo—she would act like a slayer, the role belonging to Crocell back in Hell—but the beasts were all fair game.

With a quick hop, Paimon twisted midair and slammed the talons of her feet into the brain matter of the closest Claw, waiting for the other to slam down its arms where she was standing. As it fell into her trap, she pivoted and threw the claws of her left hand through the great crab's pincer, golden knives slicing through its chitin like brittle bark.

After dismantling its arm, Paimon jumped off the other crab and gutted the creature with her right claws. Niccolo smiled at the deadly, angelic violence, but then he saw a great chimera bearing down on her. A ten-foot log was held between three of its limbs, and Niccolo knew he was too late to help.

"To your right!" he shouted, bringing his sword behind him even as Paimon reacted to his warning.

Quickly, she assessed the incoming threat and dropped down, dragging her nails along the shoulder joint of the hellish crab she had just killed and—as Niccolo heaved his sword toward the terror—Paimon picked up the four-foot-long claw and jumped. The moment felt like minutes to Niccolo, who had already released his blade like a missile, and he watched as Paimon met the chimera head on and slammed the Claw's pincer into her enemy before using it as a platform, jumping over the creature.

It was just in time, as Niccolo's bastard sword carved through the air and then tore open a massive gash in the chimera's torso, sending a wave of rotten blood pouring out of the wound. It wasn't enough—it had not been wreathed in Niccolo's fury—but the Horseman was already swinging around his bow by the time he had let go of his blade. With a quick movement he had rehearsed a thousand times, Niccolo brought his gnarled bow to bear and nocked an arrow against the ethereal string.

Focusing on his rage, Niccolo let go and was pleased to find his arrow bathed in green fire.

The arrow screamed through the air before bursting right through the frame of the chimera, splattering guts and pieces of the Claw's pincer in all directions. Seeing that his work wasn't entirely done—the chimera was made of at least twenty humans—Niccolo created another blade from his demonic hand and smiled as his old sword, the one still buried in the creature, dissolved into acid and created a puddle out of their enemy.

Paimon looked at him in wonder from the other side of the newly-made filth, but then the sickness took hold of her and she doubled over, hacking in place. Out of nothing but concern for her, Niccolo threw his bow back over his shoulder and ran to meet her, but he should have paid better attention to his surroundings. Before he was just a few yards away, something slammed into him from the side and lifted him high in the air.

Gasping in pain, Niccolo looked down to find something unlike anything he had seen in Hell. He was used to all manners of beasts from the different continents, even creatures that had never existed in his time period, but this thing was something entirely different. The closest thing he could compare it to was a rhino, but it was covered in tentacles and spines and all manners of marine life parasitically attached to its hide.

More importantly, six inches of the creature's great horn had made its way into Niccolo's side, twin tusks also keeping his arms pinned to his chest and back.

Niccolo would have liked that to have been the only problem, but it was carrying him to another part of the battlefield and away from Paimon and Plague. Panicking, Niccolo pawed at the horn buried in his torso, but after his efforts made him sink down another two inches on the creature's horn, he realized his flailing was not helping. Gathering his remaining strength, Niccolo set his heels against the monster's skull and pushed with all his might, which was enough to force himself off the horn and into the air.

Niccolo was relieved and considered his options as he was airborne, but then two of the purple tentacles wrapped around him and slammed him down on the ground, dragging him along as the creature ran through the battlefield. It was almost enough to make Niccolo pass out, but he was brought back to consciousness by the pain of an errant rock slamming into his shoulder.

Now that his arm wasn't pinned to his chest, Niccolo threw out his diseased hand and cut through the closest slimy tentacle, and he was rewarded by a deep, painful bleating. The other tentacle released its grip and Niccolo crashed to the ground, the purple flesh still wrapped around him breaking apart as he used up his momentum. After a few painful moments, Niccolo finally came to a stop and was able to look up into the bright, blue sky.

He felt like it should be cloudy and stormy, but it was beautiful and fit for a nice picnic.

Feeling forty different kinds of pain, Niccolo rolled over and prepared himself for the coming violence. There was no way this creature would give up, so Niccolo prepared for the worse and took inventory of his wounds. Luckily, only five major bones were broken —nothing that needed to be set—and the damage done by the beast's horn had already healed to the point of looking like it had been caused by a short dagger.

Disoriented by a deafening roar, Niccolo lifted his head and looked for the oncoming threat. After too long, he finally spied the creature bearing down on him. It was already just fifteen yards away, swipes of its tusks flinging errant chimera and hellhounds to the side, other less fortunate creatures getting trampled underneath. Now that he was able to see its full strength, Niccolo realized he might not be able to stop it.

However, that wouldn't stop him from trying. With grim resolve, Niccolo formed another sword in his left hand, his other hand taking hold closest to the hilt once the blade bubbled into existence. Breathing deep as his bones snapped back together, Niccolo wondered just what he could do alone and outmatched.

Fortunately, he was neither. When the creature's tusks were only ten feet away, a green blur slammed into its left side, throwing it off balance and forcing it to career over to Niccolo's left and fall, its momentum dragging it along and sending a wake of earth and blood over Niccolo's feet. In amazement, Niccolo looked away long enough to watch Plague's back hooves drop to the ground, a golden woman sitting on his grey saddle.

He didn't have time to dwell on affection for his friends. A purple tentacle whipped around, determined to ensnare him, but Niccolo was ready. Bringing his blade across his body, he cut through the middle of the creature's limb, the sword splitting the tentacle along the length until the blade finally passed through the other side, sending spurts of dark blood into the air. While he retreated back to Paimon still sitting on Plague's saddle, eyes never leaving their quarry, the monster struggled to its feet.

"Suggestions?" Paimon asked, extending her hand to help

Niccolo to Plague's back, and soon he was in front of her and holding onto the saddle with his legs. Smiling, he mentally sent the plan to his horse, whose internal sigh was so loud it should have been audible.

"Yeah," Niccolo said as Plague turned away and galloped, putting distance between them and the monstrosity. After a furious moment, Plague turned back to face the rhino, who was stamping the mire beneath him, three of its tentacles spewing blood everywhere.

"You going to tell me what they are?" Paimon asked impatiently.

"When we get close, leap when I say so. Drag your claws along its back and this should work out," he said, already spurring Plague into action. At their movement, the monster pushed off the ground and helped close the distance.

"*Should* work out?" Paimon asked in desperation, and for just a moment, Niccolo turned back to grin.

"Just trust me," he said before looking back at the oncoming beast, whose every footfall shook the earth beneath them. It seemed like no time at all before Plague was about to clash with the monster, which was exactly the moment Niccolo was waiting for.

"Now!"

When he shouted, Paimon pushed off of Plague's saddle, her momentum enough to send her soaring just above the monster's head and narrowly avoiding its tusks and horn, and she did what Niccolo had asked for. Eight deep, dark rents were torn into the flesh of the rhino's back, digging into the soft cavities of its twisted anatomy, but Paimon had always been meant as a distraction.

As soon as Paimon was free from Plague's saddle, Niccolo had dismissed the horse into a cloud of corrosive air, the remnants of his acidic body flowing into the monster's nostrils and mouth.

It was the exact same tactic he had used against Valefor down in Hell. However, this time, Niccolo sank through the cloud made by his horse and met the ground, which was exactly what he had intended. Because of the lake of ichor and mud underneath—combined with the shared momentum of both creatures—Niccolo was able to slide along the monster's underbelly and drag his wicked sword through unguarded flesh.

Fortunately, he was going so fast that he was not enveloped in the creature's entrails, but that did nothing to arrest his momentum. Soon, he was out of control and past the creature, wondering just where he would end up, but then he felt something catch hold of his armor and yank him back. When he looked up, he saw Paimon's golden face.

"You are *so* lucky I think you're cute."

CADMUS WAS SICK WITH HIMSELF; half because of the nauseating bloodletting, half because a thousand tormented screams broke through his mind. Torrents of miserable scenes tinged in blue flooded through his perception, but he was doing everything he could to ignore them and focus on the danger at hand. As he threw his scythe deep into the guts of a nearby chimera, he looked above to watch Phenex dive into a crowd of Beleth's twisted creations. From his impact crater, Phenex created a sphere of orange flames, causing the air to dry up around Cadmus.

He wished his prophetic vision was just because of his proximity to the messianic demon, but Cadmus knew he could only be cautiously optimistic. Then a mewling cry went out from his side and Cadmus looked down to see a young child, its upper half fully extended from the rest of the monstrosity's pale flesh, and that made him hesitate. In response, the child opened its mouth and released a song of pain, its jaw opening so wide it snapped the tendon. It made Cadmus see it for what it truly was; just a memory.

Summoning a forced calm and an ethereal shine to his weapon, Cadmus brought his blade across the base of its broken body and continued its deadly arc across two more of the chimera's brethren.

"Don't watch *me*, Cadmus. You have a harvest in front of you," Phenex shouted over Beleth's symphony of torture, which made

Cadmus snap his gaze back to the living inferno. Phenex was mostly covered in flames as he flew over to his partner, smiling as if he still had some good will with the reaper.

Though he resented him still, Cadmus realized that he would need to maintain some degree of camaraderie in order to make it through this battle.

"I don't believe anyone will want to see what spring has brought us," Cadmus said, looking over the battlefield to glean some notion of where Azazel or Beleth may be hiding.

"I dare say you're right," Phenex said, warmth radiating away from him. Then, the temperature decreased enough that Cadmus looked at his ally. "I feel like we need to talk."

"What is there to talk about? You said it was time for harvest, didn't you?"

"I was merely trying to find... some common ground. Cadmus, I'm... sorry," Phenex said softly, his eyes glowing brighter as he sent a spout of fire at an approaching chimera. Its flesh burned away, cremated as it stood, and soon there was nothing but ashes.

"Sorry for... what?" Cadmus asked as he swept his blue-tinged scythe through a crowd of moaning corpses.

"My behavior recently. Not only with Marchosias, but for accusations I threw your way, as well." As Phenex absorbed another chimera's soul, Cadmus found it difficult to focus on the danger surrounding them.

"Accusations?" Cadmus asked, and Phenex sheepishly looked back at him.

"I—something has happened to me since returning to Earth. Something I cannot entirely explain. There are..." Phenex paused, drifting closer to Cadmus and raising a wall of flame to guard them from enemies, "there are too many feelings and old grudges. I know the Bible has claimed that I have an endless reservoir of forgiveness, but... I am human, even if I have become a demon and am worshipped as God."

"You don't need to..."

"That is precisely why I *do,* Cadmus, and you know that. This was a test of character where I failed. When Judas failed in his first life, a wound was created. Instead of moving on and stitching it shut, I only buried it and let it fester. It colored my perception of you, as a person of betrayal rather than reason and," Phenex said, looking down as tears threatened to fall down his cheek. Instead, they evaporated once they touched his skin. "And I drove away a man I love as a brother.

"I will apologize to him later, but I can apologize to you now. Since, depending on what happens in the next few hours I may not have another chance... I am taking this one. Hopefully you can forgive me."

"Yeshua," Cadmus muttered, and all the respect he held for his messiah came rushing back. No longer did he resent the man; he only worried for his safety and for the prophetic flames soon to come.

"I am sorry that I claimed you held back, Cadmus, that you kept secrets which would harm us eventually. I never should have spoken the words, nor poisoned my mind with those thoughts. With this, I hope you can fight by my side," Phenex proposed, smiling as he turned back to face their enemies held at bay by his flames.

Cadmus felt terrible—especially since Phenex's claims had been more correct than he had known—but he also knew what Mercy was going to say before he even started.

If at all, later. No good can come of the truth now, Mercy rasped, and Cadmus agreed with him. There was no point in letting Phenex know what the future held, especially now that he seemed to be recovering from whatever madness had taken hold of him. Cadmus only nodded when Phenex let down his wall of flames, four chimera there to greet them.

"All is forgiven," Cadmus said before throwing his scythe through the air, a typhoon of energy following it as it crashed through Beleth's horrors. As Phenex set a pair of creatures ablaze, Cadmus tried to summon his blade to him. Instead, it sank into the mud behind the now-deceased chimera and stayed there, swaying back and forth as it dispersed its remaining energy.

Cursing, Cadmus saw a towering horror rushing up to him, at least five bodies making up each of its seven legs—its arm poised to slam down from the left—and realized he would be in much more trouble had he been anybody else. However, unlike the trick with his scythe, Cadmus had much more control over his other talent. Urging Mercy forward, Cadmus focused on the here and now, refusing to concern himself with the gaping mouths of each face that peppered the chimera's flesh.

It was almost too easy; when they were a few strides from their starting position, Mercy and Cadmus saw the entire battlefield slow down to a crawl. Cadmus could even see botflies and gnats suspended in the air as Mercy galloped past the stationary golem made of rotting flesh, every sound deep in comparison to their real pitch. Before he could really consider just why their screams sounded so different when time was slowed down, Mercy had already carried him to his weapon.

When he touched the handle of his scythe, time jerked back to its usual flow, but Cadmus was not worried. Mercy calmly turned toward the chimera, which had lost him after its massive arm slammed against the mud. Once it recognized that Cadmus had somehow moved behind it, the chimera turned and scrambled toward him on broken limbs. However, now that Cadmus was armed, he felt no need for terror or any emotion at all. He merely held his weapon in both hands and rose it above his shoulder, feeling connected to something much deeper than he understood.

With a determined exertion of willpower, Cadmus brought down his weapon and a vertical distortion divided the air in front of him, a wake of destruction and wind flying about the tear in reality. At first, Cadmus did not really know what had happened—other than the fact that he felt incredibly exhausted—but a thin red line wept along the entirety of the chimera's massive frame. Then, almost anti-climactically, all of the eyes of the dead souls went glassy and the whole creature stopped moving. Then, from that red line in the center, the creature split in half, its right half being propped up by the sliding flesh of its left side.

"Cadmus, I have to admit. I have a little crush!" a very familiar voice called out behind him, and it took all of the reaper's efforts to turn around.

Comfortable in a bloody clearing, as if nothing was wrong, Azazel stood beside Beleth, who was mounted on his mutilated white horse. They seemed so small and unimportant compared to the heaps of mutilated bodies and dying beasts from Hell, but Cadmus knew he was facing two of the deadliest beings to ever exist in this universe.

"*You...*" Phenex's voice came from his periphery, but Cadmus stared at Azazel, who wore his usual grin. After licking purple lips to draw out the confrontation, Azazel broke into slow applause.

"Yes, yes, Yeshua, it's me. After all this time. But seriously, Cadmus, that was... except for Nico's little burst of light down in the Overlook, I don't think I've seen a human do anything *close* to something like that. I gotta admit, I'd probably kiss on the first date."

"Azazel..." Cadmus was too weak to think up anything clever, but Lucifer's murderer could entertain himself.

"Now, I'm no slut! I'd have to get a ring on one of these fingers before I give you what's under my skirt."

"*Azazel!*" Another voice entered the conversation, and Cadmus turned to see Niccolo fifty yards to his left, Paimon sitting behind him on Plague's saddle.

"Hey! The gang's all here!" Azazel shouted, clapping his hands together and hopping in excitement. "Well, *most*, but they should be here shortly."

"They?" Paimon shouted, her teeth descending into deadly fangs already, but Azazel was unimpressed. He just waved off the question.

"Well, yeah, you pissed Adonai off real nice when you cut off Nithael's pretty little arms. I mean, c'mon, Nith spends *way* too much time looking in the mirror. He's gonna whine to Daddy when you burn his arms to cinders," he said before nodding at Phenex. "Nice touch, though."

"You don't have anywhere to run," Niccolo declared. Plague walked steadily toward their prey, but the grey demon mocked surprise and held his hand over his heart.

"Why would I *run?* I haven't seen you in months! I really would like to catch up before we get into all the blood and guts and pain. Seriously, Nico, this world is bleak enough as it is."

"Enough!" Niccolo shouted, drawing his sword and sweeping it across his body. "We will kill you for what you've done! Lucifer will be avenged!"

Azazel raised an eyebrow, or tried to underneath the blindfold, and then scoffed before looking at Beleth.

"They're—they're joking, right?" Azazel resorted to mockery, but Beleth did not pretend amusement.

"He's right, satyr. Enough talk, more pain."

It was enough of an insult that Phenex's eyes heated the surrounding air into crackling.

"*Time to die. Time to suffer,*" he said, the heat from his flames warping his voice, and Azazel turned to him with another grin.

"I agree," he said before extending his arms and sweeping them in front of him. Suddenly, the traitor's shadow poured out of him, its boundaries not limited by his form. In the confusion, none of them could react, but then something rose out of the shadow and Cadmus felt a sharp pain in his skull. After just a moment, he realized the source of all that anguish.

"What have you done, Zel?" Paimon shouted in anger, but she was more nervous than anything.

"Only claimed what you have thrown away," Azazel answered, his grin permeating through his words. Although Cadmus desperately wanted to be wrong, it became more and more apparent what Azazel had in store for them, especially once the new form became more beast than shadow.

A paw broke through first, dark, coarse fur covering every inch of its massive frame, and then a gaping mouth—at least eight feet long—pulled itself out of the shadows, followed by a powerful body packed with dense muscle. When the creature rose to its full height, most of Azazel's audience perceived a fifty-foot-long wolf, shadows racing all along its body and extending into twisted extensions and blades.

Cadmus saw it for what it really was.

"Marchosias..." The name had leaked out of him. In his darkest fantasies, he could never have thought of something this cruel.

"*Mar*—Marchosias?" Phenex asked in a stupor, looking from Cadmus to the massive wolf, then back to the reaper. Then, it finally dawned on him, and he turned back to face the living shadow. His voice continued as a weak complaint. "Judas?"

"Cadmus, you smart son of a *bitch*! Alright, fine, you persistent little devil. I'll let you get to second base, but no heavy petting!" Azazel shouted with glee, blowing a kiss to his current favorite. Before anyone could say another word, the gigantic feral demon let out a roar, shaking them all to their bones.

"How?" Niccolo asked, horrified, and Azazel was more than happy to answer.

"Well, Nico, I'm kinda *known* for turning demons feral. You helped *throw off the shroud*, if you remember. But, if we're going to be honest—and I feel like being honest—" he said before slapping Beleth's knee, "this guy helped me out."

"Beleth? You did all of this?" Paimon asked, memories of a scholarly and fair brother clashing with what he had become. With no hurry, the armored demon turned his head to regard his sister.

"Of course. The lowly little animals worshipped their beasts. I thought it only fitting they become like their petty idols. It was even more of an insult when fallen angels spurned their original forms and became something else. This Judas, who stole Marchosias' name, he is now the wolf he always pretended to be."

"That's how it works? Those who take on animal traits..."

Cadmus mused, his breath finally coming back to him, and the giant apathetically explained the rest.

"It is a relatively easy magic, only an extension of the reality hex they already placed on themselves. Even Azazel was able to learn it without difficulty."

"Wait, if Azazel has animal traits..." Nico started, which was interrupted by a disgusted grunt from Beleth and a giggle from Azazel, who pointed at him with a raised hoof.

"*These old things?* Beleth knows they're just for fun."

"Azazel is useful to me. This is a marriage of convenience," Beleth said before turning his attention on the giant wolf they had summoned.

"*You... for what you've done...*" Phenex growled, the flames around him growing more intense as he continued. "*I'm going to kill you for doing this to my friend.*"

"If you think you can, flea," Beleth replied in a patronizing tone before drawing a five-point seal in the air and setting his hand against the shimmering surface. "But you will have to kill your friend before you have a chance."

When he ended the conversation, Beleth flexed his fingers and the purple sigil shattered apart. By the time the last shard of the seal fell to the ground, another roar tore through the atmosphere, and the very battlefield seemed to resonate with the aftershock.

Marchosias had been unleashed.

CHAPTER 10
HELLFIRE UPON US

Buné scanned over the scroll Räum and Amon had scrawled in their feathered hands, taking time to note each mark and accent. The angelic language was beautiful—even if it reminded them of times long past—and each subtle scratch from their quills could hold worlds of meaning. Therefore, it was prudent to focus and try to analyze multiple meanings and implications from each statement. When he finished reading it for the third time, Buné looked up at Lucifer and sighed.

"Does he expect us to treat this seriously?" he asked, and Lucifer tried to shrug off the absurdity.

"I know. He's lost his mind. I especially like that part about the locusts with faces of men and those cute little crowns."

"It's as if he picked random traits out of a hat and tried to call it originality," Buné said before tossing the scroll onto the table and leaning back in his chair. Five fallen angels, Lucifer's small council, were sitting in his bedchambers, and it had become increasingly apparent they needed the privacy.

"What does he hope to gain? Adonai has already proven his superiority. Is he just rubbing it in?" an intimidating Fallen asked from the other side of the table. The silver-eyed giant had crossed his arms, and every time he shifted his weight, his chair creaked in protest.

Breathing out deep, their robed, grey-haired brother curled his hand over the end of a knobby staff.

"I believe Adonai is just bored, Eligos. It's been two million years since the rebellion and he's been left twiddling his thumbs. Looks like a cry for help, if you ask me," Barbas proposed, gruff as he looked to their overweight brother, who had yet to speak. Ronové continued to sit there even as Barbas waited for a reply, content to keep his thoughts to himself.

"So his boredom means the end of the world, then? Such an egotistical prick," Eligos replied, opening his mouth and making his jaw click loud enough for the others to hear. "Doesn't even care about what that means to anybody else."

"He is a **god**, Eligos. He does not need to care," Ronové finally entered the conversation, looking back to Lucifer and blinking slow. "I'm curious as to why you've called us here. What does it matter what Adonai is scheming?"

"Gabriel spoke to me after we got these prophecies," Lucifer said, shocking even Ronové out of his malaise.

"How?" Barbas asked, voice shaking as he considered the importance. There had been no contact with Heaven or Adonai for thousands upon thousands of years. Moloch had seen to that.

"The seal has weakened, and that has opened a sort of... window," Lucifer explained, hesitating on the comparison. "We still can't travel to the other dimensions—and neither can they—but it has opened a way to communicate with them."

"Get to it, then. What did our dear brother say?" Buné asked, analyzing Lucifer's every expression.

"It was a few days after Räum and Amon went about writing this... revelation. Gabe explained to me what all of this nonsense meant," Lucifer said before leaning back. "Believe me, he seemed as annoyed as we are now."

"That coward..." Eligos muttered, but he was silenced by a quick glare from Lucifer.

"He was always a messenger, never a fighter. Can't blame him for keeping his nose clean," Barbas replied for him, and Lucifer continued after another beat.

"Anyway, the short and sweet version is that Adonai wants us to cooperate and have a second rebellion. Now that Yeshua's following has really started to take root, Adonai is using it to become the god he always wanted to be, and he needs an enemy and a battle to really force it home. One last blaze of glory before he shuts off the lights and creates his new project. He figures with all the human souls popping up everywhere that it will be more entertaining than last time."

"Why the hell does he think we'd cooperate? He forced us into exile!" Eligos shouted, uncrossing his arms and setting calloused hands onto the table. Lucifer could see the wood crack once the great warrior pressed down with his fingers.

"I'm sure he thinks that we want revenge, or to try again," Buné suggested, and Ronové gave a disgusted sigh.

"A fool's errand," he muttered, looking to the armored Fallen with contempt. Instead of balking at his eye contact, Buné shrugged and looked back at the others.

"No one is debating that," Lucifer interrupted. *"Even Gabriel sympathized, but I let him continue, since it's his job and all. The main thing that Adonai wants from us is to create these Horsemen characters. They're supposed to herald this apocalypse of his, and he wants them to come from Hell to really force the point home that we're the bad guys."*

"Insufferable bastard," Eligos huffed. *"Like there's any way I'd help him out with any of his schemes. You told Gabe that we refuse, right?"*

"I told him we'd do it, actually," Lucifer said quickly, lowering his head before the onslaught of protests.

"You can't be fucking serious!" Eligos started them off, and Ronové followed.

"What could we possibly gain?"

"I misheard you, didn't I?" Barbas asked, laughing in desperation, but then their brother asked the real question.

"What's the scheme?" Buné had almost whispered it, but it forced his

brothers into silence, anyway. After lifting his head to look at them, Lucifer turned to make eye contact with each of his four trusted allies.

"You can all say no, but hear me out, first. We've all seen it, brothers,"
Lucifer said, pausing as he looked at these most noble of fallen angels. "The humans have a potential we cannot fully comprehend."

"You and your pet project," Ronové spat out, sneering at their inclusion. "What exactly are you proposing?"

"Adonai has given us an excuse to invest in these young souls, and from what we've seen through Seere and Ajax and all the reapers, they don't seem to have a limit to how much power they gain. When Adonai created us, there was a ceiling to what we could do. These humans... they're —well, maybe they won't stop."

"You want to train them and make them more powerful than us,"
Eligos spoke softly, earning a nod from Lucifer.

"Adonai won't see it coming. If there is one thing we can count on, it's that bastard's arrogance." At the remark, Ronové grunted.

"How do you suggest we create your champion? How do you suggest we fuel this human's development?" he asked, watching Lucifer for any weakness.

"Death," he stated simply, waiting for someone to react.

"What do you mean?" Eligos was the first to speak, but Lucifer was already turning to face Buné, who was glaring at his high king.

"You want to train one of my reapers," Buné concluded, closing his eyes and leaving them closed as his brothers tried to follow along.

"One of his reapers? You think that's a possibility?" Barbas asked, and Lucifer shrugged and finally sat down in one of his chairs

"I feel like that's the best option. We're supposed to create these four Horsemen, and it's pretty obvious that one of them is going to personify death. Out of everyone, I believe Buné's reapers are going to be the best candidates," Lucifer explained, but Eligos waved his hand around before setting it on the table.

"Why not any of my fighters? They're plenty strong. Seere can rip men apart without even trying."

"Because my reapers harvest and absorb the souls of every person they

reap, brother, so they have a head start," Buné explained, opening his eyes so that he could look at his fellow demons. "Lucifer and I have known this for some time, but we kept it a secret."

"You and your secrets," Ronové muttered as he looked to Lucifer, but he quickly recovered. "Well, I see no reason why we should debate this further. It is obvious that Buné's reapers shall be our candidates," he stated before facing his grey-eyed brother. "Do you have any favorites for the position?"

"No, I didn't know I was breeding souls for an apocalypse." Buné leaned back in his chair. "I'll start vetting some candidates over the next few months. But," he said before sitting forward and setting his elbows on the table so he could clasp his hands together, "in order to deceive Adonai, we need to have the other three Horsemen."

"What are you proposing?" Barbas asked.

"The city of Dis is split into four parts, as long as we don't count Lucifer's palace. If I and my reapers are to represent Death, the three of you need to pick your Horsemen," Buné said with a small nod at each of them.

"That's exactly what I was thinking," Lucifer agreed, giving a forced smile to his small council.

"I **know.**" Buné avoided eye contact and let bitterness flavor his words. "Obviously Eligos and his fighting pits are bound to be War. We don't need to delay that judgment. I'm more curious as to who should be Pestilence and Famine. Barbas has been known to dabble in disease, but Ronové... well."

"Well?" Ronové asked, raising an eyebrow. "Say what you need to say, brother."

"I believe I've said all I need to," Buné stated, cold until he turned back to Barbas. "Barbas, if you don't mind, would you treat your quarter as a breeding ground for disease?"

"I... well, it's not like Famine is any better," Barbas muttered as he shook his head. "I just don't know how we're going to choose our Horsemen. Does it even matter who **we** choose, or is Buné's reaper our only concern?"

"We have to make it **look** good, at the very least," Lucifer suggested, bringing his hand to his temple and massaging the skin. "And, who knows, it might be good to have some redundancy."

"I'm sure Ajax wouldn't mind waging war against Adonai eventually," Eligos said, shrugging before letting out a big yawn. "So what now?"

"I think we need to figure out some way to choose the Horsemen," Lucifer said, trying to make eye contact with each of his brothers. "And I have an idea for that."

"An idea from Lucifer, how surprising," Barbas said before sighing and stretching his arms above him. When he brought them back down, he noticed how Lucifer was apprehensive and staring at him. "Oh... it has to do with me."

"Sorry, Barbas. I want to create some sort of process, some bond that will be created naturally for the best candidates for these positions. I want..." Lucifer hesitated before breaking eye contact and pursing his lips. "I want the horses to choose their masters."

"I'm sorry, what?" Eligos replied first, at which point Lucifer raised his head.

"I want to create a soul hybrid between a harvested soul and a horse from Hell—just fragments—and I want them to seek out those who would best exemplify these forces of Adonai's apocalypse. Then, once they have found them, I want them to... resonate and bond with their masters," he explained, finally making eye contact with Barbas by the end.

"You want a lot of things, Scratch. Did you fall down on that shiny skull of yours? What makes you think I can do this?" Barbas asked, shaking his head as he worried the end of his staff. Before responding, Lucifer let out a heavy breath.

"Because I know you helped Beleth with... Mammon. I know you helped create the process where we joined souls together and created a new one. He wouldn't have been able to do it without you."

Lucifer had rushed through the explanation, pain clearly evident in his voice, and Barbas broke upon seeing his brother's. He closed his eyes, and he was still shaking his head as he continued.

"Scratch, this is..."

"Something we need to do and, more importantly, something you **can** *do. I wouldn't ask you to do this if I didn't think it was within the realm of possibilities," Lucifer argued, but Barbas opened tear-rimmed eyes and that shook his resolve.*

"After Mammon... Scratch, I..."

"That wasn't your fault. It wasn't... it wasn't Beleth's, either. Mammon's crimes fall to me," Lucifer said before standing out of his chair. "If we truly want to make Adonai pay for **his** *crimes, I think this is our best chance."*

"Fuck it, why not?" Eligos replied before pushing his chair back from the table and standing up to his full height. "Fighting and dying beats sitting around with our thumbs up our asses."

"As brutish as his argument is, there is no flaw in the logic," Ronové said before joining them and looking down at their brothers. "But I do not believe we should continue unless the five of us agree to do so."

"Seems like my hands have been tied," Buné admitted, but he didn't bother to get out of his chair. "I won't fight it."

"Barbas?" Lucifer asked, waiting for their last brother. After a long moment, Barbas rose out of his chair and leaned heavily on his staff. He tried to speak two or three times, issuing a syllable before giving up, but eventually he made eye contact with Lucifer.

"I'm going to need some time," he said softly, drawing a growl from Eligos.

"You seriously not up for this, old man? What do we have to lose?" he asked, but Barbas tapped his staff against the ground to take back the floor.

*"**Time** to... think about how I'm going to create these bastard souls Lucifer wants. Seems like we're doing this thing either way but... last thing I want to do is promise something I can't give. Already... already done that once," Barbas said before briefly looking at Lucifer and visually relaying a thousand apologies. Then he turned and headed to the door. "Just need some time."*

"Barbas, you son of a bitch, why can't you ever be straight about these kinds of things," Eligos said as he stomped after his brother. Seeing that the

small council had disbanded itself, Ronové nodded at his remaining brethren before following them.

After the door closed behind the squat demon, Lucifer almost breathed a sigh of relief, but then he turned and noticed Buné glaring at him.

"So what **else** did Gabriel say?" he asked, not even courteous enough to blink. With a sigh, Lucifer sat back down for his scolding.

"Why do you think he said anything else?"

"Don't even start with me. I'm already angry enough that you volunteered my reapers for your little deception. That, and I know from that little twitch in your eye that Gabriel talked to you **before** Amon said a word," he said, crossing his arms and gritting his teeth. "So you better start telling me the truth."

"I always intended to."

"Then do it."

"You're vicious, you know that?" Lucifer stalled as he leaned forward and set his elbows against the table. After interlacing his fingers, Lucifer set his forehead against his knuckles and tried not to scream. "Gabriel let me know the truth about Zel."

"About Azazel? What would an archangel have to say?"

"He..." Lucifer tried, but his rage made him shudder. "Even before we fell, Azazel has been working for Adonai."

"How do you know that? How can you even **start** to trust Gabriel?" Buné asked, at which point Lucifer lifted his gaze.

"He used the blood oath in front of me. And..." he said, briefly closing his eyes so he could collect himself. "He told me things that only Azazel and I know. He gave me all the information that Azazel has given Adonai over the years."

"Why would Gabriel know this?" Buné asked, his gaze hard but his confidence wavering. Taking in another painful breath, Lucifer tried to avoid losing his temper.

"Because he was their goddamned medium."

"This is—"

"Phenex!" Lucifer shouted, slamming his hand against the table and cleaving it down the middle and leaving ragged pieces. "Do you remember *our brother? How he turned into that ridiculous bird and how you had to stab him through his heart?"*

"You're saying Azazel had something to do with that?" Buné suggested coolly, almost not reacting to Lucifer's violence, which forced a bitter laugh out of him.

*"**That** was his latent power, apparently. Something Adonai gave to him thousands of years ago, just like your ability to harvest souls and not fall apart. Everything he did for us during the war, everything he's manipulated in Hell, even... even having his eyes burst in front of me... it was all an act. It was..." Lucifer said as he shook his head and felt tears of frustration fall down his cheeks. "It was all an act."*

"We can't know for certain," Buné tried to argue, but he saw that all the fight had gone out of his brother. Lucifer breathed in through his nose as he wiped away the tears from his cheek, but soon he was able to continue.

*"We **will**. From now on, the only information he gets is what we give him. Gabe will let us know what Azazel tells him. Then we'll know for sure. At the very least, we know not to trust him." Lucifer clenched his jaw as he considered his traitorous brother.*

Seeing the determination on Lucifer's face, Buné lowered his gaze and looked at his armored hand.

*"What if **I** am the traitor? How do you know you're not just playing into their hands?" He fully expected his brother to react logically, but then he heard light laughter coming from the other side of the broken table. Lucifer was smiling at him.*

"Buné, if I ever thought you would betray me, I would surrender immediately. I wouldn't have a chance."

"Probably not," Buné said before turning to the window that opened out to the dark expanse of Hell. "I have two men who might make good champions for your plan."

"I'm surprised it's not just one. You've always thought of all the angles."

*"Well, it just comes down to what information I **have**. Currently, my favorite would be a general from Rome, though I don't know if he has the*

drive to take on an illogical war. That sense of duty is absent," Buné explained swiftly, and Lucifer realized his friend already doubted the general's potential.

"And the other?"

"A former gladiator. It's only been a decade since his fall," he said, making Lucifer scoff. "I **know**, but there is a quiet defiance in him, still building in strength, that... it's too early to tell."

"Well, luckily, we have some time, it seems. Especially if Barbas has some trouble with the horses." Lucifer stood and walked over to a pitcher of wine, which had been on a nearby cabinet and safe from his tantrum.

"You expect too much of him, especially with that line about Mammon," Buné scolded his brother, who nodded as he poured two goblets of wine. When he walked back over, he handed one of the silver cups to Lucifer and sat back down, the ruined table still between them.

"I know, but the idea was to have him feel that need for redemption. Manipulative, I know, but otherwise he wouldn't do the work," Lucifer explained, knowing full well that his brother had already guessed his intent. Sighing with disgust, Buné raised his goblet and sneered at his brother.

"Cunning as always. A toast to your second rebellion, Lucifer."

"A toast to its champion," he replied before draining the goblet in one draught. After finishing his own, Buné sighed and closed his eyes.

"May he overcome our sins."

"JUDAS!"

Phenex's scream was enough to jolt Niccolo back to the present, and he was quite grateful for it. Before he could act on instinct, Plague carried him out of the way of the shadows reaching for him, but even then Niccolo had to duck under the dark tentacle. Once he was clear of danger, Niccolo was finally able to see the monstrosity Marchosias had become.

Dozens of shadowy tendrils extended from his massive body,

some of which were tiny and merely searching for purpose, but others were twisted extensions with vicious blades carving through the air. Even then—with all of that power clearly flowing out of him —the terrible wolf was only half-covered in his shadows, most of which obscured his front half. With the exception of his mouth and burning yellow eyes, the demon's face was hidden in darkness.

Just as Marchosias sent twin tendrils rushing toward the Horseman, flames flowed between them and sent the shadows to oblivion. Grateful that Phenex had been looking out for him, Niccolo looked to the sky and saw the shining man pointing down.

"*What are you doing? Go after Azazel! I'll... I'm taking care of Judas,*" he said before bringing back his arm. After collecting a sphere of flames, Phenex threw it down so it would crash into Marchosias' face. As the wolf roared in pain, Phenex flew in front of Marchosias' mouth and around him, a stream of fire flowing in his wake. "*Come on, this way!*"

After Phenex made the massive beast turn, Niccolo realized that he had no time to wonder at the result of Beleth's cruel magic. Looking to his left, Niccolo found Azazel grinning at him, arms crossed as he shook his head, and Beleth was still mounted on his mutilated horse. Just upon seeing Azazel's dark smile, Niccolo's blood boiled. This supposed friend had betrayed Lucifer time and time again, content to be nothing more than Adonai's secret servant.

"You," Niccolo muttered as Plague approached them, his mount reacting instantly to the Horseman's desires. Even Paimon seemed to read his thoughts and dismounted, wary of impending violence.

"Me," Azazel replied with a laugh before pointing at their feral friend. "Do you appreciate our work? It took us *all day* to break his will. Even after you abandoned him..."

"Why? Just why, Zel?" Paimon asked, her arms already shining as gold spread from her fingers and up to her shoulders. "What did Adonai give you to switch sides on us?"

"He never *switched* sides, Paimon. He's always been working for Adonai." Niccolo's voice quaked as he returned to Lucifer's

299

memories. He didn't even need to know what Lucifer and Buné had discovered after that meeting; it was obvious that Gabriel had been honest from the start.

And as Azazel stood in front of them, it was difficult for the Horseman to control his rage.

"Since when were *you* the smart one, Nico?" Azazel asked, marveling at what seemed like intuition. "I don't know what I'd do if *both* Horsemen knew my plans. There wouldn't be any more fun reveals."

"Lucifer's soul." Niccolo swung his leg over the saddle and dropped to the ground, ignoring Plague as he wordlessly argued against him. Mentally ending the argument, Niccolo turned back to the demon who killed his second father. "I inherited his memories. When Gabriel told him about the Apocalypse, he spoiled your plan, too."

"*Really?*" Azazel asked with a twisted smile, more curious than surprised. "That pretty bastard knows how to keep a straight face!"

"*When did you know?*"

Paimon's voice demanded his attention, but Niccolo did not turn. Instead, he formed the handle of his sword and kept his eye on the traitors, even as the battle between Marchosias and Phenex made the ground shift beneath them.

"Only just now," Niccolo whispered, before clearing his throat and looking back to his enemies. "Did you really think you'd get away with it, Zel? I'm beginning to see why you wear that damn blindfold."

"Please, I *did* get away with it. Lucy's dead, we're on Earth, I turned your puppy into a rabid dog, and you got off your fucking horse of all things!" Azazel laughed maniacally as he opened dozens of eyes scattered along his entire body, using all of them to stare at Niccolo. "What makes you think I'd be scared, *now*?"

"Because," Niccolo replied before lazily pointing back at Paimon with his thumb, "you didn't kill *her*."

"That's just... adorable."

"Enough of this," Beleth's voice boomed, ending the verbal sparring. With a quick movement, he made a five-point seal and then forced his arm through, where half of it disappeared. Beleth was drawing back his forearm from the ether when he was suddenly forced to duck in his saddle, and Cadmus' ornate scythe cut off a few strands of blond hair as it flew over his head.

"You should stay down. *Know your place*," Cadmus said as he kept his arm extended in front of him, blue energy warping the space around his hand. Beleth had been rising up from the horse's back, but a whistling sound forced him back to Misery's saddle and he narrowly avoided decapitation. "I will be your opponent, let's leave these three to their grudge match."

"*Reaper*," Beleth said as he slowly rose to his full height, his arm still in another dimension. After drawing it back, he held an obsidian broadsword in his armored hand. Once he was ready, Beleth yanked on his horse's reins and turned away from the maelstrom of shadows and flames occurring just a hundred yards away. "Follow me."

Without another word, Beleth dug his spurs into the sides of his mutilated horse—blood trickling out of the new wounds—and rode into a group of chimera that parted on his arrival. After nodding at his friends, Cadmus urged Mercy forward and into the gap between the monsters, which closed behind him.

Once they realized they were alone with Azazel, Niccolo and Paimon turned back to find him shaking his head.

"So much fucking drama. That's all you humans ever did for us," he mocked, sauntering toward his opponents. "Don't get me wrong—it made the time pass much faster—but sometimes it makes me want to gag."

"You don't get to talk about drama. Scratch would be *alive* if not for you," Niccolo growled, green energy flowing out of his pores as bloodlust took him. Grinning wildly, Azazel pulled on the knot of his blindfold and untied it, throwing it away and revealing the black pits Adonai had given him all those years ago.

"You know *what*, Nico? I could say the same for *you*."

That was enough for Niccolo to run forward, his sword held to his right side. From his belt, Azazel grabbed a short dagger with his right hand and rushed to meet him. Just as they were about to clash, the clouds parted and seven golden orbs appeared in the sky.

The Heavenly Host was no longer content to watch.

"*JUDAS, PLEASE!*" Phenex tried to keep in control as six dark blades burst out of Marchosias' back, heading straight for his position in the air. With a quick backhand, Phenex let out an arc of fire which intercepted the attack, but he still had to dive out of the way of two of the stronger extensions. After flying to the monster's side, Phenex let the fire retreat from his face.

"*I'm sorry! It's my fault this happened, but listen to me!*" The wolf slowly turned, its yellow eyes reduced to slits, and a low growl vibrated the air around them. With a break in the action, Phenex tried to continue. "*I know some of you is still in there, Judas. Just st—*"

He didn't have a chance to talk, as the wolf abandoned the shadows and lunged forward, his jaws upon Phenex in just two seconds. He was almost unable to react, but Phenex propelled himself up and set his palm against Marchosias' dark snout, pushing down hard enough to escape yellow teeth.

Unfortunately, Marchosias was moving fast enough that his skull still crashed into Phenex and sent him sprawling through the air. In the moment Phenex closed his eyes, he felt a sharp pain in his shoulder.

Gasping, he opened his eyes and saw that one of Marchosias' shadows—still tethered between his eyes—had plunged through his flesh as if it was air. Breathing raggedly, Phenex could only wait until the giant wolf snarled and then shook his head out of instinct.

After Marchosias threw him away and into the ground, a wake of rocks and mud formed upon impact. With so much pain flooding his senses, it was difficult for Phenex to keep conscious, let alone maintain his infernal armor. As his body crashed through the soil, his flames died out and left him a normal man.

When he finally stopped moving, Phenex was left staring into the sky and wishing he had stayed dead the first time. Rising from the ashes of Hell had not redeemed him; he had used his new freedom to throw away his friend and turn him into a feral beast. He was so involved with his self-pity and misery that Phenex didn't notice the golden light coming from above him, and instead lifted himself up to look at Marchosias.

The giant wolf was stalking toward him, his front half wreathed in shadows, and Phenex considered not getting up. After all this time, when it really mattered, *he* had been the one to betray Judas. If he had not held onto a worthless grudge, Marchosias would not be a monster outside of reason.

It was only fitting that Phenex might become his dinner.

However, when Marchosias made his way to the impact crater— walking along the trench Phenex's body had made in the dirt— instinct took hold. Phenex propped himself up on his elbows and backed away from his friend, kicking at the dirt to push himself along.

That didn't matter to Marchosias—the giant wolf more than made up for Phenex's escape with each stride—and it wasn't long before the demon's mouth was above Phenex, his teeth bared and saliva dripping onto the ground.

Being so close to death, Phenex had difficulty thinking. This behemoth above him was no corrupted friend; it was just another monster from the dark. Shadows crept along his long face, some of them becoming thin knives that would tear into Phenex, but then Marchosias cocked his head to the side and the shadows retreated, revealing dark fur as the black splotches departed. With that momentary reprieve, Phenex was finally allowed enough time to think.

Then he remembered he could fly.

Without another thought, Phenex surrounded himself in flames and condensed them into piecemeal armor before pushing off the ground with his legs. As the canine terror snarled, Phenex escaped and burst through the air, wings of flame growing out of his back as he put enough distance between him and his friend. Once he was a hundred yards out, Phenex turned to find shadows had covered Marchosias' face again.

"Judas!" Phenex shouted, his voice now clear. Although Marchosias had been so close to killing him, for that instant, something had clicked in his feral brain. "Judas, please listen to me!"

"You *recognized* me! Some part of you remembers who you were!"

Despite his hopes, the wolf jumped forward and tried to snap him out of the air, the shadows on his face reaching for Phenex even as he rolled to the side and away from danger. This time, however, Phenex would not give up on him.

"When you smelled me, you smelled your friend! Yeshua! I'm not your enemy, I'm not your prey!" he shouted just as a dozen sprawling tentacles tried to grab him out of the air. Deftly avoiding them, Phenex continued his appeal. "Beleth and Azazel did this to you!"

"But I helped..." he admitted, flying higher into the air so he would be out of reach. "And I'm sorry, but we can bring you back! I'm sure of it! Just focus, just try to be Judas again! Remember all those years in Hell! Remember who we used to be before all of this!"

Just as he finished that sentence, two flashes of gold streamed past, the vacuum created by their descent banishing the flames that protected him. As they returned to their master, Phenex looked down in shock. Two golden orbs were stuck in the ground—their surfaces shifting like water—and before he could react, they dissipated and revealed their occupants.

"I'm not sure he wants to, *messiah*," a vaguely familiar voice came from a silver-haired angel. Phenex had floated down to inspect them and he realized that this new arrival wasn't entirely a stranger.

"Who... who are you?" Phenex asked the angel who had spoken —he did not recognize the other one—and almost immediately he was met with anger.

"You must be joking! I am Nithael, an officer in the Heavenly Host! I was responsible for turning that village into walking corpses! You—*you burned my arms to ashes*!" Phenex's lapse in memory was enough insult to fill Nithael's every word with venom, but Phenex's temper flared once he realized who had intruded on his intervention.

"A very petty officer at that..." Phenex mocked the angel, whose glorious wings burst out of his back with violence, but his arms were more interesting. They were entirely silver, and Phenex watched as blades extended from his wrists until they were the length of short swords. "And if I burned your arms, what do you have attached to your shoulders?"

"You made a mistake, *messiah*." Nithael spat out the word, a conceited smile twisting his long face. "You made an enemy of *God* by harming his servant. Now you and all your friends will pay."

"Don't you know the danger of getting between a wolf and his prey?" Phenex asked as he pointed at the growling wolf, who had adopted a hostile stance and bared his teeth at the angels.

Nithael looked behind him and rolled his eyes.

"A mindless beast? I'm sure Jophiel can put him down. *Now*, if you please," he said offhandedly to the other angel, who was a petite woman with short black hair, her golden armor and axe looking far too big for her body. With a nod, the woman turned toward Marchosias and extended bright yellow wings out of her back.

"Understood." After just a word, the angel flew toward Marchosias and readied her axe, its edge reflecting the golden light from above.

Panicking slightly, Phenex forgot that Marchosias had become a monstrous beast and that they had been fighting only moments before. Instinctively, he burst into flames and screamed through the air, fire streaming behind him as he tried to intercept his angelic enemy. Jophiel had more than enough of a head start, but Phenex was not going to let anybody hurt his friend ever again.

He almost didn't make it, but as Jophiel swung her axe, Phenex let out a torrent of flames that burned through the air in front of

Marchosias. The inferno would have engulfed her if she had not abandoned her attack and rolled to the side, and even then a few feathers from her right wing burned away. Once Phenex saw that she had turned toward him, anger creasing her forehead, he realized she was sufficiently distracted.

"You will pay for that, demon!" Jophiel shouted as she pumped her wings and flew toward Phenex at great speed, but he knew he could not focus on her assault. Dropping a few feet, Phenex narrowly avoided the twin blades of Nithael, who had drawn both arms across his body with the intent of cutting Phenex in half.

"For that... and for my *arms*!" Nithael shouted, still oblivious to how outclassed he would be in a fair fight.

Phenex let the flames surround him once more and flew away from both angels, hoping to have some time to consider his options. Both the golden and silver warriors flew after him—Jophiel using her superior speed to try and flank from the left—and Phenex was almost glad to see what seemed like a hundred shadowy extensions stretching out to attack all three of them. He turned around so that he could focus on flying faster, but if he had taken time to look, only half of Marchosias' tendrils were the blades he had seen before.

Half of them were blunt tentacles.

"I burned them last time, angel. What makes you think this time will be different? You think because you brought a friend that it'll be easier to gang up on me?" Phenex shouted, hoping his insults would still reach his enemy, and he thought up an interesting tactic. Banking hard to the left, Phenex headed straight for Marchosias, whose shadows had momentarily abandoned his face.

"I care nothing for honor, demon! If you die, I will be pleased with or without the help!" Nithael shouted in arrogance.

Still flying straight toward Marchosias, who was now directing several dark tentacles at his friend, Phenex narrowly avoided an axe tearing through his back. Only by twisting through the air and sending out a wave of fire did he force Jophiel to miss, the heat enough to act as a thermal, catching her wings and forcing her up and out of striking distance.

"We are here to clean this world of your *filth*. That is all we care about!" she screamed, almost frothing at the mouth because of her incompetence.

Phenex did not care; he only wanted to distract them long enough for his idea to work. Not disoriented even though he continued through the air upside down, Phenex tried to keep his enemies close enough not to notice his plan. When he looked forward and saw Marchosias lunge, Phenex dropped through the air, just underneath the wolf's massive frame, and hoped his feral companion would do the work for him.

"*Messiah!*" Nithael shouted, which was enough for Phenex to hope. However, when he made it out from under Marchosias and looked over the monster's shadowy back, he saw that Nithael had avoided his death and was still rushing forward. "I will not delay this any longer!"

"Fine, then—" Phenex started, flames surrounding him and growing, but two golden feet slammed into his shoulder, dislocating his arm and sending him tumbling over the ground, and the bone of his left shin snapped like a twig after the first bounce.

With only a moment for frantic thoughts, Phenex tried to correct his momentum and fly back into the air, but a golden gauntlet slammed into his head and then threw him back against the mud, dragging his face along the ground. A root caught the bottom of his eye and broke the bone, but when he was finally released, Phenex did not care. He rolled over—barely able to make out what was happening in front of him—and realized that Jophiel stood over him, the head of an axe high above her shoulders.

"This is the fate you deserve, demon," she declared, and it was difficult for Phenex to argue with her. When she brought down her weapon, Phenex tried to justify it all—convince himself that this was all payment for his sins—but he was saved instead.

Before Jophiel's axe made it halfway to the ground, a giant wolf's mouth crashed down and engulfed the top half of the angel. When it clamped shut, blood sprayed out of the gruesome wounds and crushed Jophiel's arms.

After clenching his jaws further, causing Jophiel's hands to drop her axe, Marchosias lifted his head and ravaged the angel's corpse like a rag doll, blood and saliva whipping around and onto Phenex's stupefied face. He continued to stare as the giant beast slammed Jophiel's corpse against the ground again and again, but her legs finally tore away once he swiped at them with his paw.

Seeing what probably lay in store for him, Phenex could not will himself to move. He just prepared for death as the demon opened his mouth and let Jophiel's lifeless torso join her bleeding legs.

"Yesh... ua," a rasp broke through the air, and Phenex's heart started pounding. Instead of preparing for death, Phenex crawled forward and saw the giant wolf shaking as it stood, the shadows having departed from its massive frame.

"Judas? Judas!" Phenex was unable to stop himself from stumbling forward on a broken leg, the bones of his face and shoulder healing without him noticing. Tears streamed out of his eyes as Marchosias shuddered and howled in pain, his left leg shrinking abruptly.

Even though he felt for Marchosias in his agony, this was exactly what Phenex needed; this was his chance for redemption. Letting out another howl, Marchosias' front legs buckled and reformed, becoming more humanoid after the transition.

"Ye... *shua*," Marchosias started in his normal voice, but the second half came out as a scream, and then his body rapidly shrank and broke and reformed into something resembling the friend Phenex had abandoned. With five yards to cover—and his shin refusing to heal because he wouldn't stop using it—Phenex was slow on approach, but he ignored the pain. A grateful smile was on his face.

"That's right, Judas! It's me! It's Yeshua!" When he was just within a foot of Marchosias, the man had reverted almost completely, his fur departing and leaving brown skin behind. With one last surge of energy, a naked Marchosias rose to his feet and yelled skyward, but then his strength abandoned him and he started to fall.

This time, Phenex was there to help. Except for his leg, all of his bones had healed, so Phenex was able to catch Marchosias and keep him standing. Seeing that Judas had reverted and he had saved his friend from being a mindless beast, Phenex couldn't contain his happiness. The tears continued to flow, but these were from joy.

"Yeshua, I'm sorry," Marchosias mumbled weakly, but Phenex wouldn't allow an apology.

"No. No, don't you ever say that. Didn't you say that we never had to?" Phenex tried to joke, and Marchosias was gracious enough to smile at it.

Then terror filled his face and he grabbed his friend by the shoulders, switching places just in time for a silver blade to burst through his heart.

"Judas?" Phenex asked in alarm, his eyes wide upon feeling something poking into his ribcage. He looked down to find something strange coming from Marchosias' chest; deep, dark red flowing around bright silver. He was so confused that he didn't really notice that the strange thing had also punctured his abdomen, scarlet blooming along the fabric.

"Not..." Marchosias said quickly, pain enveloping his voice, and shook his friend by the shoulders. It was enough for Phenex to look up and make eye contact. "Not... your fau—"

Then the blade twisted, and Judas Iscariot was dead on his feet.

Partly in shock, partly from the force of the blade twisting and the weakness in his broken leg, Phenex fell away from Marchosias and to his knees, his world destroyed in an instant. Redemption had been so close; his friend had been saved. Without knowing why, Phenex was finding it difficult to see. He couldn't even realize that it was because of the tears pooling around his eyes.

"I'd say it *is* your fault, *Messiah*."

He had been lost, but Nithael's scorn brought Phenex back to the present. This was not some dream; that was not some strange person's corpse lying in front of him. Marchosias was dead—his best friend was *dead*—and it was only because Phenex was a damned fool. Still staring at his fallen companion, Phenex rose to his feet, the tears on his face evaporating as heat built within his skin.

"How kind of you. I can kill you without kneeling to your level," Nithael said, completely unaware of his predicament. Once Phenex was standing, the angel raised his right hand, his silver arm shining from two light sources, and then brought it across Phenex's neck.

However, as soon as it touched Phenex's skin, the silver blade melted away and splattered along the ground, leaving him unharmed.

"What? How?" Nithael shouted, but Phenex would never let him speak again.

With rage boiling within his veins, the small man extended his hand and grabbed Nithael by the jaw, immediately blackening the skin and fusing his lips together.

"I... will *not* forgive," Phenex stated simply before Nithael's entire body became a blazing inferno, his screams momentarily breaking through a new hole in his cheek before his life was snuffed out along with the flames. His enemy destroyed, there was little on Phenex's mind as he stood on the barren field.

When he looked down at Marchosias, emotion overtook him and he broke, streams of burning tears etching dark lines into his skin that would not heal. He curled in on himself, remembering the man he met on the mountain so many years ago, the first time Judas spilled blood for their revolution, all of the guilt he held on his shoulders. He remembered their meeting in Hell; all of the years they spent side by side.

After a thousand painful memories, Phenex could not take anymore and sprawled over his friend's corpse, sobbing and wishing that anything else could have happened.

Only once the sickening odor broke through his senses did

Phenex recover enough to lift a few inches and look at his friend's body. What he saw horrified him more than anything he had ever seen in life, ever seen in Hell; this pain was so much more than anything he felt while dying on the cross.

Beneath him was a burning corpse. He had betrayed Marchosias one last time.

His sanity departing from him in an instant, Phenex fell away and could not breathe. What blackened heart lay inside his rotten chest was beating faster and faster, pain assaulting him from all sides. He clawed at his chest underneath his robes, wishing that he could rip himself apart, but his nails were not sharp enough. All he accomplished were several bloody scratches in his skin that healed even as he drew his nails back. Realizing that he could not kill himself without help, Phenex had no options left.

He had *nothing* left.

Absent thought, Phenex rose through the air broken. He could not see through the steam that came from his tear ducts; his tears evaporated as soon as they formed. As he continued to float higher, Phenex had trouble focusing on any one sensation. His skin felt the air around him and his mind was far away in some lost memory, but all he could really focus on was the pain coming from his heart, even if he did not remember why he was feeling it. This misery, this rage, this agony had to be released somehow.

After taking a long breath, Phenex screamed, his powerful voice tearing through the atmosphere. With that scream came the inferno, the flames erupting out of him as if the world had never known fire before. In that terrible moment, there was no sky, only the promise of pain and death spreading out for miles in all directions.

And so it was that Hell came to Earth.

CADMUS ONLY NOTICED the hill of corpses at the last second, but Mercy was still paying attention to their surroundings. As the desecration of twenty mouths rose out of the ground to swallow them whole, Mercy jumped and set his hooves against rotten teeth, springing up further and flying through the air. Cadmus was about to thank his friend, but the horse had no patience for it.

These are distractions, master. Focus on the demon king, Mercy rattled, and Cadmus begrudgingly kept his thoughts to himself.

Seeing a giant arm swinging down from their left, Cadmus turned his blade up and dragged it along the chimera's flesh, harvesting their souls instinctively. It had become second nature, even if he felt the weight of each reaping adding to his burden.

"Beleth, this is far enough!" Cadmus shouted after the armored Fallen, who was riding his grotesque horse through narrow gaps between the monsters. From time to time, Beleth would tap against a sigil hidden in the air and summon another monster out of the ground, and it was becoming more than just annoying.

"*I* will decide when we have gone far enough!" Beleth shouted before slashing his great sword in front of him, a series of three hidden seals materializing and shattering as he rode through, and then spurred his horse to run even faster. Cursing, Cadmus kept up his guard and watched for Beleth's trap to spring. However, nothing could have prepared him for what happened next.

Mercy reared back as tons of earth burst into the air in front of them, a vast wound in the Earth splitting open as a wall of flesh screamed its way out of some other Hell. The reaper's eyes went wide as the giant chimera was unleashed and continued to rise up into the sky, blotting out the sun just halfway into its ascent. Its wails and painful echoes assaulted Cadmus' ear drums and a migraine tore through his head, flashes of blue memories flitting about his mind's eye.

"How is this, *reaper*?" Beleth's voice broke through the chaos, his interruption enough for Cadmus to focus on what lay before him.

Standing hundreds of feet tall, the chimera twisted and undulated, but Cadmus could not bear to look at it. Instead, he turned to face Beleth, who had maneuvered his horse onto a nearby hill so he could look down on the scenario he had created.

"Can you even stand to stay conscious?"

"What... have you done?" Cadmus asked, unable to sit straight as sympathetic pain rocketed through every nerve of his body. The only thing he knew was that if he could not recover from whatever this was, he would not survive.

"Nothing more than you've encountered before, insect. Paimon was not the only target of my experiments, as well you know. I mentioned this last time, if you remember," Beleth explained, a sneer on his face. "Your empathy makes you *weak*."

"You—you did say that," Cadmus replied, closing his eyes briefly so he could try to manage the agony. When the ground shook beneath them, he realized he could not waste time on the sensation. "What does that mean?"

"Did they not *bother* to explain, reaper? Did Buné in his tower not *deign* to reveal this truth?" Beleth asked with a scoff, drawing a seven-point seal in the air while Cadmus was distracted. "There is a reason why you were chosen to be a reaper, why that horse beneath you follows your commands."

"I do not... command him," Cadmus said, gritting his teeth before lifting his head and making eye contact with Beleth. "Mercy is my friend."

"Another weakness, born from a greater one. The Horses of Hell should merely be servants; tools for a greater purpose. Misery will not fail me, as she has no option to do so. But that is beside the point. Your failure to master a simple beast is unimportant."

"What *is* important, Beleth? What's important to a traitor like *you*?" Cadmus asked, his resentment enough to break through the pain. In defiance, Cadmus sat up straight in his saddle even as the giant chimera's shadow enveloped him.

Beleth merely smiled.

"*Fear*, human. Fear and the power which inspires it. The empathy you hold—what has allowed you to foresee death in others

—is not strength. It makes you vulnerable to psychic attacks. This is why I designed the chimera for *you*. Out of every one of our pursuers, you, shockingly, had the most potential to undermine our cause. That has been evident since the first time I met you hundreds of years ago, and I do not believe it an accident."

"You've got to be kidding..." Cadmus shook his head and laughed, even as his chest spasmed from mental stress. "Are you saying you respect a *human?*"

"*Far* from it, but I would never choose to ignore a threat or disregard chance. And so, when I manipulated these creatures—twisted their souls together and made their existence true anguish—I did it for this purpose. Across the threads of this and so many dimensions, I wanted them to cry out for death, to cry out to *you*," Beleth concluded, smug satisfaction plastered across his face. "I would cripple your mind before crippling your body."

"Oh, is that all?" Cadmus summoned false bravado, and he held his weapon to the side and let it shine with blue energy. "It must be disappointing to see that it didn't work."

"Reaper," Beleth said, sighing before placing his hand against the purple seal that had been waiting for his command. "It has not started yet."

When the seal broke against Beleth's gauntlet, a thousand screams burst across the dimensions and engulfed the reaper's mind, forcing him to scream along with them.

In that moment, Cadmus could only cry as if tortured, but time itself had warped inside his mind's eye. For him, literally a hundred days passed as the sympathetic pain burst through every fiber of his being, stretching his energy into painful dimensions as each individual life Beleth had used for this creation made itself known. Cadmus was stretched in almost infinite directions, his very existence drawn and quartered a hundred times. True reality was beyond him.

He had lost his way as the real-life chimera leaned over to devour and assimilate its next victim.

Pale Rider! Mercy's rattle resonated and destroyed a dozen visions of pain. *Master!* The word destroyed a hundred more. *Reaper!* Now only a few tortured souls remained.

Cadmus!

Suddenly there was only one; his own. Cadmus opened his eyes, disoriented but alive. However, when he looked up, even as Mercy turned and galloped away, he saw a pillar of flesh descending from the sky, thousands of miserable creatures mutated together for the sole purpose of destroying his sanity. A pit growing in his stomach, Cadmus focused on what lay ahead of them and realized that chimera lined each side of the path. They had fallen into Beleth's trap and there was no way out.

Hurry. Please. This is my fault, Cadmus thought, but Mercy did not answer. He only sent thoughts of disapproval that Cadmus accepted without a fight. If Beleth had not exploited this empathy—a vulnerability Cadmus should have considered long ago—they would not be so close to death.

Their situation was made even worse as the sky turned to fire and Phenex's scream broke through the pain and rage of Beleth's creations. When his companion's pain and grief slammed into him, Cadmus almost fell out of his saddle, but he could not fail again.

Pushing away his empathy, Cadmus swung his scythe at the arms and legs and screaming mouths that advanced upon them as they ran away from the giant chimera. Half the time, as soon as he had begun carving through the miserable souls, pillars of flames struck them and turned them to ash. His skin complained—pain came from second-and third degree burns which healed within seconds—but he did not have the time to care.

As soon as the thought struck him, Cadmus realized his obvious mistake. Instead of fighting the enslaved creatures, Cadmus looked ahead of him. Focusing on the narrow gap that was already drawing closed, Cadmus willed time to stop, to slow down, to do anything.

Except nothing happened.

Cursing, the reaper shook his head before trying again, calling out to a power he should have been able to control. Yet again, nothing happened, and in his frustration—as the shadow of the falling tower of flesh overtook them—Cadmus despaired. This must have been some side effect of Beleth's trap; this must have been part of his plan.

Beleth truly had crippled Cadmus before he could become a threat.

As he looked forward and saw another chimera break through the soil, blocking the last escape from the horror descending from the sky, Cadmus knew it was over. This one was twenty feet tall—at least ten humans had been sacrificed to create it—but that wasn't even important. He and his horse would be crushed before they even made it to the pale horror.

Then Cadmus witnessed a miracle. The top half of the chimera split open, a flash of something disappearing before the reaper could fully comprehend what happened, but then a creature burst out of its midsection and launched itself into the fray.

In a wake of flesh and bone, a blood-covered woman sailed through the air yelling a war cry. Scarlet covered every inch of her, but as she rocketed over him, Cadmus realized that Cimeries had come to his rescue.

Turning to look over his shoulder even as Mercy carried him further, Cadmus watched as the Amazon landed and kept running toward the massive chimera, which was almost upon her. So completely confused by her sudden appearance, Cadmus's jaw was slack as the woman planted her feet down before pushing with all of her might, jumping straight into the "head" of the falling monstrosity, pike held straight out to meet it.

"Cimeries!" Cadmus yelled once he finally recovered enough to speak, but the warrior's blade had already met the chimera's flesh.

Surrounded by pale blue energy, Cimeries impaled the creature with such force that what remained of its falling body was pushed upward, and then her spear was swallowed up beneath layers of tortured skin. As Cadmus thought she might actually succeed, she followed after her weapon and was absorbed into the giant body.

Cadmus was horrified at the sight, thinking her lost. He could only remember how one of Beleth's creations had almost assimilated him just by touching him with an arm, but then something amazing happened. In an instant, the skin closest to the ground split like a torn seam, blood and guts and bone pouring out of the wound as the top of the creature was ripped away. When the chimera's lifeless "head" was lifted high enough into the air and broke entirely from its body, Cadmus was finally able to see what happened.

There, seemingly hovering in the air and holding tons of flesh with her free hand, was a blood-covered Amazon yelling her heart out.

After Cimeries twisted in the air and threw the flesh to the side, she landed on the creature's back as Cadmus gulped down empty air. Even though he had just been assaulted by thousands of screams of pain, even though he had seen Earth became hellfire and brimstone, this single woman was more terrifying than anything he had seen in thirteen hundred years. When Cimeries stood up and turned to face him, she was calm and collected, as if nothing had happened.

"Come, reaper, let's finish this."

Mercy carried him forward, but Cadmus had lost his confidence.

"I... Beleth. I can't—I..." He still felt the echoes of psychic torture and could only look at the ground speeding past.

"*Cadmus*," she said clearly, which forced the reaper to make eye contact. Even though she was covered in gore, she offered him a thin smile. "*You* are not alone."

"Cimeries..." he murmured, already feeling a wave of confidence, and suddenly it all fell into place.

This had only been another tactic, another psychological attack. Beleth had only created these creatures so that he could weaken them before the real fight and he had made the mistake of admitting it. With this knowledge, gripping his scythe tighter, Cadmus readied himself for the coming slaughter.

He just had to remember that he was a reaper and that this was merely a harvest.

"Good. Take the left and I will take the right," Cimeries said before leaping to the side and rolling out the rest of her momentum. After she recovered, Cimeries held out the hooked blade of her pike to her left, looking back to her companion before nodding. Once he realized her plan, Cadmus urged Mercy to the creature's other side and extended his scythe. Although the rest of the massive creature was starting to pick itself up, it was already too late to avoid its doom.

Both of them yelling and brimming with different shades of blue energy, Cadmus and Cimeries dragged their blades along the sides of Beleth's monstrosity, reaping the tortured souls and freeing them from agony. Their pain joined them, their screams echoed through their ears, but the warriors from Hell could not surrender now. This was their duty.

It was only thirty seconds before they cut through the last pieces of Beleth's monster, but it had exhausted both of them. Even as fire crashed from the sky—huge, blazing whirlwinds tearing through Beleth's mutilated experiments—the human souls collapsed into themselves; Cimeries on the ground and Cadmus in the saddle.

Phenex's grief was stealing the very air from their lungs and it was difficult for them to recover, but they were not afforded a moment of mercy. A bolt of lightning struck the ground between them, forcing them to look on the armored horseman on the hill. There was a wide smile on his cruel face, the first Cadmus had ever seen from him.

It was clear that Beleth had not yet begun to fight.

CHAPTER 11
VENGEANCE FOR THE DEVIL

A blue demon knelt in the courtyard at the top of the stairs, blood covering his arms up to the elbows. Streaming down his face were bright, incandescent blue tears, and silent sobs wracked his body as his hands lay still, palms up and fingers twitching. As he neared the grief-stricken Fallen, Lucifer had a difficult time restraining his emotions.

"Do you know what I did today, Lucifer?" Crocell lifted his head, bright tears brimming beneath black eyes. "Do you know why I'm kneeling here? Why I'm covered in blood?"

"I have an idea," Lucifer almost whispered, approaching his brother but not getting too close. He had no idea what the fallen angel was capable of in this state.

"You have an idea?" Crocell asked skeptically, scoffing as he looked back down at the tile covering the courtyard. A pool of blood and tears had formed between his knees, but rain had started to fall and was now diluting the mix.

It almost seemed like Hell sympathized with Crocell's misery.

"I can guess, that's what I can do. Is it over?" Lucifer asked as he knelt to join his brother, the Slayer of Dis. Rain pelted the courtyard even harder *and when Crocell spoke, his words were drowned out. Lucifer had no choice but to ask again. "Is the Shroud dead?"*

"No! No, he's not, you bastard! He... got away," he confessed, dropping his head as his entire body trembled. Crocell held his arms across his body and tried to give himself comfort even as he was assaulted by cold rain.

"I'm sorry," Lucifer said, extending his hand so that he could place it on the slayer's blue shoulder. Lucifer considered how much of the truth he could give his brother, but then felt the rain strike against his face with even greater force. This was not unexpected; Crocell always had an affinity for water.

*"Not **that** sorry, brother. You don't sound surprised." Crocell slowly placed his hand on Lucifer's arm and then removed it from his shoulder. "Did you know what he could do?"*

"No," Lucifer said with confidence, his tone more than enough to fool one of his weaker siblings. "I only knew that he was trying to build his forces in secret."

"Apparently, he cared little for them," Crocell said as he stood up, lightning crackling around him as he revealed his true form. Water ebbed out of his back and formed dark wings, and electricity flowed along his arms. Once Crocell was standing, the skies of Hell seemingly answered his prayers. A spider web of lightning shattered the dark skies and thunder echoed throughout the small courtyard.

"He turned them."

"What do you mean?" Lucifer asked, wrinkles forming in his brow as he stood and joined his brother, who was seemingly oblivious of the storm crackling above. "Turned them into what?"

*"Into **animals**. All the humans he brought to his side, all of those pathetic, corrupted humans were transformed into mindless beasts, into feral creatures," Crocell explained, raising his arm to point back to the Famine Quarter. With all of the rain falling around them, the blood on his arms dripped away, but it was clear that Crocell would be forever stained. "Over a hundred demons had gathered there. Only three walked away."*

"Ronové?" Lucifer asked, earning a nod. "And..."

"I killed them, Lucifer. All of them. A hundred souls—some of which I

320

had known for centuries—were reduced to rabid creatures who could not remember anything beyond instinct and murder," Crocell stated, anger breaking through his normally stoic voice. "I wanted you to know that."

"Crocell..." Lucifer started, his heart going out to the blue demon, but Crocell merely shook his head. Then he walked forward and grabbed Lucifer's right hand and pulled him close enough that no one else could hear over the storm.

"I will hunt for him. I owe it to all of those souls I couldn't save. I don't care how long it takes. This Shroud will not get away with it. Until I do, however—since you will not bother to tell me **why** this happened—" he said before grabbing further up Lucifer's arm with his other hand and then wiping blood and rainwater along his skin, "I want you to know that you share this guilt with me."

"I..." Lucifer was forced to abandon his arguments as Crocell stepped back and stared hard into his eyes. Seeing that the slayer was resolute, Lucifer took a deep breath and nodded. "Just like all the rest, Crocell. You are not alone."

"If only that were true," Crocell said before turning around and jumping high into the air—his wings growing larger as they absorbed rainwater—and in a flash of lightning, the slayer disappeared.

Sighing, Lucifer closed his eyes and held out his arm, letting the rain take the blood away from him. As heavy as it was on his conscience, this new guilt was just another drop in an ocean.

"How many died?" a frail voice shouted over the storm, making Lucifer panic. He turned quickly, almost letting out radiant wings, but then he saw grey robes and a gnarled staff held in bony hands. Breathing out in relief, Lucifer walked forward as Crocell's storm started to dissipate.

"How much did you hear?"

"Enough, Scratch, though that last whisper was swallowed in the thunder." Barbas patiently waited underneath the closest awning as his brother walked through the rain. By the time Lucifer was within a few feet, the thunderstorm had been reduced to a sprinkle. "You know who the Shroud is."

"Yes, it's—" Lucifer started, but Barbas tapped his staff against the steps and frowned.

"You didn't tell me before. Don't change your mind now."

"Barbas..." Lucifer muttered, but the old man shook his head and leaned on his walking stick.

"I **mean** it. Your schemes work better when you stick to 'em. If you ever intended to let me know, it wasn't going to be like this, and it would have been damn well before any of your subjects died." Barbas yawned slightly before letting out a loud sniff. "I'm no good in a fight anyway."

"You keep saying that like it's true," Lucifer said as he dropped his gaze to the ground, noticing from the lack of rain that Crocell's tantrum had finally run its course. "Never would have made it back here without you."

"And you keep saying **that** like it's true. I've never been one for flattery, Scratch, so let's keep it simple. I only asked about the souls because... well, it doesn't matter. Guess I just have a soft spot."

"Then why are you here, old man?" Lucifer smiled despite the recent tragedy, but he realized it was in bad form once his brother sneered back at him.

"You got more than a thousand years on me, geezer, so you'd best shut your mouth," Barbas said in annoyance, but he soon gave a weary sigh. "The job's done."

"The job? You mean the horses?" Lucifer crossed his arms, and in response, Barbas tapped his staff and nodded at something past his brother. After raising an eyebrow, Lucifer turned to find something incredible.

Blood and muscle manifested in the air before twisting and combining, bones and red skin joining together as more and more tissue came into existence. Even as that continued, grey smoke billowed out of single point just a few feet away. As the new cloud expanded, dust swept in from all directions and swirled into a new form just to the right of the cloud.

Lucifer was amazed as the first creature finished its manifestation, a powerful red and black horse pawing at the ground. Before he could fully understand what was happening, Lucifer looked at its neighbor and saw a *grey, emaciated beast with sunken eyes, whining even as it stood, and was overcome with pity.*

"We pay our respects, Lucifer, High King of Hell," a rasp broke him out of his daze, and Lucifer was confused by the interruption. Looking from one horse to the other, Lucifer finally made eye contact with the white stallion on the end and understood.

Although this was their first meeting, Lucifer could tell there was great power in this Horse of the Apocalypse.

"Barbas, these creatures are incredible," Lucifer said in wonder, earning a neigh of disappointment from the red horse, which reared back and huffed out of its nostrils.

"You may be the Devil, but treat us with some respect. Don't talk about us like we're not here," a scream tore through the air, and Lucifer was stunned to find himself momentarily frightened by a mere animal.

"I... I am sorry, uh—" Lucifer started, but then he realized he did not how to address these creatures.

"This one is Fury, who should learn some damned manners," Barbas said as he walked up and slapped the red horse across the face with his staff. "You be quiet from now on."

"You—" the scream came back with force, but one glare from Barbas was enough to silence him before he made another mistake.

"He's obviously going to Eligos and his champion, whoever that is. Seere's being stubborn about accepting the position," Barbas explained before walking along the line. "This next one is Despair, who's a quiet little thing. I figure she'll be good in Ronové's company. We can't expect too much from the philosopher, and he'd rather have a docile horse."

"I agree," Lucifer said as he looked at each animal. They were magnificent creatures, far beyond anything he had expected to see once he had given Barbas this assignment.

He wondered just what went into their creation.

"And this one is Mercy. He'll be just right for Buné's reaper," Barbas said as he brought his hand up and rubbed the side of the white horse's face. Feeling affectionate, the horse closed his eyes and leaned into his touch.

"Why do you say that?" Lucifer asked, drawing out a sigh from Barbas.

"Because he's stronger. They will all grow with their horsemen, but Mercy is the most... resilient; he has the oldest soul. With all of that empathy, Buné's student will be more vulnerable. I... wanted to make sure we gave him as good a chance we could," Barbas explained before turning to face his brother. "We're practically sending them on a suicide mission."

"Well, you've certainly accomplished something. These horses... you've outdone yourself, Barbas," Lucifer said in appreciation, but then he frowned. "Though, there's only three."

"There's another, he's just lazy." Barbas grumbled before whistling and slamming his staff against the tiles, hard enough to send out a splash of rainwater.

As Lucifer watched, a green cloud materialized and then condensed, a black horse appearing within the fog. Once it was standing before them, blight and all, it neighed and shook its mane.

"What the hell do you want, old man?" a deep voice greeted them, and Lucifer was forced to smile. Even though this horse was unexpectantly disrespectful toward his creator, it was almost endearing.

"I want you to show up on time, Plague! Don't know where you got this rebellious streak of yours," Barbas argued, clearly pretending to be angry. "You realize that you're meeting the High King of Hell?"

"That guy?" the black horse asked before looking over Lucifer with green eyes. "This a joke?"

"I could get out the wings for you..." Lucifer shifted his weight to one leg and a deep rumble filled the air, and it took him a second to realize the horse was laughing.

"Nah, I trust you. Hey, Barbas, where's Glory? I can't feel her for some reason," Plague asked as faced Barbas, who stammered and looked at the ground.

"Glory?" Lucifer asked, but the old demon didn't seem to hear him. He breathed in and out with effort, clearly suffering under some memory. Although he was unable to make eye contact, Barbas finally responded.

"She's not coming," he said, lifting eyes threatened by tears.

"What do you **mean** she's not coming?" Plague asked, his voice deeper as he realized something sinister had happened. Instead of answering, Barbas turned to his brother and bit his lip.

"I made a fifth horse. I was... going to give her to someone you chose to represent the palace. Figured we didn't have to go entirely by Adonai's book. But," he hesitated, closing his eyes and breathing deep. "I couldn't do it alone, Scratch."

"What are you talking about?" Lucifer asked, uncrossing his arms and setting his hands on Barbas' frail shoulders. That close, his brother could not bear to make eye contact.

"I had to ask Beleth for help. She was his price."

"You... you gave him one of the horses? But..."

"I know, Scratch. I **know**. If anybody is going to be a traitor in our midst, it's going to be him. I just... it needed to get done, and I couldn't do it alone. I'm sorry." Barbas wiped away his tears with the right sleeve of his robe and backed away, choosing to seek comfort from his hellish children.

"Does he know why we need them?" Lucifer hoped his brother had not ruined all of their plans with this moment of weakness.

"I know better than to tell the truth. I'm sure he could see some of the threads, but I've known our brother for a long time. He's not so hard to fool," Barbas explained as he buried both of his hands into Plague's mane. Lucifer was disappointed, but ready to take the next step.

"What did you tell him?" he asked, finally earning his frail brother's gaze.

"That Glory was the strongest."

"Well, well. Someone's gotten a little tougher." Azazel's face was unnerving without the blindfold, the pits of his eyes an abyss. Even with Niccolo's considerable power, the grey demon was able to hold off the Horseman's first assault with just his small dagger. It didn't help that Lucifer's memories distracted him in that instant, but Niccolo was back with a vengeance.

"Tougher than you think," Niccolo snarled, gripping his handle tighter and pushing down, the extra force enough for Azazel to dig in his heels. Although he was at first surprised, Azazel grinned and reduced his dozens of eyes to slits.

"Let's hope you're still clever," he said before something green whipped around and seemed like it was about to strike Niccolo in the face.

With a sharp clang, Paimon's left hand struck against the object and she followed through with a rushing assault on Azazel, who ducked and dodged around each wild strike, laughing all the while. Lifting his hand to his face and feeling blood, Niccolo realized that Paimon had saved his life.

Held at the curled end of Azazel's tail was a second dagger.

"Paimon! You know better to interrupt boys when they're roughhousing!" Azazel dove forward with the knife in his right hand before using his tail to strike from his left. However, Paimon twisted and caught Azazel's wrist before lifting her armored foot and using it to defend against the second blade.

Taking advantage of the opportunity, Paimon was about to use her other hand to gut the traitor, but he was able to drive both of his hooves into her golden face, which knocked her off balance and forced her to release his hand. Although she staggered for a moment, Paimon recovered and crossed her extended nails above her to ward off a quick flick of his tail.

"Why should I care about the boy's club, Azazel? I'm trying to kill you!"

The blade struck against Paimon's fingers, chipping away at the liquid metal, but then she dove forward with her right hand, trying to impale his spinning body. However, since he was able to see in all directions, Azazel was ready. Slashing below him with daggers now held in both hands, he knocked away her arm and slammed a knobby knee into her face, sending her sprawling to the ground.

"You and I both know that's not going to happen." Azazel was gleeful as he leapt forward, all three weapons ready to slam into her prone body, but a demonic arm slammed into his side and sent him barreling to the right. He tumbled through the air, and—even though Niccolo chased after him—Azazel jumped back further, sheathing his weapons before using his hands to spring off the ground and into graceful acrobatics.

"We *will* kill you, Azazel. We came all the way to Earth to do it." Despite his declaration, Niccolo's chest was tight and his heart pounded, and he wordlessly urged Plague to help him.

Ceasing his carnival antics, Azazel landed on his hooves and shook his head.

"Oh, and here I thought you were just trying to end the world. That Black Death of yours is doing wonders, already." Azazel was goading him, picking himself up even as Plague burst into existence and galloped toward him from the periphery.

"Well, we both know I'm a miserable failure," Niccolo replied as he ran forward. He hoped he would be enough distraction while Plague closed the distance.

"True enough. And three against one, Nico? That's fucking dirty."

Azazel spun just in time to find Plague bearing down on him, only two feet away, and Niccolo almost smiled at the sight. However, once Plague was within striking distance, Azazel lunged forward and grabbed the black horse by the throat, stopping him instantly. Using his tail to wrap around Plague's hind leg, Azazel lifted Plague off the ground and looked over his shoulder.

"Heads up!" Azazel then tossed the black horse at Niccolo, who was still trying to wrap his mind around how the satyr had even stopped Plague, in the first place.

Just jump! I'll be fine! Plague's voice came to him, finally allowing him to react.

As Plague's body barreled toward him, Niccolo planted his feet and shoved with all his strength, rising fifteen feet in the air and evading the body of his own horse. As he fell toward Azazel, Niccolo took the time to glance behind him and saw a green mist spreading out from where Plague should have landed. Confident that his friend was alright, Niccolo could focus on the enemy he had thought was still on the ground.

Unfortunately, when he turned back, Azazel's grinning face was only a foot away.

"Eyes on *me*, Nico!" Azazel chided him before slamming a fist into his face, the power of the blow enough to send Niccolo flying up and backward, his momentum completely reversed.

If Niccolo had been conscious, he might have known what it was like to be weightless, but he only regained his senses as he was plummeting to Earth. He panicked slightly as the ground rushed up to meet him, but then a green cloud condensed beneath him and redirected his momentum, his horse forming in time to save him from a broken body.

"This is going to be *fun*, Nico!" Azazel shouted from a hundred feet away, his arms crossed lazily as his body shuddered with silent laughter. "If nothing else—no matter *what* happens—this is going to be fun!"

"Paimon," Niccolo muttered as he saw her rushing toward Azazel, every part of her that could be turned into a weapon extended to their deadly potential. She covered the distance between them with long, quick strides, and when Azazel finally noticed her approach, it was too late for him to be ready. When she leapt into the air, about to slash the traitor to ribbons, Niccolo felt lucky to have met her.

He was still smiling when a golden sphere dropped from the sky and opened up to reveal a small angel who immediately dropkicked Paimon and directed her back toward Niccolo. She landed hard on her left arm, but Paimon scrambled back to her feet and dug her heels in, finally stopping her momentum after several yards of dragging her nails through the earth.

"Mitzrael, you fuck—" Paimon started, but then she doubled over and hacked up blood onto golden hands, breathing heavily once the attack subsided. She looked up to see the small angel crouched down, his double-bladed weapons in his hands.

"Pai-Pai, what's wrong?" he asked, almost with genuine concern, but Azazel put a grey hand on his shoulder.

"Beleth poisoned her, Mitz. Kinda regret it now, since she's not going to be much fun to fight, but hey," Azazel said with a warm smile as he waved at Paimon. "How about I take the Horseman and you could have her to yourself?"

"*Really*, Zel? Really, really?" Mitzrael hopped in elation, and Azazel nodded before turning back to their opponents. While they spoke, Niccolo had directed Plague over to Paimon and had dropped to her side.

"Really, really, Mitz. That alright with you two?" Azazel asked, and it was all Niccolo could do to stop himself from rushing at the pair. Before he could react, Paimon slapped away his hand and stood to her full height.

"That's fine. I'm sure Niccolo will find some way to avoid being bored as he rips you apart." She was all attitude, but blood trickled out of her mouth.

Confident with this ancient warrior beside him, Niccolo was about to follow up with a threat of his own, but an explosion overwhelmed their conversation and a massive surge of heat slammed into them. Distracting him entirely, Niccolo was forced to see what had done this.

A blanket of fire lay across the sky, spreading further until Niccolo could not see the end of it. Centered over where Phenex had been distracting Marchosias, Niccolo finally saw the source of the explosion. A giant sphere of white-hot flames at least a hundred yards in diameter was floating in midair. Flares and tendrils of fire flowed out with every surge of energy, crashing and destroying anything where they met the ground. Tornados of swirling flames came into existence and dissipated after devouring the air around them.

Then the scream tore through the air, a tortured wail of misery which could only mean one thing.

"Oh, Jesus," Azazel muttered, just loud enough that all of them could hear. Scoffing at his own words, he shook his head as everyone turned to face him. "Huh, well wasn't *that* appropriate."

"What—what is happening..." Niccolo mumbled, the shock almost too much for him to bear, but when he looked back at the living inferno—as he was able to see the shadow buried in the flames—he had to admit the reality of the situation.

"Marchosias... He's dead, little man." Plague's voice wavered through the air, the heat distorting his voice. "But we'll have to deal with it later."

"But..." Niccolo tried to speak, but Paimon wrapped her fingers around his hand.

"He's right. For now, let's try to make it worth it." Then she turned her attention back to their enemies, who were settling into ready positions. His grief turning to anger, Niccolo gripped his sword tighter and advanced on Azazel and Mitzrael.

"You don't have to tell me twice."

Grinning wildly, Azazel beckoned Niccolo to follow after him before sprinting away, every stride propelling him three or four yards, and they realized that Plague was the only one who could follow. Niccolo jumped onto his saddle and, after rearing back and letting out a deep bellow, the black horse raced after the departing traitor in a wake of green fog. It was only seconds before Paimon was left alone with the giggling seraphim.

"Pai-Pai, I really do enjoy seeing you after all these years," he said as he hopped forward, too many teeth showing in his malicious grin. "We had such good times when we banished the Nephilim."

"You're a monster, Mitzrael, you always were." Paimon was nervous about her condition, but this angel would not escape again. "I'll never forget what you did."

"What *I* did?" Mitzrael crawled along the ground to Paimon's left, forcing her to mirror his actions. "The Nephilim were our *enemy*. Father said so. I did my duty, and so did you, Pai-Pai."

"Will you *stop* with that name?" she barked, her teeth extending almost to the point of distorting her words. "It was never cute. Grow the fuck up."

"Fine," Mitzrael said in a low voice, digging into the soil with one of his daggers. "Don't know why you have to spoil the fun. You were a hero, you know? They made a *statue* because of your victory."

"*Victory*?" Paimon stifled laughter. "Mitzrael, that was a *massacre*, and we were *not* in the right. I'll never forget what he made us do."

"Oh, who *cares* if it was right?" the angel asked, rolling his eyes before he rushed forward and leapt at her with spinning blades. "Father knows best!"

"Damned fool." Paimon dove out of the way, knowing that he would not have left himself so vulnerable without some trick up his sleeve. Instead, once she rolled over and looked at him, he just laughed.

"You could have killed me right there, Paimon. Shows how weak you've become. It was only two million years, you know? You should still have some fight in you."

"I have plenty." She was about to launch into a whirlwind of claws, but then bile rose in her throat and made her choke. When she finally spat it all out, blood followed.

"Plenty of *something*, at least. Beleth really wasn't kidding around," Mitzrael said in mock concern. Seeing his jokes as an opportunity, Paimon picked herself up and licked the blood from her golden lips.

"Why, Mitzrael? What is going on here? This wasn't in the revelation, so why are these two helping Heaven?"

"Because they want to? Zel was always in our corner. As for those of us in Heaven?" he explained, hopping on his ankles. "We just do what we're told. Zel told us to be ready to come down and help out with this little battle of yours, and we, simply, didn't object."

"How come it's just you? Why doesn't Adonai send the Host?"

Mitzrael looked away as he remembered his briefing, which was exactly what she wanted. Taking advantage, Paimon dove forward and slashed at the angel, who only realized what she was doing at the last second. Mitzrael hopped up onto his left arm and twisted his body, clashing his other blade against Paimon's nails and then pushing so he could leap away.

"No fair! You can't ask me questions and then attack when I'm answering them!" Mitzrael shouted as he curled in the air and landed on his feet, only for Paimon to lash out with a leg, intent on digging her talons into his midsection. Throwing both of his hands toward the ground, he parried her attack and then jumped so he could roll over her back and then spring forward, evading her next backhand of deadly knives.

"Why not? It'll make it interesting!" Paimon replied once they reached the break in their rhythm, but then a massive fireball slammed into the ground just a foot away from her. It remained there for a moment, seemingly frozen in time, but then it exploded and the force knocked Paimon off her feet and through the air.

She landed hard two yards away, her armor glowing red-hot and searing the skin underneath, but she couldn't afford to lie on the ground. Picking herself up with some effort, Paimon got to her feet and saw Mitzrael laughing from the other side of the impact crater.

"Interesting enough for you?" he asked. Breathing heavily, Paimon tried to collect herself even as another spasm ripped through her insides. She could not allow Mitzrael to see more of her weakness; she had to hide it.

Luckily, he had a weakness of his own.

"Getting there," Paimon said as she sauntered forward, slightly throwing out her hips and letting the fire all around them reflect off her body. From the way his eyes glassed over, Paimon knew that Mitzrael was still the pervert he was before the rebellion. "So you were saying? Why are you alone?"

"I'm... not," Mitzrael answered, clearly distracted as he lowered his blade from his mouth. "Nith and Jophiel were taking care of the *Son of God*," he said before motioning toward the source of all those flames. "Apparently that didn't work out."

"So just the three of you?" Paimon asked as she crouched and continued her approach, giving Mitzrael a full view of her armored cleavage. He shook his head at that and breathed with difficulty, causing Paimon's lips to curl in delight.

"I—um... stop that," the angel said as he made eye contact with his sister. "That's just cruel. You know I always had a crush."

"Oh, you don't appreciate the view anymore?" she asked with a lilt in her voice, trying to ignore the swirling flames coming closer.

"Look, if you want answers, I'll give them to you. You're going to be dead anyway."

"I wouldn't be so sure," Paimon hinted before drawing back and letting her nails extend further. Mitzrael smiled at the change in her demeanor and crouched forward, ready to strike.

"Seven of us came down, *Pai-Pai*," he said with a sneer, deciding to revert to his annoying persona. "Four of us to deal with you; three of us to kill the watcher."

"The *watcher*?" she asked in alarm, and Mitzrael giggled even as flames raged about their arena. He nodded as a column of flames scorched the field behind him.

"Dear Tamiel, he really should have stayed quiet. Adonai was not pleased, I can tell you *that*. Once Uriel is done with him... well, what I'm about to do to you is going to be an afternoon delight," he threatened, a grin plastered across his face as the inferno raged behind him. Seeing that he didn't notice, Paimon realized she did not need to be at full strength.

"What makes you think I will let you live, Mitzrael?" She let the armor fall away from her face so she could look at him with pure white eyes.

"Because, Pai-Pai! After the Nephilim, you were just never the same. How are you going to *stop* me?" he asked with condescension, which was enough for Paimon to scream in rage and dive forward with a slash of her left hand, seemingly striking out in fury.

However, she was completely in control. Knowing he would leap backward and guard with his weapons, Paimon pulled back before landing the blow and instead launched her right leg up with enough power to force Mitzrael further into the air. After striking his guard, Paimon followed through by pushing him and using the momentum to flip backward. As soon as she touched the ground, she leapt forward with a powerful downward slash using both of her hands, which would have normally been very foolish.

In fact, Mitzrael was completely confused as to why she even thought to attack in such a manner.

However, that reason became clear once the strength of Paimon's assault forced him into the column of fire that had been building behind him. Without a chance to even scream, Mitzrael was enveloped in Phenex's tantrum, his body turning to ashes as the air was driven from his lungs and every charred inch of his body was accepted by the flames. He landed within the column of fire, and Paimon knew he would never leave it.

Although satisfied with his death, Paimon realized she couldn't remain, standing next to the encroaching flames. In his grief, Phenex had no concept of control, no concept of good or evil, neither friend nor foe. The same inferno that consumed Mitzrael was now advancing on her, and even as another spasm of pain ripped through her torso, Paimon sprinted away from the flames and toward Niccolo. What Paimon saw was enough to make her gasp and double her efforts.

And even as death followed her every step, Paimon just hoped she would make it to his side before it was too late.

CADMUS, Mercy's voice rattled against the reaper's brain, forcing him to abandon his staring contest with Beleth. The demon king was still perched on his hill and grinning at the human souls below, and swaths of animated corpses were roiling about in a perimeter around them. Still, Cadmus knew he had to respond to Mercy's call.

I'm kinda busy here, he thought as he tapped his heels against the horse's flanks and prompted him to circle toward Beleth. Instead, Mercy stayed his hooves.

I need you to promise me something, Master. Whatever happens here, my sister deserves her rest.

What are you talking about?

Beleth's cruelty must end. You must sever Misery's ties to this plane. It is paramount that you lay her to rest, Mercy explained, but it only shocked Cadmus further. Pursing his lips, he watched as Beleth scrawled a sigil into the air. This conversation needed to end as soon as possible, especially with the added threat of Phenex's meltdown.

Misery is your sister! Why would you want such a thing, and can we please move? Cadmus tapped Mercy's flanks once more, but the horse refused to move, not even when a fireball exploded nearby.

Not until you promise! Her suffering must end! If you need further persuasion, her soul is tied to his. He does not notice—he likely does not care—but it will provide a moment of opportunity you can use.

As Beleth finished drawing a fifth letter into the air, Cadmus realized he did not have time to argue.

Fine, I promise! Now let's do something about this, he urged, and immediately Mercy broke into a gallop toward the demon king. Once Beleth set his hand against the shimmering purple energy, crystal shards lanced out of the ether, but Mercy was too fast and dodged each incoming missile.

"What makes you think you can hope to challenge me?" Arrogant as he spoke, Beleth dragged the sigil through the air to follow Mercy's path. "I know everything about you, your purpose, the strengths and weaknesses of your mount! With the flick of a wrist, I can send you spiraling into madness!"

"Then you should have already killed me," Cadmus replied as Mercy rounded a slope and started toward the Fallen and his stationary horse.

"And you think a head-on approach will serve you well?"

"Only to distract you," Cadmus replied with a smile, and immediately Beleth realized what was happening.

Abandoning his onslaught of ice as fire raged about them, Beleth turned to see Cimeries falling out of the air, her pike aimed at his torso. With a grunt, Beleth swung his obsidian blade to counter her attack, but it only served to launch her airborne. Seeing that he was caught in a pincer attack, Beleth spurred Misery forward and the horse jumped off the hill.

Cadmus gritted his teeth, realizing this would be much easier if he would just follow Mercy's advice, and within a few seconds they were at the crest of the hill. Once Cimeries landed behind him on the saddle, Cadmus urged Mercy to follow after Beleth, who was once again placing his hand against purple sigils laid across his path. Almost immediately, pained moans filled the air, and their wails tore through the reaper's mind.

"Focus, Cadmus. He does that only because it distracts you," Cimeries stated simply, but it was becoming more than the reaper could bear.

"You really don't understand how this feels."

"No, I do not. However, we do not have the option for you to get bogged down in their pain. We need to follow Beleth and kill him. Focus on your objective."

"You make it sound so easy."

"I know it is *not*. However, I believe in you. For a man, you are worth something."

That choice of words forced Cadmus to realize that she really meant it. With the strength of a warrior queen at his back, Cadmus turned his attention to the retreating Beleth and realized that he had a trick up his sleeve.

Throwing his arm forward, Cadmus ignored all the empathetic pain surrounding him and tried to exert his will on Beleth's back. This needed to work—Cadmus had no other real option—and so he convinced himself that it would. Then, just as he was about to give up, blue energy ebbed out of his outstretched arm. Whatever powers he had, they seemed to be returning.

With just that small expression of willpower, Cadmus realized that Misery was running slower than she had before. Seizing upon this, Cadmus flexed all of the muscles along his right arm as Mercy continued to gallop, as the tortured and mangled flesh of Beleth's chimera fell around them, as flames appeared and exhausted themselves in moments. They were only safe because Cimeries swept away chimeric appendages before they could become dangerous, but Cadmus could not count on that for long. With a defiant shout, Cadmus tried to bend the universe to his will.

The universe obliged.

In that instant, both horse and her demonic rider floated through space, the mangled corpses of his chimera paused halfway through their birth from the mud. In that same instant, Mercy continued on just like before, even if his rider was bathed in blue energy. It was torture for Cadmus—he still felt the effect of each chimera's wails—but this needed to happen. What gave him strength was the woman behind him, the arm around his midsection holding him tight.

"Just a little closer, reaper," she whispered, and Cadmus realized that he had brought her with him into whatever this was. Grateful that he wasn't alone, Cadmus breathed deep and focused on maintaining his gift, to halt the flow of time for as long as possible. If he was able to get close enough, Cimeries might be able to end it after all.

There were still ten yards between them and Beleth when Cadmus started to falter. His breath became muddy; his senses started to fail him. Five yards away from them and Cadmus' eyelids became heavy, his vision shaking and his mind feeling like it would melt away. Just a yard away from them, Cadmus felt like he would be driven from consciousness, but he knew that he was close enough that Cimeries might be able to strike.

"Now!" He hoped that he had given her the right opportunity once he felt the woman's arm fall away from his torso.

From what Cadmus could tell, she brought her feet up to the saddle so that she could launch herself, but that was when their plan went awry. As soon as her feet left Mercy's saddle, she was torn from

Cadmus' distortion of time and the shock was enough for both of them to be shunted back into the normal flow of time.

Instead of being able to thrust her pike through his black heart, Cimeries was only able to slam into Beleth's side and drive him from his seat on Misery's saddle. She landed hard on the ground, unable to grab hold of any part of Beleth or his horse, but she had been able to throw him off balance and—still attached to the saddle—Beleth listed to Misery's right side. Once gravity took hold, his shoulder landed against the ground and he was dragged through the mud as his mutilated horse galloped on without noticing.

It would have been a great opportunity for Cadmus to kill Beleth, but the trauma he endured from slowing down time was too much for his body. As Beleth protested and tried to stop his horse, Cadmus curled over in his saddle and shook violently, drool coming out of his mouth as his body rejected the experience. He couldn't even hear Mercy's thoughts or his voice.

Cadmus only knew that this felt like dying, like the lions were ripping him apart all over again.

"Stop now!" Beleth shouted, loud enough to draw Cadmus out of his fog and, once he was able to look forward, he saw the demon king wrap his fingers around Misery's front leg and snap it, forcing the living nightmare to the ground.

It was just in time, as a wall of flames descended like a curtain just a few yards ahead of where Misery came to rest. Cadmus could only watch as Beleth tore himself from the saddle and then threw his horse away, pushing himself off the ground by using the dark broadsword in his right hand.

"That is what you get... for running." Cimeries walked forward, her words labored from the pain of slamming into Beleth. No doubt, she had broken something in the attempt to kill him. "But you cannot run further."

"Why would I run?" Beleth roared, taking slow steps toward his enemies. "You are only human! I can destroy you in an instant!"

"Then why haven't you?" Cimeries asked, raising her pike as she advanced on his position.

However, before she was within forty feet of the furious demon king, a golden orb crashed into the ground ten feet in front of Beleth. Although it pushed the odds into Beleth's favor, Cimeries only glared resolutely. When the energy dissipated, a lanky angel with drawn-out features stood up, blue armor seeming black as fire raged about their battlefield. He held a plain staff in his hand, but Cadmus guessed that it only appeared innocuous.

"Brother, I have come to help you with these humans," the angel stated, almost apathetic as he turned to Beleth. The demon king was still walking forward while the angel spoke, not even turning to face someone who had arrived in such a spectacle. Trying to stop shaking and failing, Cadmus wished he could help Cimeries, but he could barely sit up in his saddle. Mercy was screaming at him, but he could not hear the horse's voice.

"So you would resort to fighting with the help of angel, Beleth?" Cimeries asked, sidestepping so she could keep both of her enemies in her sight, but then Beleth did something she did not expect. When he was within just a yard of the newcomer, Beleth finally turned to face him with rage.

"I do not need it!" Beleth bellowed as he brought his blade above the tall angel's shoulders, severing his neck and killing him instantly. When the corpse fell to the ground, he turned back to face his fierce opponent. "I need *nothing* to kill you."

Although she was at first taken aback, Cimeries quickly recovered her senses and offered him a wry smile.

"I am glad to see you have some semblance of honor. I was beginning to lose hope in you."

"I do not need your hope; I do not need your respect. My very existence is leagues beyond your own," Beleth said as he stomped forward, his sword held to his right side. He was about to raise his left hand to start drawing in the air, but Cimeries put out her left hand in a halting motion.

"Hold! If this is the case, why bother with your magic? Face me as a warrior, Beleth, not as a coward. My pike versus your sword. A true contest of arms," she suggested, which stunned Cadmus. Gulping down empty air, he watched as Beleth's expression broke and turned into a smile. Then a low chuckle broke through the air.

"A true contest of arms..." he muttered, keeping eye contact with the warrior queen. "Yes, yes I think I like that. You truly are one of the exceptional cases, Hippolyta. If all humans were like you, I may have supported Lucifer's cause." Lifting his sword into a forward guard and holding it with both hands, Beleth circled to his right, and Cimeries mimicked the movement instinctively. "Let us see what capabilities you truly have."

"I could say the same for you," Cimeries said before breaking from her position and rushing the demon king. When she was within just a few feet of Beleth, she juked to the right and was met with a cross slash determined to cut her in half. Anticipating the counter, Cimeries rolled forward and then tried to thrust her pike into Beleth's armpit.

Taking notice of the attack, Beleth knocked away the shaft of her weapon with his blade and then jumped back. Once he was able to gain purchase with his boots, Beleth drove forward with a thrust of his own and Cimeries was forced to dive to the side. Smiling, Beleth turned his blade and then drew it across his body, hoping to catch her off-guard. She was, but Cimeries quickly swung her weapon forward and crashed it against the blade, hoping it would divert his attack.

Instead, the impact was enough to throw her ten feet through the air and onto her back.

Cursing—his mind finally starting to come back to him—Cadmus tried to urge Mercy forward, but a wall of flames swept between him and the two warriors. His spirit sank as he watched shadows dancing beyond the intense waves of orange and red.

Cimeries, as strong as she was, had already failed against Beleth before. He could only just make out the woman's shadow picking herself off the ground and roll to the side in time to avoid a powerful jumping slash from Beleth. She countered, but Beleth was able to deflect the blow somehow and the shadows separated again.

However, after that exchange, Cadmus realized that he couldn't tell which shadow was which. It was just too difficult to see what was happening beyond the wall of flames, so even if he could throw his scythe forward, even if he could use his powers to manipulate time, he had no real way to help.

Cadmus.

The mental shout was enough to bring him from the brink of despair, and Cadmus turned his head to look down at the horse. When he saw Mercy's pale eyes, Cadmus realized he had been trying to get his attention the entire time.

"Wh—what?"

"Remember what I said!" Mercy's rasp tore through him and shunted him back to the present. "Remember what I said about the ties between Beleth and Misery!"

With just those words, it finally dawned on Cadmus what he needed to do. Looking away from the fire and the flames, Cadmus could see the pain-ridden and broken horse trying to pick herself up just thirty yards away from him. Although its voice was drowned out by the roaring flames and the moans of Beleth's chimera, Cadmus could actually feel the horse screaming in pain.

"I—" he started, but Cadmus realized he had absolutely no time to ask another question. With every passing second, the odds of Cimeries surviving through her battle were becoming worse. Knowing that he could not reach the horse quickly and that he could not manipulate time, Cadmus brought back his scythe and prayed that he would be able to aim in his current state.

Slinging his arm forward, Cadmus let go of his weapon and sent it into a horizontal spin. It seemed like an eternity as the scythe carved through the air, and Cadmus knew there was every possibility that he had failed in his mission. However, in that impossible second, Cadmus watched as his weapon flew to its mark and the blade sliced through the neck of the mutilated horse. It was through in an instant, and Cadmus watched as the disembodied head at first rose a few inches in the air before falling to the bloodied soil below.

Hoping against the odds, Cadmus expected to find the warriors still dancing among beyond the flames, but the curtain of fire had been drawn away. What he saw shocked him, amazed him, drove him to tears.

There, standing straight up and staring forward with unfocused eyes, was Beleth, and just a few feet away, crouched and holding her pike in front of her, was Cimeries.

Their battle was over; Cimeries' pike had skewered the demon king through the heart.

"How... what..." Beleth muttered in shock, but Cimeries didn't bother answering him. Instead, she retrieved her pike, a wake of blood following after the curved blade, and then she slammed her foot into his midsection. Once she had sent him to the ground, she stepped forward and stood above him. Even with the great wound in his heart, Beleth was still breathing.

"Beleth." Cimeries held her pike above the Fallen's head in judgment.

"Fallen Angel. Demon King. *Traitor*," she spat out the word. "I am here to avenge Lucifer."

With that declaration, she slammed her pike through Beleth's face, destroying his brain and ending his life in a flash of blue light. Even as the flames roared about their battlefield, it seemed like time had stopped and that saying a single word might defile the moment. Cadmus only watched as purple energy burst from his wounds and engulfed her. It took Cadmus a moment to realize that she was absorbing Beleth's soul, that someone so powerful might completely overwhelm her.

After jumping off Mercy's saddle, he ran toward the warrior woman, but then the purple energy disappeared and he found Cimeries still standing. When she turned to face him, her gaze hard as stone, Cadmus stopped in his tracks. She only needed one last breath before picking up her weapon and stunning Cadmus into silence with three small words.

"Only Azazel remains."

"Azazel!" Niccolo shouted as he ran forward, his bastard sword held to the side. Instead of being worried, the grey demon opened his arms, daggers held in each hand. When Niccolo swung up and across his body, Azazel ducked to the side and flipped over, lashing at Niccolo with the third dagger held in his coiled tail.

After falling back to avoid the blade, Niccolo lunged forward with his twisted arm and grabbed hold of Azazel's tail. Smiling, he pulled hard and tried to plunge his sword into Azazel's unguarded midsection, but the demon twirled to the side and closed the distance, holding Niccolo in a mockery of a lover's embrace.

"Aww, you're sweet," Azazel said before flipping the blades in his hands and dragging them down Niccolo's back. The daggers tore through his armor and into his flesh, forcing out a cry of pain, but Niccolo was able to keep his presence of mind. Throwing his head forward, Niccolo tried to headbutt his opponent, but Azazel slipped away and pushed back before launching into a backflip, the dagger in his tail slashing up the middle of Niccolo's chest.

This time, Niccolo heard the grind of metal on metal and was grateful that some part of his armor was worth something. He backed away from Azazel and held his sword in front of him, waiting for his back to heal.

"You're leaving yourself far too open, Nico. C'mon, didn't Lucy teach you better than that?" he asked, which caused Niccolo to fly into a rage. He jumped forward, determined to cut Azazel in two with a vertical slash, but the demon merely stepped to his left and let the bastard sword slam into the ground.

"Seriously? Why the hell would I get caught by something as lazy as that?"

Turning the blade, Niccolo swung his sword to the right with the hope of catching Azazel's shins, but the traitor merely hopped over the strike and then threw out his tail, slapping Niccolo in the face with the flat of his blade.

"Nico, I want a *fight*. If you keep being this awful I'm just going to have to kill you. It's just... sad," Azazel said, throwing out his hip, and it was all Niccolo could do to stop himself from lunging forward.

It helped that he was not alone in this fight.

Stop it. Think this through, Plague's voice came to him, calming Niccolo down considerably. Holding his sword in a forward guard, Niccolo listed to the voice in his head. *He's baiting you because he probably can't handle you directly. Keep your wits about you and you'll be able to kill the fucker.*

You say that, Niccolo grumbled within his mind, but he tried to maintain some sense of control. He circled the grey-skinned demon, who regarded him with curiosity.

"Oh, what you girls talk about..." Azazel said with a pout before setting his hands on his hips. He held a loose grip on his weapons, as if he wasn't currently fighting for his life. "Plague, I'd like to hear your voice, too! We used to have such good talks!"

"Fuck you, Zel," Plague's voice boomed before the horse burst out of a green cloud that appeared on Azazel's right. With both daggers, Azazel turned to face the black horse, who was using his rear legs to kick at his midsection, but that was exactly what Plague had wanted. Niccolo took the opportunity to dive forward with a cross slash aimed at Azazel's upper leg, smiling at Plague's tactics.

Seeing that he was caught in a trap, Azazel pushed off the ground with his tail and rolled away from Niccolo, narrowly avoiding both strikes. Niccolo followed the horizontal strike with a downward slash, but Azazel was able to deflect it with the dagger held in his tail. Fortunately, the power behind Niccolo's sword was enough to send the weapon flying.

Unfortunately, Azazel was still healthy and whole, but Niccolo was encouraged. From the demon's scowl, Niccolo could see that the attack had shaken him. It wasn't long before Azazel recovered his grin, but there had been a moment of weakness. Crouching down so he could spring into action, Azazel chuckled softly.

"That was tricksy. I like it. I *really* do," Azazel said, the black of his eye sockets almost hypnotizing Niccolo, but he shook it off. Taking his left hand off the handle of his sword, Niccolo used it to beckon Azazel forward.

"More where that came from, Zel," he said, prompting the demon to throw himself into a whirlwind of movement. Twisting as he leapt forward, Azazel slashed and stabbed at Niccolo's feet while he threw his tail at Niccolo's face.

Dodging the weapons by jumping forward, Niccolo slammed his forearm into Azazel's tail and swatted it away before attempting to stab Azazel through the neck. The grey demon ducked to the side and threw his right hand forward, but this time Niccolo twisted and let the blade pass by harmlessly. Grunting with satisfaction, Niccolo set his nails against Azazel's arms and then jumped away, tearing chunks out of the demon's flesh.

Although he was pleased to hear a cry of pain, Azazel's tail came down from above and slammed into Niccolo, knocking him to the earth and burying his head in mud. Before he could react, twin daggers stabbed through his torso three times before something wrapped around his neck. Without any way to fight it, Niccolo was lifted into the air, and he was just barely able to see Azazel panting.

"You know, that arm has saved you *way* too many times. I should cut it off for you," he said, but then Niccolo saw Plague rushing up from Azazel's left side. Pleased by the sight, he waited for his horse to rescue him, but Azazel had been watching the horse with a dozen eyes that were scattered across his body. With barely any effort, Azazel whipped his tail around and across Plague's face, using Niccolo's body as a makeshift bludgeon.

Instantly, Niccolo felt something torn away from him.

"Plague!" he tried to shout, but Azazel's tail tightened around his neck.

"Oh, he disappeared into that green cloud of his, don't you worry. Your bratty little ass knocked him out. You should worry about yourself."

"I—" he started, but Azazel's tail constricted his throat further, choking out the word. Still, he was able to force something out. "I don't... need to."

"Nico, *buddy*, I'm holding you by the throat, I got two daggers that I can shove through your heart *right now*. The only reason you're alive is because I haven't decided to kill you yet. Are you really that stubborn to think you're on the winning side of this thing?"

Still held in that demonic grasp, Niccolo merely shrugged.

"You... used to like that... about me."

"I did. Still *do*... but it's getting to the point where I need to end this thing. It was fun, Nico, really," Azazel said before something pierced Niccolo's heart. The Horseman vaguely realized that Azazel may have killed him, but he wasn't going to just give up. Instead, he made eye contact with Lucifer's killer and laughed.

"So... how are you going to kill me?" he asked, and Azazel's face twisted in confusion.

"How?" he asked, drawing out the blade and plunging it back in, which made Niccolo feel like he was going to fade away. Laughing softly, Niccolo gathered what strength he had and sneered down at Azazel's face.

"I don't know. I just—I just know one thing. Something you forgot," he said, feeling the creature stirring from within his consciousness. Thankfully, Azazel was so disturbed by Niccolo's continued existence that he merely brought Niccolo's mouth closer to his ear.

"*What*? What do *you* know that I *don't?*"

Niccolo let out a pained breath before chuckling, Azazel's tail easing on its grip so he could speak.

"I am a *Horseman*," he said just as Plague formed beneath them, throwing Azazel off balance.

His face was full of rage for having been tricked, but Niccolo used the opportunity to lunge forward and clench Azazel's earlobe between his teeth. Tasting the demon's foul blood, Niccolo yanked his neck back and felt skin tear, the pain enough for Azazel to unwrap his tail from Niccolo's throat and fall away.

Still weak from Azazel's attack on his heart, Niccolo fell back against the ground and looked at his opponent. Azazel was enraged —something Niccolo had never seen before—and that was almost worth the price of dying. From his position, Niccolo could see the traitor wanted nothing more than his death.

However, Plague was busy distracting the grey demon, so he did not have the opportunity to finish off Niccolo. The black horse continued to strike at Azazel, running headfirst into the demon only to dissolve into a corrosive cloud, reforming once the grey demon got a lungful of pain. Hacking up mucus and blood, Azazel collapsed to his knees and shuddered on the ground. It was enough for Plague to stop his mist assault and try to throw his hooves into Azazel's face.

Except that had been Azazel's plan all along. Not nearly as weakened as he seemed, Azazel leapt forward and grabbed Plague by the throat with his tail, heaving the horse off the ground once he could use both arms. With a frustrated grunt, Azazel turned and threw Plague toward his master, forcing him to dissolve into the mist so that he would not crush the still-healing leper.

Feeling the green air flow around him, Niccolo watched as Azazel glared at him with fifty blood-red eyes.

"That's *enough*. If I can't stab your heart, I'll just tear it out of you!" Azazel said, running at Niccolo so fast that he was unable to react. He only watched as Azazel stomped forward, his goat legs powerful enough for him to jump five yards at a time. Then he leapt through the air, his grey hand poised to dive right into Niccolo's chest. In that moment, Niccolo knew he was about to die.

Then a green mist formed in front of him and a black horse appeared from the ether, throwing itself between his master and the demon intending to kill him. Before Niccolo could do anything, the beast was thrown into him and the three tumbled end over end, earth and blood and bodies mixing together and disorienting him.

When Niccolo was finally able to pick himself up, he noticed a black shape lay in front of him, letting out staggered breaths and whining softly. Looking around him, Niccolo noticed that Azazel lay behind him, a red and black shape clutched in his hand. Seeing it beat slowly, then weakly, Niccolo realized what had happened.

Whipping his head around, Niccolo saw Plague and the blood pooling around him and panicked, hoping against hope that he was wrong.

Crawling forward and denying reality, Niccolo could not help the tears forming in his eyes. He whined unintentionally as he got closer to his horse, his friend, the one soul truly attached to him. From this side, he couldn't tell, he couldn't know, so when he got to Plague's head, he circled around to see just what Azazel had torn out of him. It could have just been muscle; it could have just been a lung or some other unimportant organ. Something, *something* that did not mean he was going to lose his friend.

However, when he reached the other side, Niccolo saw the gaping hole in Plague's chest where his heart used to be. He was still breathing, but it was only a matter of time. No matter how defiant they were, denizens of Hell could not live without their hearts.

Sniffing back mucus and choking back tears, Niccolo crawled to Plague's head and held it in his lap, hoping to see some life from the one creature he needed most.

"Little..." Plague's voice came, deep, but not with his usual strength. Niccolo could still see the green of his eyes, but they were becoming dim.

"Shush, don't you talk. We're going—we're going to be fine," Niccolo argued, his voice wavering with too much emotion. He tried to send warm thoughts of sympathy, of confidence, but Plague would not have it. Closing his eyes slightly, Plague tried to console his master.

"No, little man... I'm not. You'll have to go on without me," he said, his voice softer with every word. "Know that I'm proud of you, that you're so much stronger than you think. I love you, Nico."

"I love *you*, Plague," Niccolo tried to say, shaking his head in defiance. "But you're not dying on me."

"I am. No fighting this one," Plague said, his words barely audible by the end. Niccolo continued to shake his head and sniffed back the snot filling his nose.

"We fight to the end, Plague!" he argued, but the light had already gone out of his horse's eyes.

Goodbye, little man.

And then he was gone.

"That was touching."

Azazel's snide voice ravaged the moment, and Niccolo's grief started to transform him. Setting down the head of his beloved horse, Niccolo climbed to his feet, tears completely clouding his vision, and stood hunched over. He swayed at first, but soon he was able to turn and face the grinning demon.

Azazel only laughed at the display.

"And here I thought bestiality was not your thing."

Looking at the demon who killed his friend, Niccolo could not think clearly. Something had changed in him; something was lost, and he would never be able to get it back. Whatever it was, it had died with Plague.

And as he looked at Azazel's grinning face, as he saw the world falling apart around him bathed in fire, Niccolo decided that it would not end like this. This murderer would not get away with this. *No one* would get away with this. If anyone was going to end this, it was going to be *him*. His fury, grief, frustration, indignation, his *righteousness* unable to be contained any longer, Niccolo lifted his head to the sky and screamed.

When he did, three voices came out and light exploded in all directions.

Azazel was thrown back fifty yards by the massive surge of energy and had to close all of his eyes just to avoid being blinded.

That familiar, haunting harmony echoed in his ears. Wind tore at his skin and only by digging in his heels, hands *and* tail was he able to keep from tumbling further.

After a few moments, the light dimmed and the wind died down slightly, so Azazel opened a tentative eye to see just what had happened. What he saw astounded him. Bright, white light emanated from where Niccolo had been standing, but it was still too much to look at directly. What was even more amazing was that the fire covering the sky had been pushed back and away from the source of all that energy. Only once the light dimmed down to acceptable levels was Azazel able to see just what had happened.

There—standing in the middle of a crater a foot deep—was Niccolo, his arms held to his sides and his face lowered to the ground. However, he wasn't the same Niccolo Azazel had been fighting only moments before. Magnificent, shining wings spread out from his back, light seemed to pulse from his very skin, and in his hands were very familiar objects. Strapped to his demonic arm was a radiant buckler, and held in his right hand was a short sword brimming with energy.

Azazel was seeing a living ghost.

"L—Lucifer?" Azazel asked, so confused and disoriented by Niccolo's appearance that he honestly thought he was seeing the brother he had murdered. However, when Niccolo raised his head and opened two eyes bursting with white light, Azazel was forced to admit his mistake.

"Close."

Niccolo crouched slightly and then flew forward, using his powerful legs and wings to rush his enemy in an instant. Azazel was unable to react as Niccolo slammed a demonic fist into his face and sent him rocketing backward through the air.

Midair, before Azazel was able to recover, Niccolo used his arm to force the traitor's face against the ground and ran alongside, dragging Azazel through the terrain. Before the friction could halt them, Niccolo stopped them by stomping on the ground and then pivoted, heaving Azazel over his shoulder and into the air.

When Azazel opened his eyes, he found that he was a hundred feet in the air and still climbing. However, just as soon as he made that realization, Niccolo was in front of him and had stabbed him through the gut with Lucifer's sword.

"That is for Paimon," Niccolo said softly before withdrawing the blade and grabbing Azazel by the throat. Niccolo then threw him even higher, flying up and over so fast that the traitor could only gulp down empty air before Niccolo was above him.

Throwing his fist down, connecting with Azazel's jaw and breaking it easily, Niccolo sent him crashing back to the ground. And just as he was about to hit the earth, Niccolo used his shield hand to slam him down even harder. "*That* was for Andras."

"This," Niccolo said before picking Azazel up and turning him around, using Lux to tear through his tail and send blood spurting everywhere, "is for all the kings you killed."

"*This,*" he growled, holding Azazel by the throat so he could carve off his left arm, "and *this*. And *these*," Niccolo said as he cut through each of Azazel's limbs, "are for all of the humans you turned into feral beasts!"

"*This,*" he shouted, shoving Lux into one side of Azazel's stomach and then cutting across to the other, "is for Marchosias! *This*," he screamed as he shoved the blade into the demon's heart and twisted the blade, "is for *Scratch!*"

Niccolo withdrew the blade, and Azazel was still breathing, somehow. However, this was exactly what he wanted. Setting the blood-covered point of his short sword up against the bottom of Azazel's head, he breathed in and out with effort, his teeth clenched.

"Nico..." The nickname leaked out of Azazel's mouth, but Niccolo ignored him as tears streamed down his face.

"And this... is for my *horse*, you bastard."

Then Niccolo shoved Lux into Azazel's brain until the point broke through the crown of his skull.

Breathing sporadically, Niccolo realized that he was holding a lifeless corpse just before grey energy started to leak out of Azazel's body. Then the energy flowed into him and threw his mind into chaos.

Millions of memories flitted around in front of him, the truth behind everything Azazel had done, why he had done it, who he had done it for. Just like Gabriel had said, he had always been Adonai's man on the inside. He had never been part of the revolution; he had betrayed Lucifer, betrayed *everyone* who ever trusted him. Then the worst of it slammed into Niccolo.

Azazel had sabotaged Mammon's birth. He was the reason the Hellborn had become a monster and why Lilith had died; he was the reason Lucifer was left alone and suffering for thousands of years.

Howling in pain, Niccolo collapsed into himself, dropping to his knees and letting his wings and weapons shatter into the air. Tears were streaming down his face, rage, pain, guilt, terror—*everything* was assaulting him all at once. When he was finally able to see, to see past the memories of Adonai's servant, Niccolo finally remembered who he was. He was finally able to remember what he had just lost.

Lifting his head, Niccolo saw Paimon running toward him, but he could not recognize her. He only saw the corpse of a black stallion, a friend who had been so alive only moments ago. Plague would never speak to Niccolo again, never ridicule him again, never show him affection again.

Forgetting everything else for just a moment, Niccolo curled up beside his horse and lost himself to grief.

CHAPTER 12
NO REST FOR THE WICKED

Lucifer was sitting in a rigid chair at the edge of his throne room, a rolled cigarette of hellweed held between his fingers, and it was becoming difficult to justify taking another drag. It had become a recent habit, but it had also been decades since he was truly able to enjoy **anything,** much less smoking. Still, he raised the cigarette and pulled in a lungful of acrid smoke, letting it burn at his insides for a moment before letting it out in a heavy sigh. When he did, it obscured his throne.

Uncomfortable most of the time, Lucifer watched as the throne shifted again, new weapons and armor forcing their way to the surface and promising new pain for his back. Groaning, he lowered his head to his palm as he realized it was a new day. Another day of ruling this kingdom of refugees and pretending to be something he was not.

When he raised his head from his hand, Lucifer pursed his lips and looked to the entrance of the room, finding he was not alone. However, his guest would not need any of his masks, or need Lucifer to pretend to be some sort of authority figure.

Curling his fingers, Lucifer beckoned Buné to come closer. He was hoping his brother would take the cue to sit in the chair nearby, but Buné stopped several feet away and crossed his arms.

"It's almost time, Lucifer. Azazel is making his move on Räum soon, from the look of it, and the Council of Kings is only a week from now. He's been following the old crow ever since he came to us with the changes to the revelations."

Buné's glare burned through Lucifer and forced the angel to look down at his hands. Ash collected at the end of the cigarette, and it was a welcome distraction.

"Räum, huh? Guess it's not going to be much longer at all. We always knew he would start going after Fallen eventually." Lucifer concluded the statement by raising the cigarette to his lips and sucking in foul air. For some it was addictive, but Lucifer really just liked the pain. "Those new revelations certainly made Zel nervous, though. It's not like they changed much of the situation."

"Would you quit that?" Buné asked, causing Lucifer to look up at him with a smile.

"I'm sorry, **smoking** bothers you?" he asked incredulously, but Buné only narrowed his eyes.

"**You** smoking bothers me. It's just a stalling tactic and you know I can tell. Put it out," Buné demanded before walking to the other chair and dragging it over so he could sit opposite Lucifer. Since his friend already knew his tactics, Lucifer dropped the cigarette and ground it out beneath his foot.

"Yes, sir." He sat back in his chair and crossed his arms as Buné did the same. They sat there like that for a time, neither one wanting to venture forward a tendril of conversation, but eventually Buné leaned forward and interlaced his fingers so he could support his head.

"Is there any way to change your mind? It really doesn't have to happen this way."

That surprised Lucifer. Buné had always been a source of confidence and defiance; he would never surrender if he thought he could win otherwise. It just made his argument mean that much more.

"I don't see how, old friend. Without my death, the two of them would not find their way to Earth. Without our **failure**," Lucifer explained, accenting the word with air quotes, "we couldn't be sure they would have the strength and resolve to carry on. Humans... they love their vengeance. Without it, they're... content to survive. I'm sorry, Buné, but we can't risk it."

"You know we **can**, you're just being stubborn. You want to make yourself out to be a martyr when you could stand beside them and actually **guide**." Buné glowered. "It doesn't **have to happen**."

"Buné..." Lucifer started, setting his chin on his palm, "half the point of this is to see if humanity is really able to succeed us. If we hold their hands, if we just use this as an excuse to rise again and we fall, we've accomplished **nothing**. We have to let them reach their potential, even if that means we won't be there to help them."

"They're just boys. Infants**!**" Buné shouted for the first time in thousands of years, jumping out of his chair and throwing the chair behind him, where it tumbled until it fell on its side. "Cadmus is barely past his thirteenth century and Niccolo just finished his third!"

"Not yet, actually. Still halfway through the third."

"You're putting all of our hopes and dreams, schemes and tricks, the **weight** of the **world** on their shoulders, and you don't even have the courtesy to let them know your plan." Buné snarled, his composure completely broken.

"I'll think of something." Lucifer avoided eye contact and looked at the ruined cigarette on the floor. For a split-second, he almost wanted another one, but Buné took a few quick steps and stepped on the cigarette before backhanding his brother across the face. Lucifer let his cheek throb and remained sitting, only bothering to look at his brother.

"That's for **them.** Just for that pitiful fucking excuse. They don't deserve this," Buné said before turning away and walking over to his discarded chair. Lucifer watched him as he picked it back up and placed it where it had been before sitting down again. "You're just using them."

"No. They don't deserve this, but I'm not using them. I care too much for that."

"Oh, I'm not debating that you care for them, but you can't look at me with a straight face and tell me this isn't cruel. Niccolo looks up to you like you **are** his father and you're planning to let him see you **die**. You're planning to cause him pain he might not be able to handle."

"He'll handle it..." Lucifer muttered, the fight going out of him all at once. "Niccolo's strong. **Cadmus** is strong. They'll be able to lean on each other, to depend on each other. I wouldn't send them out into the world if they couldn't," he explained before looking into Buné's eyes. "Like it or not, our time is over."

"I'm not sure it was **ever** our time, brother," Buné admitted, his mind far away. When he turned back to face Lucifer, it was clear he had given in. "And you expect me to stay my hand?"

"You have to, Buné. When they come to you, you have to tell them to stay away from it all. Nico's stubbornness will get the better of them and they'll come to me and Azazel."

"And when he destroys the palace, I'm supposed to just sit on my hands?" Buné followed up the question, resentment coloring his statement.

Lucifer chuckled at that; his friend was too predictable.

"And you say that **I** ask stupid questions."

"You're telling me to abandon my brother, my king, and let him die at a coward's hand. It's a pretty complicated way to commit suicide."

"Don't you think I've earned it, though? At least I'm trying to make the world a better place. Is that **so** wrong?" Lucifer asked, breaking Buné's composure. Suddenly, he looked at his brother with sympathy.

"No. After all we've seen, I can't judge you for that. It's a shame I have to stay behind, though. Sure I can't be part of your martyrdom?"

"You and I both know you've always been the one to pick up my pieces." Lucifer laughed, drawing a smile out of his stoic brother. Buné made eye contact with Lucifer, and just like that, there were no more arguments. "Astaroth will make his moves, Buné. He'll turn this place into the army it needs to be, but you need to be there to guide them once they're ready to rise against Adonai."

"Since you can't be bothered to lead your own rebellion."

"Hey, I already failed once. Can't have **two** failed rebellions to my name," Lucifer said, drawing a scoff from his brother. Then the smile disappeared.

356

"Do you really think we have a chance this time, Lucy?" Buné asked, and Lucifer sighed as he turned back to look at his shifting throne.

It was about time that he gave it up to someone better.

"I think this is the only chance we ever had," he breathed out. Before Buné could do much else, there was a loud knock on the door of the throne room and it was immediately pushed open. Gathering himself quickly, Lucifer straightened his posture and watched as Niccolo marched into the room and then looked around in confusion. Once he found the Fallen sitting at the edge of the room, Lucifer smiled back at him.

"There you are, Scratch! Why are the torches out?" He had so much energy, this surrogate son, and it was threatening to improve Lucifer's mood.

"Oh, you know, mood lighting," Lucifer replied. Although Niccolo laughed, Buné was less than pleased.

"It's the first thing in the morning, Nico. What are you doing here?"

"Early morning training session. Basically, I'm here to kick his ass," he said, lazily pointing at the Devil.

"And where did this confidence come from?" Lucifer asked, leaning back in his chair and crossing his legs. "Last time we fought I'm pretty sure I blinded you and had my blade against your throat."

"Exactly," Niccolo said before rolling his solitary eye. "I need to pay you back."

"Brother, would you indulge my young friend here and allow me to shame him in private?" Lucifer asked, turning to Buné and expecting him to understand. Fortunately, Buné knew exactly why he wanted to be alone with his second son.

With only a nod of his head, Buné rose out of his chair and headed to the doorway, briefly stopping at Niccolo's side.

"Be easy on him. The old geezer's hip is about to break." Buné patted Niccolo's shoulder and gave him a small smile, and Niccolo nodded in approval before turning to face his mentor.

"Thanks for the tip. I'll be sure to target it," he responded, earning Buné's scoff. After the exchange, Buné continued on his path and hesitated at the doorway so he could make eye contact with Lucifer.

Worlds of information passed between them in that brief moment, but Lucifer just smiled and nodded, hoping that would be enough. Then Buné passed through the doorway and left Lucifer with his favored son.

"You know, Nico, I'm not sure I want to beat you up today," Lucifer said once the door closed behind Buné, motioning to the other chair with his left hand. "Why don't you sit down?"

"Seriously?" Niccolo asked, raising an eyebrow but still walking over to the chair before plopping himself down, setting his right arm along the back of the chair. "I'm calling that a forfeit."

"Eh, why not? Your willpower is obviously stronger than mine, today." Lucifer surrendered, throwing up his hands in mock display. "I'm just not particularly in the mood."

"Oh, why is that?" Niccolo asked with some eagerness. Looking at him, Lucifer felt an odd mixture of pride, admiration and guilt. Niccolo was still so young, so full of vitality, but Lucifer was about to force him through a world of hurt. Pushing it out of his head and trying to stick to the plan, Lucifer derailed the conversation from the truth.

"After two million years in Hell, I'm allowed to feel that way, Nico. Why don't we just catch up? We haven't actually spoken in some time."

"Well, there's really not much to update you on," Niccolo said before shaking his head and looking to the floor, trying to recall something interesting. "Hell's pretty boring, for all the bad reputation it gets. I mean, only eight souls fell to the Pestilence Quarter since I last saw you."

"Eight? That's not bad. You think any of them will make good soldiers for the war?" Lucifer let his arm fall onto his bended knee and tried to appear relaxed.

When Niccolo leaned forward, still looking at the floor in dismay, he reminded Lucifer of his younger self.

"Doubtful. They're having even more problems than I had when I got here, and that only fixed itself right before I became a Horseman. I wouldn't put much faith into them," he said before looking back to Lucifer. "Is it really worth it to care about all that? I mean, yeah, we're supposed to start the Apocalypse, but do you think any of these guys can take down angels? It's hard for me to see the point, sometimes."

"It's... hard for me to see it sometimes, myself," Lucifer admitted, his conscience screaming at him to reveal the truth. This army they were raising was nothing in comparison to Lucifer's plans for Niccolo and Cadmus, but Niccolo wasn't allowed to know that. Looking away, Lucifer tried to compose himself before redirecting the conversation.

"But we have to do what we have to do, Nico. So... how's Fafnir? Your dragon doing alright?"

"He's doing really well. Last week he had a cold, somehow, but he's all better and terrorizing some of the lesser souls. He **almost** bit me the other day, but I put the fear of God into him," he said with a laugh, and when the name of their true enemy passed Niccolo's lips, Lucifer realized that he could not leave him completely empty-handed.

He needed to offer **something** to the human who might fix his mistakes. After a moment of silence—Niccolo staring at him the entire time—Lucifer prepared himself for what he needed to say.

"Niccolo," Lucifer paused, pursing his lips before breathing in deep, "I want you to know that I'm proud of you, for coming this far."

"What are you talking about? I'm just a Horseman. You know, just waiting 'til the Apocalypse."

Lucifer wanted to reveal everything, but he knew he could only offer clues and vague notions or it would all be ruined.

"Just hear me out, kid," Lucifer said with a grunt. "For someone as young as you, becoming a Horseman of the Apocalypse and leading part of a demonic army is quite the accomplishment. It may not seem like this all has a purpose, but I want you to believe in yourself and what you're doing."

"Please, I'll be fine. Besides, it's not like you're not going to be there with me. It'll be your time to rise again," Niccolo said with a smile, but that made Lucifer's heart ache. Lowering his gaze, he tried to compose himself and just barely succeeded.

"There may come a time when I'm not around to help. The Apocalypse will be pretty hectic, and between Earth and Heaven, there's going to be a lot of ground to cover. Basically... I'm saying you might not always be able to count on me to help, for me to add my power to yours."

"Scratch—"

"This is important, Nico," Lucifer interrupted, his voice deeper and more serious. When he looked back at his favored son, the smile had dropped from his face. "I want you to know that when I'm gone, you're still you. You're still the same stubborn jackass who refused to die when a Horseman of the Apocalypse tried to kill you. You're still the same man who sparred with the Devil and lived. Whatever comes to pass, you have the power to keep going. I know it."

"Where—" Niccolo tried again, but a shake of Lucifer's head was enough to stop him.

"Doesn't matter where this is coming from. Don't lose that **defiance**, Nico, no matter what. You don't have to depend on **me**, on **anyone**, and even when all hope seems lost, there's always a way. You **can** depend on me, on Cadmus, but if there comes a day where we're not around, I want you to know that you have it in you to keep fighting on alone."

"You sentimental..."

"No!"

"Yes!" Niccolo interrupted him this time, lifting himself out of the chair and standing above his mentor. "You're being sentimental and mushy and it's uncomfortable. You don't **have** to tell me any of this, Scratch. I **know** I'm fantastic. I know I can depend on you and Cadmus and Barbas for anything and I appreciate it, but don't talk about it like it's already happened.

"I," Niccolo said before leaning down and slapping Lucifer's shoulder, "am going to the Death Quarter and seeing what boring things Cadmus is up to, because anything is better than suffering through this. None of this needs to be said. I know you're worried—you never **stop**—but this is something you **don't** need to worry about. The Apocalypse hasn't even started yet."

"Nico," Lucifer started to protest, but the leper had already stood back up and was walking to the doorway.

"I'm not listening to it unless you want to say it while sparring with me." He reached the doorway and placed his hand on the handle before looking back at Lucifer. "So get Lux in your hand or I'm out of here."

"Fine, you brat," Lucifer said with a smile, standing out of his chair and letting his wings and sword burst into existence. Pointing Lux at his student, Lucifer felt all his doubts melt away. If anyone could succeed him, it was this stubborn little creature smiling near the doorway. "But if I win, you have to listen to me for another hour."

At the wager, Niccolo smiled and took his hand off the door so he could summon the sword now bubbling into existence.

"Then it's a good thing I won't lose, isn't it?"

"He knew!" Niccolo sobbed it out, the revelation enough for him to lift himself off Plague's corpse. "He knew all along..."

"What are you talking about, Nico?" Paimon asked, her voice trembling as she tried to recover from sprinting to his side. She had tried to stop it, tried to help them, but she had been far too late. Instead, she had been a witness to Niccolo's transformation.

She had been there to watch him inherit the powers of Lucifer.

However, once Paimon was able to get close, he had devolved into a sobbing mess, grieving for a friend who had been attached to his very soul. She had knelt down next to him to rub his back, but now he was even more agitated.

"*Scratch!*" Niccolo slammed his fist against the ground for emphasis. "He knew he was going to *die*! He *planned* this! He..." Niccolo tried, but his anger abandoned him and sorrow took its place. "He wanted me to see him... die..."

"That's—are you sure?" Paimon asked out of sheer reaction, but she immediately regretted it.

"Yes, I'm fucking *sure*! I saw him talking to Buné about it! All of this," Niccolo swept his arm around him, pointing at Phenex burning in the sky and then finally turning back to Plague's body. "All of this is a result of their planning."

"They couldn't mean for any of *this*..."

"No... not this," Niccolo said, gulping down his misery and shaking his head. "No, this was all Azazel and Beleth. This is all *Adonai's* fault along with his fucking angels. This is..." he said, his voice turning to a whine as he realized his part in this tragedy, "...this is *my* fault."

"Nico, no." Paimon set her fingers against his arm, and he shrugged them away, but she would not let Niccolo continue to blame himself. "No one could have seen this coming, not you, not Lucifer. *Azazel* probably didn't have a clue."

"Scratch wanted the portal to open, Paimon," he muttered in a low voice. Paimon backed away, stammering, and Niccolo kept staring at Plague's lifeless face.

"He even got Buné to stay away so that he wouldn't interfere. Scratch wanted seven kings to die," Niccolo said before turning to face her. "I'm not sure you were supposed to live, Paimon."

"He wouldn't..."

"Why *not? You* know him better than most. After you fell, Lucifer's only real hope was to rise up and take back everything from Adonai. When he realized that humanity was his only shot, he planned for everything. He planned for the kings to die, he planned to use Azazel to his advantage..."

"Scratch..." Niccolo hesitated on the nickname, "he *used* me. He knew I would go out of control and chase after Azazel. He knew I would see just what Adonai was up to, his brutality and his selfishness, and he knew I would keep going."

"Since he met me, Paimon. Since he *met me*, he's just been using me."

Paimon saw the tears streaming down his face and crawled back to his side—even as Phenex's rage still burned through the entire battlefield—and grabbed his face with both hands.

"No, Scratch loved you. He loved you more than he ever loved *me*, and you *know* that. You *felt* it. Don't you dare deny that he cared for you."

"I know *exactly* how he felt about me, but that doesn't change the truth. I was his backup plan in case Cadmus wasn't strong enough.

Just another puppet for him to control," he said before feeling a sharp sting on the side of his face. When he looked up to see Paimon's arm, he realized that she had slapped him.

"Niccolo, you are no one's *puppet*. You wouldn't stand for it. I haven't known you that long, but you have always, *always* shown just how stubborn and independent humanity can really be. If Scratch put you in his plans to overthrow Adonai, it was because he *depended* on you and your strength. Your resolve and defiance."

"Paimon..."

"And he *chose* to show you this vision. He *wanted* you to know just how far back this goes, how he was willing to die, how he was willing to depend on you for *everything*. Sweetie, this was his *confession* to you. That was Scratch's last *goodbye*."

Tears pooled at the bottom of her eyes, and Niccolo realized she was speaking the truth.

"His last... goodbye," he repeated, too stunned to argue further. She nodded, wiping away tears with the back of her left hand.

"You know I'm right. You have his wings, Nico, and his weapons. Scratch lives on in you. *You* are his legacy, and I know he'd be damn proud of you," she said, but Niccolo couldn't look away from Plague's closed eye.

"Paimon, I don't know what to do. I can't even think about taking on Adonai right now. I... Plague... I should be dead..."

"I know, honey, I know," she consoled him, wrapping her arms around him for a moment and wishing they could stay and grieve. After rubbing his back, Paimon withdrew and shook her head. "And you don't have to think about Adonai right now, but we have two very real problems."

"Wha—"

"First, we have to calm Phenex down somehow," she interrupted him, pointing at the firestorm still threatening their lives. "With Lucifer's powers, I think you may be able to do it."

"I... maybe," Niccolo surrendered, looking at the white-hot

flames and biting his lip. The way he looked, Paimon felt horrible for what she was forcing on him.

"And we need to do that fast, Nico," she said, earning his attention. "Tamiel is in danger. Adonai sent angels after him, too."

"What?" Niccolo shouted, three voices echoing out of his throat in harmony as white wings burst into existence. "How?"

"Mitzrael told me before Phenex killed him. We're already late, but..."

"We'll make it." Niccolo looked to the sky with eyes bursting with light, the scarred tissue on the left side of his face not enough to hold it back. "I'm not letting more of our friends die today." After the statement, Niccolo jumped with such force that it broke the ground beneath him, and then he was soaring straight at the flames.

Trembling, Paimon watched from the rubble and wondered just how much of the Devil now lived in that poor boy.

YESHUA FELT the warmth around him and wondered what was happening. He knew there was something important he forgot, something that was being smothered by the waves of anger and heat and fire all around him. The only thing he knew was that he was grateful for it; he could remember the pain being so much, too much for him to bear. It had something to do with what he had done...

Then he remembered. He remembered just what he had done to his best friend. The flames burned hotter as his heart broke again as he recalled how Judas had turned back into a human—had abandoned his rage and fury—and looked at his friend with relief. He remembered the silver blade entering his chest and taking away every ounce of life in his body.

With that memory, Yeshua realized a horrible truth. When he had lain across Marchosias' body, grieving for the friend who had saved him from a second death, he had harvested the man's soul. Yeshua wasn't remembering this death from his perspective; he was feeling what it was like to truly die, to be betrayed by a man he loved like a brother.

Crying out in pain, Yeshua felt every scene from his friend's long life surround him, saw history from the eyes of Judas Iscariot. Suddenly, all of his own actions seemed so terrible, and at once understood why his friend had betrayed him so long ago. Then he saw how they had reconciled, how they had carved out their lives in the depths of Hell and had depended on each other.

And just as he realized what was about to come, Yeshua was back in that forest where he had thrown his friend away. He felt the rage and sorrow, the pure frustration Judas had felt; Yeshua felt his own betrayal like a knife to the heart. He felt his fear when Judas issued his ultimatum; he felt his heartache when Judas left those woods with tears in his eyes. The werewolf would never have let anyone see them in life, but Yeshua could see them now.

Letting out another bright flare, Yeshua screamed in horror and pain as Judas' memories assaulted his mind. He saw it all from the demon's perspective as Azazel and Beleth surrounded him with chimera and hell beasts, as they swarmed around him with greater numbers and pinned him to the ground. Yeshua felt every blow and every cut as Beleth twisted his body and transformed Judas into that enraged giant wolf.

"*Phenex!*"

The name seemed familiar to the airborne man, but it did nothing to take him out of his friend's memories. However, it was enough for the perspective to shift. Instead of anger and resentment and pain, different emotions surged about and confused Yeshua. Now, as he watched himself and the angels soaring through the air, he felt worried and frantic. When he relived one of Judas' last moments—as he shook his head back and forth with an angel clenched in his jaws—there was nothing but a sense of concern in his head.

Then, when his mind flowed to the memory of Judas returning to his human form, Yeshua finally understood. It had all been worry and concern for *him*. In his last moments, Judas had only thought about his friend and trying to save him. When Judas saw Nithael rushing toward them and switched places with Yeshua, he only cared about saving his friend's life.

This was what Judas had wanted to show him. In his death, he didn't want Yeshua to feel responsible, to feel like he hated Yeshua for abandoning him. Even as he was absorbed into Yeshua's soul, Judas only wanted him to understand that he had loved his brother until his tragic end.

Letting out flaming tears that scarred through his cheeks, rage abandoned Yeshua and all he felt was grief for the man he had betrayed. He did not deserve this life and he certainly didn't deserve to be here in Judas' place. After more than thirteen hundred years, Yeshua finally realized just what kind of man he had been.

"Yeshua!" the shout came again, three voices echoing against each other, and it caused him to realize one vital truth. When he had died, Phenex had given up his earthly name. Yeshua had been a man who inspired a religion, who had been responsible for so much, and he had run away from that responsibility.

However, now that he knew the truth of his deeds, Phenex realized that he could never claim that responsibility. He was responsible for the death of a good man—a *great* man, his brother in arms and the afterlife—and that he was a monster. He was *truly* more of a demon than he had really considered.

"Yeshua!" the chorus shouted through the flames once more, but Phenex would not ignore it any longer. In an instant, the inferno blazing for miles in all directions was absorbed back into the demon, who was naked if not for a scrap of fabric hanging loosely about his hips. With white eyes and tear tracks burnt into his skin, Phenex turned to face the stranger with angelic wings, who was hovering fifty yards away.

"That is no longer my name," Phenex stated simply, causing the stranger to stare at him in confusion. After approaching the flying man, Phenex realized he was looking at Niccolo, and briefly wondered how he had come to grow wings just like Lucifer. "I am Phenex. I have been reborn."

Al... right," Niccolo said, pausing halfway through the word, "sure. Are you... done?"

"No, I will not be finished until the angels pay," Phenex said, fire escaping with the violent words, but he looked down at the destruction he had wrought and grunted. "But this battle is over."

"Are you alright? Marchosias..."

"Is dead, Niccolo," he said, turning to face his companion and breathing in. "And I am responsible. Why do you have Lucifer's wings?"

"I..." Niccolo said, his fist shaking as he held Lux in his grip. "I don't know. Plague died, I..."

"Enough," Phenex said before floating over and setting a gentle hand on the shoulder of his ally in grief. "We have both been reborn, it seems. We will kill those responsible, I swear it."

"Yeshua..."

"That is *not* my name anymore, and I will not repeat myself again," Phenex said, his voice darkening. "I don't deserve that name after what I did to him. I will be judged—I will not run from it—but Heaven will be in flames before that happens. You understand, I think."

"I do," Niccolo agreed before making eye contact with his vengeful ally. "And we will make that happen, but we need to get back to the others. Tamiel is in trouble."

"Then lead the way."

Without another word, they descended to the scorched battlefield where only three figures remained standing. When Niccolo set his boots against the ground, the ground cracked and caused him to look down. The sand that had been there previously had been turned to glass due to the heart from Phenex's firestorm.

"Nico, I'm so sorry," Cadmus said. His words broke Niccolo out of his daze, and he looked up to see a face full of compassion and misery. "I know what he meant to you. I can't imagine what it would be like to lose Mercy."

"No, Cadmus, you can't." Gritting his teeth, Niccolo squared up to his companions and focused on the current problem. "But we can't stay here. Tamiel is in trouble."

"Paimon briefed us, but how do you suppose we catch up to them?" Cimeries responded, prompting Niccolo to glare at her in fury. However, Cimeries did not balk.

"What are you talking about?" he asked, but Paimon spared Cimeries from answering him.

"I think she's saying that because of how fast the angels move inside of those spheres, we might not be able to get to them in time."

"No, I mean, what are you talking about? We have a way to get there in time," he said before turning his gaze on Cadmus. "Cadmus will slow down time and we will get there."

"Nico, I..." Cadmus stammered as he collected his thoughts. "I don't know if I can do that. That's more than a day's travel away."

"Don't let me down now, Horseman. You've been able to slow down or stop time *how many* times in the last week? I'm not letting Tamiel die if we have any way to stop it," Niccolo said, but Cadmus shook his head.

"That is... I almost *died* carrying Cimeries with me just now—"

"We are *not* letting Tamiel die!" Niccolo interrupted before light burst out of him and stopped Cadmus mid-sentence. "*Almost* is still not dying, Cadmus. We have to do everything we can. We have to use all the powers at our disposal. I just need you to get me there."

"Nico, I'm not sure I can take all of us like that," Cadmus argued, caution filtering into his words, but Niccolo stomped forward until he was by Mercy's head.

"I didn't say *us*. I said *me*. You're taking me, you're slowing down time, and we're going to save Tamiel. *That* is what is going to happen."

"You're asking too much," Cadmus argued, but Niccolo grabbed his left hand and yanked down hard so their faces were inches away.

"I'm not going to let more of our friends die today! Marchosias died because of our mistakes. Plague died because of *mine*. Look at me and tell me that Tamiel deserves to die." His voice shook as grief bubbled to the surface.

Cadmus was about to argue, but once he saw the pain in Niccolo's face, he couldn't refuse him. Sighing, he looked north and motioned behind him with a nod.

"Get on, then," he said, and Niccolo immediately complied and jumped into the saddle, his wings disappearing in an instant. Before Cadmus could urge Mercy forward, Paimon ran up beside them.

"What are you guys doing? You can't go alone! We just need to figure out..."

"Paimon." Cadmus looked down at her in resignation. "This is the only way. I just need to get him there."

"Cadmus..."

"I can't tell him no, Paimon. Not today. Hopefully the next time you see us, we'll still be alive."

"Cadmus!" Paimon shouted, but she was silenced by fingers falling against her cheek. She looked up to see a human gazing down at her with Lucifer's eyes.

"I'm not letting our brother die," Niccolo said as Mercy reared back—an angry rattle issuing from the ether—and before anybody could react, the horse and his riders blinked out of existence. When Paimon turned to face what was left of their group, she knew they would return.

However, she also knew they would not return unharmed.

As he strolled through the clearing, Tamiel tapped his shepherd's crook against an errant lamb. It was a timid little thing and walked back to the rest with only a small squeak of complaint, which forced a smile out of the exile. They were cute when they weren't straying too far from the rest of the flock, and that was the main reason he kept them around. It was a nice distraction from all the pain and death he could see happening around the world.

Reaching the end of the clearing, the lamb followed the other sheep into the pen attached to Tamiel's hovel, rushing headlong into the wall of complaining animals. Tamiel followed lazily behind, closing the pen behind it before resting his hand on the old wood. This was a time of peace in Tamiel's life, but he couldn't fully enjoy it; he knew Niccolo and all the others were facing all kinds of danger.

Although he had thought about watching the events from afar, Tamiel decided against it and kept himself ignorant of what was happening on the other side of the Rubicon. He had seen too much death already; he didn't need to see what Azazel and Beleth would do if they were victorious. After all this time on Earth, Tamiel had decided to rely on hope. He had made a contingency plan in case the humans fell and the others came to finish him off, of course, but he decided that it would be best to wait and see who would arrive at his door.

Pushing through into the dark confines of his hovel, Tamiel walked over to one of the feed bags and picked it up to his shoulder, grunting as it weighed him down. It seemed that after two million years of living on Earth that he had lost some strength, but that was fine. He had never truly needed it.

As he walked back to the entrance of his house, Tamiel thought about Cadmus and the power lurking within him. The reaper had more than just a feedbag weighing him down; Lucifer's plans and the souls of thousands threatened to break his back and his will at any time.

After letting out a heavy breath, Tamiel hoped his friend would be able to help the poor Horseman. When he had gone to visit the old reaper, he had seemed wary but interested. It was another issue Tamiel would have to leave to hope.

Tamiel walked into the sunlit field and breathed deep the fragrant air. The springtime temperature was quite pleasant and he tried to enjoy the warmth of the sun on his skin. He remembered the old days, the first few millennia where he and Sathariel had explored it all. It seemed like only yesterday that she had stood in this very field and looked back at him with a mischievous smile.

Almost immediately, that vision was replaced by her face twisted in pain, her back arched to the point of breaking and the bloody stumps of her wings propping her up against the floor. He trembled as he remembered his part in that, how he had shriveled with his back against the wall as the Amazon had given her peace. That was Tamiel's greatest shame; why he would never be able to leave this clearing.

This was where he had last seen her happy, and he could never abandon that.

Tamiel calmed his nerves and lazily walked over to the pen, hoping the small lamb would be able to cheer him up with its antics. Except for Lucifer's avengers, those creatures were the only thing Tamiel really cared about. Even at his worst, their affection was enough to bring him some small comfort.

However, when he finally reached the pen, he found every single sheep dead, their throats slit and their bodies lying in a mix of blood and dirt. Except for the lamb. The lamb's head was cut off completely except for a small piece of flesh that connected it to the rest of its frail body.

His sorrow was so great that Tamiel could not react fully, but he also knew that he had no time to grieve. Dropping the feedbag from his shoulder, Tamiel turned to face the three angels standing nearby.

"We figured it would be best to kill them now, brother. Once you're gone, they won't have anyone to feed them and, well, you've coddled them with the life you gave them. They wouldn't survive in the wild," the shortest angel said lazily, his hands hidden in the long sleeves of purple robes as he stood to the right of his brothers. His face was rather unremarkable except for an appearance of perpetual boredom.

"A cruel sort of mercy, Sabrael. Must you always kill those who cannot fend for themselves?" Tamiel asked, crossing his arms as he slowly walked toward his brothers. He stopped once he was within ten feet and squared up to them.

"If they cannot fend for themselves, what is the point of their existence? Not everything needs to live," Sabrael responded, looking straight into Tamiel's eyes. "If it makes you feel any better, we didn't feel any joy in the slaughter."

"Oh, I suppose that relieves you of any sort of guilt, then," Tamiel said sarcastically, which drew a scoff from the long-haired angel standing in the middle, who he easily recognized as his brother Uriel.

"Why would we feel guilty about slaughtering anything, Tamiel? We are ordained by God and our duties are beyond your judgment. If a sheep gets in the way of God's will, there will be a *dead sheep*." Uriel held his spear loose in his right hand, the point closest to the ground dripping with innocent blood.

"You are a proud example of our race. How I feel so *blessed* to count you among my siblings. Why are you here, Uriel?"

"It's a simple thing," the last angel spoke, causing Tamiel to look to his left. The angel was naked from the waist up, short brown fuzz etched into angelic runes along his scalp. His legs were covered in thick, billowing trousers, but the blood-covered axe in his left hand drew Tamiel's gaze. "We're here to kill you."

"Oh, that's all, Camael? I never would have guessed." Tamiel closed his eyes and sighed. When he opened them, he looked at his brothers with disdain. "I asked *why* you are here. You're here to kill me, obviously, but why?"

"You are a problem," Sabrael ventured, still looking with half-closed eyes at his exiled brother. "Although Azazel and Beleth have likely bested your human friends, there is still a possibility of a powerful uprising from Hell which would be... less than beneficial. If you were around to lead them, it could be troublesome."

"I'm sorry, *what*?" Tamiel asked in shock, uncrossing his arms. "After two million years on this rock, you think I'm a threat *now*? Why?"

"You were *always* a threat, Tamiel," Uriel answered, a frown on his face. "Why do you think I deigned to persuade you to join our righteous side? Lucifer was not wrong to think that you could sway the masses, that you would have made a difference in the war. You still have that charisma and capability, even if our father rightly tore off your heretical wings."

"That was a long time ago, guys. And if—if what you say is true," Tamiel argued, hesitating as he thought about how Niccolo and Cadmus and all the others could be dead, "then I don't have an army to muster. If those kids died against Azazel and Beleth, I wouldn't have a chance."

"Well, it doesn't really matter," Camael said with a grunt as he heaved his axe onto his shoulder. "Orders is orders, and it's not up to us to question them. Just consider this your very belated execution for crimes against Adonai."

"Please, brother, regain some small amount of dignity and go quietly," Uriel said as he turned to look at a noise coming from the forest, disgust evident on his face. "My opinion of you would improve."

"Because that means *so* much to me."

"It should, *watcher*. So much death was caused by your betrayal, by your standing on the sidelines. Tell me, how did it feel to watch as your dear Sathariel succumbed to madness and begged for death you would not give her? If you would not die for your crimes against our father, perhaps you could die out of shame for *her*," Uriel spat out, making Tamiel's eyes go wide.

If it had been before the war—if it had been before he had been cast down to Earth and forced to watch as humanity struggled and was then subjugated—Tamiel may have rushed forward and killed his brother. Instead, he felt the weight of it all; he felt his guilt and grief for his lover.

He felt the need to atone.

"That was low, brother," Sabrael's voice broke through, causing Tamiel to look at the squat man in the purple robes. Sighing, the angel shook his head and motioned south. "However, his list of crimes is not over. Perhaps, Tamiel, the Horsemen may have had a better chance fighting Azazel and Beleth if you had been there to help."

"That... you don't..." Tamiel fingers curled into fists, but he realized his brother was speaking the truth. So much had been lost because he had stood by; so much had been destroyed because he was too scared to pick a side. When he looked at Sabrael—his apathy making him appear confident in his claims—Tamiel realized he may have doomed those poor souls who had come to him for help.

Falling to his knees, Tamiel let himself drown in guilt and grief. He trembled, his eyes watered, his fingers curled and uncurled without volition as Camael approached him. All he could think about was Niccolo and the ghost that haunted him, about Cadmus and the terrible burden tied to his very soul, about his sister and the love that had never been returned to her, about the Amazon and the revenge just outside of her reach, about the werewolf and his quest for redemption, about the messiah and the mockery of a faith that had been built in his image.

All of those thoughts were replaced by the horror of Sathariel's pain-ridden body, and Tamiel realized he never should have lived this long.

"Won't hurt a bit, brother. I'll make sure of it." Camael's voice came to his ears, but the haze of guilt and grief was too much. Tamiel just stared at his hands and imagined all the blood covering them. So much had been his fault, and maybe this was exactly what he deserved.

"Good, Tamiel. At least you have come to your senses," Uriel's snide voice broke through the ether, and suddenly Tamiel's mind was filled with memories that had not surfaced in thousands of years.

He remembered Lucifer and his easy smile, his joy upon finding that humanity had the capability to learn. That memory was replaced by that of meeting Sathariel for the first time, the fire in her eyes enough to make him fall for her instantly. He remembered the speeches she gave, how powerful her spirit was as she convinced her brothers and sisters to lay down their arms.

And as Camael swung down his axe, Tamiel remembered her smiling in the very same meadow where he was about to die.

Without another thought, Tamiel brought his left hand above his neck and summoned a golden broadsword that had not seen light for two million years. It was just in time; the blade of Camael's axe was only inches above his neck and struck against the shining sword with a loud clang before bouncing off and into the ground nearby.

"Wha—what are you doing?" Camael asked in surprise, not bothering to withdraw his weapon. Tamiel felt bad for what he was about to do, but it changed nothing. With a quick movement, the exile propped up his left leg and pivoted, holding his sword with both hands as he impaled Camael through the chest with a swift thrust.

"Finally standing up for something," he muttered as he rose up to his feet. Then he threw his leg into Camael's torso, pushing away his dying body and withdrawing his sword so he could deal with his murderous brothers.

"What have you done?" Uriel was too shocked to move as he spoke, but then he recovered and held his spear in front of him. "Camael was your brother!"

"So was Lucifer, so was Astaroth, so were all the others!" Tamiel shouted, grabbing hold of his grey robes with one hand and tearing them away, the cloth ripping easily to reveal his shining torso and a loose, white skirt that drifted past his ankles. As he stood there, two golden, mutilated stumps grew out of his back, but Tamiel didn't notice the pain that came with them. "I let them fall to Hell when they deserved Heaven. I will not *watch* another second of this farce!"

"This is the most foolish thing I've ever seen!" Uriel screamed, his brown wings creeping out of his back as he advanced on his exiled brother. "You are fighting for a dead cause! Lucifer is dead, the Horsemen are dead—their Apocalypse is *dead*!"

"No," Tamiel stated, shaking his head slightly. "You wouldn't have come here if the Horsemen were dead. No need to lie. Though I may not be able to kill both of you, I will not let you win without a fight *this time*."

"What makes you think you can beat us? You are powerful, Tamiel, but you are not strong enough to win against both of us." Uriel hovered a foot above the ground, his wings flapping lazily.

"I don't need to. It's just you and me. Sabrael will watch," Tamiel said, drawing his sword into a forward guard and directing the blade toward the floating angel. Uriel shook his head before looking at the bored angel to his left.

"What is he talking about?"

"Oh, he's right," Sabrael responded before giving a lazy yawn. "I've never been one for fighting."

"It appears I know our brother better than you, Uriel. He never dirties his hands."

"*Why*? We could finish him easily." Uriel said, but Sabrael laughed and shook his head.

"Are you just as pointless as those sheep? If you cannot handle a mutilated angel, I don't quite see the point in your continued existence, either. Fight. If you lose, I'll consider finishing the job myself," Sabrael said before withdrawing his right hand from his robes and waving off the entire affair.

"*Father* will hear of this."

"And Father will approve. Go on, little brother."

Uriel glowered in frustration, and once he realized that Tamiel was still watching, he shook his head and tried to regain some semblance of order. Then, without another thought, he flapped his wings and rushed toward the mutilated angel. However, Tamiel was prepared and jumped forward, his sword at the ready.

And with a brilliant clash of arms, Tamiel finally joined the fight.

———

"Faster!" Niccolo urged, his arm still wrapped around Cadmus' torso as the world bent around them. At first it had seemed completely unnatural while they tore through the Italian countryside—birds frozen in midflight, no sound coming to his ears except for Mercy's footfalls and Cadmus' breathing—but Niccolo had gotten used to it. Once he had, he had become more demanding as well, which was more than just taxing on Cadmus.

"Trying," Cadmus replied with great effort, his mind completely consumed by the task at hand. Niccolo had been right; without the chimera, he was able to maintain this state for longer, but it was extremely difficult. Once they arrived at Tamiel's hovel, Cadmus doubted he would even stay conscious, but he understood the risks.

Without this sacrifice, they had no chance to save the exiled angel.

"Try *harder*," Niccolo said.

"Let him concentrate. I will not tell you again," Mercy rasped, which was enough to stop Niccolo before he could get flustered. Mercy was less forgiving than his master, and even with all of his newfound power, Niccolo was easily cowed.

It seemed like it had been hours since they had started riding—and it probably had been hours for them—but Niccolo could tell that almost no time had passed. He half-expected to see three golden spheres flying above them, that maybe they had completely overtaken Tamiel's hopeful murderers, but they had not been so fortunate.

Instead, Niccolo had been forced to stay quiet and wait, which tore at his nerves.

"How much longer, do you think?" he asked, but Cadmus was unable to answer. About to ask again, Niccolo leaned slightly to the side and finally saw why.

Cadmus' face was pale and sweat poured from his brow; his eyes were half-closed and his lip quivered. Only then did Niccolo realize what he had asked of the reaper. He felt awful for forcing Cadmus through it, but then Niccolo looked ahead and saw a familiar outcropping of woods.

"Almost there! Just a little longer, Cadmus!" he shouted in glee, but then his spirit fell as he realized that they could already be too late. The angels may have already killed the watcher and left; Tamiel's body could already be cold.

Gulping down his apprehension, Niccolo tried to lower his expectations as Mercy tore around the bend, through the path in the woods and then across the clearing next to Tamiel's hovel. Once they cleared the crest of a hill, Niccolo was able to see what was waiting for them.

He only had a second of relief—able to watch Tamiel as he was midway through swinging his sword—before Cadmus finally ran out of strength. Just as they were past the top of the hill, the reaper's eyes rolled back in his head and he fell to his right side. That jerked all three of them back into the normal flow of time and caused Mercy to trip, sending the horse and his riders tumbling through the meadow.

After a few painful seconds of rolling along the ground like a ragdoll, Niccolo gathered his senses and slammed his arm down, throwing himself into the air and allowing him to correct his trajectory so he could land, stopping his momentum by dragging his feet through the soil. When he finally stopped moving, it took Niccolo a second to realize he was alright.

Coughing up particles of dirt and grass, Niccolo looked behind him to watch Mercy lying on his side before scattering into dust. That worried him slightly—thinking his friends were wounded—but Cadmus was still breathing. Passed out, but breathing. That was enough for Niccolo to turn his attention back to the struggle behind him.

What he saw made Niccolo smile for just a moment. Uriel and Tamiel were trading blows, each of the angel's thrusts met with a swipe of Tamiel's golden broadsword, each cross strike from the exile swiftly evaded by the hovering angel. It wasn't fair—Uriel's wings gave him the advantage—but Tamiel was still holding his own. Now that they had come to save the exile, Uriel did not stand a chance.

"*Uriel!*" Niccolo shouted in three voices as he formed radiant wings from his back, Lucifer's sword and shield in his hands. With a strong flap of his wings, Niccolo rushed toward the brothers locked in combat.

"Lucy..." Tamiel was stunned to hear his brother's voice after two million years. He even let down his guard as he turned to face the new arrival, but so had Uriel. They only watched as the silhouette of an angel flew closer, but then Tamiel realized his mistake. For a moment he smiled in shock, but then he realized what had happened and cursed under his breath.

"Impossible!" Uriel shouted, his long hair obscuring his face. He had never expected the Horsemen to escape Azazel's traps, but Lucifer's wings and weapons were the cause of his surprise. As the human mockery of an angel flew toward them, Uriel felt something close to fear.

However, a loud snap reverberated through the air and Niccolo crashed into the ground, a deep trench forming as his body was dragged through the meadow. The wings, Lux and Morningstar all disappeared once he came to a stop, but Tamiel could only watch as the Horseman writhed in pain, gasping for air. After a second of curiosity, Tamiel finally saw why.

Niccolo's demonic arm—what had given him so much power in Hell—was twisting, warping and bending like a snake, as if he had no control over it.

Then Tamiel realized that he *didn't,* that this was all part of Adonai's plan. He slowly turned to face Sabrael, whose left arm was extended and exposed after snapping his fingers.

"*Really?*" Violence poured out of Tamiel, but Sabrael shrugged and slowly approached the pain-ridden human.

"What... is... happening?" Niccolo gasped out, somehow able to maintain his consciousness as his arm bent and broke in unnatural contortions. He was barely able to turn over and sit on his knees, desperately trying to hold his arm down with his human hand and failing.

"A contingency plan, young Vespucci. This game has far too many pieces, but they are all useful from time to time," Sabrael explained as he came closer, the sun framed behind him and hiding his face in his own shadow.

"Who—who the fuck... are you?"

"Niccolo, don't listen to him!" Tamiel shouted as he ran forward, but Uriel wouldn't have that. The angel stabbed at Tamiel with his spear, forcing the exile to deal with him. Throwing his blade across his body, Tamiel knocked away the thrust, but then Uriel's knee found its way into his gut and forced the air out of his lungs. Jumping away, Tamiel had to avoid Uriel's continued assault and was forced to abandon hope for intercepting Sabrael.

"Oh, you know me, though it has been quite some time," Sabrael said as he continued forward, his purple robes dragging along the ground. "I dare say you've looked better, *young Vespucci*."

"That... no one... only..." Niccolo tried to think through the pain, tried to muster some sort of resolve he could use, but his thoughts were scattered and his defiance had abandoned him. He looked up at the approaching angel as his demonic arm writhed outside of his control, and when Sabrael finally stood above him and the veil of shadows fell away, Niccolo could only say one word. "Innocenti..."

"Good, I'm glad you still recognize me, Niccolo," Sabrael said, satisfaction making his dark eyes sparkle. "It would have been a shame to explain who I was to you."

"How? Who?" Niccolo muttered, his entire world falling down around him.

"Always. I took the guise of Lorenzo Innocenti for only one purpose," Sabrael said before kneeling down beside him, setting a pudgy hand against the twisting demonic flesh of Niccolo's left arm. At the touch, it was as if someone had lit Niccolo on fire, and he only just barely maintained consciousness.

"To give *you* a purpose."

"Nico..." Cadmus' voice came weakly from a few yards away, causing Sabrael to look over at him in curiosity. The reaper was crawling forward, his eyes barely open, but Sabrael still looked at him with admiration. Bringing back his hand, the angel clapped softly at the Horseman's efforts.

"Don't expend too much energy, reaper. You won't be able to stop this," Sabrael said before turning back to his former student. "Niccolo, I feel some small amount of guilt for the life I gave you, but it was for this purpose. I gave you your leprosy. I tore you away from that comfortable merchant's life so you could become someone greater. So that you could play your part in God's plan."

"God? This is... God's plan?" Niccolo asked, his confusion just barely overcoming his rage and indignation. Smug, Sabrael smiled and nodded his head.

"Yes, Niccolo. We needed someone to manipulate among the Horsemen. We knew Lucifer had some kind of plan. The firstborn always did. I trained you and gave you this blight so that when the time came—as it has—you would be able to end this world the way Adonai intended. In blood, disease, fire and death."

"*Nico!*" Tamiel shouted, causing Niccolo to turn in shock and watch as the mutilated angel ran toward them. His sword was held in his right hand and he looked worse for the wear—he had sustained some injuries along his arms and legs in the last few seconds—but he was still whole. "Don't listen! He's not—"

"I'm not *what*, Tamiel?" Sabrael interrupted softly as he turned to face his brother. He stood up straight, calm as could be, as the exile bore down on him. Just before Tamiel was within striking distance, Sabrael smiled. "I'm sure you know Uriel is behind you."

Frantically, Tamiel turned just in time to block a powerful thrust from Uriel's spear with the flat of his blade, the force enough to push him four yards back, where he stopped within reach of Niccolo. Uriel wasn't finished, however, and drew back slightly before flapping his wings and rushing forward. Realizing that he had no option, Tamiel held his sword to the side, point forward, and gambled everything on one last thrust to end his brother's life.

However, a snap filled the air, and almost immediately Tamiel felt something tear through his back and out his stomach. Looking down, Tamiel saw a blood-covered, diseased hand with black nails sticking out of his flesh. Then, before he could react, Tamiel felt Uriel's spear enter his chest and pierce through his heart, ending a conflict that began two million years ago.

"*No!*" Niccolo screamed, his arm still buried in Tamiel's back, but it did nothing to change the reality of the situation. When Uriel pulled back on his spear, Tamiel's body slid off Niccolo's arm and then fell to the ground, the exile's breaths coming with great effort once Uriel retrieved his weapon.

"Yes, Niccolo." Sabrael knelt and grabbed the leper's jaw with short fingers, turning his head so they could make eye contact. "However defiant you are—no matter what you really want—you are here to fulfill Adonai's wishes. That arm is not yours. It is *his*. And it is your duty to end this world."

"That goes for you, too, reaper," Sabrael said as he pushed off the ground and stood to his full height. "Whatever Lucifer's plans were, they never mattered. We own you. Adonai *wanted* you to come to Earth along with your fellow Horsemen. He wanted you to cull his flock, to prepare this world for the final act."

"In short, you work for *him*," Uriel added, wiping his spear point off on Tamiel's clothes. "And we expect you to keep working. That is your purpose. Fulfill it, and maybe you will be part of the next world. It really depends on how much mercy God wants to show you."

"And you will be grateful for whatever he chooses to show," Sabrael said. "Goodbye, Horsemen. We will meet again."

Even though he wanted to tear them apart with his nails, his fists, anything he could use against them, Niccolo did not have the chance. Before he could stand, both Uriel and Sabrael were wreathed in golden light and spheres formed around them. In seconds, the spheres jettisoned up and then disappeared into a hole in the sky which reformed immediately.

In just a few minutes, they had thrown everything into chaos.

"Tamiel..." Niccolo uttered, the name painful to his throat as he crawled forward, cradling his demonic arm as it healed from Sabrael's exercise in cruelty. When he reached Tamiel's side and found him still breathing, Niccolo allowed himself hope.

"Nico." The word leaked out from between Tamiel's lips, but when he opened his eyes and saw the expression on Niccolo's face, he slowly shook his head. "Don't..."

"I'm sorry," Niccolo whined, refusing to look at his arm covered in Tamiel's blood. "I came to help, I didn't..."

"Don't listen... to him," Tamiel said with difficulty, grabbing hold of Niccolo's collar even as blood dribbled from the corner of his mouth. "Sabrael... doesn't know."

"Doesn't know what?" Niccolo asked, unable to comprehend that these were Tamiel's last words. His denial at losing yet another friend was too much for him to fully cope.

"You'll... know. And you stay back!" He turned his attention to Cadmus, who had stumbled within earshot by using his scythe as a crutch.

"What? Why?" Cadmus was confused, but the watcher continued after coughing up blood.

"You don't get mine... you can't handle it. My soul's... different," he explained cryptically, and Niccolo was the one who decided to argue.

"But... you'll be a ghost! We can at least give you peace!" Niccolo placed his hand on Tamiel's shoulder and forgot who he was for the moment. "Please, brother, let him."

"I can do this, Tamiel. I can at least do this." Cadmus coughed as he came within a yard of the dying angel, but Tamiel shook his head.

"I won't let you. Sorry, not after what I've seen." He then looked past them and jerked his head, the effort enough to make him tremble. "That's why *he's* here."

"He?" Cadmus asked before turning in place and finding they were not alone.

Walking slowly toward them, grey robes billowing around his frame as he approached, was a figure holding an ornate, white scythe in his left hand. Gulping down their fear, Niccolo and Cadmus could only watch as the tall figure came to a stop, white hands holding onto the black handle of his tall scythe.

"This is Solomon." Tamiel winced as pain tore through his body. "He's going to help you, Cadmus."

At the introduction, the figure cocked its head to the side, but eventually grunted in agreement. Soon enough, it raised a hand to the hood obscuring its face and drew it back, revealing short white hair and a well-kept beard framing his stern face. His eyes were a pale blue and they stared straight at the dying angel.

"You always make promises for other people, Tamiel. Who is to say I won't break this one?" Solomon asked as he drew closer to inspect Tamiel's wounds.

"Because you owe me?"

"You have never let that die, old friend." There was slight annoyance in Solomon's tone, but it was obvious that he was more concerned for the exile on his deathbed.

"It dies when I do, *Solomon*." Tamiel stressed the name before turning to face Niccolo. "You're going to want to step back."

"Tamiel, I didn't mean to..." Niccolo motioned toward his already-healed arm, but Tamiel scoffed blood at him.

"Of course, you didn't. Don't be stupid. Now get out of the way and let me die. Solomon will take it from here," he said, pushing weakly at Niccolo with the strength left to him. After standing up, Niccolo slowly backed away from Tamiel, maintaining eye contact the entire time.

"Tamiel..." he muttered, but the exile shook his head one last time.

"I'm alright, Nico. I... have wanted this a long time. Now you," he said before turning to look up at the ancient reaper. "Do your job."

"Without pleasure."

Then Solomon drew a shining, blue blade through Tamiel's body and tore soul away from body. Niccolo and Cadmus watched, nursing their wounds, as one of the most powerful angels in existence was turned into little more than residual energy.

The three of them stood there for a moment of silence, but soon Cadmus heard sniffling beside him and turned to see tears streaming down Niccolo's face. His heart going out to his friend, Cadmus tried to console him.

"Wasn't..." he tried to say, but Niccolo slapped away his hand before burying his face in his human hand and wiping away the tears.

"Don't you *dare*, Cadmus! My hand went through his stomach. If we hadn't come here, if I hadn't interrupted, Uriel would never have had the chance to kill Tamiel. He was *better* than that. *I* am the reason he's dead."

"Not all the guilt is yours, Horseman. It was not your blade that entered Tamiel's heart," Solomon stated in grim fashion as his fingers wrapped around the handle of his scythe, but Niccolo would not entertain the thought.

"I am not a *Horseman*, anymore!" he shouted, Plague's death coming back to him in vivid detail. "They took that from me! Just like they took my arm, just like they took my life, just like they took Scratch!"

"You are being dramatic. Stop it," Solomon commanded like an annoyed father. At the insult, Niccolo's blood boiled in his veins and he stomped to the tall reaper with violent intent.

"I'm allowed, *Solomon*, and you better be careful the way you speak to me. Even if that bastard took my arm, I can still kill you with no problem!" he shouted, pointing a bloodied finger at the old human. In response, Solomon stepped forward and towered over him.

"You have no idea who I am. Back away," he said calmly, which was enough for Niccolo to reconsider his options. "You do not want to kill me, Niccolo. I am one of the few hopes you have for avenging your fallen friend."

"What?"

"There is a reason I am here, and there are plenty of reasons for you to avoid the guilt of Tamiel's death. I did not come here by chance. I came here because Tamiel asked me a favor. He *asked* me to reap him," he said, looking to each Horseman throughout the statement.

"He asked you?" Cadmus asked.

"From his gifts, he knew it was likely he would die today. And he did not want you to reap him, Cadmus, because he did not think you had the capability to do so. He knew of your difficulties, of your questions. In fact, he asked those same questions of me. And however much you *want* to blame yourself, Niccolo," he explained before turning pale eyes on Niccolo, "you cannot. His death was predetermined. He wanted to die."

"I..." Niccolo tried to make sense of the chaos in his mind, but Solomon was not kind enough to wait.

"We can grieve for our fallen brethren, but we must also look ahead. I am here to guide the two of you, to guide Cadmus on his path, but I must know what the angels said to you. You must trust me."

"Why should we?" Cadmus asked, skeptically. The old reaper didn't bother turning his head.

"Because Tamiel did, and you trusted him. Now, if you will, *what* did Sabrael and Uriel say to you?"

"They... wanted us to continue with the Apocalypse," Cadmus interjected, trying to relieve Niccolo of the burden. He had already dealt with so much in just one day. "They want us to end the world. To prepare for the final act."

"Interesting. Well, then we should deny their wi—"

"No," Niccolo interrupted, making both reapers balk with one word.

"What?" Cadmus asked, and Niccolo gritted his teeth.

"No. We'll do it. We'll tear this world apart," Niccolo said, his eyes unfocused as he considered his vengeance. Cadmus looked at him for a moment, speechless, but eventually he approached his friend with caution.

"Nico, that's what they want—"

"No, that's what they *think* they want." Niccolo snapped his gaze back to his friend. "But we're going to kill as many people as possible. You and I, we're going to bring this world to its knees."

"Nico—" Cadmus started, but Niccolo swept his arm out to his side and Lux formed in his hand.

"But not because that's what they *want*. We're going to kill as many people as possible because we need as many *souls* as possible," Niccolo explained, turning his gaze from one reaper to the other. "We are going to raise an army, we are going to train them—we're going to make them kill each other for all I care—as long as they're powerful enough to kill angels. When we rise up against Heaven, we will have all the strength of Hell and all the strength humanity can offer us."

"Horseman, that is ludicrous," Solomon argued, but Niccolo turned his rage on the tall reaper and let his new wings out in their full glory. Morningstar formed on his wrist and waves of powerful energy flowing away from him.

"*I told you, I am not a Horseman!*" Niccolo shouted in three voices before calming down and gathering his senses. "They took that from me, just like they took my past, just like they took my future. Whatever plans they have, I will *destroy*! I will *not* be anyone's puppet, not *Lucifer's*, not *Innocenti's*, not even *God's*! This is *my* life and this is *my* war and I *refuse* to let anyone control me ever again!"

"They wanted a Horseman, but I will give them a *Devil*. I will kill anyone who gets in my way. *Anyone*." Murder laced every syllable, and that promise remained even when he turned his radiant gaze on Cadmus.

"Niccolo..."

"Don't lie to me again, Cadmus. Never again."

"I haven't..."

"Don't!" Niccolo shouted, a burst of energy coming from his eyes. "Don't expect me to believe you didn't see any of this happening!"

"I..." Cadmus paused, remembering his vision of Tamiel running to kill Sabrael, of Phenex's explosion in the sky, and knew that Niccolo was right.

He also knew that he was not going to stop lying now.

"I didn't."

"Never," Niccolo growled as he closed the distance, coming within just a foot of his best friend. "Never again. If you do, I will not hesitate."

Doing his best to hide the terror he felt, Cadmus realized Niccolo meant every word.

EPILOGUE

Cadmus bit his lip, doing what he could to absorb the day's events. When he looked up, he found his companions gathered around the campfire. Phenex and Solomon each sat alone to his left and Cimeries with her back against a tree to his right. Across from him sat Niccolo and Paimon, the demon king's arm around Niccolo's shoulders. Although the flames of the campfire distorted his view, Cadmus looked at his friend and noticed his eyelid flicker before a green eye stared back at him.

Immediately, Cadmus broke eye contact and retreated to his thoughts.

As much as he wanted to tell the truth, Niccolo had become incredibly volatile since inheriting Lucifer's powers. Before all of this, Cadmus had been tempted to reveal his secret, but now there was no chance of reconciliation or forgiveness. If he told Niccolo the extent of his betrayal, it was possible that he would attack Cadmus without mercy.

Cadmus could not have that; he had to keep Niccolo in the dark. There were no options left now, especially since his friend had decided to wage a war against God and begin the Apocalypse in earnest. It was foolish—even if it was exactly what Lucifer intended —and Cadmus worried they would not be ready when the time came. Everything seemed to be spiraling out of control.

Sighing, Cadmus leaned back against his stump and closed his eyes, his mind retreating to those few minutes after Lucifer's death. It would do no good to relive it, but he had no choice. When his exhausted mind finally gave up on consciousness, Cadmus returned to that throne room and his last day in Hell.

CADMUS.

Coming to a stop just above the new pit in Lucifer's throne room, Cadmus looked up to see blue wisps of energy rising from the Devil's corpse. As he watched in wonder, the energy rose and condensed, eventually forming into an ethereal shadow. When its eyes opened and stared at him, Cadmus knew the ghost of Lucifer was speaking to him.

"Lucifer... I'm sorry, I'll reap you—"

No**, Cadmus. **I want you to leave me.

"I... what?" he asked, completely forgetting that a battle determining the fate of Hell was occurring beneath him. He only stepped forward so that he could stand within a few feet of the shade.

I... wanted to die. I wanted to... be—come... this. It was necess —ary.

"I don't understand," Cadmus mumbled, shaking his head as the wound in his shoulder healed. Mammon's nail had done a number on him, but the pain from it was nothing to the confusion he felt.

You will foll—ow. Onto... Earth. I will... become part of him.

"Part of who? What do you mean follow to Earth?"

Patience... reaper. I... will tie my soul to Niccolo. I will give him my power. You,** the ghost paused briefly before shining brighter, **will help him. You and Niccolo will succeed where we did not. You... will make sure he lives. Depend on each other.

"Lucifer..."

But do NOT tell him. He cannot know. The plan... will only work if he gets there... on his own. For him to fully ab—sorb my power... he will need to suffer. I am sorry. Trust... me.

"I'm supposed to keep this a secret?" Cadmus asked, his conscience already fighting against him, but then the ghost's eyes flared and shocked him into silence.

He cannot know! Promise me, Cadmus. I am trusting you with the fate of the world. I am trusting you with... my son. Don't fail me. Promise me.

"I..." Cadmus said, looking down and cursing himself for what he was about to do. "I promise."

Thank you. Go... go and help him kill Mammon. But... one last...

"What?" he asked, anxious at what this ghost of the Devil might want from him, and it was only made worse by Lucifer's hesitation. When he finally responded, Cadmus heard exactly what he did not want to hear.

Once he absorbs my power, if... he falls, if he is corrupted, you will have to be the one to stop him. If he becomes... a monster, it's up to you to...

However, before Lucifer could finish his request, the shade dissipated and the energy flew down below, down to where Niccolo was still fighting Lucifer's son. Cadmus would have demanded answers, but he already knew what was expected of him. For now, he would have to push it out of his mind. As he jumped over the edge and started falling down to help Niccolo, he heard Lucifer's voice one last time.

If he becomes a devil, you will be the only one who can stop him.

With a start, Cadmus gasped awake and found himself back in the present. Frantically, he looked at his surroundings and saw that everything was just the same as it was when he had fallen asleep. Only the fire burned a little lower. Breathing deep with relief,

Cadmus tried to forget what he had just seen. It was far too much for him to handle.

However, when he looked across the fire, he found Niccolo still staring at him. Cadmus was slightly surprised by the attention, but then he gave a soft smile to his old friend, trying to lighten the mood. Instead, Niccolo stared hard for a moment before breaking eye contact and gazing back at the fire.

As Cadmus watched the fire reflecting off Niccolo's eye, Lucifer's last request echoed within his mind. He wanted nothing to do with it —tried to convince himself he would never need to consider it—but his friend had changed. With Plague's death, with all the tragedy of this day, Niccolo had lost a great deal of his humanity. To hear him talk about killing millions of people to raise an army was insane. Cadmus wondered how much humanity still remained in his best friend, but he feared it was not enough. This time, he did not ignore the echoes of Lucifer's voice within his mind.

If he becomes a devil, you will be the only one who can stop him.

Facing this darkness, Cadmus doubted he could.

DRAMATIS PERSONAE

Adonai: The creator of Earth and Heaven, and that only served to inflate his ego.

Ajax: The Horseman of War, and in life he was known as Ajax the Greater from the Trojan War. He spends most of his time in the War Quarter fighting, drinking or both.

Amdusias: A King of Hell and the stoic twin brother of Asmodeus. He is known for weather manipulation, and he rules over a kingdom suffering through an eternal winter.

Amon: One of the Demonic Seers, along with his brother Räum, Amon relayed the prophecy for the Apocalypse. He has a raven's head along with other avian aspects.

Andras: A former human who abandoned his shape to look more like an owl. He is known as an information broker throughout Dis, the capital of Hell.

Antonio Gherardini: A successful merchant in medieval Firenze and the father of Camilla Gherardini, Niccolo's first love.

Asmodeus: A King of Hell and the light-hearted twin brother of Amdusias. He has access to pyrokinesis and has taken on draconic aspects since his fall to Hell, suiting himself to his volcanic kingdom.

Astaroth: Lucifer's more martial twin, Adonai created him to be a general in the war against the Nephilim. Even though he is not one of the Kings, he works diligently to keep Hell from falling apart.

Azazel: One of Lucifer's best friends, he is a Fallen Angel who appears as a satyr with a reptilian tail, and he generally keeps Lucifer company in the palace.

Bael: A King of Hell who appears as an anthropomorphized toad with venomous horns. He generally does not commit to either side of a conflict and focuses on self-preservation. Most of his realm is silt and swampland, a breeding ground for all the insects he loves to eat.

Balam: A King of Hell who appears as a gigantic humanoid hybrid between a bear and goat. He is known for his strength and lack of intelligence, and his kingdom resembles a redwood forest with sparse wildlife. Balam has a habit of hunting anything that moves.

Barbas: The leader of the Pestilence Quarter in Dis, the capital of Hell. He acts as a mentor for Niccolo, helping him find his place in Hell after his death.

Beleth: A King of Hell, known for his intelligence and sadism. He always wears obsidian plate mail, and he has mastery over many schools of magic. He had a giant fortress built in the center of his dark kingdom, surrounded by a deep network of mines where his subjects endlessly toil.

Belial: A King of Hell, called the Eveningstar to serve as a foil to Lucifer. He appears as a reanimated corpse, and he consistently blames Lucifer for their fall to Hell. His kingdom is a cold, barren wasteland, and his ostentatious palace is the only permanent structure.

Buer: The Head Librarian in the Famine Quarter and the preeminent scholar in all of Hell. He appears as an aged centaur, though that is purely an affectation.

Buné: The leader of the Death Quarter in Dis, the capital of Hell. He acts as a mentor for Cadmus, and he is one of the only angels who could ever reap souls.

Cadmus: The Horseman of Death and Niccolo's best friend in Hell. He was an early Christian who was executed via gladiator combat.

Camilla Gherardini: The daughter of a merchant in medieval Firenze, and Niccolo's first love.

Carlo Vespucci: A wealthy merchant in medieval Firenze, and Niccolo's father.

Cimeries: One of two Hell Knights, former humans who protect Lucifer from lesser threats. She claimed Cimeries after her first life as Hippolyta, the legendary Amazon.

Crocell: The Slayer of Dis, a Fallen Angel tasked with exterminating feral demons so that human reapers are not in danger. He wields a trident and is attuned to electricity and water.

Diogenes: The Horseman of Famine. In life, he was a Greek philosopher who rejected the norms of society. He is often accompanied by Manes, a stray dog, and Despair, his horse.

Eligos: The leader of the War Quarter of Dis, the capital of Hell. A giant warrior with a shifting weapon, he generally spends his time presiding over the fighting pits.

Furcas: One of two Hell Knights, former humans who protect Lucifer from lesser threats. One of the older humans to fall to Hell, he still wears the trophies of monsters he has killed.

Gabriel: One of the archangels, and he is generally seen as a messenger throughout Heaven.

Giovanni Simonetti: A minor noble in conflict with Niccolo during his time as a leper.

The Leviathan: A terrifying entity from another dimension who acts as a deterrent for violence between the Kings of Hell.

Lilith: The first angel to ally themselves with Lucifer, eventually becoming the High Queen of Hell. She dies in the process of giving birth to Mammon.

Lorenzo Innocenti: An enigmatic merchant who operates out of medieval Firenze and Napoli. While he seems to assist Niccolo, no one else finds him trustworthy.

Lü Bu: The first Horseman of Pestilence, and a legendary warrior from the Three Kingdoms period of Chinese history.

Lucifer: An archangel who rebelled against Adonai so he might enlighten humanity. Currently rules as the High King in Dis, the capital of Hell, but he is also known as the Firstborn and the Morningstar.

Mammon: Known as the Hellborn, Mammon is the only child born to Lucifer and Lilith, who he killed during childbirth.

Marchosias: A former human who usually appears as a werewolf wreathed in shadows. For more than a thousand years, he worked for Astaroth along with Phenex, his longtime friend.

Marco: A man who enjoys life too much, he is often seen offering unsolicited advice to Niccolo, his best friend in Firenze.

Mercy: The sentient horse who serves as the mount for Cadmus, the Horseman of Death.

Mitzrael: A sadistic Seraphim who took great pleasure in fighting against Lucifer and his allies, even after they had surrendered. He was sent to Earth along with Nithael to stop the Horsemen.

Moloch: A refugee from another dimension, like the Leviathan, who made his home in Hell long before Lucifer and his armies fell.

Niccolo Vespucci: The current Horseman of Pestilence and a former merchant prince from medieval Firenze.

Nithael: An officer from Heaven sent to Earth along with Mitzrael to stop the Horsemen.

Paimon: A King of Hell who appears as a seductive blonde woman. Before the Fall, she was known as "the Butcher" for how savagely she fought against the Nephilim. She has made her kingdom along a tropical beachfront where she can remember the warmth of Heaven.

Phenex: A former human who acts humble despite an immense capacity for pyrokinesis. For more than a thousand years, he worked for Astaroth along with Marchosias, his longtime friend.

Plague: The sentient horse who serves as the mount for Niccolo, the Horseman of Pestilence.

Purson: A King of Hell who appears as a hybrid between snake and human. He rules over a desert kingdom, so he often seeks reasons to visit anywhere else.

Räum: One of the Demonic Seers, along with his brother Amon, Räum relayed the prophecy for the Apocalypse. He had a crow's head, and his prophecies were considered more accurate.

Ronové: The leader of the Famine Quarter of Dis, the capital of Hell. Appearing as a squat demon with a long staff, Ronové is considered a master of rhetoric.

Sathariel: A pacifist angel, she was romantically linked to Lucifer before the rebellion, eventually becoming a Watcher along with Tamiel for the sin of staying neutral.

Sitri: A former human who took full advantage of their second life and became a shapeshifting socialite. All gossip eventually goes through Sitri, usually for a price.

Tamiel: Considered Adonai's favorite before the rebellion, he and Sathariel were considered Watchers and were banished to prehistoric Earth.

Uriel: The most violent of the archangels, Uriel is more than happy to punish anyone who has displeased Adonai in any way.

Valefor: An aggressive Fallen Angel who was considered powerful even before he turned feral.

DRAMATIS PERSONAE

Viné: A King of Hell who comes across as an implacable shrew, but she can form blades from her bones that will rip most people to shreds. Her kingdom is a lush rainforest, and seldom few souls who venture into those depths ever return. Whether or not Viné is involved is a mystery.

Zagan: A King of Hell who appears as a giant with bull horns, and he consistently maintains a buzz off a bottle of wine that perpetually refills itself. His kingdom is mountainous and he holds court in a hollow within the central range, but grapes grow freely within the valleys.

WATCH FOR...

Niccolo and his friends will return for <u>In Defiance of Heaven</u>, so you can jump right into the rest of the series as soon as you'd like!

If you're curious about some of my other writing, I've re-released my novel <u>Ouroboros</u>, a political standalone about hallucinogen abuse, through 25&Y Publishing, and my first series, the <u>Icarus Trilogy</u>, is a science fiction trilogy about futuristic gladiators stuck in an endless cycle of death and rebirth.

Currently, I am working for Yoton Yo Studios as the Narrative Director for the Exfinitum TCG, and I have a few titles under contract with 25&Y Publishing. First is Daytrippers, a paranormal science fiction series set in the same world as Ouroboros, and the next one in the queue is Evenin' Flow, a short story collection that covers multiple genres.

And if you literally just want something to watch, I have a YouTube channel based around <u>Beat Saber</u>, where I review custom songs and try to guide new players. Once I get back to streaming, my handle on Twitch, and most platforms, is Kkauffany, so feel free to say hi!

www.ingramcontent.com/pod-product-compliance
Lightning Source LLC
Chambersburg PA
CBHW072300020726
47501CB00002B/333